EXIT STRATEGY

INDIGO CITY DARKER BOOK 3

A.J. DOWNEY &
JARED KINGPACAL LAIN

COPYRIGHT

Text Copyright © 2021 A.J. Downey, Jared KingPacal Lain

ISBN: 978-1-950222-36-0

Edited and book design by Maggie Kern @ Ms.K Edits
Cover art by Dar Albert at Wicked Smart Designs

DEDICATION

To Vicki Bartle, for helping me get my house in order and for encouraging me to go for it on the cult aspect for this storyline. For keeping me grounded during all the chaos. Thank you for being my sister and chosen family. -A.J.

This one is for my traveling family, with whom I've spent many a Summer in Kentucky, Walker Stalker Con in Atlanta, and beyond. Their love of travel and friendship were an inspiration for the road trip that this book is. So, to Heather M, Jackie R, both Kelly's, Stacy L.K., Francis K, and my wife and love of my life, my Moon and Stars, Heather. -Jared

PROLOGUE

alanthe…

"You look just beautiful."

My mother plucked at my long red hair, bringing some of it forward over my shoulders to frame my face. She was beaming with pride, and I couldn't help but smile, too. It was July, my birth month, and I was just a few days past my fifteenth birthday.

The Presentation of Youth and Purity was an incredibly important event held once a year at the New Eden Centre. It was a debutante cotillion, a presentation of the young women of the faith, committing themselves to the teachings of Elijah Ellison Emerson and the vision of New Eden – blue skies, clear water, and a verdant and green Earth. All of the year's debutantes were waiting for the August, Elijah Emerson to appear.

Before the actual Presentation, before the cotillion with the music, and the lights, and the beautiful dresses, we were *presented*, a sort of inspection. My mother said it was a formality and I had nothing to be worried about. To be here was to have already passed everything that had to be passed. To get this far meant that I was in the very top. I knew I was in the top. I was a Youth Leader in the

Youth Corps program, something I accomplished in just four years. I was a Goodwill Ambassador for the New Eden Centre and had not just gone on missions. I had even earned the right to sit at the planning table and help organize one.

There were a dozen of us, and I knew the others. They were Youth Leaders, Goodwill Ambassadors, Ristars who were expected to attend higher learning than the New Eden Academy could provide. They would become engineers, lawyers, and doctors, and then return to us.

The floor was cool under my bare feet. We were all barefoot, wearing the same snowy-white satin robes, our purity as a symbol.

It began in the morning with a private audience with Master Maxson, the Majordomo of the New Eden Centre. None of us knew what to expect, just that we were to file in and stand aside while the Majordomo had some words of wisdom for us. The hallway was rich and opulent, and each was attended by a designated chaperone—our mothers, older sisters, aunts, or a woman who was a patron to us. My chaperone was my mother. I fidgeted. August Emerson was on the other side of that door, waiting. I barely heard the rote speech the Majordomo was giving.

What words of wisdom would he share with us?

What secret words would he share with me?

So exciting!

"Okay, stop fidgeting. Remember your posture, eyes forward, smile, for Eden's sake, smile," my mother whispered hurriedly as the double doors to August Emerson's office opened. The line of us girls fell into a hush, our excitement quivering in the air, the thrum of it running through each of us as we tried to hold still and not fidget as a man in a sharp suit stepped out and turned.

"His holiness, the right hand of Uriel, the prophet of the New Garden of Eden, August Elijah Ellison Emerson, will see you now," he declared and when he nodded, the lead chaperone to the left of their charge touched their charge's shoulder. I waited at the end of the line, the last to go. When it was my turn, I felt my heart lift in my chest as though lighter than air as I stepped forward, the gossamer skirt of my robe swishing against my thighs.

We filed in along a set of rich, wooden shelves lined with leather-bound books; the gilt lettering on their spines glittering in the morning light through the tall windows opposite them. I stopped and turned, my mother just behind me and to my right.

Oh my God, it's really him! I thought. Emerson was the founder of the New Eden Centre and stood behind his heavy wooden desk as the man who announced he would be seen shut the doors behind them and put them to his back.

August Emerson smiled at us all and came around his desk.

"Good morning, First Daughters."

"Good morning, August," we chanted back to him.

He clasped his hands in front of him and eyed us all. His gaze settled on me. I felt myself flush lightly. *August Emerson was looking at me! Me!* I almost couldn't believe it.

"Oh, now look at you," he said, smiling, and came to me. He settled his hands lightly on my hips, and I froze. "Aren't you *all* just lovely?" he asked, and I felt myself blush harder.

He dropped his hands to his sides and said, "You may all disrobe."

I blinked and would have jumped as I felt my mother's hand tug at the bow holding my robe closed, but her other hand was firm on my shoulder. Panic bloomed inside me.

I flushed for a very different reason as my robe fell open. Underwear wasn't part of the ceremonial morning dress, so I was completely exposed. More so when my mother took the insubstantial-to-begin-with dressing from my shoulders and swept it down my arms. I snuck a glance down the row of girls. Several were blushing, like me, with embarrassment, their chaperones all having done the same thing. August Emerson paced in front of us, staring, eyes never blinking.

I felt my eyes go wide when his holiness dropped to one knee in front of me. I looked down into his twinkling blue eyes, and it felt like my heart crawled into my throat as his fingertips traced the side of my face, down to my shoulder, and further down. Then he ghosted up the outsides of my thighs.

"You're an exceptional young woman, Calanthe, a First Among First Daughters," he said, and then he was touching the inside of my knee. I jumped when his fingertips skated up the *inside* of my thighs, fingertips lightly brushing my sex. I felt my eyes brim with humiliated tears.

"Most exceptional." He rubbed over the lips of my sex, and I tried not to quail from the invasive touch.

A small sob bubbled out of my throat and the tears fell. I blushed hotter when his finger slipped inside me. My mother's hand clamped down harder on my shoulder, and I could feel her willing me to silence, to stillness.

"Oh, yes..." he breathed, his eyes closing. "You'll make a great man a very fine wife indeed. So nice and tight." I felt myself clench involuntarily.

His touch was gone almost as fast as it'd invaded me.

I stood, shaken to the core, unable to think a single coherent thought, my synapses misfiring.

The next thing I knew, my mother was helping me back into my robe. All of us girls were standing, weeping silently, some sniffling. All of us were silent as we were led out of August Emerson's office and back out into the hallway. My mother hugged me around the shoulders and rubbed me up and down the arm.

"Oh, I'm so *proud of you*, honey."

Proud of me? For what?

"Mom?" I asked, and I sounded far away, even to myself.

We girls were whisked to separate rooms of the New Eden Centre and were left to meditate. I showered, scrubbed between my legs, and cried.

When my mother returned to get me ready for the ball, I asked her, "Mama, how could you let him do that to me?"

She lowered my dress and gave me a reproachful look.

"Honestly, Calanthe! You've been bestowed a great honor. Are you really going to stand there and *complain* about it? He named you First Among First Daughters. There is literally nothing higher than that. You will wear the Emerald Dress, the Vestments of New Eve."

I stood in open mouthed horror... I couldn't fathom...

I don't remember being zipped into the green dress, or who put the crown of laurels on my head. I don't remember being led back downstairs into the ballroom. I don't remember being introduced. I don't remember anything except his smiling eyes and rich melodic voice as he said, "Well, hello, Calanthe. It's so very nice to meet you. I'm—"

"Arik Rex, yes, I know."

I thought he was my salvation. That he could and would be my way out of the New Eden Centre.

Boy, was I wrong...

1

---

*K*urt...

It seemed, as of late, that my life had been a series of bad choices.

The most recent of those choices was to enter the arena of personal protection, becoming the organizational manager of a certain celebrity's bodyguard and entourage. He was well known, immensely popular, and his action-oriented, politically savvy, and environment/socially messaged movies were guaranteed money-makers at the box office.

Arik Rex was the new ideal in Hollywood movie stars – strong jaw, sparkling eyes, perfect gelled hair, the best one-liners – and his movies appealed to the explosion and stunt crowd, the action series crowd, and women in the fourteen to fifty-five demographics loved him for his simmering charisma, cool awareness of social trends, and being a woke actor, without being a *woke* actor.

I only knew this because there were plenty of times where nothing went on requiring my attention, and the only thing to pass said time was flipping through pages of celebrity tabloids, waiting and watching. The content was shallow, the interest was transparent, and it was frankly deeply and fucking *boring*.

But it was a job. Importantly, it paid well. My last job had left me floating on three months of back payroll that wasn't going to be made good on, mostly since it had been a mistake working for a heroin cartel. Like I said, a series of bad choices.

Arik Rex was an actor of no small skill. His real acting wasn't for the Hollywood cameras, it was for the journalists and tabloid cameras. I knew a few things about him. He had no problem spending *special time* with his fans, despite being married to a beautiful, younger woman. He also had something of a cocaine habit, but I had certainly seen worse – both in terms of worse drugs, and worse drug usage. He was somewhere between a method actor and a character actor, and when something or someone forced him to break character, the man fucking lost it. The *"no phones on set"* rule wasn't to prevent leaks from filming, or of the set itself, it was to make sure that no one caught one of his tirades and shared it.

Audio of one of them had leaked before my time and it had been *weeks* of scandal on the celebrity gossip shows and in the gossip rags. It was also one of the things that had ushered my predecessor out of my current position and provided the opportunity for me to step into the role in his stead.

It was impressive, really – one of Arik's tantrums. He would be completely in character, whatever would happen, and then next thing you knew, he had broken out in a sweat, eyes bulging like he's choking or about to shit himself, and then it's screaming and throwing things. Everyone else would roll over and show their bellies, not literally, but figuratively. There would be people scurrying away, hiding. Some would attempt apologies, sometimes things would be thrown at *them* instead of just in general for their trying.

It might have been impressive even to me if I hadn't been through boot camp for Her Majesty's Royal Marines and hadn't spent years in Afghanistan and Iraq. Listening to some polished American dandy pop off was nothing particularly intimidating. When it came to people screaming in my face, he wasn't even on the top ten list for anything other than maybe being the wealthiest person to do so.

And that seemed to earn me some credit with him, gained his respect. Indifference about his sexual escapades and drug use cemented the deal.

The job was a paycheck and that was something I needed. My previous employers had certainly been worse people, less reliable on payday, and much more intimidating to deal with. The other nice part was that the people I did have as *enemies* now were paparazzi, and fans, and sometimes people who were part of production. Again, Arik was prone to throw things; anything he could lay hands on could become a projectile. He was a terrible shot, but that meant that when he did decide to play human catapult, it was bluster and show, but the people who had a hammer thrown at them didn't know or assume that.

"There's a woman in my trailer, Worthy. She needs to be expedited," Arik said. I nodded and gave my cigarette butt a flick away.

"Consider it handled," I said.

"You know, it takes a decade for a single one of those to decompose," he said, eyeing where I had tossed the butt.

"*Uh-huh,*" I barely responded before heading toward his trailer. The last thing I would take from him was his moralizing on the environment. Hard to take some of that seriously from a man who owned six houses, forty cars, four personal aircraft, and two yachts.

"Quick and clean. My wife will be visiting the set this afternoon," he added. I nodded, said nothing, and went to his trailer.

It wasn't really a trailer, it was a half million-dollar RV, REX1. "Rise and shine, decent or not, I'm coming in," I announced myself as I was taking the steps inside. I heard a flurry of movement and a few soft curses. There was a woman in the first bedroom, which was no real surprise. This was a regular occurrence. Enough so that we had a protocol for it, and there was even a non-disclosure clause in the security contracts. If anyone talked, leaked anything, even mumbled about it in their sleep, it was job forfeiture, monstrous fines, and a possible civil lawsuit.

"Get out of here," the woman said, clutching the top sheet to her chest.

"That's the idea. Let's go," I said.

"No, you get out, I'm a guest of Mister Arik Rex." Her tone was hot.

I grabbed the sheet and jerked it out of her hands. She squawked indignantly and by trying to hold on; the momentum toppled her over. It wasn't surprising that she was naked underneath. I spotted a pile of clothing that had a bra strap sticking out of it, so I grabbed that and tossed it at her. "Here are your clothes. Put them on. This is the express service, and I'm the head of his bloody security detail," I added.

She looked at me, a mixture of confused and startled. That was maybe the only hard part – them realizing the betrayal. That there would be no soft murmured goodbye, no lingering kiss, no long gaze into his magnetic blue eyes while an orchestra chord rose... *Fuck me, I've got to stop reading the tabloid stories. They were affecting my head.*

Her next action was predictable. She dug her phone out from where she had it tucked away. The phone was the thing that had to be caught. Her face was illuminated by the screen, and it flickered color, and then I snatched it from her hands. "Hey, you can't do that!" she shouted.

"Get dressed before I carry you out over my shoulder and give everyone a good hard look at that fanny," I said. She lunged for the phone, but I caught her, flat palm against the base of her collarbone, the smack of skin against skin audible. I pushed her back onto the bed. "Dressed, now, unless you want everyone on set to see your pink bits, eh?"

With my other hand, I opened her photo gallery and started

deleting every pic in the last 24 hours, wiping out her evidence of having been in his presence, in his trailer, and anything else that was a breach. She lunged at me again, and I almost lost the phone. She evaded the palm, tried to go inside, and ended up tangled on the floor, twisted in the sheet. I dropped a knee against her shoulder.

There were still rules – no knees to the neck, not that I would do that to even a deranged star fucker.

I pulled up her social media activity and started deleting that as well. She struggled and threw a few punches against my thigh and then several that were decently aimed at my cods. Her fist connected with the cup, and it made a twin-coconut clacking-together sound. "Sorry to spoil that. All you groupie types and angry actress types are super predictable. You all go for the knackers and the eyes."

I finished with the phone while she struggled under me. Satisfied with the *sanitizing* of the device, I tossed it on the bed and let her up. She was red in the face, chest heaving with anger. It made her tits really pop out. It was a shame she was pissed. I didn't pick up Rex's leavings, but the thought did cross my mind on occasion; they were never shabby, always easy on the eyes.

"Clothing, now. If you're not dressed in one minute, you're going out that door naked," I said for the last time.

She threw her clothes on with trembling hands, her eyes sharp like daggers. I was wary of her. Women were by far more dangerous than they were given credit for. If there was something she could have improvised into a suitable weapon, she would have used it. Anything sharp could go between the ribs, or be used to slash at arms, face, or hands.

Most were fighters, the ones that managed to make it this far. The wallflowers and the shrinking violets didn't make it through his vanguard. Rex liked his conquests to be independent, strong willed, aggressive, and assertive. They were nothing like his mouse of a wife. That woman might as well have been a marble statue for as much as she projected herself or made herself known. She was shock pale to boot, fire-red hair, tits like a teenage girl – nothing like his taste in groupies.

It was something to do with his church, lots of words about purity and environmental shit. It was religious noise, and that was something that I had long since learned to tune out.

His piece du jour was still fighting with a shoe when the minute timer I tapped on my watch went off. "Time's up, chippy, time to go." I grabbed her by the elbow and started moving her toward the door. She grabbed at her phone, leaving behind a shoe and both of her stockings.

"No, wait," she pleaded as I kicked the door open and started pulling her down the stairs. She bucked and pulled back, but that was fine. I turned halfway down the steps leading up and pulled her off her balance. This was a maneuver I had perfected over the last few weeks, with a little practice from one of the women from legal. The woman pitched forward and would have face-planted at the foot of the stairs, if I wasn't in the way. Instead, she collapsed over my shoulder, and I caught the backs of her legs before she could flip. Two steps down and I was on terra firma. Rotate to the left but pull short so no skulls smack the side of the RV, and then it's the goat path around the front of the vehicle, down to the security tent, and then one of the lads stuffs the wildcat in a golfcart and takes her to front of the set, or to her car, whichever is closer.

By that point, it was out of my hands and handled.

I passed the angry woman off to one of my guys, a chisel-faced kid from Arizona. He wanted to be a cowboy actor but missed the genre by sixty some odd years. He took the woman and showed her that he had hand restraints and a taser, both of which went a good distance to calming her right the fuck down.

"Let me know when you've finished your run to the Humane Society," I said.

"We'll get this lost cat back home," he said, throwing a passable Hollywood salute, but there was nothing military in it. He meant well, so I wouldn't bust his bollocks over it.

I went back inside and swept the vehicle for anything the woman might have left behind that was compromising – drugs, drug paraphernalia, lingerie, weapons, etc. Satisfied it was clean, I thumbed my phone.

"Housekeeping, aye? ... Hey, Maria... Aye, it's Kurt. We've had a stray cat get into REX1. I need a full cleanup... Oh, I know how often they seem to get in. I might need to call maintenance and have them look at the closer on the door." I laughed.

One of the things that had astounded me about picking up the Hollywood gig was just how many open secrets there were, and how, despite no one talking about them, everyone knew. The amount of screwing around that went on, the scads of drugs that were being consumed, and there was more than a little bit of deviant behavior going on past even just coke and star fucking.

I ran a tight ship in Rex's security.

My detail had a monthly drug screening, weekly depending on who was going to be on set. I had learned that some certain types who shall go unnamed are much more into the party scene than others. That was another thing that had gotten the previous head of Rex's detail removed from his position.

Can't do a good job of perimeter security while doing lines of coke off a certain runner-up Actor of the Year's dick. A certain actor that Rex himself disliked having around.

Rex had been part of my interview, and there had been a bit of pomp, where he had a bunch of nearly naked women come parading through our interview. The men who turned their heads to watch the women had their interviews cut short. The men who didn't turn their heads were asked questions after the women left. They were odd questions. Some were trick questions, but it was all attention to detail, and quick wits.

Then I was in charge and getting a regular paycheck.

My lodging was part of my compensation package, so I didn't have to sleep in my truck, or face a three-to-four-hour commute between what I *could* afford and the Hollywood Hills that my charge resided in. I had a small apartment, courtesy of his New Eden Centre. It was some sort of fancy super-green commune plan. Everything was close to self-sustaining – solar panels and solar water heaters on the roof of the apartment complex, green planning, and a communal high-efficiency laundry service.

The place was annoying as shit, and the neighbors were just fucking unbearable.

Work kept me busy, and I didn't spend much time there.

"Hey, Sarge," my radio chirped. It was my second, Madeline Oberisk, a tall blonde woman with boxer's hands and a paramilitary background in SWAT.

"Go ahead for Kurt," I said.

"Cardinal is inbound, ETA thirty minutes," she replied.

"Copy that. I'll expedite housekeeping. You queue up a vehicle for Cardinal and I'll make sure we're ready here." I thumbed the mic.

"Copy for Obe," she said, and the line closed. Cardinal was Miss Calanthe Quinlan. Like the bird, she was small and red, and tended to arrive in a small aircraft. She probably would have choppered onto the set except that Rex was working on some sort of big-budget time-travel sci-fi thing that involved Roman gladiators, and the set was no fly. A helo setting down would ruin film, sets, the works.

I went to work, checking the perimeter, tagging my men on the ground, and the man posted to the guard tower, watching everything from a portable thirty-foot elevated shoebox. Like the well-oiled machine we were, Cardinal's driver was directed to one of the service entrances, missing the crowd of snoops and paparazzi who stalked the edges of the set, armed with telephoto lenses the size of sniper rifles.

"Skyfall, is the air clear?" I thumbed my mic again, watching the large hybrid sedan make the turn through the blackout fencing around the set.

"Air is clear, Kurt," the call came back. "No drones within two miles of the set."

"Good, let's get the air clear. We don't want eyes on Cardinal or Tomcat," I said.

"Copy that," he responded.

Moments later, the car pulled up in front of what security considered the headquarters. A cluster of smaller trailers created a partition, blocking cameras that could see above the blackout wall, and pop-up walls made another side, concealing the area from set cameras. The big green walls could be edited out easily with computers. Green room, makeup trailers, and the common area took up the rest. The area had initially also housed a double row of plastic porta-johns, but I got those moved to a new latrine area where we could have sandwiches and smokes without having to smell taco shits and wine piss all day.

The complaints about the long walk were still being registered and promptly discarded. No one was complaining about the common area smelling better. Maybe they were used to that, but me, no. I couldn't take that stink packing itself in my nose.

I stepped forward, opened the door of the sedan, and offered the passenger inside my hand. I had met Cardinal a few times, but always in passing, and never exchanged anything more than a polite nod or bow of the head. She reached up, accepting my hand, and I *helped* her rise from the car. That was the role I had to play, almost like SAG rules. Don't speak unless spoken to, and if someone did bother to notice my existence, it was a good idea to keep everything to five sentences or fewer. Five words or less was better.

"Miss Calanthe, welcome to the *Sandal Paradox* set." I smiled.

"Thank you, and I prefer Callie, please," she said.

"Of course, Miss Callie," I offered.

"*Sandal Paradox?*" she asked.

"Working title of the set. The last screenwriter's meeting I was called into, they still hadn't settled on a title for it."

"So, you're the head of security?" she asked, purely a social nicety. She was always a textbook of prim and proper, always with polite questions that she already knew the answer to.

"Aye, Staff Sergeant Owen Worthington, but everyone calls me Kurt," I said.

"How do you get Kurt from Owen?" she asked politely. She seemed like the sort who did everything politely and might faint if someone spoke too forcefully in her presence, or, Heaven forbid, let out a bit of blue language. Cardinal didn't fit her. Those birds were aggressive and territorial, and she looked to be neither. She made me think of the old stories of elves and Fae ghosts, translucent with hair made of fire.

"It's a nickname I picked up years ago when I was on deployment. I read a lot," I said.

"Maybe Kurt doesn't mean what I think." She raised an eyebrow.

"I didn't have many books on hand, so I was rereading the same ones over and over. Most of the books I had were by Kurt Vonnegut." I gestured, and one of the security people nodded and waved the car to leave the common area and move down to the motor pool.

"Oh, Kurt Vonnegut…" She paused thoughtfully. "I did read *Cat's Cradle*, before the library was sanitized."

"*Slaughterhouse Five*. It seemed relevant when I was in Afghanistan," I added. "You read much?"

"I don't read as much as I used to," she said. "The physical library was torn out and everything was digitized or was tossed for not being of value or interest."

"Vonnegut didn't make the cut?" I asked, surprised.

"Quite a bit didn't make the cut," she said, sounding a tint sad.

"I have a few books in my bunk, if you wanted to borrow one. It will probably be a while before Tomcat is done on set. I mean, Mr. Rex."

"I'm familiar with the callsigns, Mr. Worthington. What's mine?" she asked.

"Cardinal, and please, just call me Kurt," I added.

"Gladly, Kurt." She smiled. "And I'll take you up on that book offer."

It only took a minute to duck into our bunk trailer, grab a few dog-eared books from the footlocker, and drop them off with Cardinal.

It had been nice meeting her formally and finding out that she was literate.

Half of my detail was barely literate, and on the set, it was less than that. They could read, but they chose not to. It was something that I had a hard time processing.

Shooting lasted another hour or so. There was shouting, green screens were moved around, a stagehand was fired for wandering into a shot while on his phone, and the general ongoing noise that was the business. I kept an eye on the detail. There was something that had me feeling squirrely today.

The first clue that shooting was over was when Rex appeared stomping up the hill, flanked by his entourage. A man held an umbrella over him, giving him shade. A pair of personal assistants chased him, garbling about emails, texts, and calls, which he waved away.

When he reached Cardinal, he actually looked the part of a bloodied Roman gladiator, but one now wearing an earpiece and smartwatch. These guys, they loved their tech.

"Radiance," he said, greeting Callie.

"Husband," she replied and rose to meet him. There was a pause, like they would have embraced, but then they noticed each other – him, her cream dress, her, his oil, fake blood, and dirt-covered breast-plate. They stopped and instead, exchanged chaste lip-to-lip kisses.

"Makeup would have a fit if they had to match my blood makeup again," he apologized.

"Of course." She smiled.

"I see you've met my head of security? Worthy is a good man and has a very fitting name." He gave me his Hollywood-side smile, the sort the hero throws to his sidekick. I gave him a grunt back.

"Miss Rex will be staying with us the rest of the afternoon and we will be attending dinner together this evening. Let's keep this clean and tight, no photographers, no intruders."

"Ever vigilant," I said, and he beamed. It was some stupid catchphrase from one of his older action films. I gritted my teeth and told myself the bonus pay was worth it. He took Calanthe's hand and led her toward his trailer.

"Worthy?" he asked.

"Present, sir," I replied.

"Make sure that no one bothers my wife and I for a while. Nothing short of missiles falling from the sky, understand?" he asked. I nodded and said nothing. They went inside and pulled the door shut. There was a soft hiss as the lock partially engaged, but there was no click of the bolt. Maintenance still hadn't addressed that. I turned my back to the door, pushed my shoulder into it, and then heard the *snick* of the latch engaging.

"Tomcat and Cardinal are in Rex1, elevate to orange," I said into the general security channel on the push-to-talks. One by one, the detail acknowledged the threat level, and made the appropriate changes in posture.

"Test six," the tower chimed. "Assets to G3, assets to G3 thirty minutes."

I watched as a drone lifted off from the tower and swung north toward the main gate.

"Sarge?" The tower chirped me on my private channel.

"Go ahead, tower," I replied.

"Bogeys are moving from G1 toward G3. Delay was about thirty seconds," he said.

"Copy that. Let's see about scrambling the channels at the end of the day. Those only lasted about three days. They're getting faster at cracking the signals."

"At least the Taliban wasn't that good," he said.

"Aye, and they were just shooting at us." I laughed softly and pulled a cigarette from my crumpled pack. "Kurt out."

I puffed the smoke a few times. I kept my eyes moving, and tried not to listen, without putting in music or something else to drown the sounds coming from the RV out. Rex was not a gentle man, and I could hear both of them, the slap of skin against skin, choking and gagging noises, and what could only be her weeping.

Not my concern. What my boss did with his wife was beyond none of my business.

I flicked the butt, pulled another cigarette and lit it.

These people were fucking animals.

2

Calanthe...

I heard my husband coming. It was hard not to with his entire entourage. It was just enough time to hide Kurt's books away. He didn't know any better, and I didn't want to cause him any grief or trouble for the small kindness. Small kindnesses turned into big kerfuffle's around the New Eden Centre with a depressing regularity.

Our public greeting was brief and awkward. I smiled and laughed for our audience, as it was expected of me, but Arik had that predatory look in his eyes, that set to his shoulders. He was in a mood, and I was about to choke on it, surely.

As soon as the trailer door shut, he dropped all pretenses.

"Take off your dress and get on your knees, Calanthe."

I hesitated, and he scowled at me. "*Today,* woman. I only have a certain amount of time between shots, and I don't need you wasting it."

I felt myself color and his smile became wicked.

I disrobed and he worked his cock out of his costume. I made to move closer, but he stopped me with an, "Ah, ah!"

I went slowly to my knees, and he smiled.

"That's a good girl," he murmured and stood, hands on his hips, cock rising as I crawled toward him.

"Don't fuck up the blood or makeup," he warned me as I reached him.

"No, Husband," I murmured, and I took him into my mouth. I could have gagged from that alone, but he grasped me by the roots of my long hair and did that for himself, thrusting himself past my teeth and into the back of my throat. I choked at the unexpectedness and cruelty of it, tried to swallow around him, and sobbed. He wasn't particularly *big*, or *long*, but it was enough.

I tried to blank my mind, to go somewhere else, but that was a lot harder to do than it sounded with the insistent, painful tugging at my hair and the choking and inability to get a full breath.

I gagged especially hard, and he pulled back, allowing me to breathe a moment which ended on a strangled sob.

"What did I say about costume and makeup, Radiance?" he asked me, and I stumbled out an apology, hating myself for it. Hating all of this. Hating everything.

I just wanted to die.

They wouldn't let me.

How did I know? I'd tried... last year.

"Up," he commanded, and I fought to get my legs under me. Arik was cruel, liked it when girls flushed and colored, liked it when they cried, which is precisely why I'd been chosen for him.

Apparently, I was pretty, even when I cried.

"Don't want to nut in that pretty mouth of yours, not when we're trying to make a baby, right?" he asked, and I obediently bent over the end of the bed. He didn't bother bringing my lace panties down, just moved them aside and shoved inside me.

This was easier to deal with in some respects. He, at least, wouldn't be getting what he wanted out of his prized broodmare. I made sure of that.

He fucked me with never a care about getting me off. In fact, the few times that I had were a deep source of shame, as though my own body had betrayed me. I closed my eyes, gripped the covers beneath my hands, and let him ride me. It was over faster when I didn't resist.

I hated how he'd suckered me in the beginning. Always sweet, so respectful, until he'd slid the ring on my finger, and I'd discovered too late that the gold band was a pair of shackles in disguise. I was forever chained to Arik Rex and, by default, the New Eden Centre and I hated it. Hated myself for being so naïve and wishing that I'd been born into far different circumstances.

The wet slapping of his cock driving into me ended in a crescendo of his satisfied grunting. He slipped out of me, slapping me on the ass with a cruel smirk.

"Clean yourself up and get back to the mansion," he said. "We'll go again when I get home tonight. App says you're primed."

I hated that fucking app – the one that tracked my cycle when I was ovulating, all from the convenience of *his* phone.

Part of being beholden to the New Eden Centre was to be a good wife and mother to the next generation charged with the continuation of the healing of our planet. The planet was life and Mother to us all, and we were charged with her protection and care into the future, into the beyond...

All lies. All to keep men like Arik and August happy and content with young pussy.

He threw my dress down into my hands and said, "Don't even think about showering before you leave. Gotta give my little swimmers time to reach their goal."

I nodded mutely, and he left the trailer. I looked after him, cringing when Kurt looked past my husband to see me on the floor in my underwear.

Humiliation was par for the course.

I dressed and took the time to settle myself before I went back outside. Kurt was waiting and I handed him his book.

"Thank you for letting me borrow this," I said.

"You finished?" he asked, steely blue eyes skating over my face. I couldn't meet his eyes and just shook my head. He seemed nice.

"No," I answered. "But Arik wouldn't like it if he knew I had it. You don't know any better... I took advantage. I apologize," I said.

"It's no trouble, it's just a book," he said.

I nodded and took a deep, cleansing breath.

"Shall we?" I asked.

"Your makeup... the paparazzi are around the bend," he said, and I sniffed and pulled my big, bug-eyed sunglasses out of my purse and put them on my face.

"Sufficient?" I asked.

He gave me a strange, lingering look and nodded. I put a dazzling smile on my face, and he sort of reared back. I asked, "Shall we then?"

He nodded. "Right you are, Miss Callie. This way."

He escorted me back to the waiting car – my prison transport back to my gilded cage.

3

____

*K*urt...

One of the first things you learn about major cities is that there are a lot of strange people who live in them, living their own lives, doing their own weird thing. Then you learn that regardless of what that weird thing is, you stay the fuck out of it. People lying on the ground are something to be avoided. Over in Afghanistan, and some other countries that we were officially never in, you might see someone lying in the road or next to it. The humane thing is to stop and render aid, or just drag the body out of the road just out of respect and not driving over it with a convoy.

That's when the snipers start picking your guys off, or the bomb that they're wrapped around detonates. Urban encounters are similar, but they don't explode. You end up being part of a performance art piece, blood thrown in your face while another asshole you didn't notice uploads it to social media. It's a homeless person and you've rolled a crazy over, and they decided that the best course of action is to take a bite out of your face, or maybe take a couple fingers.

The lessons are quickly learned.

Sometimes it's a mugger with a concealed gun, and then it's in your belly button while they're telling you to hand over the goods. Sometimes it's a revolver, sometimes it's a flashlight, but who rolls those dice?

The same thing is applied with couples. There are people who seem like they have no reason to be together, the chemistry makes no sense, the dynamic isn't there. But that was in public and there was no telling what they were like when no one was watching. That's what it was like with Arik and Callie. In public they were a celebrity couple, pretty in all the pictures. In person, their relationship was cold, cold like ice. She said things sometimes that were disturbing, that painted a dark picture. Unsettling to me...

Then they'd be in REX 1, and I could hear them going at it like animals, gagging and gasping, groaning, and shouting.

Afterwards, Arik would come strutting out like King Shit, Lord of the World. Callie would come out later, looking like a scalded lobster. It was the pale skin. It was like that for people who were that pale – they only had the two colors, glacier and lobster – it didn't mean anything. There had been a lad in the company, skinny ginger kid, and he joked that he put on sunscreen before bed, so he didn't get moon burn. Or there was the joke about turning the screen brightness on his phone down because he was getting tan lines on his face from the display.

He was a funny kid before a Taliban RPG turned him inside out.

I considered worrying about Callie, she seemed nice enough. If there was a problem, she was always with women from that New Eden group. I hadn't read any of the New Eden books, but it was mostly like a church, and church women were there for each other.

I actually take that back. I didn't consider anything; I *did* worry about her. But it just wasn't my place. Not until she said something, and even then? *Bloody hell...*

Filming ended late and getting the assets from the set back to their mansion up in the hills was an easy task. We scrambled signals, sent false instructions out on the compromised network, and then watched as the paparazzi went chasing after three sedans, while Tomcat and Cardinal left moments afterwards in SUVs.

Once they were away, my shift was over, and I logged out of the network. I wouldn't be on call again for hours. The house detail at the mansion would take over once they were secure, and in the morning, I would resume my duties. After having listened to Rex lay into his little ginger like she was a Bangkok whore, I needed to get rid of some of that mental noise. I needed to get her out of my mind.

The cure for mental noise was actual noise, and that meant hitting up one of the bars close to the set. There were also two effective methods to stop thinking about a woman – one was to get smashingly drunk, and the other was to pick up another woman for a night.

The first part was easy enough, there were several dozen in walking distance from the studio gates, ranging from dirty dives up to high-end places that offered a dirty-dive chic experience for the Kristal and caviar crowd. I picked the former, a dirty hole-in-the-wall with a shite live band, and a blinking neon sign that screamed topless servers after eleven.

The plan was simple, assault the frontal lobe with high-grade alcohol and provide support with loud music. It was a simple plan.

As for the second option, there was always a chance that I could run into the regular – a shallow needy woman who's just broken up with her piece of shit boyfriend and is looking for some rebound dick to remind her she was still young and pretty and could have any man she wanted. Being tall, broad-shouldered, thick in the neck, an overly serious expression, and the military tats on my arm drew them like flies to honey.

Most of the time I blew them off.

The cocky arrogant ones who came up to make demands were told to fuck right off with their twatty nonsense. There were some who were given the hard no when they walked up – the ones with the incredibly obvious baggage, signs of hard drug use, or seriously lacking personal hygiene. My personal least favorites were the slightly above-average good-looking ones who would come up, trailing their reluctant partner behind them, wanting me to play the bull for their cuckold fantasy.

Hard pass on that.

On occasion, though, the right one would come along.

Plastic free, natural hair color, that *girl-next-door* vibe, no outrageous makeup, a few hints that she had more going on in her life than being a barfly. Those were the ones that I would take back to their own places, put their ankles behind their ears, and give them the old two, six, heave until they were shaking.

The main point was that I didn't look for any of these women. I didn't hunt for them. There was a whole city full of self-important dude bros with identical haircuts, hunting and chasing everything with a pair of X chromosomes. They reminded me of the feral dogs that I had seen in Afghanistan, and during a brief stint in South Africa. They moved in packs, sniffing out the sick, the weak, the vulnerable, and made them their targets. Women almost instinctively recognized them and avoided them.

I pounded a shot of Jameson, then drank my beer. The rest was listening to the band as it struggled through a few songs and watching a few of the different screens around the place. It was a fucking mess – one had streaming news, another had some sports' shite playing, another was running vintage cartoons. The place was a madhouse. I was three drinks in when eleven rolled around and the bags and jubblies came out.

Pity.

Some of them should have stayed up. The next time I went out drinking after a day on the set, I would have to pick somewhere else.

None of the wankers in the bar cared too much. There was a lot of wolf whistling and pounding on tables. For a pair of tenners, one of the topless waitresses would come over and give your face a good bap beating.

I wasn't having any of that.

There was something about just wanting to be left alone that seemed to make people relentless in bothering me. Maybe that was part of the big city, I guessed. Everyone was supposed to be part of the hive, part of the human swarm – whistle at titties, harass women, get in fights with other dude bros whose collars were popped at different angles from your collar. Staying out of it made me a target, of sorts.

The news did catch my eye. I saw the flashy colors and logos. There was the symbol of New Eden, and then it turned into a mushroom cloud. Then, there was a woman with short auburn hair, shaking a fist and shouting wordlessly. The only sound was the reverberating wail of the band, and a waitress hitting me up – twenty for a titty beating or if I wanted another beer. I waved her away with an order for another shot of Jameson and I pulled out my phone.

It didn't take long to bring up the local news affiliate and link to the story.

FALLOUT Spokeswoman and Founder Marion Tate Puts New Eden on Blast – the headline was scrolling across the screen. I read a little into the story, some bint was going on about how she had been sex trafficked by the New Eden Centre in San Luis Obispo.

It wasn't a new story, and not the first time that I had seen that woman. She had been in the news a few times, trying to stir up shit against New Eden, but the best she could manage was some topical outrage. Hard to get traction against an organization that was all clean air and electric cars, techno-socialism for everyone. Believing that New Eden was into human trafficking was as laughable as those assholes chasing Bigfoot or the local loons who went tromping off into the marshes looking for the fucking snallygaster.

"Everyone is looking for something to believe in, you know," a woman said, sliding into the spot next to me at the bar. Her sudden appearance put me on alert. I wasn't a fan of sudden things.

"Pardon?"

"You know, New Eden, Jesus, Oprah, everyone is looking for something to believe in." She gestured to the muted screen of the ranting woman next to the mushroom cloud icon, and then my phone. She had looked over my shoulder.

"No atheists in a foxhole," I replied, a familiar enough expression.

"Army?" she asked.

"Royal Marines." I nodded.

"Can I buy you a cup of tea?" She gave me a smile.

"Last time I checked, it was the lad's duty to buy the pretty girl a drink at the bar."

"Oh? You think I'm pretty and you want to buy me a drink?" She smiled. She had walked me back into a corner and knew it.

"I'll buy you a drink if you come off the hard pitch," I said. "I'm not looking for anything other than some noise, and a few cold beers." As if sensing my conversation, the band took that moment to launch into a thrash session that was as loud as it was poorly executed. I looked over to see what they were doing to make such an awful racket. It seemed that the problem was that the lead singer and the guitarist were trying to match their head flails while facing each other, and the guitar player was either drunk or one of his hands had gone numb, possibly from doing whatever the hot drug was for shitty bands.

"There's plenty of both here, Big Ben." She laughed, a little forced, her eyes a little tight.

"What's the angle, boyfriend piss you off?" I asked.

"I don't have a boyfriend," she replied, and I gestured for the bartender to bring us two more. "I'm not on the rebound, but I think I might have misread you."

"If that is an apology, I'll take it," I said.

"Look, you are a prime slice of beef and I want to take you home. Maybe you can make me need a handicap tag for my car for a few days." She raised her eyebrows a few times, licking her lips and then biting on one for a moment.

"You know what? Sure. Why the fuck not?" I said.

Fifteen minutes later, we were in her apartment. It wasn't too bad, I had seen worse. She wanted to talk, wanted to make out, then talk more. Her big talk wasn't so big when we were alone, and not in the bar. She was asking about friends, family, what part of England I was from. I answered a few questions, but my mind was somewhere else.

Chunky sunglasses.

Thick foundation.

Always wearing a scarf, or shawl that covered her neck, shoulders. Almost like a chic hijab.

Calanthe was still firmly pressed in the back of my mind.

"I was under the impression you wanted something very specific," I said. "I'll not put you on, that's the only reason I'm here. You're pretty, and you cut straight to the point. So, are we going to do that, or do you want to chitchat yourself to a solo night with your good vibes?" She seemed taken aback, and that was fine. If she didn't want to get down to business, I could leave as easily as I came.

"I'm not used to it really going like this," she said.

"Are you ready to go?" I asked.

"Go?" she asked.

"Go, shag, fuck. Are you ready to do that or do you need a minute?" I asked. I felt pieces sliding into place. Those ugly fucking sunglasses might as well have been the international symbol for domestic abuse.

Thick makeup, Arik's entire attitude... was he really a wife beater? More than just cheating on Callie, was he physically abusing her?

"I think I need a minute," she stammered.

"Go on, get yourself ready, I'm going to have a smoke," I said and put my hand on the doorknob.

"You don't have to go," she said softly.

"It's rude to smoke inside someone's apartment," I said. She nodded, and I stepped outside the door, pulled a smoke from the pack, and lit it. It was a sweet kiss of relief. Standing in the cool air, smelling the distantly foul stink of the city, I found that my mood was gone. Instead of getting Cardinal out of my mind, I had half a buzz and had focused on her. Everything she did was to cover bruises.

The last thing I really wanted was this. Oh, sure, the woman inside was pretty enough, and there was no doubt she had some baggage going on. Was a good dicking going to do anything to make that better or worse? I also had the visual image of Callie in my mind, what Arik had likely done to her. I knew he was a right bastard, and that he liked doing some kinky shit, but this wasn't Hollywood perversion.

Her blurry makeup, snapping those big sunglasses in place, the remarkable smile she'd plastered on in a blink... It made me angry, and anger made me focus.

Almost as angry as I had been when she handed the book back to me, saying it was because he wouldn't approve. What did it matter what she read? She was a grown woman. Might not look like it, sure she would have gotten carded to go into an R-rated movie, but that didn't change anything.

And if he could raise a hand against her?

If the woman had come to the door, anytime during that smoke, things might have gone the way she wanted. After I tossed the first butt, I considered lighting another one, but there was no need. I didn't know what she was doing to get ready, but my patience was just gone. I left the front of the apartment, walked down the stairs, and to my car. I had thought too much, and now I needed to act.

I stopped and looked back. Maybe there would have been a flicker of movement, a sign of the woman. Maybe she was just fucking sitting on her couch, waiting for me to piss off, or she might have been furiously dry shaving her lady garden, or twisting into some ridiculous lingerie. The best thing she could have done for me was drop the pretense, drop her knickers, and show me her bottom.

But everything had to be involved and difficult.

I pulled the door of the car shut and pressed the start button. I hated that. Just give me a bloody *key*.

I sighed.

Bad luck seemed to follow me through every job I had ever had, and it seemed that nothing had changed. I had been hired to be the head bodyguard to a leading Hollywood celebrity, and now, I knew, if what I suspected was true? I had just become his number one threat.

If I didn't end up in jail after this job, I needed something that literally could not be fucked up.

I put the car in gear and headed toward the Rex mansion, up in the hills.

4

*C*alanthe...

I was sitting at the table, working on a jigsaw puzzle, one of the few things I was allowed to do, but pretty much only nature scenes – which was honestly fine for me. I liked them well enough, sometimes daydreaming about the sounds that would come with actually being there. The rushing water, the rasp of the leaves in the trees as the wind swept through them... you know, just transporting myself into the scene and away from here if I could.

It was a long way from where I thought I would be, though. I had been First Among First Daughters, a Youth Leader in the Youth Corps, I had dreams. I hadn't dreamed of being a doctor or a lawyer, or a judge. There were plenty of First Daughters who were better suited to that. What I had dreamed of had been to become a politician, a leader. My goals hadn't been so lofty as Madam President, but becoming a congresswoman? A senator? Totally attainable. I could have used my connections with the New Eden Centre, with August Emerson, with the celebrities we knew – junior senator, then senior senator. *A career...*

What cabinets and committees could I have been attached to?

Ways and means?

Oversight?

The possibilities had seemed endless.

The number of puzzle pieces was not endless, and I put the last piece in place. The rolling hills and flowers were complete, and it was another puzzle finished. There was at least a sense of peace and purpose when I did these puzzles. I sighed.

Of course, that sense of peace wasn't to be. Not for long anyway, especially when Arik was home. Usually, it was just him talking on his cellphone, loudly through his Bluetooth, or laughing obnoxiously at *TMI Newz*, the gossip show after the nightly news that he was watching in the other room. I, of course, wasn't *allowed* to watch, even though the volume would be turned up loud enough that it was impossible to miss a thing.

Everything had to be loud, over the top, in your face when it came to the Arik Rex.

He had a thing for watching the celebrity gossip programs. I hated it when he did that. He took such delight in the misfortunes of his A-list celebrity compatriots and was so quick to fly into an incandescent *rage* whenever he himself was caught at something or featured in a way he didn't like.

The only thing that seemed to make him angrier was when the paparazzi and the gossip mags focused on *me*, his much younger and beautiful wife. He loathed it when the attention was off him and placed on me as I was supposed to merely be an *extension* of him and not my own person.

Misogyny thy name is Arik, I thought to myself.

"Trouble in Paradise?" I heard the annoying and smarmy Miss bitchy blonde, Heather Dee bleating loudly from the living room.

"Looks like it," her lumbersexual male counterpart, Rob Dee, agreed.

"Last week, we showed you footage and photographs of Calanthe Rex, Arik Rex's young wife, going into a fertility clinic popular with the celebrity jet set due to their strict confidentiality and secrecy."

"That's right, Heather. Except now, we've got an exclusive and confidential source that says Mrs. Rex isn't going to the clinic for fertility treatments as has been widely reported."

"Oh, no! Robby, I thought according to Rex and his people, Calanthe was trying really hard to conceive," Heather declared.

"Apparently not," Rob said. *"According to our source, Mrs. Rex has been trying just the opposite and has been receiving injections for birth control!"*

"I wonder if Mr. Rex knows that," Heather said, laughing. The television went silent, and then I heard him stand. A few moments later, his rage exploded from the living room. He screamed, all venom and bile. How dare they spread those stories, not without speaking with him first. The audacity of going live before even thinking of talking to him. Something was thrown across the room and shattered. I jumped and scattered the puzzle pieces I was trying to put back in the box. There was more screaming – how he would cut them off, make the calls he had to, to make sure they lost their jobs.

Of course, none of what he blustered about would really happen. Sometimes it did, but Arik wasn't as all powerful as he liked to think. I sat in frozen terror and listened to Arik rage some more.

There was something about insulting Rob Dee's strap-on beard, and that if he wanted, he would have the plastic surgeon repossess Heather Dee's fake tits so he could use them as paperweights on his desk, because that was all she was good for. I couldn't guess who was on the other end of the line, but he fell silent as he listened, and whoever said what? Well, he seemed to be placated by it. He stopped screaming, his tone dropping, emanating from him scathing and acidic. Then there was a final reprimand that if they pulled a stunt like this again, he would personally show up to fuck all of them in the ass, and then beat them to death with their own microphones.

There was a long pause, a foreboding like a pending storm.

I felt Arik's seething gaze fall upon me.

I looked up slowly. The puzzle box lid I had been holding fell from my suddenly nerveless fingers.

I'd seen Arik angry; I'd even seen those eyes wild with a combination of alcohol, drugs, and raw emotion, but the coldness that radiated from them now terrified me in a different sort of way, as though the fire of his anger had gone out, as though the tide of his emotion had been pulled back from the shore and this silence, this deafening silence was simply the calm before all of it came rushing out, came rushing back in and I was right in the path of his impending tsunami of rage.

Arik wasn't the tallest of men, quite average in height and build in person, actually, but right now? He positively loomed in the doorway that separated my sitting room from the rest of the house. I stood up slowly and he asked, voice hollow, "Is it true, Radiance?"

"What? Is what true, Husband?" I asked, feigning as though I hadn't heard.

"Don't fucking play with me, *Callie*."

Oh, oh no, he never used my preferred nickname over my given one unless he were absolutely *enraged*.

I went to brush past him casually, to get out of the room and hoping against hope that I could make it, saying, "I don't know what you're talking about Arik. You'll have to tell me."

He caught my arm and fixed my eyes with his and I felt my mouth go dry. I swallowed hard, my throat very nearly clicking with the effort when he said, voice the embodiment of winter itself, "Don't play with me, *child*."

"Arik, I don't know what you're talking about." I frowned and his hand flashed, faster than light, lighter than air, but when it crashed into the side of my face, it did so with the force of a cinder block. I cried out and put a hand to the stinging print of the back of his hand and tears stung my eyes. I felt the color creep and he threw me out into the living room and down the two carpeted steps. I put my arms out and gritted my teeth as the heels of my hands slid across the carpet, stinging with a burn almost right away.

I scrambled to my feet before he could start kicking and the tsunami crashed. He was screaming at me, my ears still ringing from the slap. When I turned to face him, I turned right into his closed fist, crashing into the same side of my face he'd only slapped the moment before.

I screamed and he came at me. Both of us tumbled to the carpet. I think I was screaming, his fist crashing into the side of my face, my head, boxing my ear. I had my arms up, trying futilely to protect myself, but there was no protection from Arik when he was this angry. There never had been.

"Are you not entertained?" Arik screamed. "Everything I do, everything I put up with, and that is the garbage that won the awards?" My head might as well have been underwater for all I could hear, all I could see.

His fist crashed into the side of my jaw, a strike that for a moment I could appreciate. It was almost his signature move, his finishing strike for different fights his different movie personas all ultimately used. My vision winked out for a few seconds, and everything seemed to be caught in slow motion. That was bad, but it didn't hurt. Everything started to shift, like the sun was moving in the sky.

I was falling, my legs were gone.

Consciousness would chase quickly after that.

I wanted to thank whatever higher power there might be that existed, but I didn't really believe in any. I couldn't. Not when there were men like Arik Rex. Not when there were men like the ones who put me with him. Not when my own *mother...*

There was *darkness.*

Silence.

Then a jarring intrusion into this floating museum of intro-spection.

"Callie?" I put up my hand and tried to pull myself away from the masculine voice. I wept; my own voice as broken as the rest of me as I feebly tried to pull myself across the blood-smeared carpet.

"Oh, no, love. You're safe. I've got you now."

I shrieked at a touch on my arm, strong fingers wrapping around my forearm. I couldn't breathe, chest heaving, breath sawing in and out of my lungs, head pounding with heat. The taste in my mouth – metallic with blood and fear – made me nauseous.

I was hoisted to my feet and everything rushed and whirred, swirling in a miasma of color and then blessed calming black. The last thing I remember was fetching up against something hard and covered in cloth, the sensation of floating.

The Woodrow Linea couch. I'd fallen against that awful, hard, modern couch in our living room. With my face pressed against it, I could make out the pattern in the upholstery, the tasteful use of different colored fibers making up its limited-edition Warhol orange fabric, and my blood smeared across it.

I hurt, everything hurt, so I welcomed the ensuing oblivion with open arms and prayed that this time would be the time I wouldn't wake up.

5

———

Kurt...

The Hollywood mansion wasn't the first war zone I had walked into, but it was the most upscale, and the least lethal. I entered the house and immediately heard screaming and ranting. Arik was under a full head of steam and was spouting lines from his less successful films. I knew enough of his filmography to know that the movies he was quoting were the ones that held more or less to the New Eden philosophy, a green and pure earth, all that shit, and had tanked. Critically panned, or the thing that filled him with bile, his Raspberry nominations, and awards.

When I stepped into what amounted to Callie's recreation area, the scene was shocking. She was face down against the overpriced sofa; blood smeared across it. There was more blood all over the carpet, and it was obvious whose it was. Arik turned to face me, his face a mask of ruddy rage, eyes bulging and bloodshot. He clenched his fists around the base of one of his awards, an angel made of gold. There was blood on it, and the wings were damaged. Had he struck her with that?

I moved quickly, my first instinct being to discount him as a threat and the need to assess if Calanthe was still fucking alive. A human being could take a lot of damage and keep moving. She might have been a wisp of a thing, but that meant she had to be tough, have some core of iron inside her.

She wouldn't have lasted with Arik Rex otherwise.

I felt him approach me, before I could kneel next to her. She was breathing, ragged, and hitched. She was sobbing. "Callie?" I asked, and she recoiled from the sound of my voice.

That meant she wasn't dead and didn't need CPR or the defib machine that hung in the hallway linens' closet. Arik was filled with the sort of rage that only celebrities seemed to possess. It made sense, really, they were never held accountable for their actions. Men like Arik Rex could commit felonies, and at the end of the judicial system, their victims would end up in jail.

The golden angel struck me in the shoulder, near the base of the neck, and it sounded like Arik was screaming at me like my name was Quintus, or Jenner? I wasn't sure. I rolled with the hit, away from Callie's prostrate form, and across the carpet. I needed the space, and a few seconds to figure out what I was going to do.

Draw my sidearm? No good. He was full of himself, and if I shot him, I went to jail. I went to jail for a long time.

I couldn't strike him, and if I did, I couldn't leave a single mark on him. A jury would see a discharged Royal Marine sitting across from the man that they loved through two dozen movies, voice-over jobs, and several famous cartoon characters. I would be treated like a third world dictator caught trying to flee his own country.

I rose, adopted a fighting stance, and beckoned for Arik to come at me.

He took a step, and then a second, his eyes glazed with a rage that seemed unnatural. I had seen eyes like that before, but they were buried in the face of a man who had spent months living cave to cave, carrying nothing but a rifle and his own fury, to fight the Western world for invading his country.

It was surreal seeing that same intensity in the eyes of a man who had a personal esthetician on staff around the clock. He brandished the damaged angel at me – a heavy, poorly balanced, misshapen club.

"I'll destroy you, boy," Arik hissed through his teeth. I felt the urge to smash those perfectly pearly whites down his throat but knew that couldn't happen.

"I'm not afraid of a man who cares what the Dees on *TMI* say or cried when the Man with the Golden Thumb approved of his pet miniseries," I said. The taunt struck and he gave a shout and lunged with the poorly shaped improvised weapon. Basic hand-to-hand and self-defense would have served him better than all of the Hollywood choreographers and stunt coordinators had. I struck inside his wrist, forcing him to drop the gold-plated monstrosity to the floor.

There were a half-dozen moves I could have followed the disarming with, but I couldn't. This was a challenge because I knew I couldn't leave any marks on him; nothing he could use as evidence of assault. One bruise could be enough. I let his lunge pass me. Instead of any of the throws, leg sweeps, or actual close quarter combat, or CQC, I knew to be effective, I grabbed him by the belt and the back of his custom-fit overpriced polo. He gave a choked scream, and immediately threw an elbow back. I took the hit on the shoulder, a solid one at that.

He twisted to try throwing his Hollywood haymaker at me.

Bad angle, no momentum, but still caught me in the side of the head and broke my sunglasses.

He screamed something too. He could scream all he wanted. What staff was here bunkered down or hid when he was in a rage like this, and no one called the police in this household. That mistake had been made once, and from what I'd heard, that poor woman had been deported to San Salvador. She wasn't from San Salvador, she was from Wisconsin, born and raised. His lawyers were either just that crooked or just that good, as were all his connections.

I took another blow to the cheek before I could get an arm under his to pull him into a grapple. We both went to the ground, and I took the force of the fall. The glass-top table cracked, and then broke. The glass part had the decency to not shatter until it was already against the floor. Arik flailed, but I stayed wrapped around him and worked until I could loop an arm around his neck, and then pulled him into a sleeper choke hold.

Thankfully, the screaming and ranting stopped, but he kept throwing body blows with his elbows, and kicking. But cut off from breathing, he started running out of steam really fucking fast. His last few seconds of activity was all body tension and clawing at my arm around his neck. At this point, the cocksucker should be graying out, or seeing spots in his vision, all that fury kicking his ass harder than I had. I felt him tremble, flail a few more times, and then he went limp.

I kept the hold for a few more seconds. I had seen a particularly salty American Marine come out of a quick release choke hold like an absolute bear. Later, I found out he liked to fake going limp, and when the hold was released, jacking up the guy who got him down. He was a hell of a wrestler.

I rolled Arik off of me and pulled myself to sit against the sofa.

Callie was still breathing, thank fucking fuck. I contemplated a smoke but decided that wasn't the best use of my time. I would be better served checking myself and getting her back on her feet, and out of this place. When I tried to move her, she shrieked. It was an ear-piercing sound, but God only knew what sort of condition she was in. I pulled her upright, and her head rolled on her shoulders. Her eyes were closed. The bruises were going to be hideous when they fully bloomed. She guttered out a thick sob.

"Oh, no, love. You're safe. I've got you now," I said, but I don't know that she heard me. She went slack in my arms, going uncon-scious. "Well fuck," I grunted.

I picked her up like she was a child, surprisingly light in my arms, and carried her out of the crime scene. I was thankful she was light; my neck hurt, and I could feel my back sticky with blood. The table? The award? I wasn't sure, but it didn't matter at this point. Forward action, always forward action. I sat her down in the front foyer, in an overstuffed chair that seemed more decorative than for sitting. She had several shawls and stoles in the front closet, and those would be useful for keeping her warm, and hiding her injuries for the time being.

What a fucking arse he was, striking a woman as beautiful as her. *Bloody hell, to strike any woman!*

Disgusting.

I took one of Arik's oversized coats meant to fit over his full costume off the back of a chair and pulled it on, concealing the worst of the blood. I needed to get her out of here, get *us* out of here. I had a plan earlier, and it had seemed like a good plan, but that was before the fight, before several hits to the head, and definitely before there was a woman beaten bloody. Fuck all, what was I doing? There was the Little Free Clinic a few miles from here, but they might recognize her. I couldn't stay. We couldn't stay. My mind was starting to chase its own tail.

Forward action. I opened the door, picked up Callie, and carried her out to the sedan. It took almost everything I had to get the back door open and her inside without dropping her or setting her down next to the car. It was awkward as fuck getting her settled in, and once I shut the door, I looked up to see two of the housekeepers standing in the doorway of the house.

"Mister Worthington?" the taller of the two women spoke.

"Yes, Esme?" I asked.

"Are you taking her somewhere safe?" she inquired. I nodded in agreement. "Far away from here?"

"Yes, I am," I said. "She's not safe here."

"We'll clean up the mess," the shorter woman said. It looked like she was on the verge of tears. Concern for Callie? Concern for themselves? I didn't know.

"When someone from security comes, tell them to send me an email, my phone is broken," I said. They both nodded. "And be careful. It's easier to find a new job than it is to wake up in the hospital."

For a moment I could see, I could understand. They had their own world, where it was them on one side, and the wealthy and powerful on the other, and people like me, the security people and the guards, we were a foot in both. But right now, blood on my hands, I was firmly one of them. I had turned on the man that had hired me. The very best thing I could expect was to be fired and blacklisted from the industry. Worst case, bounty hunters? *Who knew what a man like Arik was capable of doing?* There were hired killers, I knew several personally. The last thing I wanted was for one of them to come after me, to recover her.

To haul her back into that golden cage of misery and brutal beatings.

I drove us out of the Hollywood Hills, down into the thick of Los Angeles. It was a mess of traffic, snarled roads, and the persistent stink of the city, of the smog. While driving, I took my phone, powered it down, and popped the back off to pull out the SIM card. The card was easy to snap, and then discard the two tiny pieces of silicone out the window onto the side of the freeway.

The next stop was a storage facility a few miles from the apartment where I occasionally slept. Old habits die hard, and there were several exceedingly important things kept in the double-locked unit. The largest and most important was my truck. The short bed '68 was patina red, with a rollbar, lift kit, and was romantically American. It was the first vehicle I had bought that hadn't been a rolling piece of trash, or German. I had bug-out bags in the back, and several locked cases in the bed. Those were highly questionable in California, as they contained a sizeable arsenal of firearms. I was sure most of the guns were illegal in this state, but it was California, and it was only a matter of time before the legislature started passing measures limiting the number of knives a steakhouse could have or limiting the size of tools for being too dangerous.

I moved Callie from the back of the car to the passenger seat of the truck and secured her in with the seatbelt. Her pulse was steady, and she didn't seem to be in any sort of life-threatening distress. Lord knew I had seen enough of that in my life. I swapped the vehicles out, backing the sedan into the unit. I took my travel bag from the trunk of the car, tossed it in the back of the truck and winced. He must have really nailed my shoulder with that fucking award.

Last thing before dropping and locking the door was popping the hood of the car and disconnecting the battery. Power killed, and parked inside a metal shell, it might take them days to find the car, if ever. I locked the unit and got into the truck.

This was mental, just fucking mental.

I put the truck into drive and pulled out of the storage facility. An hour later, we were heading toward Las Vegas, and there was nothing on the scanner other than the usual dystopian chaos that was Los Angeles and Southern California – gangland shootings, a few police high-speed chases, helicopter chatter about traffic problems, a pair of Amber alerts ongoing, but nothing close to us. We might be in the clear.

We cleared Pomona, then through San Bernardino, and Callie came to as we were heading north, finally on I-15, aiming for Barstow, and passing between the forests that hemmed in the urban sprawl. She sat up slowly, pressing a hand against the window, and then the side of her head.

"Where am I?" she asked.

"Safe," I said. "You're safe."

"Arik?"

"Nowhere near you, and you never have to see him again," I said. "I'm working on putting distance between you and him."

"Kurt?" she asked.

"Yes, Callie?"

"Did you kidnap me?" she asked.

"I would like to think *rescue* is more of what I had in mind," I said. The thought had occurred to me, but it was less pressing than getting away from Hollywood, from Arik, from the security people who technically worked for me, and that I helped hire. "I'll take you anywhere you want to go if you have somewhere you want me to take you. You are very specifically not a prisoner, captive, or anything like that."

"Oh, okay," she said, almost sounding let down.

"Is there somewhere you want me to take you? What about your family?" I asked. Callie shook her head, and immediately put her hand to her temple. I could see the instant regret.

"No, no." Her voice was soft. "I don't have anything, nor anywhere to go."

"I'm sorry," I said.

"It's not what you think. They're not dead... they're on his side," she said. "If I went to my family, they would give me back to him, and he's furious."

"Can I ask what happened?" I asked.

"Arik found out I've been receiving birth control at the fertility clinic," she said, her voice soft and ragged. "And then, well, you know."

"I thought you two were trying," I said. She snorted indelicately.

"*He* was trying. I don't want any kids. I was getting contraceptives from the clinic specifically *not* to be their broodmare. That's why he was so mad."

"Oh fuck." I whistled.

"Yeah, and if I go back, I'm pretty sure he'll kill me."

"I won't take you back to him," I vowed. "I have this pesky conscience that won't let me do things like that, no matter how much I get paid."

"I appreciate that, but where will you take me?" she finally asked.

"I have a place, it's completely off the grid," I said. "A cabin, outside Indigo City."

"Completely off the grid? What are you, some sort of militia nut?" she asked, her eyes focusing better than they had been.

"No, Afghan war veteran, and I found that I really liked living alone and not relying on anyone for anything," I said. "My last job, it paid really well, but there were some problems with HR, and I didn't agree with some of their business practices."

"I need a shower, and my clothes are ruined," she said, distracted again.

"You do, and I do too. How's your head?"

"Feels like I've been hit by a truck."

"I can get us a motel room and get you some clean clothes. You can shower and make sure you don't need medical treatment."

"I'll be okay," she said. "My head just hurts, and I feel disgusting and sticky."

"It will be slumming compared to what you're used to, but it is a start to something better," I promised, and I think part of that was for myself. Once again, I had fucked up a job. I fucked up working for the Escadrille Cartel, and for the Royal Marines before that, and college before that. It was my own personal fucking MO, get involved with the wrong person, the wrong group, and then rather than make the smart decision? Ruin everything.

Strike an officer.

Sign on with a heroin cartel.

Abduct the wife of an A-list celeb.

Could this get better? I was sure it could.

It was close to nightfall when I picked a small town off the side of the interstate and noted the historic Route 66 marker as we left the new pavement for a road that seemed like it hadn't seen a department of transportation truck in decades. I cruised another fifteen miles down the access road before finding the first town. It wasn't much, but they had everything that I was hoping to find. There was a motel, sunburned and rundown, a thrift store, and a place that looked like it might serve food.

We pulled into the parking lot of the proudly named *Motel*. That was it, just Motel. If it had been closer to the interstate, it would have fit the bill for a no-tell motel that rented rooms by the hour. Out here, no. This was still a seedy-as-fuck place, maybe somewhere drug deals went down and coyotes made their deliveries.

Callie seemed to take the place in stride as I used an actual metal key to open the faded door and let her into a room that had cost us thirty dollars for the night. The clerk hadn't blinked as he told me the pool was closed, the shower might or might not work, and there was no breakfast service. It was obvious the pool was closed, due to fact that there was no water in it, and rather than being covered with a tarp, it was closed off with overlapping sheets of chain-link fencing.

It reminded me of a prison, from a post-apoc movie.

I bolted the door and started checking the room. I looked at Callie who was at that point staring at me. "What are you doing?" she asked.

"I don't trust the place. Making sure there aren't any false doors, no recording devices, nothing like that," I said. I felt paranoid as shit, and I wasn't sure if it was from the events of the day, from the vibe of the place, or just the amount of blood I saw every time I looked in a mirror, or at her. "Why don't you take a shower, get cleaned up. Then I can make sure none of those injuries is more serious."

"I don't have any clothes to wear," she said, looking at me, and then her feet.

"Don't worry about it. I have a few things you can borrow in my bug-out, until we can get you something else," I said.

"Do you have women's clothing in your bag?" she asked.

"Well, no," I said. "You can wear one of my undershirts and a pair of sweatpants. We can run those clothes through the wash. There should be a laundromat somewhere, and there *is* a thrift store here. You can get some different clothes there."

"Well, I'm pretty sure this is Fenty and has to be dry cleaned," she said. "And the rest of that, I'm not really fluent in... that."

"Fluent in that?" I asked.

"I kinda know what some of those words mean, but I don't really know what they are," she said.

"Look, go take a bloody shower. I'll leave you some clean clothes on the bed. While I'm out, I'll find us some food, and see if I can find you some clean clothes more suited to you. If you want to run away while I'm gone, the phone is right there but I'm not sure if the line works. Like I said earlier, if you want me to take you somewhere, you say the place, and I'll take you."

"Except back to the mansion," she said.

"I can't go back, I choked Arik Rex unconscious in the middle of a shattered table. If I poke my head back up in Hollywood, I'm pretty sure the police will have me in cuffs faster than you can blink," I said. "I would rather take my chances on the run."

She nodded.

"While I'm gone, maybe don't take a nap. You took a hard enough hit to knock you out, and while your pupil response looks okay, and you don't seem to be exhibiting any signs of brain trauma, I don't trust it. I will see about finding you an anti-inflammatory for the pain and potential swelling."

Her expression reminded me of some Afghan children I remembered. The other side of the Yank's shock-and-awe campaign. Their homes had been hit by bombs bigger than anything this side of a plutonium-fueled weapon, and they had that same glazed expression, that same contained trauma. Most of them had been okay, and I thought that Callie would be too. There were some who weren't okay, and that would take time to sort out.

I left her alone, somewhat reluctantly, to go get the things we needed. She probably didn't need to be left alone, but there was no way I could drag her out into whatever this nameless stain on the side of the road was. No matter how jaded and numb people in Los Angeles were, people outside of the city would look twice at a woman covered in blood and bruises and the questions would begin, blame would be assigned. I sighed and found the thrift store closed – maybe tomorrow, maybe somewhere else down the road. I did manage to grab some food from a burger joint with a cracked yellow sign, and a bag of medical supplies from the gas station. The clerk seemed as bombproof as the horses on one of Rex's action movie sets.

I would have killed to find a dive bar, maybe grab a beer or two, and to be able to sit and watch a television news broadcast. I didn't know how hot the authorities were on us, and that was a concern. It would dictate what direction I needed to take. It was probably more important that I talk to Callie though. We had to have a plan, an understanding. Fuck, if it turned into something like abduction or kidnapping, crossing state lines, it would make assaulting Arik Rex look like flirting with prison.

The restaurant didn't offer much, so I took a paper bag of hamburgers and fries back to the room.

Calanthe was sitting on the foot of the bed when I came in. She immediately flinched away as I opened the door, but relaxed when she saw it was just me. "Hey." She gave me a lump of a smile. "I was wondering if you were coming back."

"I didn't think I was gone that long," I said.

"It wasn't that long, no. I was just worried that this wasn't real." I sat the paper bag down on the aged table, opened it, and handed her one of the burgers, and a paper cup of fries. "I was worried that eventually I was going to wake up with my face mashed into the carpet, and everything tasting like blood."

"I'm sorry," I said softly. "It took me way too long to figure out what was going on."

"No worries," she said. "Arik was very good at being discrete, probably better at hiding his temper than his infidelity."

"You know about that?" I asked.

"I have known. I'm a lot of things, but neither dumb nor blind." She gave me a half-smile.

"I take it you are feeling more yourself?" I asked.

"I am, and I have a single question."

"Shoot."

"Why Indigo City?"

"I have a cabin there," I answered.

"You said that already." She looked at me. Her eyes were sharp now.

"I bought a cabin there, awhile back. My last job paid really well, and I wasn't overly fond of living in the city itself."

"What happened to that job?"

"Well, I found out I was working for bad people, and had to resign."

"Worse than Arik?"

"Yeah, you could say that. They were into heroin trafficking, gun smuggling, international terrorism, all that. The people in charge had a change in management, and then things got interesting. A lot of people ended up getting shot. Hard to keep a job when your employers have been filled with bullets."

"That's frightening," she said.

"Yeah," I agreed.

"So, you're not a very good bodyguard?"

"I'm an excellent bodyguard. The cartel decided to not pay me the last few months of my employment. When the angry people with guns showed up, I had no reason to fight them. I took a few things, tossed them in my truck, and left. Called in a few favors and got a new job, working for Arik."

"Oh," she said.

"So, this is what I have to offer you. I have a cabin, outside of Indigo City. It's off the grid, and no one will find you there, if you don't want to be found."

"It's just a cabin?"

"It's just a cabin, a little Thoreau, but not without some comforts," I said. "I have books, a kitchen, that sort of thing. It's not a wooden box with no electricity or running water."

"That doesn't sound too bad, actually," she said.

"After that, it's figure out a new plan. I know people who know how to do new identities, start new lives, that sort of thing."

"Like a private sector Witness Protection Program?"

"Just like that," I said. "There are entire industries operating like that, in open secrecy."

"That is a lot to take in, really."

"It is. Private doctors, people dealing in merchandise like guns and body armor, custom cars, handling finances, tech stuff, they even have their own email system, Cryptonet. If they don't have them yet, I'm sure they'll have cryptophones that can't be tracked or monitored by the government – ghost phones, I guess."

"That's insane."

"That's the world we live in. You've just become aware of it."

"Who recommended you to my husband?" she asked.

"I can't tell you who, but I can tell you that he's a professional assassin."

Callie's face paled even further.

6

———

*C*allie...

I was quiet after that, trying to let everything that Kurt had told me sink in. It was terribly hard to think with how thoroughly my brain had been rattled in my skull, but it wasn't the first time I had had a concussion and it probably wouldn't be the last. It was a grim thought, knowing that I was likely on borrowed time, but I had learned, time and time again, just how long New Eden and Arik's reach was.

There was no escaping. Not for long, anyway.

To his credit, Kurt didn't feel the need to fill the silence between us with a bunch of questions or chatter. He just let me be, which was nice in a way, and scary in another. Arik seemed to always be talking, mostly about himself, and usually at a mile a minute to make it harder for the people listening to pick up on his grift or his bullshit.

It was hard to ask questions when you can't get a word in edge-wise. Kurt's strong silence was pleasant but still unnerved me because when Arik was quiet, he was calculating, and when Arik calculated, typically something cruel followed.

God, my head throbbed and ached. It didn't help that I couldn't sleep. I mean, all I wanted to do that first night *was* sleep, but any time I drifted off, it seemed like it was all too soon Kurt was gently shaking me awake. I knew he wasn't trying to be malicious – he was trying to protect me or save me. I'd been through this once or twice before. Wake up every hour on the hour to make certain I *would* wake up.

I knew that I was fundamentally changed by the injuries to my head, the previous ones at any rate. I didn't know how much more change I was in store for with this one. It didn't even surprise me anymore that I found myself wishing I wouldn't wake at all.

I didn't think I could take anymore, and simply not waking up? It seemed like the kinder way to go versus what Arik would do to me, and possibly what he would do to Kurt when he caught up to us.

"I'm so sorry," I said dully, and Kurt startled from the other bed and looked up from his battered paperback and over at me.

"For what?" he asked.

"For dragging you into this. For what he'll do when he catches us. For what New Eden will do."

He set the book down, frowning slightly and asked, "And just what will they do, Callie?" he asked me.

I sniffed and tried to keep the sob bubbling up my throat silent.

"I don't know, exactly... but I'm sure it will be bad. It's always been worse than what I imagined, so I try not to imagine those things anymore."

He grunted, a thoughtful yet noncommittal sound and stared for a time at nothing at all before returning to his book. I closed my eyes and cried quietly, the tears hot against my battered skin, the salt making it itch, but I knew better with all the bruising than to try and wipe them away.

The next day, when Kurt decided it was time to move on, he brought me a pair of gray sweatpants and a white tee shirt.

I went into the bathroom and showered. I hadn't the night before, scared I would pass out or fall and cause more problems. I'd said as much when he had returned to the hotel room and asked. He'd simply nodded.

The hot water felt good, but my face felt swollen beyond measure, and it was entirely too uncomfortable. I didn't feel like I could get a good wash on my hair – it was too long, almost to my knees, and the water pressure out of the shower was barely a trickle. At least it *was* hot, although I don't think hot was the right thing for my face or the swelling. I couldn't remember the word for the right thing readily, my brain foggy and every time I tried to think of it, the word eluded me. I could picture the thing, like glass, in cubes, and I could think of the word's synonym – *ice*, but I couldn't think of the word for the opposite of hot. Such a simple thing to forget, and so maddening that it was just out of my thought's reach.

I didn't look in the mirror. I didn't want to see if I couldn't think. I didn't need to fuel my nightmares any more than they were already fueled. I had plenty of fodder for the rest of my days.

When I came out dressed, Kurt looked up from the foot of his bed. He looked different. Very different. Gone was the suit and in its place, a pair of worn but comfortable-looking jeans with a few paint stains, and a white tee peeking from the collar of a plaid work shirt. Instead of loafers, he had on a sturdy brown pair of work boots, and he looked... I don't know... more real this way. Like suited Kurt had been an illusion all along. A costume.

He looked me over and frowned slightly at how I had to hold the sweatpants with one hand to keep them from falling.

"Did you use the drawstring?" he asked.

"Afraid so," I said, nodding carefully and slowly and he frowned.

"That's bloody unfortunate," he said, brow wrinkling. "I'll work on getting you something more suitable to your frame."

I nodded and murmured, "Thank you."

He did something unprecedented then and kneeled at my feet.

"A bit bloodstained, I'm afraid; but it's all you've got for now," he said and cupped my heel gently. I raised my foot and he slid one of my ballet flat house slippers onto my foot then just as carefully did the other.

He stood up and turned like he hadn't done anything at all and I just sort of stared at him for a moment, trying to decide what had just happened.

"You alright?" he asked, eyeing me a moment later.

"Um, yes, sorry..." I shook my head slightly as though to clear it and he frowned again.

"Let's get you in the truck," he said. "Some fresh air and a little sunlight might do you some good."

I inclined my head in agreement and followed him outside, wincing as the harsh sunlight lanced through my eyes and raked the back of my skull. My head instantly set to pounding, my brain feeling like it was throbbing and too swollen on the outset of the throb to fit inside my skull.

"Oh, God!" I gasped and covered my eyes, stopping and swaying on my feet. A shadow overtook me and I risked a peek, Kurt standing in front of me, blocking the worst of the light.

"Here." He slipped a pair of wraparound sunglasses over my eyes.

"Thank you," I murmured.

"Is that why you always wore those big, bug-eyed things?" he asked casually.

"Um, sometimes to hide bruising, most of the time because I couldn't for the life of me perfect lying with my eyes. The truth is always there." I sighed. "Probably another reason why I was chosen," I murmured.

"Chosen?" he asked, opening the passenger side of his truck, and holding out a hand. I put my hand in his and leveraged my aching body up into the passenger seat, holding onto the waistband of the borrowed sweats for dear life.

"That's right," I said, settling onto the bench seat, "you really have no idea how things really work inside New Eden, do you?" I asked.

"Apparently not," he said, and he was thinking about that, I could tell. I looked down at him from my perch and sighed.

"When you're ready, ask your questions," I said. "I'll uh, do my best to answer them."

He frowned slightly again and nodded, shutting me inside the truck. I sighed and melted back into the seat, leaning against the door, resting my forehead against the warm glass, the desert wavering with the heat outside the window... or maybe that part was in my head. There really wasn't any telling.

We only went three hundred and fifty miles or so, cruising out of, I think, California and through Arizona, before detouring north. I didn't honestly know precisely where we were, and I didn't really care as long as it was away from New Eden. I didn't make any small talk. I didn't feel well obviously, and Kurt didn't want to push it. Rather, he decided we should find me some suitable clothing and just before leaving what I thought was Arizona, he pulled in at a second-hand store; one of those places I distantly remembered from my childhood – before New Eden.

"Keep your sunglasses on. Try to hide as much of that as possible with your hair, yeah?" he asked.

I gave him a weak smile.

"I'm an old hand at this, even when I feel like death. Don't worry," I said.

We went in and I held my head high but did keep the glasses on. At the first set of startled looks, I smiled and said, "Car accident." I got a few nods and just like that, it was magically dismissed. It usually was.

I fell. I shouldn't read and walk. I tripped over our beloved pet. People would take just about any excuse so they didn't have to face the reality. Their favorite actor being abusive and an awful human being was a reality no one wanted to face, which is how so many Hollywood elites got away with it for years on end.

Kurt stood by as I pulled several things in varying sizes that looked like they would fit off-the-rack and I went into a fitting room.

Sizes established fairly quickly, we snatched the bare necessities and got out of there. I ended up with several worn tees that might have cost a few hundred dollars at a Rodeo boutique, but here they were a buck each. The material of the tees was thin and didn't seem like it would hold up for very long, but by the same token, it was soft and felt good against the skin. There was a single pair of jeans, a pair of shorts, and some sandals that had the previous owner's toe prints in them – not glamorous, but better than what I had. I wished I could change here in the store but as soon as Kurt had us hustled past the cashier, he whisked us out and back into the truck.

"I thought we were going through Arizona," I said, and he grunted.

"Traveling in a straight line is a bad plan," he said. "People will be looking for us, and if we don't follow a linear path, we're harder to track. We're out of California. Arizona is pretty hot property, lots of development in Tucson, Phoenix, Flagstaff. I really only know because of those property flipping shows, the one Arik liked."

"Oh, right..." I said trailing off and staring sightlessly out the window for a time.

"You alright?" he asked.

I nodded mutely.

"I'm okay," I lied – because I wasn't. There was nothing about this that was even remotely okay.

By the time we stopped, I was so grateful. I didn't want to eat. I wasn't thirsty. I just wanted *sleep*. Kurt let us into the roadside motel's room and I went to one of the beds and sank onto it gratefully.

"I'll get us some food," he said, and I looked up at him almost beseechingly.

"Can I sleep now? Like for real sleep?" I begged.

"How do you feel?" he asked.

"Like my husband beat the shit out of me," I answered soberly.

He nodded and said, "I'll wake you up when I get back. You can eat, then go back to sleep."

I nodded miserably. I would take what I could get.

"Hey, Kurt," I said as he went to go out the door. He looked back. "I don't know if I've said thank you, yet," I murmured, frowning slightly.

"It's no trouble," he said, and I felt my frown deepen.

"It's a lot of trouble for you to go to and you don't even know me," I said.

"We have close to three thousand miles to resolve that last, yeah?" he said. I forced a weak smile and nodded slowly and carefully. "Be back in a bit," he declared and shut the door.

I laid down gratefully, but the bed was as hard as a rock and didn't provide much in the way of comfort.

THE NEXT DAY was much of the same. We passed through a good portion of Utah and stopped. Most of the driving was made in silence as I tried to recover my scrambled wits which was easier said than done. I'd stared at multilayered rock formations and marveled at the oranges and reds they contained. Some of them were even more varied than that – the stone layered in tans, browns, a deep burgundy, and even greens as though the stones had been set to spinning and someone had taken a paintbrush and painted bands of colors throughout the formation. I didn't understand how something so beautiful could be formed naturally, but I assumed it had to do with tectonic plates, and centuries upon centuries of wind erosion. I'm sure it was all very scientific, which used to be a subject I excelled at, but for the life of me, I had no interest now.

It was as though I gathered up all my thoughts and threw them at the wall and whatever stuck? Well, good, but not much was honestly sticking.

It was frustrating. I knew I wasn't the same person I had been before Arik Rex, but by the same token, I couldn't for the life of me identify what had been lost, which maybe, in its own way, was a mercy. I don't know.

I sighed, a heavy thing, and Kurt misinterpreted it.

"We'll stop soon," he said, and I tore my gaze from the rocks rising to either side of us and looked over at him.

"I'm just tired all the time right now," I said. "I'm sorry."

"It's alright," he said. "That was quite the beating you took. I've known grown men who couldn't take half as much in Her Majesty's Service."

"You were a soldier, then? Before all of the bodyguard stuff?"

He laughed to himself.

"Aye." He nodded. "I was a soldier."

I didn't say anything. I mean, what was there to say?

"What about you?" he asked a moment later. "What were you before Arik Rex and New Eden?"

I shrugged and sighed. "My mom joined New Eden when I was like six or seven," I said. "I honestly barely remember a time that was *before New Eden*. As for what I was before Arik Rex... I was a high school student... valedictorian... um..." I trailed off and shrugged lamely.

It was all Kurt could do not to slam on the brakes. He certainly took his eyes off the road.

"Just how old are you?" he asked.

I blushed and looked away. "Old enough," I said defensively.

Which was a lie.

I had just turned eighteen, but no one was supposed to know that, and I didn't want Kurt to know. I mean, I trusted him, but I was ashamed. Deeply. It just didn't seem like something I should tell the truth about yet and so with a deeper shame than what I could previously fathom, I had to keep Arik and New Eden's secret a little longer and felt sick for it. Guilty even.

"That's not a number," he said.

"No, it's not," I replied testily.

"Oy," he said. "It's no reflection on you! I'd just like to know what a fifty-year-old man is doing marrying a girl that looks as young as you."

Getting himself some nubile pussy, I thought to myself, but I could never say it out loud. It wasn't even my thought. It was Arik's. Something he had said to me once about how he never expected getting himself some nubile pussy would cause him such a headache.

I closed my eyes against the wave of nausea that threatened to overwhelm me.

"You gonna be sick?" Kurt asked me and I felt the truck lurch as he took his foot off the accelerator.

"Yes," I said through gritted teeth.

He pulled over, and I threw open my door just in time for the contents of my stomach to paint the side of the road. It wasn't nearly as pretty as the way the earth and universe had painted the Utah rocks.

I couldn't blame my head injury for throwing up. I just had that much to be sick about.

7

*K*urt...

The miles rolled by under the wheels of the truck. It was a pain the first few hours, getting out of California and the bloody awful traffic. Back on those roads that were a half-dozen lanes or wider, and the cars crawled bumper to bumper. Progress was torturous, and I spent more time on the clutch and brake and fighting the urge to shout and throw rude gestures, than actually getting anywhere. Now that we were free of California, the road was much narrower, two lanes in most places. And it was desolate. Desert and rocks; it was the stuff of Americana.

If I was going to possibly go to jail for the things I had done, I was going to throw a few bucket-list items down before it all possibly went sideways. There was also the fact that I *knew* who was going to be tasked with finding us, finding Callie, and bringing her back. Madeline Oberisk, and she was nothing if not professional and efficient. I hadn't picked her to be my second by accident.

She wasn't my first choice, but anyone who was going into the security detail had to be approved by the New Eden inspectors, and several of my first-round choices had been quickly vetoed. But

Maddy had been a New Eden acolyte, and her chops had looked solid – non-combat deployment in the U.S. Army, short stint in law enforcement after that, changing careers after coming up crosswise with the boys in blue in an internal affairs' matter that she wouldn't talk about, but whatever had happened spoke to me of her character.

She was also nearly unbeatable in hand-to-hand. She had tremendous reach with her kicks, and top marks on the firing range, and in handling hot situations.

That was who was going to be leading the hunt for us.

And she lived and breathed New Eden.

But, being something of a religious zealot, and a by-the-book soldier and police officer made her one specific thing – predictable. She would assume that I would act like she would and move as quickly and efficiently away from Hollywood as possible. That was where she would look, and the areas where she would send the resources allocated to her.

LAX and any of the local municipal airfields would be scouted and watched. Calls would be made to various law enforcement agencies to come as close to an all-points bulletin out for us, and for the lame-ass car Rex had me driving. Maddy didn't know about my truck, or how much I had lived for Americana as a kid.

The last thing she would expect me to do was to pick the old path of Route 66, the Will Rogers Highway, as my getaway route. If she did somehow come up with that, she would certainly not expect me to detour off of the highway to cut north through Monument Valley. I knew this place; I had seen it dozens of times, hundreds of times. Of course, it had been on a theatre screen, or on my television. Gods of American cinema had ridden horses, slinging pistols, chasing desperados, Indians, Mexicans, other cowboys. John Wayne, Clint Eastwood, all the spaghetti westerns with the bad soundtracks. It was something my old captain and I had bonded over to begin with – a love of old American cinema.

Callie was distracted, or bored, or she drowsed through the drive. The truck didn't have the amenities of a new car. There was no satellite anything, no touch screens, nothing streaming or internet, no distractions except for an AM/FM radio and an 8-track player. The player technically worked, but I had never gotten around to finding any of the blocky tapes it played, or doing the infinite wanker move of trashing the vintage equipment and replacing it with a cutting-edge Bluetooth streaming radio system capable of syncing with my phone.

No. My perfect truck was as dumb as I was.

So, the radio popped and crackled as we moved away from civilization, the bright hubs fading away as we plunged into the desert. There were the familiar mounts and buttes – the ones that I had seen so many times. They were even larger in person than they seemed on the screen. The desert was so much vaster than I could comprehend and it was beautiful in its alien starkness.

Everything I had experienced could vanish into this expanse of rock and sunbaked badlands. Really, the only thing I could imagine being larger than this land of fantastic vistas was the Pacific, which was really a vast and trackless waste of salt water, rolling blues and grays for thousands of miles. Both had their own beauty, in their extremes.

Afghanistan had been similar in its starkness, and closer to what I was feeling emotionally. The westerns had been a distraction, a happy figment from my childhood. This – being pursued, violence, bad decisions – felt more like the fights in the 'stan.

I both hated it and felt an appreciation for its sense of purpose. When I looked at Callie, I knew that there was a reason for this, a good reason. I was rescuing her, saving her from unspeakable horrors. There was no doubt about that.

There were plenty of people I had failed to rescue.

Some I had failed to protect.

Fuck, this was never easy.

It was also rough sitting next to Callie. She seemed so frail, and her bruises so livid against her pale skin. She hid it under her mane of red hair and thick sunglasses. There were very definite signs of post-concussion syndrome, the most notable ones being lapses in memory and concentration. I knew soldiers who had been like that. They would pick up that thousand-yard stare or drop off mid-sentence because their mind just quit putting words together.

You couldn't let them get lost. You could see them when they started to fade out, and that's when you'd give them something to bring them back into the moment – toss a rock at them, grab them and give them a hard shake; anything to break that mental blue screen. I saw Callie's eyes take on that look, and that was when I would do something to get her attention – ask her a question, offer her a drink. If I couldn't think of something, I would let the truck wander over the wake-up bars on the side of the highway, or aim for a rough spot, bumping her chin off of her hand.

The one thing I didn't do was engage physically. I didn't know how gun-shy she was and didn't want to give her a reason to be even more traumatized.

She did seem to be hanging together, at least functionally.

There would be time to put her back together, and there was a place that we could do that. I would have to make a few calls, and that would be dicey. I couldn't use a regular phone, and I didn't have one of those fancy encrypted phones. It was a bane of the modern world that almost every phone call made could be tethered back to its GPS coordinates, and there were people I didn't want to know about my plans, and people who didn't take unsecured phone calls.

And all this had to go on inside my head in silence. I couldn't discuss it with Callie. She was still hazy from the knock to the head, and God knew how much untreated head trauma. There was no reason that she should be burdened with the things I knew.

It was near nightfall when I pulled into the parking lot of the Grosjean Hotel, a large block of a building designed to look like a rustic ski chalet. The curtain wall of mountains that flanked around the hotel gave it a majestic look, reminiscent of what an American castle would have looked like if they had ever had need of building them. In stark contrast to Arizona and Nevada before, everything was draped in snow, and the air was brisk, our breath steaming in the night.

The lighting made it easier for Callie to get through the lobby without too much attention being drawn to her. The few people who were there were more interested in drinking in the bar, looking at the mountains and snow, flirting – the usual oblivious pretense of tourists. The staff was likewise morose, the sort of glazed and disinterested expression from young people and retirees who worked the late shifts. As long as no one was on fire or screaming, they didn't care.

Callie's thick glasses and bruises didn't raise the first eyebrow.

Her nipples poking through the thin material of her shirt drew no attention.

Well, a very small amount of attention, and I felt a stab of disappointment in myself for noticing something so petty.

"So here is the plan," I said, as I shut and bolted the door of the suite on the second floor. "Hot baths, showers, whatever, room service, and a full rest. Maybe a couple of days."

"A couple of days?" Callie sounded incredulous, but also relief tinted her voice.

"Yes, we're nearly in the middle of nowhere. This place is nice, but its ultimately a fourth-tier ski and mountain resort in Mormon country. We can rest. No one is going to look here for either of us."

"How can you be certain?"

"There is no trail, no cellphone traffic, no smart vehicle tracking, no credit or debit cards, and most importantly, taking a detour away from the most direct, or most efficient exit strategies is the second to last thing that they should expect us to do." She nodded thoughtfully.

"What is the last thing they should expect us to do?"

"Not make a play at all, to have stayed in Hollywood, or just Los Angeles in general."

"If that was the last thing they would expect, why didn't we do it?"

"Because you're something of a celebrity and it would take Arik five minutes to get every paparazzi and celeb-stalker in the city looking for you. If they can catch that stalker who stole what's her name's Frenchies by recognizing the dogs, you would be easy to catch."

"My hair?"

"Is beautiful and noticeable." She clutched at it, her face screwing up into a scowl. "And there are plenty of women with red hair, so it's not an issue."

"It feels like it *is* an issue," she said.

"We're going to employ something that celebrities are awful at, urban camouflage. We're going to make you look like a normal person, just any other woman, and they will be so busy looking for Calanthe Rex they won't notice Callie—"

"I've never been normal," she said.

"Don't worry, the hardest part about it is that it's boring." I smiled.

"What would you know about pretending to be normal?" she asked.

"Callie," I said. "How much do you know about me?"

"Some?" She shrugged.

"How about you hop into the tub and relax? I'll get some room service heading this way. I've got a few emails to send and will find out what we can do to normalize you."

THERE WERE ONLY a couple of emails to send through the crypto server. I needed a doc to take a look at Callie and had no way to get a hold of one of those underground operators, but I knew people who did. Hopefully by morning, I would have some answers on that front. RedRoan was an upright guy, and it would be worth owing my old captain again if it meant that I was sure that Callie was going to be okay.

Food and booze came quickly, but room service was a hit-or-miss affair. I had seen some hotels border on being psychic delivering food.

There were other hotels that took hours to get mediocre microwave-level shit to a room even when they knew they were bringing it to one of the highest-grossing stars in the industry. The paparazzi camped in the parking lot, celeb stalkers in the hallways, security bogged down, and Mister Rex having booked the entire floor or even wing of the building, and still an hour for a shrimp cocktail.

That had been a truly epic rant.

He had sent his personal helicopter to fly to a beachfront bar, pick up a phoned-in order, and flew it back faster than the hotel could deliver the saddest five shrimp in a plastic wine glass cocktail to his room. He had screamed and then thrown the cocktail on the hotel manager.

Should have been a clue, really.

He had threatened violence, something about shoving the lemon wedges up the chef's ass and fucking his wife and daughters so they would know what a real man was. The entire security detail had a laugh at that. It was easy to laugh. The non-celebrities were looking at three-to-four-hour waits, and most everyone at that point had decided it was better to send runners on foot to get food through the blockage of groupies and New Eden protesters.

Fucking Fallout, they were almost always around, with their picket signs and chanting. Half of our job in security was keeping them contained. At least I didn't have to deal with them now. Praise fucking God.

"Room service is here," I said, knocking on the bathroom door. There was nothing but silence. I knocked again and still no response. I shouldered the door open, adrenaline surging through my body as nightmare scenarios strobed in my head. She had fallen asleep, or had a convulsion. She was slipping under the water, drowning in steaming hot water. The door banged against the counter, and Callie startled in the tub hard enough to splash water everywhere.

"Jesus, I'm sorry," I sputtered. She stared at me with huge eyes, her hands clutched over her shoulders, concealing her breasts under a cloud of bubbles and red skin. Bubble bath?

"Is... is everything... okay?" she asked.

"Yeah, I just thought, fuck, I don't know what I thought," I said. "Room service is here. There's a bottle of pinot and some food, and you didn't answer when I knocked."

"Oh, I probably had my head underwater." She gave me a smile.

"I'll go. I've been in here too long."

"It's okay, Kurt. You've seen me nude before, haven't you?"

"I have, but that doesn't really justify my being here now," I tried to explain. She gave a shrug.

"So many men have seen me naked, what's one more? How about you give me some company and maybe some of that wine?" Her smile was sweet and almost impossible to refuse. How could Rex raise a hand toward her? That I could not understand.

Or forgive.

I cleared my throat, still uncomfortable.

"Sure," I said. I fetched the wine and then poured some in the water glasses sitting next to the sink. When I brought the wine to her, she accepted it with a polite thank you, and then sank back down into the tub, to where only her head was sticking up out of the water. I was thankful for the bubbles. "I think this is the most I've seen of you since Barcelona, when there was the security breach in the private pool area."

"I remember that," she said. "It was always relieving when Arik was mad at someone else and not me."

"I wish it hadn't taken me so long to figure out what was going on," I apologized.

"Don't feel bad about it, Kurt. There are plenty of people who are fully aware and have known for years, and yet did nothing."

"That's awful," I said. I covered my awkward silence with a long thoughtful drink of the wine.

"It was, but I've accepted it. It was in the past, and nothing can change that. I just hope I have a future. Not that I doubt your ability," she said with an apologetic smile. "I just know how they are."

"Who knows and would allow this to happen?" I asked, the point sticking in my brain.

"You said that I didn't know you that well. How about you tell me about you, and then maybe I can tell you some of the stuff I haven't told anyone?"

"Fair enough," I agreed quickly.

"You said you know about pretending to be normal?"

"That, yes, that I know a lot about. Getting out of the military and reintegrating into civilian life involves a lot of pretending to be normal. I spent years of my life training, in a uniform, everything organized, every chain of command clear and obvious, and everyone had a rank. Salute higher ranks, lower ranks salute you. Everything is a horribly inefficient mess. There's red tape everywhere, but compared to civilian life, it's simple."

I sighed and went on.

"Coming back means picking what you wear again, and having to realize that there are no ranks, no order, no organization, and it's all incredibly boring."

"How is it boring?" she asked curiously, cupping a heap of bubbles in her hand.

"No adrenaline rush from being shot at, never being shelled by an enemy. I haven't been inside a military vehicle in years, and riding in civilian helicopters or private jets? It's just not the same. I haven't felt an explosion since I left Afghanistan."

"How do you feel an explosion? Like, without getting hurt."

"You have to be pretty far away from it. Really far away if they're big. I've been about a mile away from a bombing sortie – big thing came over and rained fire on an enemy position. It was like thunder, a rock concert, and an earthquake all at once and it just went on and on. I could feel it in my bones and my teeth. Then it was over, and the air was full of dust and smoke."

"Wow," she said, then blew the bubbles across the water.

"It doesn't bother you?" I asked. "Me, just sitting in here, while you're in the tub. You know, naked?"

"I told you, a ton of men have seen me naked, what's one more? Plus, you aren't going to hurt me, are you?"

"I would die before letting someone hurt you ever again," I said, feeling like some of those words shouldn't have gotten out.

"You aren't cruel," she said, and she sounded so certain.

"How do you know?" I asked. "I'm a combat veteran, Royal Marines. I've killed a fairly large number of men."

"You're not pretty enough to be cruel. Pretty men are cruel." Her cheeks flamed almost as bright a red as her hair and she put a hand over her mouth. She wouldn't look at me, but I wasn't offended. I knew what she meant.

"Like Arik?"

"Arik is very pretty," she said. "That was why at first, I was able to put some of the bad things aside. He was very pretty, and rich and famous. What dumb girl doesn't want to marry a wealthy celebrity?" I didn't say anything and studied the grouting of the tile on the wall, the backsplash on the sink, the sink handles, anything to not look into the dissipating bubbles, to the clear water. "I was really dumb, then."

"I doubt you were dumb," I said.

"No, if I was smart, I would have figured out the trick. I wouldn't have fallen into their game, and I would be free now, not hiding in a tub nursing a concussion."

"Can I ask? Or if you prefer, I can absolutely mind my own business—"

"Your own beeswax?" She smiled. "No, it's fine. I trust you enough to tell you, maybe not all the details, but enough. New Eden is a cult, you know that now, right?" I nodded.

"I didn't know, growing up in it like I did, but after my fifteenth birthday, it didn't take me too long to figure it out." She looked sad and then the silent and grim bravery was back in her expression as she shrugged again. "By the time I did, it was too late."

"Yeah, they sell that bit about the environment, living green, save the planet. I bought that line. I thought that bit was legitimate – just a bunch of hippy green freaks out to save the planet. That the job was a safe bet. Nothing shady there." I shook my head. "I know that New Eden talks about green stuff, but the longer I was around? Well, I didn't really see any of it in practice. That should have been my first clue."

"There really isn't terribly much to see," she said and then looked as though she was gathering her thoughts. "So, its environmental lobbyists and green lawyers funding people through college to turn them into scientists and geoengineers, hydrologists, botanists—"

"Right, everything you would need to save the world from turning into Mad Max smoking angel dust," I said. She nodded.

"I thought that was where I was going to go, really aiming for a judicial appointment or even public service as a representative in the house, work my way up, maybe become a senator. In my dumb fever dreams I thought I could be Madam President, the first Green President of the United States. I wanted to change the world, turn the oceans blue, the forests all green, save us from poverty and crime, pollution, everything."

I smiled, hearing the vibrancy come out in her words.

"I was blessed. I was the First Among First Daughters, a Goodwill Ambassador for the New Eden Centre. My Presentation of Youth and Beauty was to August Elijah Ellison Emerson himself. I was... groped, inspected like a horse being sold at auction, and then I was given, as a gift, to Rex. He is one of the New Eden Centre's largest supporters."

"That part I know," I said. "Tithes his box office to the Centre, always selling the green angle."

"I was given to him when I was 'legal' by state laws." She put "legal" in air quotes with her fingers, raising her hands from the bath, the water streaming and tinkling as it fell back into the tub. "I was married the literal day I turned sixteen. He took my virginity that night, but my innocence had been stolen long before the first time he mounted me." I looked away. This sort of candid confession left me feeling helpless and awkward, wanting to punish these assholes for what they did to her, and Lord, God, knew what they had done to other people.

"I'm sorry it makes you angry," she said. "I'll be quiet."

Her words made me look up sharply, the math I'd been doing forgotten.

"You aren't making me angry," I said.

"Your body language changed. You're angry," she said again.

"What they've done makes me angry, not you, I promise."

"Maybe some more wine, and less talking?" she suggested. I agreed and poured another round. The wine was middling at best, but the offerings were limited to the cash I had on hand, and that would run out quickly, trying to play at the celebrity level. My cash would have to last until I could get somewhere that was advanced enough to let me cash out some of the EdenCoin I had been given as a hiring bonus.

"Help me up, and towel me off," she said, sliding up in the tub after depositing her now empty glass on the side.

"Pardon?"

"I've had wine, and a knock in the head. There is no one else here but you," she said, looking at me like I was being obtuse.

"Okay," I said hesitantly. "Don't you do this yourself at home?"

"Well, actually, no," she said. "I have two ladies-in-waiting that do everything with me., I'm never left alone. Someone is always watching."

"Oh," I said. She was being serious. She stood with my help and stepped out of the tub, and waited for me to literally buff her dry with the towel as she swayed on her feet, trying to concentrate on keeping them under her. I kept my head turned and tried to be as non-involved as possible. This was too strange; she was so petite, and I felt incredibly awkward. I could feel the flush in my goddamn face. I had handled being shot at by a sniper better than I was handling this.

She laughed.

"Kurt?"

"Yeah?"

"Pay attention, you aren't going to break me. I know I'm pale but I'm not a bone China doll. If Arik didn't break me, you aren't going to cripple me with a terrycloth towel." I looked at her, and she gave me a hint of a grin. "Dry me off. C'mon now. I don't like to drip dry, it's bad for my skin."

I did so, and feeling her body through the towel, the sweep of her back, her hips, the swell of her small breasts, I couldn't tell if my heart was racing because it thought I was handling a bomb or racing because I was excited. Maybe both.

I had been trained for violence. My hands were accustomed to hand-to-hand combat, the familiar weight of knives, the stocks of guns.

Not the slender body of a beautiful woman.

She showed me how to wrap a towel around her hair as she held a hand against the edge of the bathroom vanity, wrapping it tightly, sweeping it up in that weird turban looking thing that women with long hair were fond of. Keeping my mind on the task, ignoring her reflection in the mirror, that had been as tense as cutting a trip wire hooked to a landmine, or pulling the fuse from the roadside artillery shell rigged to blow.

Her breasts were small, but flawless in shape – pale pink rose-buds for nipples – and she was completely bare between her legs. Part of me stumbled inside, seeing that. There was something almost scandalous, almost forbidden, about the way it looked, about the feelings it stirred up inside me.

There was also an almost disappointed college lecturer voice that echoed through the back corner of my mind, that it was a shame that a woman with such fiery gorgeous hair would be completely bare. Something-something, a woman's glory is her mane, and it seemed a pity that there was no fire down there.

"It's okay, Kurt," Callie said. "You can relax."

"Sorry," I mumbled, and reached for a second towel, accidentally knocking the entire stack over onto the floor, but grabbing one before it completely escaped. I unrolled it and felt a stab of embarrassment.

It was one of the medium-sized towels, the one you tossed down on the floor to walk on, and not one large enough to wrap around her body. "Fuck," I grunted, and grabbed another off the floor, the one on top of the spill, with the least contact with the ground.

"Here, why don't you take that towel and take yourself a shower?" she suggested. "You might need a cold one?" She laughed lightly, and I gave her an edge of a grin to take any nervousness she might have at what I did next.

"Bloody fucking hell," I groaned.

8

———————

*C*allie...

I was trying to put on a brave front. The combination of the hot bath, a little too much wine, *and* the throbbing ache in my head from being knocked about by Arik... I was trembling as I stood for Kurt to dry me off and I had a death grip on the edge of the sink as my vision swam.

I tried to play it off as normal, which for me it certainly was, but I really did need his help. If I bent to dry my own legs, I would surely give myself another head injury from keeling right on over.

I didn't like this; I didn't like feeling this way. I mean, I never had before. I'd been beaten, sure, but he usually avoided my head and my face. I'd never been this concussed, though I am sure I'd been concussed at least once, maybe even twice before.

"Callie?"

"Sorry," I mumbled. "Feeling a bit... weird. Maybe that second glass wasn't such a good idea."

"Come on, let's have you lie down," he said and guided me with a gentle hand out into the suite, which was a king-sized bed this time.

"Up you go," Kurt urged gently, pulling back a triangle of blankets and sheets. I slipped between them and when he dropped the covers over me, I slid the towel out from under me and them. He took it without a word and casually tossed it into the bathroom.

"You going to be alright for a bit?" he asked, and I nodded, wincing slightly as it felt as though my brain were sloshing around in my skull and that was *not* a good sensation.

"Eat something," he said and brought a tray of food over. "As much as you can."

"Thank you," I said, and he smiled with a slight nod. He disappeared into the bathroom and shut the door. I sighed.

I liked his company. He felt... I don't know... *safe.* I think safe was the word I was looking for. I believed him when he'd said he would die before he would let New Eden take me back and that honestly worried me.

Kurt seemed like a good man, and the world was in such short supply. It would be a shame for the planet to lose him.

I picked at my food as worry gnawed at my guts and I finally ended up setting it aside after only a few bites.

I was tired. Very tired.

Perhaps after a little more sleep...

9

———

*K*urt...

Sleep was slow coming, but once it hit, I was out. The wine helped, being exhausted helped, but what helped the most was sitting and watching *TMI News* on low volume. It was Rex's favorite celebrity news outlet, the one he dealt with the most. They came by and visited him on occasion, enough so that the dingbat anchor was on his approved list. Pretty sure she had been on her knees for him, definitely on her back.

There had been a single bit from the set, a blurb that due to personal reasons, Arik Rex was going to take a few days away from filming the already overbudget swords and sandals epic that the studio was sure would not only be a summer blockbuster but also major award bait. There were a few flash interviews with a few people on set, and they all spoke about Rex's absolute dedication to character and that he needed to take a brief break.

Nothing was said about Calanthe, no word about being assaulted in his own home, nothing. One of the people at the press conference was the towering figure of Maddy. If she was there, maybe he was more afraid of a follow-up or reprisal, not angry and sending his cult hounds after Callie and me. Or, if they were, they were going to wait.

Or, they were calling in outsiders, third party contractors or bounty hunters.

I wasn't worried about any of them.

They were as often as not, fucking amateurs.

Knowing that we were in the clear, for the time being, was relief enough. My sleep was deep and dreamless.

CALLIE WAS awake before I was and was familiar enough with room service to have it brought up. She seemed a little better, which was good. Most of the time, the only thing you could do for a concussion was rest. We could stay here, maybe another day, before moving on. I was waiting for a reply email from the Cryptonet, setting us up with an underground doctor, and possibly a financial conversion. Eden-Coin was trading high but there were other things running in the mix, things that could be more valuable.

And I had to do something to address the fact that my cash on hand was very finite.

I was checking my email through a burner phone and blew out a breath of relief. There was a doc who was available, but I would have to meet them partway. They were in a place called Lake Valley, New Mexico – a Doctor Holoke Carter, an address, and the pertinent contact information.

And what it was going to cost.

The captain hadn't mentioned that these people, who worked outside the system, were brutally expensive. I could take her to one of those walk-in clinics, drop a few hundo, and then we could be on our way, so long as no one recognized Calanthe, and so long as no one decided to play the advocate and call the police, or a domestic abuse counselor. That would be my luck, trying to get her medical aid and the police would be on my ass because some busybody tagged me as the potential abuser.

Or I would have to let go of something like ten thousand dollars' worth of crypto. Fucking hell, that was expensive.

I sent an acceptance email, and an estimate of when we would be arriving. The response came quickly. Thankfully included in that cost, graciously accepted from my online account, included accommodations for the night, possibly longer depending on the patient's condition.

I sighed.

I hoped it wouldn't be long. I wanted to be somewhere secure.

She needed to be somewhere safe.

Away from New Eden and Arik. There was no way they would let this go. Arik's ego was too big, and she was too well known. They wouldn't want to deal with the scandal of their poster boy and number one donor being an abusive asshole, womanizer, and worse. The damage to Rex's career might be salvageable. There were plenty of women who would forgive a man's monstrous behavior if he was rich and charismatic enough. But the New Eden Centre would be gutted by that revelation.

They wouldn't let him just abandon them, no. It would be like two monsters dragging each other down rather than letting the other escape or win. Something there about a squid and a whale, or a crazy guy and a whale? I wasn't sure.

"We're going to head south, when we head out," I said.

"Where are we going from here?"

"Place called Lake Valley, in New Mexico. It's between the Ute and Navajo reservations. Native American country."

"Why are we going there?" she asked.

"There is a doctor there who is going to look at you, make sure that you're okay, and maybe get you whatever meds or treatment they can give you," I said. "Did you order all this room service for yourself?"

"No, most is for you," she said. "The rest is that my stomach isn't right, and I can't seem to handle much of anything, but a little bit here, some there, it's okay."

"Nerves, maybe a touch of the head injury. If your inner ear is upset, it can throw your balance off, your appetite. It's nuts how much that part of your body is connected to," I said. She nodded and nibbled at what looked like a parfait. "That's why hearing people sick up can make you sick up too."

"Who says sick up?"

"Well, I do?" I said, and she gave me a smile.

"What is the itinerary for the day, since I don't think we're leaving today?"

"You rest, take it easy, and I go do some shopping for you, so you don't have to wear my old clothes or those terrible clothes I purchased from that Goodwill three states ago."

"That sounds okay. I know about shopping, but I didn't see anywhere when we were driving up."

"Callie?"

"Yeah?"

"You didn't notice the Grand Canyon when we went through a corner of the park."

"Oh, well... fuck." I let out a laugh. Seeing her there, spitting out the daintiest curse word, had me smiling.

"Also, we are not going to any of those boutiques that you're used to shopping at."

"Where are we going?"

"There was an Omni-Mart we passed about twenty miles back. They sell everything but houses, cars, and military hardware."

"Omni-Mart? The big box store?"

"The very one."

"New Eden has an anti-big-box-store initiative because of the environmental impact they have. Their carbon footprint is enormous, and the harm buildings that large cause to local environments, its staggering." I nodded. It didn't really matter to me, but the way her demeanor changed, it was impressive, a glimpse of maybe who she had been before. "Did you know that they deliberately buy question-able valued property because it's cheap and they don't care if they have to backfill or drain a swamp, or flatten ten acres of forest for parking lots and *green space* to be around the store?"

"I know now," I said. "But we're going there because the only other options are going to the ski shop in the lobby or driving however many dozens or hundreds of miles it is to find a city with a mall or outlet center. I have some cash, but its limited right now."

"What about a card? I know that all of the security personnel have a charge account."

"That is true, and the locations that we're approved to use it are all in LA. The moment we swipe a card, our location is made, and the bad guys are on top of us. The cards are locked in an RFID sealed container in the bottom of the bug-out bag."

"You seem to have all this in hand," she said softly. "Like you've done it before."

"Your safety is my number one priority, and if they find us, it won't be because of something we did wrong. It will be because of something we had no power over," I said. "Now, let's get you ready, throw a braid in that mane, and let's get some things taken care of."

She nodded and finished picking at her food while I bolted down what Americans had the audacity to call bacon, a bowl of thick oatmeal, and a few hard-boiled eggs. I missed having proper break-fasts, but that couldn't be helped; no one here knew about comforting things like black pudding or beans with breakfast... or gammon... Gods how I missed my gammon.

Americans were true savages with how they treated breakfast.

I drove us down from the hotel to the instance of a town that served it and the cluster of other resorts and cabin rental places around the rough bowl-shaped arm of the Rockies. There wasn't much there – a few sundry shops, a couple of squat apartment blocks, the Omni-Mart and an incredibly basic level of service industry. There were places to eat, but it was all local mom-and-pop opera-tions, and a single token effort from the outside world, a Burger

World. It seemed like the most forlorn BW I had seen, flanked by an abandoned retail warehouse and a used car lot with six vehicles for sale.

It had to be off season, so many places were closed.

The Omni-Mart was ancient. It looked like it might have been one of the first generation to be built – the ones that hadn't been custom built from the ground up with their engineered floor plans and smart design to keep people shopping for an hour when they came in for milk and bread. It was also maybe a quarter the size of a regular store, and everything seemed old, from the patina on the clothing fixtures to the people who worked the registers.

For a bit, Callie seemed lost in the sea of basic offerings.

"Let's start ground up and move from there," I said, grabbing a pushcart and moving us through the women's clothing toward the back corner of the department.

"What's ground up?" she asked, following close enough to keep a hand on the cart. She sometimes used it to hold herself up, and I made a point of pretending not to notice the moments when her balance faltered.

"Shoes, socks, panties, bras," I said.

"Oh, well, yeah," she said. "How do you know about stuff like this?"

"Two sisters, my mum," I said. She nodded, and I wheeled the cart into the pocket-sized shoe department. Ten minutes later, she had a single pair of pink mock Converse in the cart, a bag of pastel socks, and was in the underwear department, picking at the lacy things and colorful things. "Omni-Mart lace is infamous for being scratchy. Stick to something that comes in a plastic bag." I gestured away from the racks and toward a wall display of bagged underwear, each displaying a crisply smiling generic-looking woman wearing the contents of the bag like it had been dipped in Valium and rolled in Percocet – serene, smiling, accepting the luxury of ten pair of panties for a tenner.

The clatter of the cart's one bad wheel was starting to worm itself into my head, and I could feel a tension headache starting. It was hard to keep my vigilance up and help Callie. It was strange; she didn't have any familiarity with shopping in a regular store. I wondered how much of her life had been like this, trapped inside a gold cage, a prisoner of the wealth and insanity of the New Eden cult.

Regular clothes were less difficult. There wasn't much difference between designer labels and off-the-rack stuff, other than the price. She ended up with several pairs of leggings, a few oversized sweaters, some shirts, most being more basic patterns, and a single character tee of some anime character.

It made her smile, so good enough.

I wasn't empty-handed myself, adding a few new shirts, and some new underwear and socks to the cart. The rest of the cart quickly filled up with snacks, drinks, and then entertainment. She grabbed several books, magazines, and other things that I hadn't been able to keep up with. It was fine, really. I had been able to afford it.

When the bug-outs were repacked, after this, I would have to evaluate how much bail money I had in the bag, and have a way to access my online money, maybe have a quicker option to move it into other accounts, where it couldn't be tracked. In a few years, it might not even be an issue. More and more places were accepting cryptocurrencies.

We hit the faded plastic Burger World, and Callie seemed genuinely shocked by what the place was like. "What, you've never been into a B-Dub?" I asked.

"Well, no," she said. "I've never been in a place like this, any of the fast-food franchises."

"Am I going to learn about their environmental problems?"

"If you want, I can tell you, but really, it's because the food is cheap, and Arik and the New Eden Centre were more interested in *haute cuisine*, you know, farm-to-table and sustainable food practices. We almost always had a chef on staff. I don't know the first thing about cooking, which is probably going to be a problem."

"It's not hard. I can cook a few things, enough to feed myself without relying entirely on drive-thrus and food-delivery rackets," I said. "And when we get where we're going, I will show you some food that doesn't come wrapped in paper."

"What, you know how to cook?"

"Fish, and meat. Nothing fancy. I can manage a goulash, spaghetti Bolognese, chips, that sort of thing. Learned a lot in Afghanistan, ate a fair bit of camel. I don't recommend it."

"I can't imagine eating a camel."

"They taste like they smell, and then it's the devil's choice – the same tired MREs, or local burnt camel, ugh."

"That sounds awful."

"There were some days that I would go without because being hungry was better than having stomach cramps. When I ended up back in civilization, all I wanted was honeybuns, chips, and hamburgers."

"There were some days that I didn't eat either, but it's not the same," she said, brushing a few strands of hair out of her face. "I sometimes didn't eat because there was a lot of pressure to remain a certain weight. I am a celebrity's wife. I have to look the part of the trophy. There was a chef, a dietician, and a sports coach to make sure my stomach stayed flat. My job was to stay as pretty as possible and get pregnant as many times as possible."

"I wouldn't want to live like that," I said.

"I *won't* live like that. Not again." She sighed, and her wobble was noticeable enough that I moved to catch her. I ended up just putting a hand on the small of her back, bracing her. She recovered quickly, and I knew that we needed to get this wrapped up and head back to the hotel.

"Burgers and a milkshake, then back to the room?" I suggested. She nodded, and mostly leaned against the cart for what remained of the shopping excursion.

Callie's appetite seemed to surge in the presence of chips from Burger World, I mean, *fries*. I still stumbled calling chips by their proper name when everyone here insisted that they were fries. There was one thing that B-Dub excelled at was consistency. The burgers were almost identical to the ones that came from the joints in California. The same vaguely sad patties, questionable quality meat, wilted lettuce, and the secret sauce that was really just some orangish salad dressing.

The milkshake was also well received, and it might have been the single largest intake of calories I had seen her consume. That did make me feel a bit better. The rest of the evening was quiet. She seemed to be well adjusted to long periods of being as small as possible with her books. She would look up from time to time, like a meerkat. I recognized that nervous situational awareness. She was used to trouble appearing from any direction, at any time. I wanted her to be able to relax, and not have that anxiety.

The best I could do was put on the television, the volume down, and then just sit quietly, making as little movement as possible. Clearing my throat could make her jump, or even just shifting in my seat would have her head of fiery red snapping up in alarm, fixing me with a worried look, a cautionary *what is he going to do next*, in her eyes. I could only imagine the hell she lived in to have these sorts of ingrained behaviors.

The next morning, we left out early, putting tires to pavement before the sun was up. It was easy to do. With nowhere to go, and nothing to do, we turned in early. It was difficult, pulling up the discipline to not let my mind wander to what she wore to bed, a hairband. She seemed completely unaffected by me being there, occupying the far side of the large bed.

It made the next day of driving a special sort of hell with nothing but the nagging memory of it to dwell on as I drove.

There was a certain austere beauty to the states we drove through – desolate and empty. There were colors to be seen in the rocks, and perhaps, if I had been a poet, I might have been more appreciative.

Instead, it reminded me of Afghanistan.

I had gone through those mountains, being shot at by snipers, mortar shells lobbed at me, and never knowing if any rough patch in the road was just a rough patch or a buried artillery shell with a compression trigger wired into it. It made me tense.

The upside was that the roads were better here, and the chances of being shot at seemed less.

My nerves left me feeling exposed, and the only thing I could do was turn the radio on and listen to country music, or whatever else the antenna could pick up.

Lake Valley was one of the worst named places I had come across in a very long time. There was no valley, for starters. After driving for over twelve hours, traversing three states, it was barely a bowl. It wasn't even a basic, a depression, it was a plain that was sad in the middle. There was no lake either; it was simply dust and scrub.

What there was, was a cluster of buildings – a school, a store, a town hall, and a number of houses.

It was fully part of one of the Native American Reservations, and it boggled my mind that a place like this could exist inside the United States. It reminded me even more of the villages high in the Afghan mountains. The people wore different clothing, but the feeling was the same – desperate and defeated. I could feel this place pulling at me, reminding me of the weight of my flak vest, the discomfort of the armor, the harness, the helmet strapped to my head.

I could feel beads of sweat popping up on my brow that had nothing to do with the heat.

"Hello," a woman said, walking up to where I had parked. She was tall, with black hair and wearing a white coat. This had to be the doc.

"Doctor Carter?"

"Yes, you must be Owen," she said.

"I prefer Kurt, but yes."

"Let's see my patient, eh?"

10

―――――――

**allie...**

"...should have brought her to me sooner."

"I should have, aye, but I couldn't."

A heavy sigh.

I slipped back under.

I felt like I was surfacing like a deep-sea submarine, the weight of the ocean over my head making my ascent slow.

"...permanent damage."

"And what's that going to look like?" Kurt asked quietly.

"I don't know, only time will tell, but she can't take any more hits to the head or face like that."

"She won't." His voice was hard as steel, his resolve impressive, but I didn't know how it would fare against Arik or New Eden.

"How long have I been asleep?" I asked weakly.

"Don't try to get up." The doctor came to the little hospital bed's side and I raised my hand to my head. I froze and squinted at the IV in the back of my hand.

"Imaging revealed that you've had a small brain bleed. We've been keeping you sedated, letting it heal on its own further. You'll be alright."

"Please don't lie to me," I murmured. "I just heard you say that I have permanent damage."

"Perhaps motor sensory issues, maybe memory – it's hard to say," the doctor told me while she adjusted things. "Sleep for now, Callie. It won't be so bad tomorrow."

My vision blurred, from medication or tears I couldn't tell.

"Kurt?" I asked and my voice cracked.

"Aye, I'm right here," he said, and a large warm hand slipped into mine.

"I don't want to stay here," I said and sniffed. "Can we please go?"

"Not just yet," he said and squeezed my hand firmly.

"Then will you stay?" I asked. I squeezed my eyes shut and felt hot tears slide down my temples.

"I'm not going anywhere, Love."

"Promise?" I asked and the fact the word slurred scared me.

"I promise."

The world faded away again.

11

———

*K*urt...

Doctor Holoke Carter was not what I had expected. Bunkered down in the middle of what looked like a Mad Maxian nightmare in the middle of literally nowhere, I really expected a weather-beaten old man, skin like saddle leather, eyes like flint, maybe a little of that Native American chic I saw in Hollywood fashion, silver and turquoise jewelry, a few beads, a suede leather jacket. Definitely a cigarette in his mouth.

That was probably the biggest assumption I had, assuming Doc Carter was going to be a man. I was wrong on every single one of my expectations and felt a bit of embarrassment for it. Doctor Carter was indeed of Native American heritage, Ute tribe, but she was mid to late thirties, shoulder-length black hair, gold-rimmed glasses, and was dressed like a doctor would be, slacks and a lab coat. There was no doubt that these were all well-worn, as was the medical facility she had.

But that was superficial. For the middle of nowhere, her facility was exceptional. There was an aged pet scan machine, and a newer MRI system, X-ray equipment that looked like it remembered the

90

Great War, and an array of smaller lab machines that all looked to be cutting edge and new.

Doctor Carter was brisk and efficient, and after taking one look at Callie, was frighteningly professional. Her one nurse, orderly, was instantly on hand and they were going over her with the speed and efficiency of a Formula One pit crew. Callie's vitals were taken, her pupil response tested, a blood sample drawn. While the machines purred, processing their samples, Callie was stuffed head first into the MRI machine and a flatscreen hanging on the wall produced the images generated by the machine.

Callie's skull appeared in stark relief, and there was a good deal of animated discussion between the doctor and her nurse, in what I could only assume was Ute, or whatever Native American dialect the Utes spoke. My ignorance was frustrating. I could fake my way through a bit of Spanish, just from being in California for as long as I had been, and then enough Afghan to get into, or stay out of trouble, certainly enough French to get into trouble.

They started saying words I didn't like.

Cerebral hemorrhage, cranial trauma, and all those other words that medics shout over your head in the helicopter when you're being flown back to the military hospital.

I had never been the bloke on his back, but I had seen it too many times from the door position on the helicopters. Carter pushed different medications, and eased Callie into a medically induced sleep, and had the nurse set up an IV to rehydrate her.

"You're going to be staying here at least forty-eight hours," she said, looking at me over the printout from the blood-testing machinery. "She needs to rest without being shaken or vibrated in that *thing* that you call a vehicle."

"We are on a bit of a timetable," I said.

"She has a serious brain injury, and it is only by the grace of whatever god she believes in that her cognitive ability is still present. It is fairly common for people to die from brain bleeds. It's the fifth most common killer in North America."

I shuddered.

"So, you both will be staying here until she's medically released," Carter said and crossed her arms over her chest. The posture was obvious. She was going to fight for her patient, and it didn't matter what was coming after us. "Or, if it's that much of an issue, you can go on, and we will take care of our patient. The only reason you aren't on the floor right now with a needle sticking out of your neck is because I know that you didn't do this to her."

"I would never—" I started but the doctor interrupted me with a fierce expression and cutting hand gesture.

"This is domestic violence. I've seen too much of it, and you would be *astounded* how often the abusive partner brings their victim to get medical attention, and it's almost like they," she said, her eyes dark and penetrating, and I could feel her deliberately swapping the accusatory "you" for the non-targeted "they". "It's almost like there is a single script, and all the men who like to drink and talk with their fists have a copy."

"I've never struck a woman because I was angry or drunk," I said.

"Have you struck a woman?" Carter asked.

"Doctor, I've shot several, and yes, I've done hand-to-hand combat with too many." She gave me a look that would have cracked a stone. "In-country, the local women sometimes pick up their husband's, brother's or son's Kalashnikovs or RPG-2 and start shooting at the Americans or us Royal Marines. When you pick up a weapon and start shooting at uniformed soldiers, you become a legally recognized combatant and rules of engagement say legally recognized combatants are to be met with appropriate force."

"Oh," she said and lost around a half inch of height as her inflated sense of indignation deflated a little.

"An unfortunate side effect of being a soldier is that you don't get to pick who does and who doesn't try to kill you. I was lucky. I was never *seriously* injured, and I never had to deal with shooting any kids."

"I thought we were going to have a discussion about domestic abuse, and now we're looking at American foreign policy?" she asked with a tart edge to her tone.

I gave a laconic shrug.

"I'm a naturalized American citizen, and technically, I still have my dual citizenship and British passport," I said. "You Americans are the international cowboys, and at the time our prime minister was your president's wingman."

"Then the question is, why did you join the military then? You knew what they did." She crossed her arms.

"I want to say I don't understand this hostility, but I think I do. We learned a bit of American history back in Yorkshire, and I know that the cowboys and Indians stories we were told were the versions that were more American propaganda than any attempt at real history. I can only compare it to the sins of the Empire. But to the point, the reason I joined the military is that there were only three ways out of the village I grew up in – you got a job at the coal pit, you got accepted to Leeds, or you joined the military." I paused and gathered myself. "I wasn't smart enough for Leeds, wasn't dumb enough for Kellingley, so the only option was to join up."

"Economic reasons, then," she said.

"Yes, economic reasons. I spent six years in the Royal Marines, and I've seen the ugliest parts of the world and some of the worst of humanity. Now, I am a freelance contractor who seems to be incapable of making decisions in my own self-interest. By every right and drop of common sense, I should not have stepped between one of the most powerful men in Hollywood and his wife, regardless of how hard he was beating her. Even if he pulled out a gun and blew her head off, I should have stayed where I was until I was tapped to act. That was literally my job. Instead, I choked Rex out and dumped him on his own thousand-dollar glass coffee table and fled the state with his wife."

"What is she to you? Have you been intimate with her?"

"You are just seriously looking for a place to stick a knife, aren't you?"

"I have plenty of reasons," she said.

"After seeing this place, I think I understand," I said. "But I would appreciate it if you put the verbal knives away. I think I've been chivalrous to a fault, and I am beholden to none of the American sins."

"What are the American sins?"

I rolled my eyes.

"Slavery, genocide, resource exploitation, international adventurism, military support of oil? There are the Hollywood sins – sexualizing children, human trafficking, drug abuse. There is literally a laundry list. That doesn't even touch wanker shite like the cults of personality like New Eden, that does shite like groom teenage girls to be sold off to their elite celebrity backers, and God knows what that place does away from the eyes of media."

"Are you going to do something about that?" she asked. I thought a moment about that, hesitating before I answered, but I already knew what the answer was.

"In all likelihood, yes. Not by my choice. They will come to retake their perceived property and it is my intent that they draw back a bloody fucking stump, or nothing at all."

"That is an answer I approve of."

"Finally," I said.

"You should probably get in contact with Fallout. They would likely *love* to get interviews with Calanthe, get the inside word about the New Eden cult out."

"That is a good idea, but right now, we need to make sure she doesn't die, or when she wakes up, she can talk, doesn't drool, doesn't drag a foot or have to wear diapers." The doc gave me a harsh expression.

"Are you questioning my abilities as a doctor?"

"Fuck, no. I've seen enough head wounds and veterans with lingering trauma." I held up a hand. "That concern has literally nothing to do with you or your abilities as a doctor."

"I've had enough people question me and my credentials," she said. Lord, the proverbial chip on this woman's shoulder was the size of a boulder.

"Doctor, have you ever worked with the Veterans Administration, have you treated combat wounds? Battlefield triage?" She shook her head no. "It's nothing like this. It's chaos and screaming, and blood, and if you're close enough to the front, you can hear the fighting still going on as you watch medics trying to put blood back in a kid faster than he can bleed it out. Mazar-i-Sharif, Marjah, Kandahar, it was a goddamn mess. Afghans killing Americans with weapons they were given to fight the Soviets decades ago. So I've seen more horror than you would care to see. Please take care of my friend, and we will leave as soon as we can, but not before you say it's safe to go."

I could feel my pulse thundering in my ears, and I left the doc's office as quickly as I could without running. Was it reliving the memories, was it how similar this part of the U.S. was to being in-country? Was there something about her, her dark hair and angry voice? I could feel the weight of the flak jacket on my shoulders again, the heft of the rifle in its sling, the heat pressed against my skin because there was nowhere for it to go. My sinuses were full of dust again; my eyes stung with it.

Fuck this place.

I thought I would enjoy seeing parts of the country that I had only seen on television, and cinema, but it was completely different than what I had wanted, had wished it to be. I looked up at the mountains to the north and there was no difference – the color of the rock, the rainbow sunset, the vast miserable emptiness.

The outpost of the reservation was a deeply depressing place and it seemed we weren't going anywhere for a while, so I had time. Given the layout of the land threats would be visible for miles away, and unless New Eden had attack helicopters and GPS coordinates, there was no way they could surprise me. It was time for some self-care, as the Centre called it. Except that it was my self-care, and not that meditate on a leaf or a clear-blue wave shite. No, it was a bottle of cheap whiskey and my gun cleaning kit.

I dropped the tailgate on the truck, and one by one went through my collection of weapons. Each weapon was broken down, cleaned, meticulously oiled, and reassembled. Each pistol was given special attention. Some were well used, including the 1911 I had carried as a sidearm all the way through Afghanistan.

The captain had given it to me the first night we were on the same patrol. He would probably be pissed when he found out how I fucked up the job with Rex and the New Eden Centre. He was the one who had gotten me an in. Did he know what they did? Surely, he couldn't have known. If I survived this mess and ever got to talk to him again, I would have to ask.

I sighed and drank more of the cheap stuff.

It was working. The stress was leaking out of me, and I felt something akin to normalcy creep over me, but it wasn't the calm and casual cool I was used to. No, it was the nerved-up always watching, bordering on paranoid normalcy that had kept me alive through years in the Afghan mountains. I reached up and scratched at my chin; it had been too long since I shaved. In-country I had let my hair grow long and my beard grow out. It was just easier, and it made us stand out less among the locals. To them, beards had something of a social standing and meaning.

"She's going to be okay, you know," the doc said. "And I want to apologize," she said, holding her hands up and taking a few steps back. I slid the 1911 back into its holster on my hip and gave a nod.

"Apology accepted. Sorry about pulling down on you," I said.

"You really were over there," she said.

"Yes."

"There is a fair bit of stolen valor that goes on around here," she said. "Lots of people like to impersonate soldiers, or cops."

"There is a bit of cult worship, isn't there?" I asked. My eyes lingered on the horizon, watching the ball of the sun as it was starting to cross the horizon. The colors were fantastic, but part of my rational mind knew that was from the shield of pollution that domed over California, to our west.

"There is, but for some of the boys on the reservation, joining the military is often their only way out of this life, and I don't blame them. There's nothing here. There is no opportunity, just a lingering demise."

"Why are you here then?" I asked.

"Because my people need me," she said, her voice calm and plain for about the first time. "And because it's what I can do. The only reason I can do that is because of the hidden contracts I have with people like you. I don't charge anything for the locals. I soak all of the cost myself."

"Hence my ten-grand bill, eh?" I asked.

"Yes, but it *is* fully discrete. I won't turn your information over to the authorities. Fuck the Federal Bureau of Intimidation – as far as I'm concerned you were never here, and there's no record of anything that's been done. After you leave, all the records from this visit go into a burn barrel. Callie gets the only copy on a flash drive for her future medical needs."

"Other people come here, same angle?"

"Obviously, but you know I won't tell you anything about them. The confidentiality goes both ways."

"I appreciate that," I said with a nod.

CALLIE SLEPT FOR TWO DAYS. Not entirely on her own, but it did her no harm. Holoke, she preferred that to being called Doc, made sure that she was recovering and not sliding into a vegetative state, something about brainwaves and an oscilloscope, whatever. Callie was recovering. She had two IVs, a catheter, and there were several injections of drugs to reduce blood pressure, address swelling, and a few things she said were technically experimental and not available on the general market, and probably wouldn't be for years. Nothing critical, but something about stem cells, I wasn't sure.

All I cared about was Callie getting better, not worse.

12

––––––––––

*C*allie...

I stared out the truck's window grimly as we left the good doctor and the reservation behind. I had a bag full of pills – steroids, anti-inflammatories, and the like – jiggling on the bench seat between us. Kurt was silent, and I was miserable... *permanent brain damage* swirling around in my mind.

I was damaged. Beyond repair and I didn't even know how badly yet.

It was scary. It was depressing. It was... it was...

I squeezed my eyes shut and huffed a frustrated sigh.

"What's wrong?" he asked, and I shook my head slightly.

"I lost my train of thought," I said.

"You're going to be fine," he said.

"You don't know that. The doctor didn't either," I said.

I turned and looked at him and he took his eyes off the road and looked me in the eyes. His were a beautiful blue, almost as blue as the sky outside his window behind his head.

"You're going to be fine," he repeated, and his tone brooked no argument.

He stared at me intently for longer than a few seconds until I turned my head to look out the windshield first.

"Will you please just drive?" I pleaded softly.

He turned his attention back to the road, which thankfully was straight, and we hadn't deviated at all in our lane. I swallowed hard at the sincerity in his expression, those eyes of his burning into mine. I shifted on my seat, and he sighed.

"You're alive, Callie, and you're strong. You'll be fine."

I swallowed hard and whispered, "Not if they find us."

"You let me worry about that now, yeah?"

I stared at his profile – the strong jaw, his thick neck, and the set of his shoulders under his plaid shirt – and I nodded slowly.

"Yeah," I whispered and went back to staring out the window at the arid-brown flat ground meeting such a brilliant blue sky it almost hurt my eyes even from behind the dark lenses.

We were in the truck for a long, long time this time. I asked where we were going, and he said we would stop in Amarillo tonight. I felt like I should know what state Amarillo was in, but for the life of me, I couldn't seem to recall. It was upsetting and worrying and when I asked, it must have sounded in my voice because Kurt simply chuckled and asked me where the city of Kent was located in England.

"I don't know," I said.

He smiled and said, "The U.S. is a lot bigger than England. You can't be expected to know where every city is located on the map. Amarillo is in the Texas panhandle."

"Okay, and where are we now?" I asked.

"Albuquerque," he answered. "Just about the back side of it, really."

"Albuquerque, that's New Mexico," I said, and his smile grew a bit more.

"See, not so daft as you think," he said. "Tell me, Callie..."

"Yes?" I asked, pulling my eyes away from the city rolling by outside the window.

"Why are you really afraid of perhaps, and that's a *big* perhaps, being a little forgetful?"

"You don't want to forget things around Arik, or the rest of New Eden," I murmured and he put his hand over mine where it rested on the seat between us and gave it a gentle squeeze.

"You aren't going back to New Eden, or Arik, Love. I know you've got no reason to, but you can trust me on that."

A time later, maybe an hour, maybe two, I didn't really know – time was all fuzzy with the endless rush of pavement beneath his truck's tires – we started passing through an area rippling with rough black stone in the freeway medians and to either side of the highway. I frowned slightly and leaned closer to the glass as though it would help me see better.

"Kurt," I said, and he glanced my way.

"Ah, yeah?" he asked.

"What am I seeing out there?" I asked. "It looks like old hard lava but—"

"You would be right," he said with a smile. "We're driving through the New Mexico lava beds."

"There aren't any volcanoes in New Mexico," I said frowning.

"Not anymore, Love. This one is extinct, from back in the time of the dinosaurs, I think. Which incidentally, there are a lot of those around these parts as well. All through Utah, Colorado, and New Mexico, they dig up old fossils and bones."

"I vaguely knew that," I murmured. "A footnote on the lessons about the fossil fuel industry."

"Ah, yeah." Kurt nodded. "Never understood that," he said.

"Understood what?" I asked, tearing my eyes away from the rippling black stone thrusting up toward the sky in waves that reminded me of rough seas frozen in time.

"New Eden being so anti-fossil fuel and the like, and yet how many movies their poster boy has starred in with car chases and explosions."

I smiled and it was a bitter thing.

"I pointed that out once," I said.

"Yeah, what'd they say about it?" he asked.

"Nothing," I said and turned to look back out the window. "Arik backhanded me in the mouth."

I heard a squeaking, like leather twisting, and I turned back to see Kurt's large hands all but strangling the steering wheel.

"Sorry," I said softly. "I shouldn't talk about those things."

"Why not?" he asked.

"Because they upset you," I said.

"You talk about whatever you'd like, Love. Whatever makes you feel better."

I lapsed into silence again, turning those words over in my mind.

I couldn't remember when it'd happened, but I liked that he was calling me "Love" even if it was just a generic thing that Englishmen said. Like an American "Sweetheart" or "Darling."

While I sat in my silence, I thought about that, too. I felt like I should be vaguely unsettled for liking it, but I didn't. I really liked it. I didn't know what that meant. I didn't know if that really *meant* anything.

It was dark by the time we pulled off the road to get a room. I waited in the truck, inspecting my reflection in the night-darkened glass of the passenger side, staring at the bruises that were fading from wine to coffee stains under my skin. The red was leaving, the brown coming through more, but I hadn't quite gotten to the sickly green and yellow phase of things. That's when it became easier to cover it all with makeup. A little red to balance out the green, just a slightly thicker layer of concealer for the yellows – oh, and it hurt a lot less to apply and remove it all.

Except I didn't have any makeup to hide behind. No high-end cosmetics. Not even low-end drug store quality anything. Just my wild mane of red hair that dipped past my ass but wasn't quite to my knees.

The truck's door opened behind me, and I jumped.

"Easy," Kurt said. "It's just me."

"Sorry," I apologized automatically, and he shook his head.

"No need for that. You save your apologies with me."

I nodded carefully and he drove us around closer to our room. I frowned slightly when he brought everything that didn't have a lock on it inside with us.

"Are we staying for a few days?" I asked.

"Nah." He shook his head. "Just tonight."

"Oh," I murmured, my curiosity eating me alive.

"Ask the question, Callie," he said kindly.

"If we're only staying the one night, why bring everything in?" I asked.

"It's a bit sketch out there," he said.

I looked out of our motel room door, across the cracked asphalt of the parking lot, rippled by heat and whatnot, reminding me of the lava beds we'd traversed earlier in the day.

"I don't understand, what makes it... off?"

He smiled at me and shut the door, throwing the locks, and swinging the little arm over the ball that seemed to replace the old chain-style locks in recent memory.

"A lot of things you've never had to deal with in the secured confines of New Eden. We'll have to work on your situational awareness."

"Okay," I said perking up. "I like learning things."

"Aye, I somehow knew that about you," he said, dropping onto the edge of the bed beside mine – the one closest to the door and the window, which he'd insisted upon from the very first night.

"I never asked, but—"

"Go on," he said.

"Why do you always take the bed, or the side of the bed closest to the door and windows?"

He smiled and it was tired. "Lesson one, then, I do that to protect you. If anyone is coming in, they have to get through me to get to you."

I blinked slowly. I had never thought of that.

"Oh," I murmured, taken aback.

"It's been a long day. I'm going across the parking lot to that diner over there and getting us some food. You rest now."

"Okay." I nodded. "Kurt!" I called as he was halfway out the door. He leaned back and looked me over. "Thank you."

He smiled, nodded, and went out. I got up and locked the door behind him and waited nervously in the chair at the little desk for him to come back.

When he went to open the door and it caught, he cursed.

"Call—?" I had the door open before he could finish my name.

"You said it was a bad area," I said and shrugged weakly.

"I did, that was good of you." He nodded his approval.

We shared a meal, and I was ravenous, something that seemed to encourage Kurt.

"Get some rest. Showers in the morning before we leave."

I nodded.

"Okay."

I was feeling much more myself and though the prospect of permanent brain damage was scary, everything seemed a lot less scary with Kurt by my side.

We were both sound asleep when it happened. The door came crashing in on its hinges and what could only amount to a tactical strike team entered the room. Kurt sat up, gun in hand but was shot immediately. The gun was loud and fired in a burst of hellfire and smoke. I jerked and screamed as blood arced movie perfect from Kurt's beautifully muscled and broad chest and he collapsed onto his back in the bed. Somehow feathers were flying, falling like snow, and the person who came in behind the one who had shot Kurt came fully into the room. Their mask and gear a black carapace, rendering them faceless, genderless, a modern horror as they advanced, arm outstretched to snare one of my wrists in their gloved hand.

I screamed, and drew in tighter on myself, squeezing my eyes shut and already curling into a ball to ward off the coming blow.

"Callie!"

I jerked and chest heaving opened my eyes.

Kurt's face was inches from my own, stricken with worry.

"Kurt?" I asked in soft disbelief.

"Aye." He nodded fervently.

I felt my face crumble, the tears that welled in my eyes, ones of relief.

"Oh, there you go," he said as I unclenched my muscles one by one. "A bad dream is all."

I sobbed a little, and in a desperate bid to ward off the nightmare, practically crawled into his lap to hide from it.

He gathered me up and hugged me tight.

"That's it," he said gently. "You're alright now."

I cried.

Was I? Was I really? Would we ever be?

The answer to that was a resounding *no*. Not as long as New Eden and Arik Rex were looking for us. I had zero doubt in my mind that they were and that eventually we would be found.

As much as I didn't want to die, the thought of getting Kurt killed just for helping me?

Well, I had a whole lot to cry about that night, but by the same token, I couldn't cry forever.

13

---

*K*urt...

The nightmares weren't a surprise, just the force of them. Dealing with them was more difficult because it brought up the issue of personal boundaries. I was no therapist. I had no understanding of the treatment process for the various flavors of PTSD, but I remembered what helped me when I was at this point – just not being alone.

Being alone was the worst part.

During my reintroduction to society, the counselor suggested I find a support group and to get a pet. The support group ended up being a veteran's support group at a pub, owned by an ex-pat living in Maryland, and I had run into my old captain. It was incredibly reassuring to find I wasn't alone, and the place could finally make a fucking proper English breakfast down to having the right bangers and real bacon, not the sad stuff Americans seemed obsessed with. I wasn't much for taking care of a pet like they should be taken care of, but for the short amount of time I had owned a cat, an old stray. It had made a difference for the both of us, at least I'd like to think so.

Casual dating seemed to provide that sliver of human contact I needed, especially the ones that would stay the night.

After her first round of nightmares, I scooted closer to Callie in the bed, with my back turned to her. She was thin, and there was something I had those skinny women had loved – body warmth.

In her sleep, she moved closer until we were lying back-to-back. I felt her sigh and then for lack of a better term, subside. I had no idea how Rex and she shared a bed, and that felt strange, but once she pulled in, it felt more natural.

I didn't face her, wasn't going to make her the little spoon. Putting my arms around her was as likely to come across as constricting or threatening. I also didn't need to wake her up halfway through the night with something rude poking her in the bottom.

I definitely tried to not think about that. Her penchant for sleeping in nothing more than one of my shirts and a pair of panties made my blood stir. I chastised myself. I didn't need to think about her like that. She had been abused and beaten and the last thing on her mind was having a toss with a madman who choked out her husband and was dragging her across the continent.

Continent, that was something to focus on.

Thinking about the U.S. as a country messed with my sense of perspective. Some of the states seemed like countries to themselves, and in my mind, that's how big countries were. This was a continent, a great landmass bracketed by oceans.

I let myself ease back to sleep.

I HAD SEEN many places in the world that I had considered empty and desolate. Stretches of the Maghreb were vacant of any vestiges of humanity. The Afghan highlands were likewise a wasteland of rock formations and the wreckage of decades of war. There were places where we drove the shells of cities that had once been thriving and cosmopolitan, before the Soviets invaded, before radicalized Islam, before twenty years of American occupation.

This didn't prepare me for the desolation of Oklahoma.

The land was flat, and I could see the signs of ranching and agriculture, but that was all there was. The only concession to the existence of America was that sometimes we would see the stillborn corpses of towns, collections of static caravans, American mobile homes. My parents had one of those, up on a hill near the sea, and they leased it out to tourists who didn't have the money to own one themselves. But that was a vacation destination, not a place they ever lived full time. These things, they were long and narrow, almost mean with their cheapness and the way they were packed into parks.

We had been driving through a light welter of rain, watching storms race ahead of us when we came to the first disaster.

It looked like the roadside park had been hit by a Coalition strike package. The trailers were torn to pieces, some rolled on their sides. One particularly struck me because it looked like it had been opened like a tin, the roof curled up and missing. There were a handful of emergency vehicles, their lights strobing against the destruction. I felt an intense wrongness, because the air was clean, and all I could smell was the dampness of the rain and the ozone scent of thunderstorms. This sort of carnage usually came with the stink of fire, burned metal, and the particular chemical tang of detonated explosives.

After the first year in-country, you could start telling what was used in the strike by the way it smelled.

But there was no chemical smell, just wet.

We drove on, and had our sights set on making it to a town in Arkansas, where we would stop for the night. It was a longer day's drive than what we had been making, but there was something about the state that screamed at me to get out. When my gut agreed with the almost passive hostility of the environment, I listened.

"It's behind us," Callie said, looking over her shoulder.

"What?" I asked and looked in the side mirror. There was nothing behind us other than a few vehicles.

"The storm," she said softly.

I adjusted the rearview mirror and behind us the sky was so dark gray it was almost black. "Well, fuck me sideways, that is going to be a hell of a storm. No worries though." I put my foot down and trusted in the V8 under the hood to get us out of the inconvenience of the storm. I pushed to eighty. After a few minutes, the storm was larger, growing closer.

I pushed harder and the speedo ticked up to ninety, and then I noticed that Callie was sitting white knuckled and grim in the passenger seat, almost turned to pale stone by fear. I eased off the accelerator, and the speed dropped back down to match the posted signs. She relaxed, but only slightly.

The storm threw an awning of clouds over us, and then the sunlight started to fade. How bloody fast could these things move?

We were passed by the craziest thing I had seen on American road. It looked like the unholy fusion of a sneaker and an armored personnel carrier. Storm Hunters...

Storm Hunters... those were the crazy bastards who went driving into the worst storms. If there was one of them here, we could be in trouble. "Just how serious are these storms?" I asked.

"They can be bad, tornadoes and stuff."

"Stuff?"

"Like hail, and..." she paused, her mouth twisting in thought. "Bad... storm... air."

"So, these don't happen where I'm from, what's the drill?"

"Seek shelter," she said quickly, and pointed, at of all things, an overpass.

These were something I had seen that were unique to this part of the country. They had built a bridge over the highway but had to make hills on both sides to make it happen. Traffic, I guessed? There were a few motorcyclists pulled over with their bikes, sheltering behind the pylons and the bikers themselves seemed to have gone up the concrete berm of the overpass. This seemed like a prudent thing to do. I engaged the all-wheel-drive in the truck, took us off the pavement and onto the shoulder and slowed.

The rain wall hit with the force of a monsoon, but I let the truck ease its way between the last pylon and the berm. The passenger side lifted as the tires gripped and I started a slow climb. It only took a minute to wedge my truck under the shelter of the overpass, and in that time, it had gotten dark enough to justify burning the headlights. Wind buffeted us, and the storm roared overhead. I could see the shitstorm of ice it started throwing and the sky was an absolutely insane greenish-black color.

"We have to get out of the truck," Callie said.

"Are you mental?"

"No, the wind could..." she made a sweeping gesture with her hands, and the intent seemed obvious.

"The wind could pull the truck out from under the bridge?" I asked. She nodded seriously. "Fuck me," I grunted. "C'mon then, let's get to where this storm fuckery can't give us a toss all the way to Oz." She nodded and tried to push her door open. The wind kept jamming it back against her, so I had to go around the tailgate to help her get out. The rain instantly soaked me to the skin, and I had to use both hands to get her door open.

I blocked the wind as best I could, letting it batter me instead of her. "Grab the medic bag," I shouted. Of all the things in the truck that could or couldn't be replaced, the bag with her meds in it was the most important. She nodded and looped the bag over her head, strap across her body, settling it on her shoulder. We moved toward the front of the truck. It was a tight and cramped fit between the concrete ribs of the bridge over our heads, and it was obvious that nothing came here except spiders, windblown debris, and some more spiders. I shuddered in disgust but ignored them.

The wind died down, and the rain seemed to slack.

Then there was a roar. The entire sky seemed to be filled with its horrid noise. The ground seemed to vibrate with the force of it, and it reminded me of the big American cargo planes flying low, touching the ground with their back wheels, and just letting cargo slide down the ramp. Except rather than one of the big Galaxy's landing, it was a dozen, or a hundred, and the roar took my breath away.

Callie wrapped her arms around my chest and buried her face in my shoulder. It was going to be okay, I wanted to tell her, that we were perfectly safe.

Then the truck groaned, and I heard the squeal of rubber sliding across concrete and the rear end of the truck started to move. The wind had it, and I felt my mouth go dry and stomach tense. The grill shifted and instead of the GMC logo staring me in the face it was facing Callie.

The protest of tires was brief, because the wind took the rear of the truck up and off the ground and then it was pitching down and away from us. We were exposed to the fury of the storm, and I saw it – a finger of darkness stabbing down from the sky and cutting a path along the side of the highway. A black cloud of debris hid the point where it touched the ground, but there was no doubt in my mind, it was coming straight for us.

It would certainly be black humor for us to escape New Eden, and pursuit, only to end up caught by something like this. I held her closer against me, and would have said something encouraging, but I had no words, just awe and fear. The bridge shuddered, the massive concrete braces felt like they were flexing, and I felt like a fool for picking this spot. If it all came down, they wouldn't find our bodies. Debris spewed through the underpass, and I felt like we had been caught in a danger-close artillery strike, with gravel and trash everywhere. I stung my exposed arms and my back, but I braced against the concrete and the berm, and prayed.

Then it was over, and the roar was fleeing east, away from us.

"Are you okay?" I asked.

"No," she said, and I saw she was crying. I held her and we just sat in the dark.

"Let's get back in the truck. The rain will be here in a second." She looked up and I could see she was trembling. "It's done and gone, and the heater in the truck works nice like." She collected herself, nodded, and we crawled out from our shelter.

"You're bleeding," she said. I looked down to see that my arm looked raw, and I *was* bleeding.

"Some stuff hit me, nothing big," I said. "Gravel? Maybe hail?"

"We should take care of that," she said.

"Let's get somewhere first," I offered. "I need to find something on this radio, so we don't get bollocked by a storm like that again."

"You drive," she said, picking at the debris and blood stuck to my arm. "I'll find a weather radio. I'm sure I can figure the buttons out."

"You got it," I said, and we limped our way down the embankment to where the truck was sitting. Thankfully it was on all four wheels and looked only slightly worse for wear for being pushed down the road. There was a crack in the windshield, and the passenger side mirror was nowhere to be seen. That was annoying and would be expensive to replace. I sighed, but it was momentary. The engine turned over easily, and I put it back in gear. Crossing back onto the road was easy enough, after a long run down the shoulder.

We drove past more carnage – a few flipped cars, and a lorry that had been ripped apart, the cab thrown into one of the rock strewn and dusty fields. The tornado left a path of destruction that ran for almost sixty miles, and it was something that I couldn't imagine happening anywhere, let alone here in America.

The road leading out of Oklahoma seemed endless, and when we finally crossed the state line, there was an almost supernatural sense of relief. "Someone mentioned that tornadoes are really bad through here, and everyone lives in trailer houses, but no one has an underground shelter," Callie said. "It makes me wonder, what lives in the earth that's so much worse that people would rather face the storms?"

"That's some right fucking weird shit, right there," I said. She never turned her head, and just watched as the scenery faded into darkness. It was a late check-in when we finally surrendered to exhaustion. The hotel was nothing more than a sunbaked wreck on the side of the road, but the town showed signs of life – a few street-lights, and businesses that didn't shutter when the sun went down. They weren't upright places, but seedy types – topless bars, dives, and a few pull up places for food.

We hit one of the pull-ups and indulged in some of the greasiest hamburgers I had ever eaten, served with onion rings bigger than I had ever seen. Callie declined to have the same and instead had one of the strangest chicken salad sandwiches I had ever seen. It was packed full of bacon and slivered almonds, and she held it like it was a life preserver.

The mulberry milkshake was something different, and Callie seemed to enjoy it more than I did. I found it to be floral and almost sickeningly sweet.

I was happy to see her get more than a few bites down.

The hotel room was the depressing sort we were used to. The shower worked, and I was able to toss my storm-battered clothes in the bin. Judging by the look of the room, they wouldn't call the police over some bloody shirt. This seemed like the sort of place that unless there was a body, they didn't do anything other than toss some more bleach into the laundry.

This was reminding me of the worse parts of North Yorkshire, but if nuclear war had removed the trees, and burned the streams away, and left nothing but burned rock and the shells of buildings behind. I was looking forward to being back in Maryland, and my place outside of Indigo City.

"Did you know that the mountains we're going to cross tomorrow are the siblings to the mountains of western Europe, and specifically, Scotland?"

Callie looked thoughtful for a moment, working to dry her hair out after the shower. The trivia seemed important because it let me have something to say, somewhere to put my attention rather than directly on her.

After the shower she was in her usual attire, a pair of the cheap cotton panties from Omni-Mart and one of my shirts. Each time she moved the towel in her hair, the hem of the shirt rose. She kept showing me the front of her panties, and that place that caught my breath, the span above her waistband and below her bellybutton. That was a weakness of mine, along with a nice shoulder, or delicate neck.

These were better to focus on rather than the way her nipples showed under the thin fabric of my shirt.

Fucking hell, she was stunning.

"Mountains in Scotland, huh?" she asked. "I thought you were English."

"I am English, but Yorkshire, North Yorkshire specifically, is close to the Scottish border, the highlands, all that."

"I know there is more to England than London, but that's what I know," she said. "That's also the only place in England I've ever been. Back for the press junket for Arik's movie. What was that terrible one where he was a steampunk pirate in the flying ship? He had that stupid hat and wore those contacts that made him look like he had crystal eyes?"

"I've only seen one of Arik's movies – the one with the fighting tournament but had time travel for some bloody reason."

"That one, it was the opposite of good," Callie said. "Even Arik said that one was terrible."

"He hasn't done very many good films," I said. "It's no surprise the Academy has stonewalled him for all these years."

"He won't do anything that isn't a big-budget action film, or something that's tied to New Eden where it shows a ruined Earth. He's been offered roles that might get him consideration. I know there was one being floated about Stonewall, but he turned it down and said some words that I won't repeat, but they were ugly."

"I can imagine," I said.

"I'm tired," she said, and did a stretch that showed off her smooth, tight stomach. I looked away but grunted in agreement.

I let her get in the bed first and after a few minutes, I gave up the watch, double-checked the locks on the door and the safety on the pistol I put on the bedside table. I turned off the light and started to settle in.

"Kurt?" she asked.

"Yeah?"

"Would you face me tonight?" she asked.

"If you want," I said hesitantly.

"It would make me feel safer," she said.

"Sure," I said, again responding slowly.

I faced her, and she put her face against my chest. She went to sleep quickly, and it was a long time before I felt the day creeping up on me. I was distantly aware, as my consciousness faded, that she turned, put her back against me, and pushed close.

She felt so small, and so warm against me.

14

─────────

*C*allie…

I woke with a soft jolt as we rolled to a stop along a gravel drive. I blinked and stared up at a large cabin in slight confusion, then fright as I wondered if I had lost time. I could have sworn Kurt had said we had at least two more days before we reached his cabin and yet, here it seemed, we were.

"Is this it?" I blurted in surprise.

"What?" he asked, hand on the inside doorhandle of his truck.

"Your cabin?" I asked, still fuzzy from my restless sleep. It was hard napping in the truck. While I slept, it was far from restful.

Kurt chuckled. "Ah, no… afraid my place isn't half as nice as this."

"Oh," I murmured, vaguely disappointed. I just wanted to be done. The miles wore on me, and I just wanted to know what it was to be still.

"Callie?"

"Hmm?" I asked, dragging my eyes from the looming cabin outside the windshield.

"You alright, Love?"

"Huh?" It took me a half second to process his question. "Oh, yeah! I'm just tired is all. Ready to be still."

"I see." His gaze flicked over my face, his blue eyes deep with concern, and I tried a wan smile. His brow crushed down under the weight of a fresh surge of worry, and I leaned back against the bench seat.

"I'm alright, Kurt," I said gently. "I promise."

"Wait right there," he said, popping open his door. A wave of humid air, like from the inside of... *shit,* what do you call that thing? Um... the glass house thing that you grow plants in. *Greenhouse!* Yes, humid air scented with green and growing things pushed into the cab of the truck along with frog and insect song. The warmth and natural music were just about instantly soothing to the soul.

I closed my eyes and listened as he left his door open and came around to get mine. It was something he did, insisting on getting my door for me, standing close, walking with me to and from anyplace we happened to stop or be, keeping me in the shadow, the shelter, of his much larger frame.

Instead of intimidating or imposing like it had been with Arik, it was something almost completely different with Kurt.

Intent, I believe, had everything to do with it.

He put a gentle palm to the small of my back and guided me to the door downstairs. Entering a code into the lockbox hanging from the door's knob, he retrieved the keys to let us in.

The cabin was fancy, large, and had a wraparound porch and a balcony above it that wrapped around too.

"A nice change from roadside motels," I murmured as he closed the door behind us. Vaulted ceilings awaited us, a large river rock fireplace with the horns of some great beast mounted above it. The light hanging over the living space was likewise a tangle of antlers, and it was all very rustic chic.

"I think we could both use a real bed tonight rather than a concrete slab, yeah?"

I groaned and said, "Absolutely, you absolute gem of a man."

"You can have your own room if you like," he said casually, and I hesitated.

"Do I have to?" I asked softly. "I mean, is that what *you* want?"

Kurt searched my face and I felt like anxiety radiated off of me with an almost radioactive glow. I don't think I could or would blame him for wanting a break from me. I chewed my bottom lip with nervousness, and he reached out, head slightly cocked and gently used the pad of his thumb to pull my lip from between my teeth, slightly grazing my chin with a light touch that almost made me shiver.

"We can both take the master suite," he said gently.

"Thanks," I whispered.

He broke eye contact with me and said, "Go get comfortable, Love. I'll bring in your things."

"Thanks," I echoed myself again and stared a hair too long at his broad retreating back as he went back out into the music of the night.

I let out a breath I hadn't realized I'd been holding, my lip and chin still tingling from that light touch of his.

I went for the steps to the second floor and trailed up them like some Victorian ghost – except wrong setting for that, I think.

I discovered the master suite of the cabin quickly and made an additional discovery of a deep, triangular corner tub – the kind with the jets. After several nights of hard beds and several days of being jostled along poorly maintained highways and roads in Kurt's stiffly riding truck, a hot bath with those jets sounded like the absolute *height* of luxury.

"Callie?" Kurt called out from the bedroom as I worked to pin up my mass of red mane with whatever I could scrounge. Mostly a pair of hair ties and a few stray Bobbie pins I had found and kept on the hem of my shirt.

"In here," I called back over the rush of water.

Kurt peeked in the doorway and when he discovered me still clothed, relaxed, and leaned against the frame.

"You hungry, then?" he asked.

"Starving, actually. What did you have in mind?"

"You just leave that to me, eh?" he smiled, and it was such a rare thing when he did. It transformed his entire face. He went from so broody and severe to almost boyishly handsome and I felt butterflies take off in my stomach.

"Okay," I murmured. "I trust you."

He paused for a moment after pushing off the doorframe and looked me over. Those three little words held weight, and I think he knew it. The serious look was back on his face as he gave me a single nod, one that said he took grave responsibility. I felt my lips twitch and lift, my heart lightening and letting go some of the burden that weighted it in my breast.

"Thank you," I said again and the gratitude in those two words went far beyond what it should take for simply scaring up a meal. He nodded again and turned to go. I closed my eyes, listening for a moment to the rush of water from the tap.

Sinking into the hot water up to my chin was pure bliss. Muscles lost tension in places, and it took work to consciously relax for some others, but I managed to a degree.

I shut off the tap and started the jets and sighed in contentment, taking the time to reflect on all the things that had led me to this point.

All the useless academia, the years of building me up, and for what?

For what?

To proverbially fatten me up; make me their prized pig to lead off to auction for the highest bidder. I had no doubt that Arik had paid handsomely for me – a most generous donation to New Eden Centre. Money had to have changed hands somewhere. It was what I had heard, anyway. That was how the August, I mean Emerson, funded his prized "church" and his lavish lifestyle.

New Eden was no better than a cult. I saw that now. And that cult peddled in flesh, *my* flesh and I had gathered I had fetched a handsome price.

I was little better than a whore. Arik hadn't been remiss in reminding me of that fact as often as possible, and I couldn't even say it was to my own benefit. I certainly hadn't seen any monetary benefit. There was no upside for me.

I dipped my hands in the water and cupped them, bringing them to my face, washing away the day and my tears, scrubbing at imaginary dirt I felt would never come off my skin; my *psyche*, no matter how hard or how often I scrubbed.

"Calanthe." Kurt's voice was gentle and concerned from the doorway and I jumped with a little shout of startlement.

"Don't call me that, please… anything but that," I said, hugging my knees and decidedly *not* looking at him. I didn't want to fall apart. I *wouldn't* fall apart.

"Hey now, what's this?" he asked in a hushed tone and came over, sitting on the step leading up into the tub, reaching out a hand and hesitating.

"It's okay," I said, and he rested it lightly against my back while I breathed.

"That's it now," he encouraged. "Breathe, just breathe."

"Sorry," I said with a shaky laugh. "I'm not sure what's wrong with me."

"Something's triggered you, it seems," he said softly. "Just focus on your breathing. Slow it down, Love. That's it."

"I'm sorry," I said. I caught movement out of the corner of my eye as he shook his head resolutely.

"None of that, now," he murmured and took up a washcloth from a basket of them nearby. He rolled up his sleeve and dipped it into the water behind me. I closed my eyes as he ran it across my shoulders, warm rivulets tracing down my back.

"What were you thinking about?" he asked softly when my calm had returned.

"That—" My voice trembled and I hated it. I swallowed hard and bit my lips together and he shook his head.

"You know what, it doesn't matter," he said. "All that does is that you're safe now, Love."

"Am I?" I asked, finally looking up at him. He blinked and stared at me, his face as stoic as stone, carved from fine marble or maybe granite even.

"Am I safe, Kurt? Or have I just put you in as much danger as me?" I hated that. That this was a distinct possibility. A reality that went unspoken between us.

"I'm more capable than you think, Callie girl," he said with a kind of sad smile.

I closed my eyes. "No, I know that, Kurt. I'm not doubting your ability. I promise, I'm not... it's just..."

"Perhaps, if I may," he said, and I nodded without looking, simply listening to his rich velveteen voice wrapped in its decadent if slight British accent. "Perhaps you may not be doubting my ability to keep you safe, but you overestimate their propensity for violence, yeah?"

I shook my head. "I wish that were the case."

"What is it really, Callie?" he asked gently, and I sniffed and looked up at him. With a sigh, I realized precisely what it was...

I was afraid.

Not for me, but for *him*.

I think I had given up on me ever having a fairy tale ending, and fairy tales weren't meant for men like Kurt. He wasn't some prince come to rescue his princess... but a brave knight? That I could get behind, but knights didn't get to marry the girl. They were forever in service to the King, pawns in the grand scheme of things and pawns?

"I'm afraid they'll hurt *you*," I said softly, and he dipped the washcloth again and ran it up my back.

"I can take care of myself," he said with a wry grin, and I nodded, but I think he was intentionally missing the point that had suddenly become glaringly obvious to me.

"I don't *want* you to get hurt, Kurt." I raised my hand from the water and reached out to touch the side of his face. He cleared his throat sharply and stood abruptly, handing me down the washcloth as though that had been my intent all along, to reach for the wet cloth and not for him.

"I've fixed some sandwiches from the cooler," he said. "Take your time here," he said. "They're ready when you want some."

"Thank you," I murmured, cheeks flaming.

Jesus, Callie, I thought savagely to myself. *You're no end of trouble for the man and look at you. Of course, he wouldn't want anything like that...*

"Any time, Love," he said and ducked out the bathroom door, making for the exit to the bedroom. I could hear his heavy boots as he clattered down the stairs as though the devil himself was on his heels.

I sighed heavily and hugged my knees a little tighter for a second before lowering my legs.

"Way to go, Callie," I whispered. "Throw yourself at the first man that's shown you even the slightest kindness," I murmured to myself, my voice full of derision.

I mean, hadn't that been precisely how Arik had caught me in his web in the first place?

Except Kurt's not Arik. Not even close, and you know that...

And I did know that. The men were legitimately like night and day from one another. Arik was the blazing, punishing sun. Unforgiving. Relentless. While Kurt? Kurt was the cool light of the moon. Soothing. Patient... and sometimes just as distant.

I sighed. I was as clean as I was going to get after washing with the light and fragrant soap provided by the accommodations that we were in. Which, I had to admit, the soap here was a far cry and imminently superior to the drying, waxy, soap-scum-leaving motel bars I had been using.

I got out of the bath and let the water out, wrapping in one of the large towels and availing myself of the moisturizer available, lightly rubbing it into my skin, up my legs and down my arms, across my chest and an even lighter, thinner layer into my face. My thirsty skin soaked it in quickly.

I went out into the bedroom and smiled. Kurt had laid out one of his shirts and a clean pair of my panties on the bed. I donned them, and took down my hair, taking the extra time to brush it out at the room's vanity, staring at myself in the mirror, and sighing, my stomach rumbling and gnawing at my backbone for lack of anything in it.

I was ravenous. I was also stalling.

I got up and went downstairs.

Kurt was sitting on the couch and had turned on the gas fireplace, the cheerful orange flames flickering among the fake logs and making the big, stark room almost homey.

"Hey," he murmured and gestured at the coffee table and the paper plate with a sandwich and chips on it.

"Thanks," I said softly and lifted the tab on the can of soda next to it, sweaty with cold condensation from the cooler. It hissed and crackled as I opened it and took a drink, the carbonation burning all the way down, the liquid soothing my parched throat, nonetheless.

"You alright?" he asked curiously, and I put on a brave smile and nodded.

"Yeah, thanks for this," I said.

"Mind if I go on up and shower before bed?" he asked. I pasted on my smile and shook my head.

"I don't mind at all, why would I?" I asked.

"Just making sure," he said, and he put his foot down off the nearby chaise end of the couch and got to his feet. "Come on up when you're ready," he said.

"Is the door locked?" I asked.

He diverted his path from the bottom of the stairs to the front door and checked.

"Yeah," he said, and I nodded.

"Thanks," I murmured.

"No one knows we're here, Love. You can relax tonight."

I nodded and let out a shuddering sigh.

"I feel like I'm microchipped, you know?" I asked with a nervous laugh.

"You've had CAT scans and MRIs, I would know," he said with a smile, his hand on the banister. "I also wouldn't put it past those bastards," he said and banging his hand lightly on the wood a couple of times, he started his ascent.

I watched him go and said to myself and the empty room, "Yeah, me either."

The sandwich was good, even though I barely tasted it. The chips thick cut and salty with the tang of vinegar. I finished up, and sat drinking my soda, staring into the flickering flames in front of me. After a time, they went out and I smiled. It must have been on a sleep timer. I yawned and went upstairs.

I could hear the steady hiss of the shower head and the irregular patter of water hitting stone. Kurt was still in the shower, and though I know he valued his privacy when he showered, I couldn't resist a peek. I glanced around the corner into the bathroom to see him leaning, arm braced against the gray slate, his forehead braced against that arm as the water beat against his back, running down his body, over the absolute perfect globes of his ass.

I felt myself blush, and jerked back into the room, willing my heartbeat to settle.

I turned and looked at the wall of glass overlooking the balcony and plucking the light throw blanket from the corner of the bed, opened the sliding glass door.

"Callie?" I heard from the bathroom.

"Yeah, just stepping out onto the back deck!" I called.

"Alright," he called back.

I wrapped the throw around my shoulders and stepped out into the cacophony of spring peeper frogs and crickets. At least, they sort of sounded like crickets. I guess it could have been something else.

I closed my eyes and immersed myself in the warm, sultry evening air and the sounds of nature all around; jumping slightly when Kurt made a sound coming through the open door behind me. I looked back over my shoulder at him in a pair of black drawstring lounge pants, rubbing a white towel over his short hair. His finely chiseled chest flushed from his hot shower.

"Feels cooler out here, now," he said, clearing his throat.

"I like the sounds," I said, turning back to the darkened treetop view, the branches and leaves rustling in a slight breeze that picked up. I laughed nervously, acutely aware it was just him and me after I'd shamelessly peeped on him. "That was magical," I murmured.

He nodded but didn't say anything, just stood beside me, towel over his neck, hands hanging loose at his sides. I slipped my hand into his without thinking and he looked down at them for a second before gradually holding my hand back.

"I could get used to this," I said softly, and I could feel the color in my cheeks, across the bridge of my nose.

"It's a good place to be," he agreed.

"Is your cabin like this?" I asked, looking up at him.

"Ah, no." He laughed slightly. "I'm almost embarrassed to take you there. It's not a quarter so fine as this."

I smiled up at him. "I don't need fine things, Kurt," I murmured and he looked down at me, the look in his blue eyes stealing my breath.

"Aye, you may not need them, but you deserve them," he said quietly.

I shook my head silently and drew up onto my toes, pitching forward slightly, catching myself against his chest. He turned slightly into my touch and without a word, dipped his head to meet me halfway. Our lips touched, silently, a whisper of a touch, a slight whimper of desire escaping me. He pressed his lips slightly more firmly against mine and I *melted* into him. He let go of my hand and straightened, putting his arm around me.

I blinked and leaned into him, lowering myself flat on my feet against the smooth wood of the deck. I rested my head against his chest and closed my eyes, listening to the nature around us and the equally wild throbbing of his heart from within his broad chest.

Well, alright then.

15

---

*K*urt...

It seemed that life was full of curveballs. The cabin in the Smokey Mountains had been an easy enough luxury. There were still plenty of places there that were almost off the grid. That was one of the things I had found charming about the region, the deep and almost pervasive mistrust of government and a refusal to embrace fads of technology and fashion. Tradition and family ties ran deep in the folded green mountains.

And there were tons of places that didn't give two shits if you paid cash and didn't give them six pieces of personal information so their software could assemble a profile or find your data for information mining. There were places out west that were looking into facial recognition software so that they could create better in-store patterns to make people stay longer and spend more, producing a digital footprint everywhere they went.

I almost shuddered at the thought.

It was like they were completely unaware of the implications.

Callie sighed, her breath hot against my chest, tearing me out of my thoughts. Her behavior since we checked into the cabin had been strange, maybe even going back to the overpass. It had almost been flirtatious, in an awkward way. It was... endearing.

I was very much aware of how small she felt in my arms, and just how little she was wearing – one of my shirts again, and a pair of light purple panties that seemed impossibly thin. I knew it was because they were a cheap, ten pack in a bag off the shelf, but there was a definite effect.

This wasn't the first time she had slept like this. She had insisted, in that slight manner she had, that we sleep together, and that she was to be the little spoon.

What did Arik do to her? What had he done besides beat her like a drum?

How had he abused her, – gaslit, psychologically coerced, or just outright manipulated her?

I stroked her hair, and she tensed for a second and then relaxed. She still did that, but it was not as prominent a reaction as it had been before. At least she didn't jump and let out a little scream. That had been disturbing. She tucked in a little closer as I caressed her shoulder and her side. Just small, positive attention. Maybe if that was normal, she would start shedding that fright response. I could smell her, that hint of muskiness under the faint chemical floral smell of the cabin's soaps and shampoos.

I liked that, and I knew that really, I shouldn't.

I shouldn't notice.

My cock certainly shouldn't notice. But I did, and it did. With her pressed against me, it was hard to keep that thought out of my mind, especially now. Before, it had been easier. The bruises on her face had been raw but they were faded and almost gone now, and she seemed less a woman and more a terrified creature then. The fact that she was beautiful under the abuse, under the bruises, was just a coincidence. What sort of monster would I be, holding her then, everything in her life wrecked, and giving her a nudge in the backside with my bits?

But bloody hell, it was different now.

The question of had she been flirting with me had been answered when she'd kissed me, and I couldn't decide what it bloody well made me that I'd kissed her back.

Her hands pressed against my chest felt like she desired more, but she was asleep. That didn't count. I let my hand wander a bit lower, down her side and to the swell of her hip. She felt nice, but that was obvious. I had never been side by side with a woman, felt her body and thought, well this one feels like the rough side of a dead tree. My heart felt like it was racing. This was close to trespassing. She was asleep, for fuck's sake.

That didn't matter downstairs, my business was all the way up and starting to throb. It had been a good while since the last time I had such company, and she was easily the most beautiful woman I had in bed. I withdrew my hand and pressed a small kiss to the side of her head, near her temple. I felt her fiery red hair against my lips.

Then she moved.

I froze.

"You missed," she said very softly. I felt her turn her head up to face me.

"I'm sorry, I didn't mean to wake you, or upset you," I said softly.

"You didn't," she said. "You can try again, though."

I kissed her on the lips. They were so soft, and I could feel her tremble in my arms. "This shouldn't be happening," I said in a pained whisper.

"Why not?" she asked, her words almost a foreign language, dark and heated.

"Because you're still married, because of what he—" I was going to protest, but she pressed her lips to mine and silenced me. Her lips were still soft, but there was more force behind her kiss. There was a heat, and a need there too. She shifted and instead of knees and elbows against me, her full body was pressed into mine. I didn't have a chance to shift so that my aching need wasn't pressed against her stomach.

"Don't say that," she said. "He doesn't own me anymore."

Before I could respond, we kissed again. This seemed to go on, her lips parting, and then I felt her tongue. I felt like a filthy commoner, all coarse and crude, kissing a princess. I was in no way worth this sort of attention, this affection. No, I was meant for commoner women, with thick thighs and low-wage jobs, the sort who ate fried food, and smoked.

"Be gentle," she said, stroking my chest with her hand. "I want to know what that's like."

"What?" I felt like whatever grounding I had under me had been suddenly washed away.

"He was the only man I've ever been with, and he was cruel. I don't know how this is going to turn out, but I want to know what it's like to make love..." she let her words trail off.

"Okay," I agreed, hesitantly. My cock wanted me to rush in, but that was absolutely the wrong thing to do. Making love to her was the slightly wrong thing to do. The wise thing to do would be to apologize for all of this, and retreat to the couch in the cabin's living room, or maybe to the front deck, where the cold mountain air would steal my overheated enthusiasm. I kissed her neck and her shoulder and started pulling my shirt up and off her. She moved to make that easier, and then it was a memory tossed to the floor. Her breasts were small, and even in the dark, I knew how pale and pink her nipples were. They were already firm before I touched them. When I did favor the first one with my lips, the noise Callie made seemed almost unnatural.

"I don't know what you're doing but I like it," she said, her voice breathy. I stopped and looked up at her. I could barely make out the hint of her face in the dark, but knew she was looking down at me.

"Should I ask what you *do* know?"

"I only know two positions. Both involve me being on my knees, and I hate both of them," she said.

"Good to know, we'll avoid those," I said. "But is this okay?" I gave her breast the slightest squeeze.

"I think I like that, but it feels weird." She let out a breath. "It feels weird that I like it, not weird what you're doing."

"Okay, good," I said. "If I do something you don't like, please tell me, alright?"

"Okay." I could feel her smile even in the dark.

I knew he was a bastard, but I didn't suspect him of being that sort of bastard, but really, why was that a surprise? Arik cheated on her relentlessly, physically abused her, emotionally manipulated her and the whole New Eden cult. Why was it a surprise that she hadn't experienced anything remotely resembling foreplay?

I kissed her body, light and soft, and slowly worked my way down to her panties. The thin fabric was the only thing between her and my affection. I kissed along the waistband, and then down the front of the sheer fabric. She let out another groan, and her entire body shuddered. When I moved her leg, she relaxed, and spread her legs for me. I felt a shudder of excitement run through me like electricity. I knew that I was working a wet spot into the front of my boxers, grinding against the sheets as I kissed against the crotch of her panties. I could almost taste her, and her scent filled my head.

I pulled her panties to the side and kissed her on the lips.

She shuddered and let out a high-pitched almost-animalistic sound. I started slowly, exploring her, and teasing her. I followed the contours of her body, finding her secrets with the tip of my tongue.

Had I been thinking about this?

Maybe I had been, but kept it buttoned down under a professional veneer.

This was how she should have been treated – lavished with tender affection, and protected. I ached, and the only thing that would ease that was to get out of the confines of my underwear and off of the bed. I reluctantly pulled away, feeling her hands caress the sides of my head. She was panting and sighed when I stopped.

"What are you doing?" she asked, breathless.

"Taking off my underwear," I said. "I want you, if you're ready."

"I don't think I've ever been this ready," she said with a little giggle in her voice. "Which is a first."

"That is a crime," I said. I climbed back on the bed and felt her move.

"Just be gentle," she said again.

"As you wish," I said, and positioned myself above her. She felt so small under me, and I moved closer. For a moment, I was thankful the lights were out and it was almost completely dark. If the lights were on, I was sure I would loom over her, and she responded poorly to physical dominance. As much as I wanted to just slide into her, that was more blind luck than magically common. Instead, I had to pause, and use my hand to guide the tip between her lips.

I felt a quiver of excitement, some mine, some hers. Callie gripped my arms, and I heard her breathing, her breath a hot plume against my chest. I eased forward, and there was a moment of resistance. She was tense, but almost dripping wet. It felt like I moved at a glacier's pace, entering her so very slowly.

It was probably more like a minute, but it was one of the longest minutes of my life.

"Don't," she whispered in my ear. "Not yet."

"Are you okay?"

"I just... let me... let me enjoy this for a moment." Her voice was almost silky in my ear. "There's only one first time, you know?"

"I do know," I said, and without moving my hips, I kissed her. She moved her hips first, after a few moments, the only other movement being my cock throbbing inside her. When she rolled her hips, I did too, sliding out, and then back in. We rocked against each other, slowly at first and then quicker.

The pace was never fast, and I made sure that I was gentle.

"I didn't know it could be like this," she said, and gave a small laugh. I felt her body tense and relax as the sound came out of her.

"It's supposed to be like this. You're supposed to enjoy it," I said.

"I am, are you?"

"Why wouldn't I?"

"Because you're not going all fast, and you've not yelled, or made a mess of me."

"Made a mess?"

"You know, made your business, the mess, that comes when you're finished."

"Love, you've been done wrong, so very wrong," I said.

"Then do me right."

"Absolutely, Love, absolutely."

I thought about easy positions, things that weren't demanding, physically or emotionally, and it was bracketed with what she said about two positions. I knew Arik enough to guess that those two positions were doggy style, rough and hard, and on her knees while he used her mouth as cruelly as he could.

I had seen how he treated some of his groupies and fans.

Callie would never have to experience that again, so long as I had something to say about that. I could read her, the sound of her breathing, the way she started to tense as she drew closer. Making a woman reach climax usually took more than this one position, and straight missionary was not usually a home run.

But she came. It was petite, small like she was, but undeniable.

"Oh fu-fu-fudge," she stammered, and I let a laugh out.

"That's alright, let me show you something else," I said. I pulled myself off her, and then a moment later, my cock popped out of her, and she let out a satisfied groan.

"Okay, show me something else."

I eased her over onto her side and lay down behind her. It only took a second to enter her again. I was usually luckier about pleasing my companions when they were in doggy style, but she had mentioned not wanting that position. This wasn't quite the same, but the angles were the same, and it was more relaxed. I took her gently, slowly. I worked her toward a second round. I knew I could do that. I had to concentrate on that, because if I let that focus waver, I would be undone by her innocence and heat.

That would happen eventually, but what could I do to make this special for her?

Her second orgasm came more easily than the first and was a bit stronger. Was she going to build toward larger and larger orgasms? That would be something.

"Callie?"

"Yeah?"

"Would you like to get on top?"

"I'm not sure," she said. "He never let me on top."

"It's like riding a bike, or a horse."

"I can do that," she said. I rolled onto my back and felt her move hesitantly on the bed. She straddled me awkwardly, putting a knee in the middle of my stomach and I flexed rather than grunted. The last thing I wanted to do was spook her. For a painful moment, I was caught in the gap between her thigh and pelvis, but she moved quickly and muttered several apologies.

She hovered above me, trying to find the angle. She missed, and rather than sliding down on me, she pinned my cock between her lips and my stomach. I groaned, and she did too. I reached down and guided myself into her. She took all of me and then sat there, shuddering. This was fantastic. It let her pick the pace she wanted and find the angles she needed. She seemed at a loss for a moment and simply sat on me. I took her hips and started lifting her and moving my own hips. The amount of movement was limited, but it was enough to push her in the right direction.

"Oh shit," she said softly, as she found her rhythm. "Can I go faster?"

"You can go as fast as you want," I said. She did and went from what had been our fairly casual pace to one that was quicker, much quicker. I was not going to last very long under this onslaught. "Cal," I grunted. "Cal, I'm going to come."

"Go ahead," she panted, not slowing.

"I'm going to come," I said again, more urgently. She didn't respond, but I felt her shift and it seemed like I was deeper inside her than I had been before. I grabbed her by the hips and attempted to dead lift her. I was seconds away and there was no condom. I had no idea if she was still taking her birth control, or if she even still had it, and getting her knocked up was the last thing I needed to do. She let out an awkward squawk as I managed to get myself out of her. I felt the first hot pulse shoot onto my stomach, and I relaxed.

She wrapped her hand around me, while I was still going off, and guided me back inside her.

Shit.

I grunted, and my balls drained inside her, while she almost immediately went back to her rabbit like pace. She rode me like I was a racehorse, and when she came, it was impressive. Callie pitched forward, off of me, and face-planted into the pillows, shrieking like a bloody banshee. I could feel her kicking and twitching on the bed next to me. I reached over to hold her, but she let out more shrieks and then an almost hysterical laughter, recoiling from my touch.

For a split second, I was afraid that something was wrong.

"Oh my God," she finally rasped out. "That... basthole, assgard, buzzard..." she stumbled over words while still shaking.

"Bastard? Asshole?" I offered. I felt her trembling hand on my chest.

"Yes, those words, those words. All this time, oh my God. All this time, this is what I've been missing?"

"I think so, yes," I said. "I mean, I'm not a professional at that or anything, but my complaints are few and far between."

"My compliments to the cock, I mean... no, I think that's right."

"Usually its compliments to the chef," I said, and felt myself relaxing.

"Compliments to him too," she said breathlessly, and after a moment, she moved close to me again. "Sorry, I was just really... excited. My skin was really excited."

"Ticklish?"

"Mmhmm."

"I'm sorry. I didn't mean to finish where I did, since we're not taking any precautions," I said, and stroked her hair.

"No worries. I never stopped taking my birth control. I mean, it's a shot. One that lasts a whole three months," she murmured into my shoulder.

"That's good to know." I kissed the top of her head.

"Thank you, Kurt."

"You're welcome?"

"For everything."

"Yeah." I smiled in the dark.

THE NEXT MORNING reminded me of the first time I had been with a woman. Everything seemed more vibrant. There was greater clarity, and a certain lightness of spirit. I had thought I was in love with her at the time, and maybe that was what made it different. It didn't feel like this the mornings after when I had picked some woman up at a bar or off the set. Those mornings were tinged with something not quite regret, maybe a hint of annoyance. There had been no connection, just the fulfilling of some base biological urge.

But the grass seemed brighter and greener, and the birds seemed to sing a happier song. Part of that was where we were, the Great Smokey mountains, surrounded by green as far as I could see, almost like the trees were reaching up to engulf the sky. It was a welcome change from the hundreds and hundreds of miles of desert and badlands, and the near post-apocalyptic wasteland that had been crossing the Panhandle and Oklahoma. We couldn't stay, as much as I longed to. I was down to only a few hundred dollars in my stash, and the cabin had been pricey, even during the off season. It was huge, not meant for a couple, but for a family, or a retreat for a group of friends. The place easily slept eight, ten if you were willing to use a pull-out sofa.

My cabin was so much smaller than this one, but that was okay.

Mine was off the grid and unregistered. It had power from a generator, and I had plans of getting some solar panels set up, but I had to find work and money for that. I had ended up losing that heroin cartel cash, which really, that was for the better.

Callie seemed in a much brighter mood as well. That might have something to do with the sex, it might also have had something to do with the showers the cabin had, steaming heat and solid pressure. Not like the various showers we used crossing the country. Few things are worse than hotel showers. No heat, no pressure, or the heat was so hard to dial in it was roast or freeze.

I carried our bags to the truck, and then hefted the locking gun cases from where I had hidden them. If worse came to worst, most of these were worth moderate to serious money. In California, they had been a liability. Several were outstandingly illegal, here they were a commodity. I could trade some of these even for a motorcycle, or a boat.

She was a little reluctant to leave the wooden fortress of the cabin, with its tall windows and its view of the river, and the distant mountains turning blue in the distance. It was really quite stunning, and if things worked out, a place that I would have to come visit again.

"There are some people I know in Indigo City who can help us out," I said as we traded the unpaved roads and county roads of the mountains for the main interstate heading east. I had tried to avoid these roads, but here it was nearly impossible.

"What can they do?" she asked.

"Cash in some of my crypto and find out what's been going on back west. You haven't been on the news, nor on social media. Rex and his people aren't visibly looking for you."

"That's good then, right?"

"Probably not. That just means they aren't wanting to get the police involved, or it's more important for them to keep this out of the news," I said.

"It should be obvious that I will be getting a marriage breakup."

"A what?"

"A marriage breakup. I won't be his wife after this," she said.

"Divorce?"

"That's the word, sorry."

"Don't worry about it." I smiled. "And I think that is a good idea. My friends might have some ideas about where we can turn to get you some protection. I'm sure that even with whatever prenup you had, you'll be entitled to something, and it will be bad press for the New Eden poster boy to get a divorce."

"There isn't a prenup," she said.

"That's insane, and dumb on his part," I said.

"Well, the Centre created false documents to make me appear older than I am. When I was married to Rex, I was still technically a minor, and anything I signed wouldn't be legally binding in the state of California."

"How old were you?"

"At the time the documents were falsified, I was five weeks away from sixteen. *Nubile pussy* has an expiration date, you know? I was married on my sixteenth birthday."

"That's news to me, and I had no idea about Rex really playing the cradle robber, no offense."

"None taken. My mother groomed me to basically be his child bride. The Centre has been talking about expanding into other countries, especially those with lower age of consent laws, so that they can get the pussy before it turns."

"Is this some of that, what was his name, the guy with the island and the underage girls?" I asked.

"I can't remember his name, but I do remember him. I met him once or twice at the Centre, and then at Arik's afterparties. Do you know what the magic number is?"

"Am I going to be upset?" I asked.

"I would hope so, because if you weren't, that would mean you were one of them, and since you helped me, you aren't. The magic number is fourteen."

"Fourteen?" I spat.

"Yes, that is when they say we are at our most nubile. They like that word, nubile." She rolled it around in her mouth like it was a foreign phrase.

"What does that make you?" I asked, hesitantly.

"Something like a near-barren hag. Couldn't you tell last night?" She giggled a little.

"Well..." I wanted to make a joke, keep the mood light, but I stumbled to find anything suitable.

"It's okay. I'm being a bit silly, sorry."

"Please don't apologize. Your smile and laughter are beautiful," I said.

She let out a sigh, and her eyes seemed larger, dewy. Was that really a thing?

"Because of all the forged documents, and bribes, and all that," she drew in a slow breath, "my ID card says I'm twenty-three. It is all a lie because I turned eighteen on my last birthday. In a few months, I'll be a withered-up husk of nineteen years."

"Twenty-three." I shook my head.

"Surprise." She smiled sadly.

"Oh, don't make that face at me. You're much too sweet for that sadness," I said, and brushed some hair from her face.

"You're the first person I've told, out loud." There were the beginnings of tears in her eyes. "It means so much to me that you haven't pulled away or grinned like a monster. Thank you, Kurt..."

We put Appalachia into the rearview and headed toward the coast, toward Maryland and Indigo City. I would have to make arrangements to see if the captain would meet me, and if he could help. If he would even be *willing* to help. Surely, he would. That brunette had changed him, and maybe he would see that maybe, maybe Callie was doing the same to me.

My God, what was I thinking?

There was no way she would be willing to stay with me when this settled.

If this settled.

If I were still alive and not sitting in a federal prison.

16

———

*M*adeleine Oberisk...

The scene had been grim, and it looked bad. It looked really bad. The fact that Kurt wouldn't answer his phone or texts made it look about as bad as something could look. The ambulance had come quickly enough, and Arik was whisked away to the hospital with a speed that would have put race car drivers to shame. It was a lot of show. He wasn't injured, and there were barely any marks on him. Certainly less than should have been on a man who had been choked unconscious and put through a glass-top coffee table. The amount of blood was shocking. Whoever had been on the other side must look like a piece of road-rashed meat.

Calanthe was missing too.

When I dialed Kurt for the thirtieth time, the ringer went directly to his voicemail. I was going to have to start making serious calls. Where was Calanthe? Where was my head of security? Who choked Mister Hollywood action star out in his own living room, and whose blood was all of this?

What a fucking mess.

"Mackenzie, this is Obe. I'm in charge for the time being. I need you to run some checks, pronto," I said, holding the phone to my ear and giving the room the most serious look that I could.

"What do you need and where is Worthington?"

"He's MIA, and that is part of what you're going to find out for me. I need a trace on his phone and see if you can ping the LoJack in his car. I want to know where he is."

"I'm on it," Mac said.

"Can you access the security system for the house remotely, or do we need to be in the panic room to do that?"

"Either. Panic room is easier, but if it's locked, that's an act of congress to get it to open from the outside, or you have to convince whoever is in there to open up," she said.

"It's open. Can you walk me through it?"

"Yeah, no problem," she said. "I'll have to use Kurt's code to access it, and I can only do that if I have alpha-level clearance from someone at the top."

"Can you consider me at the top, since our head is missing, or do you need someone else to confirm that?"

"Can anyone else do that? I could but it would be more solid if you had Mister Rex or his head agent's permission."

"They're both at the hospital right now, and I have no idea what happened. Clear it and I'll accept full responsibility for it. You can note me on it." I heard the keys click over the phone while I walked through the kitchen, into the pantry, and then pushed the concealed lever to pop the door on the panic room. The door swung in with no incident. The room was empty, and none of the security triggers were activated. Whatever had happened, it had been quick.

"I'm in, walk me through the system," I said. Mac's voice was almost clinical as she walked me through the monitors to bring up the internal security cameras. There was a first level of security that I was able to pass with my login, but then half the house had a second layer of additional encryption. That seemed unusual. I didn't know that there were two layers. Fuck, there might be more. I guess being second in security didn't count for that much. That was a bunch of bullshit, and I was going to talk to Anderson about that. If I was number two, I should have at least known about this.

The system responded, and I started scrolling through the recordings. There were hours and hours of nothing happening, empty rooms, and feeds of trees swaying in the wind, cars moving down the street. Then, Kurt's sedan pulled up. He keyed the door, entered, and walked through the foyer. There was a pause as the feed switched to a camera that was inside the second layer of security.

"Where are we on getting through this second layer?" I asked.

"A few minutes, I can probably sus this out. Anderson and Soren aren't that creative," Mac said. She gave a laugh of victory, and then a litany of obscenity. "The internal feeds are being deleted. I'm actually watching the files delete out in real time."

"What about backups, offsite? Tell me there is some hack bullshit you can pull off to save something, anything?"

"Yeah, I'm doing that. I've been doing that." She grunted. "The good news is whoever is deleting the files is a fucking scrub. They are deleting the files one at a time instead of trashing the entire folder. This is something being actively concealed. What the fuck happened?"

"I'll see if they will let me talk to Tomcat. Maybe he'll tell me what happened, or what he remembers."

"Unlikely," Mac said. "Not considering that he'll have his agent and his emissary from New Eden with him."

"Soren is a fucker," I said. "And Anderson is a puppet."

"They were both picked by the August, Obe, both of them."

"Yeah, I can forget that." I ground my teeth; they did outrank me. Both of them did, in the eyes of the August, and in the New Eden Centre. I was lucky enough to have gotten a special bye, to be allowed to remain in the organization even though I had failed out of being a First Daughter. Since I screwed up my attempt at the Cotillion so bad that I didn't even get to appear before any of the Centre leadership. I clenched a fist. I was only allowed to remain because I was the absolute best at what I did.

Even Kurt admitted that, that I was a better shot than him, and that in hand-to-hand, I had beaten him in all three of our serious sparring matches. I was *better*. I had to be. I wiped a hand across my face. "Go ahead and send me copies of the files you were able to save."

"They aren't decrypted," she said.

"Doesn't matter. I'll hold on to them until we can deal with that."

"Consider it done."

An hour later, the mansion was swarming with New Eden publicity managers and a black-label cleaning service. I watched as they methodically cleaned away proof of everything that had happened. No photos were taken, no evidence gathered. They didn't even try to get samples of the blood, to see who it belonged to.

I called Kurt again and immediately got his voicemail. *Fucking shit, man, answer your goddamn phone.*

"This is what is going to happen," Soren said, hands crossed behind his back, chest stuck out like a tinpot dictator. "Nothing, and I mean *nothing* is to be said about anything you've seen. Everyone in this room has signed a minimum of two non-disclosure agreements, which are ironclad. If there is a leak, I will find out who did it, and will prosecute them to the full extent of the law."

"What are we going to do about Worthington and Calanthe?" I asked.

"Miss Calanthe is a missing person, and we are going to handle that internally. Owen Worthington is considered the primary person of interest."

"We should reach out to the police and the FBI," I suggested.

"Absolutely not." Soren turned to face me, snapping like a flag in a sharp breeze. "Our first priority is to preserve the integrity of New Eden and the image of Arik, is that clear. If there is any question about what has happened, your official answer is no comment. Those are the only two words you are legally allowed to say, do you all understand me?" Everyone in the room nodded.

"Madeleine?" He gestured for me to come to him, and then pointed for me to sit. I knew it irked him that as a man, he had to tilt his head up to look at me. If he tried just cutting his eyes up, he couldn't make eye contact. This way, me sitting, I had to look up at him. That was the way it was supposed to be, and he had told me more than once. Too tall to be a First Daughter, too strong, too muscled, too independent.

I had done my best, proved my devotion, my loyalty, and faith to the order. There were only a few holdouts who didn't accept that, and Soren was one of them.

"I think I'm going to let Wilson take point on this, Maddy," he said, looking down at me.

"Oberisk," I said.

"Pardon?"

"Oberisk," I repeated. "If you are going to refer to everyone else in security by their last name, you should use mine as well. If you call me Maddy, then you should call Wilson by his nickname, Woody. Do you want Woody to take point? He's been on the job less than three months. He can't find his post some mornings, and the only thing he has going for him is that he's six three and none of the felony counts stuck. He's an idiot, but an intimidating one."

"He projects confidence," Soren countered.

"He won't find Calanthe or Worthington," I fired back. "I fucking will."

"You fucking will," he said, his tone dripping with sarcasm. "What makes you think you can find anything?"

"Because Worthington trusted me. He brought me in, and he confided in me. I beat him in hand-to-hand, and my balls are bigger than yours," I said, standing and facing him. Confidence, physical dominance, intensity, things Kurt had taught me, I used them. I wasn't their ideal. I wasn't a dainty and delicate princess.

"You don't have... those," Soren spluttered.

"They're so big I have to keep them in my bra," I said. "Give me point on this, or you can kiss Worthington and Calanthe goodbye. How long do you think it will take *TMI News* or any of the other gossip outfits to find out that Cardinal is missing, and Tomcat is flying solo?"

"One chance, Oberisk, one," he said, pointing a finger toward my face. The training I had, before and after Kurt, made me want to grab his finger and pull his hand into a submission hold, feel that little bine grind in the joint, and the stress it would put on the nerve. He would scream and cry and possibly piss himself before I let go.

"I'll take it," I said.

"If you don't bring Miss Calanthe back, you're done. You're out of security. You can either go work on one of the mud farms or take your chances being turned out into the city, out of New Eden completely.

"Lexy," I said, slicing through his manly name of Alexander. "I know exactly two things – New Eden has been my life since before I can remember, and I will bring Calanthe back to you. I'll accept your apology that day, your full apology." I considered putting my finger in his chest, but I was angry, and I didn't know if I could trust myself. How fucking *dare* he threaten me, expelling me from New Eden? He hadn't been a member since he was a child. He had just showed up two years ago, been anointed by August Emerson, and suddenly was part of the inner circle, personal attaché to Arik.

"I'll have your head if you fail, Oberisk."

"I'll have your balls in my hand when I bring her back, and you will thank me," I said.

"This is why you were never accepted as a First Daughter."

"No, this has nothing to do with it, Soren. I was too tall, by an inch. I failed the inspection in my own living room because my growth spurt started earlier than most girls. Everything after that has just been a bonus."

I turned on my heel and walked toward the door. Outside, I grabbed two of security who I knew could be trusted and weren't incompetent. "Cullen, Jacobson, with me." I gestured as I was walking toward my hybrid SUV. "We've got work to do."

"What's the plan?"

"We assume the worst. Worthington is the number one suspect in the abduction of Cardinal. It is our task to find them both and bring them back here. We are not taking this to the authorities. This is staying in-house and off any devices. No texting, no calls, no email. Everything will be face-to-face. Any problem with that?"

WE DROVE to the Nerve Center where Mackenzie and the rest of the Technology and Communications team would be working. Most of what they did was PR, programming for New Eden. They had the ludicrous job of selling people on the notion of not poisoning the one planet we can live on, and they had a hard time selling it. It boggled my mind, really. I could understand men like Soren, their egos were fragile.

Hey, let's not set our house on fire and shit in the middle of the living room? Is that so bad?

Apparently, it was really bad because it seemed the world was dead set on setting itself on fire, and shitting on all of the furniture, and killing all of the pets. I sighed and grabbed a cup of coffee from the station. I picked up the recycled paper container next to it, organic, free trade, carbon neutral.

Good.

"What have you got for me, Mac?" I asked.

"Not much. Worthington has gone to ground. His cell is dead, the SIM card doesn't respond to a ping, and the only way it won't respond is if it's buried in a dead zone or the card has been snapped in half."

"Not conclusive," I said.

"Agreed, we could lose a phone fairly easily, especially if it ran into something that destroyed it, like a fire, wood chipper, acid." I gestured for her to get on with it. "Right, so I did a signal trace on his car, the sedan has a tracking device, two actually."

"Do all of our vehicles have that?"

"Yes, one in the GPS navigation system, and a second in the software of the drive system. Same for every hybrid in the fleet, three in the full electrics." I nodded. "I put the sedan on continuous ping, since you mentioned Owen being missing. It's returned a signal from a location that the net says is a private storage unit. We can be there in less than an hour."

An hour and a half later, I popped the lock off the storage unit, and rolled the door up. The sedan was sitting right where the GPS said it was. The facility manager hadn't been very forthcoming with information, but a small bribe got him talking, and the name didn't match, but the description did. The car was empty, the battery cables were popped, but the electronics console was intact.

"It was a bug-out," Cullen said, shining his flashlight around inside the unit. "There was a different vehicle in here, I can smell it."

"Can you?"

"Fuel stabilizer, it's an old vehicle. Probably something with no GPS. From what I knew of Kurt it probably had a carb on it, like old school, *American Graffiti* and all that."

"So, we're looking for a British Royal Marine in an old vehicle with Cardinal stuffed in the trunk?"

"Possibly?" Jacobson shrugged. "It's what we've got."

"Soren has several other teams out looking, you know," Mac chirped in my earpiece. I grimaced.

"I'm not surprised. What can you tell me about my competitors?"

"Wilson is leading Team Echo down to the Mexican border, and Arizona is leading team Charlie to canvas LAX and any other avenues to leave the country quickly," Mac said.

"What about Bravo, or Delta?" I asked. "Where are they?"

"Bravo and Abel are handling security at the mansion and the set respectively, and we've been designated Team Delta." I smacked my fist into my palm.

"Does Soren have to be that kind of bastard? What the fuck is his problem?"

"He wants you gone," Cullen said.

"You aren't pretty teenager enough for him," Jacobson agreed. "Those inner circle guys are like that. If you wanna be on their good side, and a woman, you need to be about five feet tall, and no more than a hundred pounds."

"All of Soren's personal valets are young women, so are August Emerson's," Cullen said.

"Look, I know that, fuck all," I growled. "So, let's assume that at least someone is going to be monitoring everything we do, so that they can keep an eye on us. If we actually pick up a lead, Soren will have a fast track to throw another team into it ahead of us. We keep communications face-to-face, no electronics. It's worth noting that our target is the guy who trained us, and he knows what we are going to do and how we're going to do it."

"He won't go to LAX or Mexico," Mac said.

"Bingo. One is too easy to get him flagged, the other is an extradition country where the rules don't apply all that well. He won't go either way."

"Where then?" Cullen asked.

"Let me hold those cards close to my chest for the moment, but we will be heading east. Mac, I will need you to hit car titles and find out what he is driving. That can be a big help to us. People notice old cars – old cars are cool and stick out. Plus, if we know what he's got, it will give us an idea of where he can't go, and where he is likely to."

"Ma'am?" Cullen raised an eyebrow.

"A lot of the older cars that people own for cool factor don't always have good performance. If he's got a two-ton fifties cruiser with a straight six and only a hundred horsepower or so, he's not going over mountains, and probably not crossing the desert. Small engine car goes north, Pacific Northwest, northern California."

"Good to know," he said.

"I'm not finding him owning any vehicles under a California

registry," Mac said.

"He's not an American, and has lived and worked all over the country. Check his resume against those states. Whatever it is, its registered somewhere. Kurt isn't the sort of person to own an unregistered vehicle, or an illegally tagged one. Guns, that is another matter."

"What about guns?" Jacobson asked, his voice rising in alarm.

"The boss was a Royal Marine. He collected firearms, including military hardware. We are going to consider him exceedingly well-armed and accordingly dangerous. None of us in Delta have military experience, so even with what we've been trained to do, we aren't going to be fully prepared to deal with what he can do if he becomes hostile."

"Fucking hell, do we even have a plan, then?" Mac asked.

"Yes, you're going to stay here and coordinate from the Nerve Center. Jacobson and Cullen will be with me, and if we can find a fourth to peel away, we'll take them too. Mac, see if we can find someone from PR or even the New Eden Centre itself – a negotiator or something, maybe someone pretty that Kurt wouldn't shoot in the face the moment he saw them." Mackenzie nodded and I knew she would have me a fourth by the time I was ready to go.

Who could I trust here? As much as I wanted us to be a brotherhood and share the trust and camaraderie that Kurt talked about with the Royal Marines, we weren't. Some of us were mercenaries, some belonged to New Eden, some belonged to people inside New Eden. I had to do this perfectly, and not just for me. Calanthe Rex was out there somewhere, and she was perfect, she was the ideal. She was everything that I wasn't, but because of that, I could rescue her. Calanthe would be a mother to New Eden, with beautiful healthy children who would have a green and pure world as their legacy, either to help restore it or inherit it. That part depended on us, and how well we did or how badly we failed.

"We will need to requisition one of the hydrogen-cell vehicles," I said. "Let's see if Rex will let us take REX3. He's not going on any junkets for a while."

"We could probably fly a lot faster, you know," Jacobson said.

"Know of any hybrid jets, electric aircraft, solar-powered stuff that doesn't have a top speed of sixty miles an hour and is the size of a sports store?" I asked. "We will find both of them without burning a tanker truck of fossil fuel doing it. We have more than one responsibility."

"What's the point of those carbon credits that New Eden promotes?" Mac asked, looking up from her computer terminals.

"We aren't shilling environmental indulgences. The carbon credits aren't prepaid forgiveness for environmental sin." I gave her a stern look. Apparently, there were no religious studies or history majors on my team. That was regrettable.

CALIFORNIA TURNED to Nevada under the wheels of REX3, a forty-foot, ten-wheel, hydrogen-cell electric-touring bus. We had a brief rendezvous with Team Sigma, the personal security detachment for his eminence August Emerson himself, in Las Vegas. This in and of itself was no major deal. New Eden held many summits and conferences in Vegas. The number of facilities there that had gone green more than suited our green and pure Earth agenda, plus, it was an easy place to get to.

Things were turning into a mess back at the set. Rex had packed his things and thrown a fit before removing himself to his personal retreat, a chalet in Colorado. I watched the gossip packet where paparazzi caught the celebrity couple boarding a personal jet and flying out of a municipal airport. I didn't know who was with him. Her face was covered, but the red hair was obvious.

"Claire?" I asked. "From human resources?"

"I'd bet money that it's Frederika, from accounting. She could be a body double for Calanthe," Cullen said.

"It's Carson Lovell," Mac said over the earpiece. "He works in the motor pool and logistics section."

"That's a guy?" I asked.

"Yup, a really short, skinny guy, wearing a wig," she chirped.

"That's so lame," our HR coordinator, Lisa, groaned.

"It's what needs to be done, and there is a good reason for all of this," I said. There was some grumbling, but it wasn't unexpected. This was going to be a long drive, and there were certain places we had to stop to recharge the hydrogen cell in the bus. We might have lacked top speed, but we had something that Kurt didn't. Endurance.

By switching drivers, we never had to stop moving, and with the accommodations on REX3, we didn't have to use hotels or motels. If he had arranged any sort of electronic counter surveillance, he wouldn't see us coming.

"Good news, Obe," Mac chirped, when Vegas was six hours behind us. "Found his registered vehicle, and I don't think you're going to like it."

"Shoot."

"It's a 1968, short bed, GMC pickup truck, off-road capability, with a solid V8. He can go pretty much anywhere."

"Where did you find the registry?" I asked.

"Maryland, of all places."

"It would be too obvious for him to go there, wouldn't it, Mackenzie," I said, hoping that she would follow my lead.

"That would be literally the first place we would look, and Kurt isn't dumb enough to run to ground like that," Mac chirped in quick agreement. "I did a search of the state and there isn't anything there under his name. *Kurt Worthington* doesn't own any land in Maryland," she responded.

"Copy that," I said.

"Cullen?"

"Yeah?"

"Are we still set for Omaha?"

"Yeah, everything okay?"

"It's fine."

Nevada turned to Arizona.

Charlie Team turned up empty-handed and were diverted south to assist Echo team with the nearly impossible task of trying to keep one vehicle from getting into Mexico, when they didn't know what they were looking for, and refused to reach out to authorities. That part made my ass itch. Feds could be discrete when the people doing the asking were highly public figures.

Arizona turned to New Mexico.

New Mexico turned to Texas.

Sigma Team turned up the fact that Worthington owned a red GMC truck, and they gave the plate information out to everyone involved in the search, even us. It only took them two days to figure that out.

Texas turned to Oklahoma and a brand-new fueling station in Oklahoma City.

"Where are you, Kurt?" I asked the sunset. "And Calanthe better be okay, or I'll kill you myself."

"What's your status, Delta?" Soren's personal-attack chihuahua, Florian Sanchez, demanded in my earpiece. I winced and reached up to dial his volume down.

"Status is Memphis, heading east," I answered.

"Why are you heading east? All of our projections have Worthington's trajectory running due north. It's likely that he is attempting a Canadian extraction point."

"Copy that. We couldn't be back in your time zone for maybe two days. I have a hunch, and we're investigating it."

"The Dragon has reminded me to tell you the stakes of your operation, and that if this hunch of yours doesn't produce results, your contract with us is done, and you're to be expelled from New Eden."

"I'm aware, and I haven't forgotten." I ground my teeth in frustration. "Do you have any more information on Worthington's vehicle, anything tied to it?"

"Negative, Delta. The vehicle was registered in Maryland, where his last job was. We have discovered that his previous employer was a narcotic trafficking organization, and that he has no friends or assets in the state."

"No property?" I asked. This was odd. I knew he had something there. He had mentioned it once or twice when he had a few too many shots of whiskey, and his lips were loosened. Never quite got that belt loosened though. I wasn't his type, but that wasn't a surprise.

I was no one's type.

That was my normal, and I was used to it.

"There is no property registered to Kurt or Curtis Worthington in Maryland. Well, that's not one-hundred-percent accurate, there are six property owners in the state with that name —none of them are British ex-pats, three of them aren't Caucasian, and the other half are too old, too young, or otherwise not our missing head of security."

"Good to know," I said.

"Did I uncover your hunch, you chasing black cats in a dark room, Oberisk?" he asked.

"My hunch is still solid, don't worry about that. Good hunting to the rest of the teams, but all they're doing is burning resources for nothing," I said.

"Where are we going?" Lisa asked.

"I'm going to have to hold that for now," I said. "I'm going to be honest, I don't know who I can trust right now, and the only thing as important as getting Calanthe back is that I'm the one that does it."

"If you don't, are they really going to expel you from New Eden?"

"They will," I said. "The *Dragon* doesn't make idle threats, and there have been other people kicked out before. Heresy isn't new, Lisa."

"Oh, I guess," she said.

"C'mon, where do you think Fallout came from? Half the

members of that organization used to belong to New Eden, but they lost their way, they were cast out. They failed, and now they blame us for their failure."

"What's the difference between them and you?" she asked.

"They failed because they didn't believe. I will not fail. I will find Calanthe and Kurt, and I will bring them both back." Do you remember, Kurt? Do you remember telling me about the mountains, and the cabin off the grid? About your pals in Indigo City? You did drink a lot that night, before you left with the woman with the tattooed sleeve on her right arm. The one I thought looked like a piece of shit, but you decided was good enough to take back to her place.

I pulled out my phone and sent him an email.

Kurt
I'll see you soon.
You better have a goddamn good explanation for this.
If she's harmed, it will be bad for you.
If you shoot at me, it will be very bad for you.
Love
Madeleine

Sent.

I sighed and put the phone back in my pocket. The chances of him checking his email were slim, and if he did, he was smart enough to either use a burner phone, or an encrypted one. I didn't really want to surprise him. That would be a good way to end up dead. I didn't want him to know I was coming either, but he had to know. He had to know that I wouldn't let him go, and I would certainly not let Calanthe go.

I would march into Hell itself to bring her back.

I might have to do just that.

17

Callie...

"Mmm." I smiled and shifted against the mattress and the crisp sheets on the bed, Kurt's familiar hard weight beside me though he was sitting up by now. I pushed myself into a similar position beside him and turned to look at him as he scowled at his phone's screen. My heart instantly dropped into the pit of my stomach at his expression.

"Kurt, is everything okay?" I asked hesitantly, my voice soft.

Apprehension filled me as he glanced up from the phone screen and squinted off into space for a moment before setting the device aside and turning to me with a reassuring smile.

"Everything's fine, Love."

I didn't believe him, but I wasn't about to let on about that.

"Okay," I murmured, and he smiled, reaching for me. I didn't flinch. I was proud of myself for that, but I did stiffen a bit until his touch fell gentle around me, pulling me into the side of his chest as he lay back with me.

He pressed his lips to my forehead, and I closed my eyes, cuddling close.

"How far have we got left?" I asked, hopeful that today would be the final day of travel. I needed to be still for a while.

He caressed the side of my face with his thumb gently and my eyes slipped closed in pleasure, some of the tension in my body easing as I melted further into his side.

"Not far, Love. We've one stop the other side of the bay from Indigo City, then we leave for the cabin."

"Yeah?" I asked, vaguely disappointed that we had yet one more stop to make.

"Yeah," he murmured and pressed another kiss to the top of my head, and I admit to soaking up his affections like a sponge. I was starved for it, and I realized with what wits Arik hadn't beaten out of me yet, just how pathetic that probably made me – which made me angry to a degree.

Sure, I was angry with Arik, but not nearly as much as I was with myself. I mean, I had been a clever girl, top of my class – *first daughter*, and yet, I still let this happen to me. I tried to work within the proverbial system and while I had rebelled in small ways, I had never tried to *escape*. I was so very sick and tired of being *afraid* all of the time... and yet... and yet as smart as I was and as smart as I probably still could be, I couldn't for the life of me figure out what to do about it.

"Callie?"

"Hm?" I looked up against Kurt's shoulder and he frowned at me vaguely, concern coded into his blue eyes.

"You alright, Love?"

"Hm? Yeah! Why?"

"You didn't hear anything I just said, did you?" he asked, and a grin overtook him.

"No, I'm sorry. I guess I was lost in my own thoughts." I frowned. *That* certainly wasn't like me. I mean, it *had* been, but I'd quickly learned not to let it happen anymore.

Kurt chuckled and gave me a squeeze.

"Alright, Love. No matter," he said, giving a luxurious stretch beneath me. I disentangled myself from my new lover, which just *that* thought alone made me smile, and watched as he got up from the bed.

He had an amazing physique, riddled with small scars here and there, thin white lines almost lost in his pale complexion which wasn't quite as ghost white as mine.

Some curved and wicked, some long and thin, punctuated to either side with a neat row of dots where he'd been stitched back together again. One on his ribs, another along one hip, but nowhere was he as scarred as much as his big hands, which *those* scars were much more apparent; standing out against the rich golden hue his knuckles had taken with the kiss of the sun.

His hands were a roadmap of violence and pain that'd been dealt to what could have been countless foes. Scraped and abraded, a million and one little splits and cuts from punches thrown. All it took was one look at Owen "Kurt" Worthington's hands to know that he was a man of action – a man used to *using* those hands. To work, to punch, and secretly to pleasure. I knew that secret first-hand now and I wouldn't trade that insider knowledge for anything.

"A lot to think about, yeah?" he asked me, and I looked up at him from where I hugged my knees beneath the crisp, thin, white sheet of the hotel's bed.

"Yeah, sorry," I murmured.

"Don't be," he said, leaning down and kissing my forehead. I closed my eyes and let myself drown in that comforting touch, well aware that they could be lost to me at any moment. My heart dropped into my narrow ass at the thought... that we were on borrowed time. That this big, strong, beautifully rugged man was likely going to die because of me.

I sniffed, the tears hot, furious, and immediate at the mere thought of it. My nightmares full of the images of Kurt lying in a pool of his own blood, those eyes that looked at me with such tenderness and care staring blankly, sightlessly. His life stolen before my mind's eye and all because of *me* and my cursed existence under New Eden's thumb.

"Hey now, what's this?" he asked, thumbing one of the errant tears away and sucking it from the pad of his thumb. I blinked up at him and said the only thing that came to mind – the burning need to know driving the words past the lump of fear in my throat.

"How bad is it really, Kurt?" He stared at me, the silence stretching between us, the calculations going on just behind his eyes as he searched my expression as earnestly as I searched his. "And please, don't lie to me to make me feel better," I begged. "The not knowing... it's killing me."

His generous lips thinned down into a grim line and his chest swelled with a slow, deep breath that he let out as a resigned sigh.

"They're looking for you," he said. "We both knew that."

I nodded. "And?"

"They've got Madeline Oberisk leading the charge."

I swallowed hard.

"Maddie?" I echoed, my mouth going dry.

"Aye."

"Is that what you were looking at when I woke up?" I asked. I felt hot and cold and hot all over again within the span of a blink of an eye as panic slowly fizzed, foaming and bubbling like acid through my veins.

Never was there another more devoted to New Eden's cause and doctrine than Madeline Oberisk. She'd been such a sweet soul as a little girl but had been made hard very quickly when she realized she would never be one of the chosen daughters. Too big, too rawboned, not delicate enough... I could tell these things had hurt her deeply, had put quite the chip on her shoulder, but Madeline wasn't one to sulk or despair.

She was too hard, too determined for that. When she'd realized she could never be first or even second among daughters of her generation, she'd decided to become first among *soldiers* in the war against climate change and the environmental agency. She'd quickly and eagerly bought into the ignorance of humanity being a plague upon the planet and had become militant in her training to become something like the sole protector of New Eden and its mission to save the planet from the destructiveness of its inhabitants.

She had begun to ruthlessly believe, within New Eden's teachings, that there was only one true way and that if things came down to force, if necessary, that she would be all in and at the forefront of the charge.

She had begun climbing within the ranks accordingly, in her own way, and her fanaticism was as downright terrifying as she was physically imposing.

"That's utterly terrifying," I blurted without thinking, and Kurt, who had sunk back down to the edge of the bed, put his hand over one of mine where it grasped my knee over the sheet.

"Aye," he agreed. "Which is why I didn't want to tell you."

"Thank you," I said. "For telling me. I don't want to be kept in the dark anymore."

He nodded slowly.

"I thought that might be the case," he said gently, and he moved his hand from over mine to tip my chin gently with his finger. I looked at him and his face was carved from stone, an almost fanatic determination to what I'd seen on Maddie's face overtaking his expression.

"You'll be alright, Callie," he swore to me. "No matter what, I'll be here, and I'll protect you."

I pursed my lips and nodded, but I knew better. Against Madeline?

"Don't make promises you can't keep, Kurt," I said gently, reaching up and cradling the side of his face with my hand. "I appreciate the sentiment, but I don't want to watch you die, and with Madeline at the helm..." I trailed off.

He turned his head and pressed a kiss into the palm of my hand, breathing me in for a moment.

"I don't make promises I don't intend to keep, Love," he told me.

But as confident as he sounded, by the powers that be, I couldn't help but still have my doubts.

THE FEELING of existential dread that'd overtaken me that morning had somewhat eased by the time the landscape had begun to change. We left the tobacco fields of Virginia in a beeline north, hitting an hours'-long snarl of traffic through Washington DC.

I'd been to DC on several missions as both a pre-teen and teen for New Eden, lobbying with politicians – congressmen and senators alike as one of the First Among Daughters of New Eden's Youth Initiative Program or Y.I.P. for short. Laughingly, it was a sort of unofficial tagline that'd been printed on tee shirts that it was *Time for Y.I.P. to nip climate change and pollution in the bud.*

God, I'd been so foolishly naïve back then. All the fancy parties dressed to the nines, serving and dining on sustainably sourced, vegan, and vegetarian fare to rich politicians on fancy China plates, drinking from equally fancy crystal glasses, and for what? Token efforts, a few lines here or there slipped into some bill that honestly was a drip or drop in the bucket when it came to the massive amount of carbon dumped in our atmosphere, poisoning our lungs from giant... what was the word? Not conglomerate, but that was like it. I knew it started with a "c"... militant, suit and tie, soulless...

"*Shit,*" I swore softly out loud.

"What's wrong?" Kurt asked, taking one hand from the wheel to put it over where mine rested on the bench seat between us.

"I can't remember the word for something," I said.

"Aw, yeah? What's that?" he asked.

I frowned.

"If I knew, I would tell you," I said and immediately felt bad for how annoyed and biting that had come out. "I'm sorry," I apologized immediately. "I shouldn't take it out on you."

He chuckled and picked up my hand and brought it to his mouth.

I stiffened out of reflex, and he kissed my fingertips, leaning over closer without taking his eyes from the road.

"You need to be a little more patient with yourself, Love," he chided gently.

I sighed out in a rush and said, "It's just so frustrating."

"I know," he said, and it was with all the sympathy in the world coating his tone. I smiled a bit sadly.

"I used to come here a lot, you know," I said, staring out over the urban landscape, at the Washington Monument in the distance, stabbing its way skyward, a declaration of defiance from man, that man would conquer all... at least that was always the feeling I got from staring at the obelisk.

Obelisk... Oberisk... they had their parallels. Maddie was just as strong, just as defiant, and to be honest, for a woman, nearly as tall as the damn thing.

My mood plummeted again, and I sighed, shifting restlessly in my seat.

"We're almost there, another couple of hours," Kurt declared. "Are you hungry?"

I shook my head. "Just restless," I said.

"Aye, traffic isn't – oi! You should have thought of that back when you first saw the sign, you bloody wanker!" he shouted as a tiny Porsche cut him off just before the lane to our right ended due to construction.

I smiled and had to giggle a little. His accent became thicker, something a bit less refined when he got irritated like that.

"Bollocks," he muttered unhappily as he had to brake hard for another such wanker.

I shook my head and sighed.

"It's going to take more than just a couple of hours at this rate," I declared and looked over at Kurt whose lips were pressed thin and whose knuckles were white and mottled where both hands now gripped the steering wheel.

"Aye, well, I can only go as fast as the arsehole in front of me."

I chuckled and shook my head. "Not your fault," I said with a shrug, and it hit me.

Corporation. That was the word I had been looking for. I rested my temple against the cool window glass and stared at the concrete urban jungle crawling past it at a snail's pace.

~

I STARTLED AWAKE. I hadn't realized I'd fallen asleep.

"Aye, yeah. We're approaching the bridge now," Kurt was saying into his phone, and I perked up. Just who could he be talking with?

"You want I should just get a hotel tonight, sir? Meet in the am?"

A voice I couldn't make out droned on the other end of the line and I cocked my head. I couldn't make out what was being said, but whoever the voice belonged to, it was rich, deep, and decidedly British, just not quite the same British as Kurt's. Like the difference between an American midwestern and southern accent.

"You're certain?"

Another pause.

"Aye, Captain, see you in a bit."

He ended the call and swore, hitting his turn signal and checking before skirting across two lanes and diving off the next exit.

"What happened?" I asked. "Who was that? Where are we?"

"Nothing's happened, Love. That was an old commanding officer of mine, a friend now, and we're in Maryland."

"Oh." I sat up and stretched, stiff from my nap and still tired, like I could just go right back to sleep. The sun had set outside the truck and Kurt had turned on his headlights, but I don't know how long ago. There wasn't a clock in the truck. It was old like that.

We took a winding path through tree-lined streets. The big old oaks lining either side in their manicured patches of grass between road and sidewalks were impressive, and the only reason oaks that big and that old remained where the roots could disrupt the street or sidewalks, yet neither appeared to be a problem? Well, that meant one thing and one thing only... that meant *money*.

We were in a *very* rich area and by God, we must have stuck out like sore thumbs in this truck in a place like this.

"Kurt," I said a bit nervously. "I feel like we're going to draw a lot of attention driving through an area like this."

"We're alright, Love. Just trust me." He covered my hand with his and gave it a reassuring squeeze.

My heart was practically in my throat when we pulled up to a set of fancy iron gates and Kurt leaned way forward, looking up through the windshield and waving at what I had to presume was a camera.

It did whatever trick because the gates started their slow mechanical swing inward.

I jumped slightly when the truck lurched forward to clear those gates, and staring out the back window, I watched them swing ominously shut behind us, the clatter they made as they closed making my mouth go a bit dry.

Kurt swept the truck around the drive and stopped it right in front of the mansion's twin front doors, putting it into park and shutting off first the engine and then the lights. I stared at those doors for a long moment, and almost jumped when they opened, a small dark-haired woman in a silk dress standing with her arms crossed, waiting.

She didn't look like the help. I mean, the help didn't dress like that anyplace that I could remember. Kurt got out of the truck and shut his door and I remained frozen in my seat, staring up the broad front steps as a large, bearish man with a cane limped up behind the woman who looked up and back at him. She smiled and said something, crossing her arms over her chest, and rubbing up and down her arms with her hands, the large man behind her looking down at her and placing a hand on the back of her neck, fingers curling both protectively and possessively.

My view of the couple was cut off by Kurt appearing in front of my window, and I admit, I jumped. He gripped the handle on the outside of the truck's door and pressed the button with his thumb, opening the door.

A rush of cooler air filled the cab, heavily scented with saltwater. I breathed deep, always having loved that smell, and let him help me down from my seat, my body groaning in protest, stiff with the ride and unyielding to the position change from sitting to standing at first.

"Take your time," Kurt murmured, and I looked up at him.

I wanted to know who these people were, and where we were, but I was struck dumb, almost too afraid to ask.

"Kurt," the man intoned with a nod when we turned.

"Hey, Kurt." The woman curled her fingers in a wave, her voice bright, confident, and plucky.

"Captain." Kurt nodded at the man. "Sadie." He inclined his head in the direction of the woman.

Footsteps came from behind them, and another man appeared. Not quite as tall as the captain, his frame slighter, wirier, and his hair dark. He looked over Sadie's head and frowned.

"Visitors?" he asked. "We never have visitors."

"Kyle." Sadie drew out his name in a warning tone. "Be nice."

The man smirked down at the back of her head.

"I'm always nice," he said, and he lifted his chin in Kurt's direction.

Kurt inclined his head back and the second man, Kyle, turned and went back into the house.

"Well, don't stand out there all night. Good God, man! Come inside!" the captain declared.

Kurt guided me forward with a hand on my shoulder, closer to my neck, almost the mirror for how the captain held Sadie. I stumbled slightly at first, before finding my coordination and we moved forward.

I was sweating lightly by the time we reached the top of the steps, and I couldn't tell you why. I swallowed hard, my heart racing, my tongue feeling stuck to the roof of my mouth, my teeth gritted. I barely dared to breathe. I could feel the rising color in my chest and face, and I hated it.

I was close to a full-blown panic attack, and I didn't know why other than I didn't know these people and they weren't Kurt.

"Easy, Callie," Kurt murmured into my hair near my ear. "You can trust them, I promise." He stroked the back of my neck with his thumb, back and forth, back and forth, a reassuring little touch and I realized, I didn't trust *anyone*. I *couldn't*. New Eden had absolutely obliterated that ability for me.

It was painfully tragic when you stopped to think about it, but I couldn't. Not right now. Not with this giant imposing bear of a man standing in front of me, and this woman shorter than even myself, standing there smiling at me, something behind her brown eyes that I couldn't quite place.

"Hi, I'm Sadie," she said, and her lips curved into a smile.

"Callie," I managed, and her smile grew a bit more. It finally hit me what that look in her eyes was all about – *understanding*.

"And I'm Roan," the man introduced himself. I looked up into a kind face despite his imposing frame, the golden red shadow of stubble along his jaw and hair nearly as red as my own.

"Calanthe," I said. "But please call me Callie." I would *not* be some shrinking violet. I would *not* let New Eden win. I stood a little straighter and Kurt gave the back of my neck a little squeeze.

"Come on in," Sadie said cheerily. "I'll show you to a room and let you decompress for a little bit. I know I can always use a few minutes to recalibrate after a long road trip."

She and Roan turned sideways to let me and Kurt pass.

"Thanks for this, Captain," Kurt said gratefully.

"It's no trouble, mate. And stop with all this captain nonsense," Roan said, closing the door behind all of us.

"Aye, sir," Kurt said out of what was clear habit.

"You good to go with Sadie, Love?" he asked me, and with more bravery and aplomb than I knew I possessed, I nodded.

"Be along soon," he said and kissed my temple and let me go.

"Okay," I murmured.

Sadie smiled at me and padded barefoot across the foyer's white marble floor. I followed suit in my cheap tennis shoes, feeling utterly self-conscious in my thrift-store clothing among all the opulent wealth.

My how far you've fallen. The derisive voice in the back of my mind made an appearance. I forced a smile back at Sadie as I trailed her deeper into the mansion and thought to myself how utterly alright I was with that, given the alternative reality that was living under New Eden's thumb.

18

––––––––

Kurt...

Getting to Indigo City was easy enough, after getting through the horror show of DC traffic. It was one of the few times that I regretted having the stick shift in the truck instead of the electronic tranny that the sedan had. But I didn't drive that car – I sat in it and could tell it where to take me and the thing would actually drive itself, for the most part. I didn't like being a passenger in my own driver's seat. Crossing the Chesapeake was a slightly different matter, either heading around land side and going through Annapolis or skirting south to pick up the Chesapeake Bay Bridge. That meant getting into the outskirts of Norfolk.

DC was just busy, lots of traffic. I didn't like the idea of going through places that were deeply tied to branches of military. Senators and lobbyists liked their anonymity and privacy to do the shite they did. Given some of the things that were in those other cities, there would be security, smart systems, and the sort of things a tech savvy group could access one way or another. I didn't want to go through either of those, but it wouldn't be that big of a deal for us to hit Indigo and see about a ferry crossing over.

But that wasn't important. What was important was meeting up with Captain Roan. He was the one who knew about making good on a bad situation. We both left the military at the same time, on the same slate of shite, and I was a cross-country fugitive with a few dozen dollars left to my name, an old truck, and enough weaponry to arm a small insurrection.

And Calanthe.

The reception was warm, much more so than I had expected.

The new house was impressive too. I had been in it before, back when I was working for the Escadrille Cartel, but I didn't recognize it. There was almost nothing left that I recognized other than the smashing full-length windows in the kitchen, facing the Chesapeake Bay. Bloody hell, that room had to have turned into a sauna every morning.

Maybe it was for the view?

The last time I was greeted like this, it was just outside of Kandahar, Afghanistan. The situation had been a bit better. Sure, there were a few thousand Taliban racing to engage us, and we had lost half of our vehicles, were almost out of ammo, and the last chopper supporting us had flown away trailing smoke, but we had reached an American firebase.

That was what this felt like. Sadie was the medical staff rushing out to grab our wounded and pull us back in with painkillers, and bandages, and a surgical hospital to turn the walking dead into decorated heroes ready to go home. Lachlan, he didn't say much, but I had seen that sort of face. Men who looked like him were the wolves who went tearing into the middle of any opposition with attack helicopters and tanks, or nothing but their bare hands, and they came home and told everyone they were safe. Then the captain, with his bum leg, was the CO sitting at the desk, wanting to know just what in the bloody hell had been going on for the last seventy-two hours. Any other officer might have yelled and thrown things. Instead, Roan would steeple his fingers, give you a sideways look, and suddenly it was like sitting in an exposed confession booth.

～

"You can relax," Roan said. "They know how to pour a proper pint here."

"I'm not sure if I'll be able to relax for a while, sir," I said. The pint was properly poured and even more, it was the right temperature. That was one of the charms of the Black Watch. I could feel a calmness moving through me, not relaxing, not yet. Being back at the pub, reconnecting with the captain, a second time even, and knowing that things should be stable now, put me at a sort of ease but I couldn't let my guard down. Not knowing New Eden.

I took another sip of Guinness. God, it was so wonderful having a proper pint, almost like my own personal reverie.

So many Americans were obsessed with getting the beer as absolutely cold as possible. The colder something was, the less you could actually taste it, which made sense for so many American beers. A cool, but not cold Guinness and Harp, and a full English breakfast down to the beans and black sausage, it was almost like being home again. I let out a breath. "As nice as this place is, I'm surprised it's not you wiping down the bar."

"You'll never catch me on the backside of a bar, mate," he smiled. "A little too much temptation on that side."

"I can't thank you enough, sir," I said.

"Why don't you start from the beginning. The emails have been a little chaotic, and don't call me sir, we're not in the Corps anymore."

"That just feels off, but as you say," I said, biting the sir off at the end. "So, I took that reference and got on as security chief for Arik Rex, through New Eden. First couple of months, easy peasy. Most everyone was professional – followed orders, though there were almost no other people with any military experience. Lots of ex-cops, mall-security types, some bouncers looking to move up into legit work, things like that." Roan nodded.

"Then I found out what sort of person Arik Rex is."

"Womanizer?" he guessed, taking a drink of his own pint.

"And then some – physically abusive and controlling."

"Did you play *The Bodyguard?*" he asked.

"No, I was literally going to Arik's office to confront him about beating his wife, and to tender my resignation. Legally it was all I could do, since I signed several NDAs to not publicly disclose any of his personal business, or the production company, or New Eden."

"This is where it went tits up?"

"Yeah, to say the least. Arik was in a full rage, had Calanthe down on the couch and was using her head as a punching bag. Full knuckles to the skull, like I'm sure he was breaking his own fingers the way he was hitting her." I paused and drained the pint.

"You need another?"

I nodded. He gestured and the barkeep bobbed his head.

"Then what, lad?"

"I pulled him off her and put him on the ground and to sleep. He got in a few licks, hit me with one of his awards, but I didn't leave any marks on him. That seemed important at the time. If he had like a broken nose or dislocated shoulder that could be medical evidence."

"That's spot-on thinking, well done, but do go on."

"Yeah, si-so I grabbed Calanthe, put her in my car, and bugged out. She was in terrible shape, and I think at that point I was panicking, so I pulled a full bug-out – ejected my phone, dumped the sedan, and picked up my old truck and kit, and hit the road. Went with following the old path of Route 66, instead of going for the obvious or quickest paths out of LA."

"Seems to have worked," Roan said as our second round of pints were delivered to the table. "And don't worry, everyone who knows about this place, they're our brothers, eh?"

"If you say so, sir," I said and looked down at my new pint. It finally felt like there was someone in this besides me, someone else who could shoulder some of this mess I had made.

"I do say so." He gave my shoulder a squeeze. "So, you made it across the continent, got Miss Callie fixed up with an off-the-grid doctor, and got here for the best pints this side of the pond."

"Yeah, all that, and now I'm not sure what to do."

"What was the plan when you were on the road? Oh, and what is Calanthe's take on this?"

"The plan I guess was to go to my cabin and wait it out."

"The one across the bay, out in the middle of the forest?"

"That's the one. It has a well and between the generator and eventually solar panels, I have plenty of power without being hooked to the grid. Between hunting, fishing, and a stock of MREs, I could live out there for a long time."

"Yeah, almost any former Marine could live like that, and live happy," he agreed. "But what about red-headed lasses?"

"She's different. Arik kept her cloistered and controlled everything she did, and apparently, New Eden is a bloody fucking cult."

"What do you mean a cult?"

"She told me that her parents groomed her to be a child bride, for whomever New Eden decided was important enough to warrant such a prize. If she was willing to tell me that she was traded to Rex when she was a minor, what is she not telling us? What goes into grooming teenagers to be married to wealthy assholes, thirty and forty years older than they are? It feels ugly and wrong."

"I'll have some of my people look into this, but it does shine a light on that batty woman on the news who says all that about New Eden only caring about green cash and pink girls."

"I saw her on the news. Seems like maybe we should reach out to her? She has an organization and they're public, and New Eden hasn't gotten rid of them."

"What sort of response do you think they're going to mount, lad?" Roan asked.

"They have a full security force, enough that they can send large numbers of armed men and women after us, and their new commander was my previous second, a monster of a woman. She's a zealot at heart and she knows where we've gone, somewhat."

"What do you mean somewhat?"

"She knows I have a cabin near Indigo City, but that's all."

"Well, that makes things difficult, doesn't it? So here is the new plan unless you have a problem with it." I nodded in agreement. "You and Calanthe are going to stay with us for a few days, get you rested up, and give her some civilization. She looked a touch feral."

"Fair," I said.

"While you are in repair and refit, we can find a way to reach out to the short-haired woman with whatever that group is called and circle the wagons there."

"It won't be like Escadrille," I said. "That was ugly business all over." The captain gave me a dark look.

"You have no idea how ugly that was."

"My apologies," I said.

"Don't worry about it, lad."

"Fallout, but they spell it all caps like they're shouting," the barkeep said. "And yeah, they're usually shouting. The short-haired woman is Marion Tate. Used to be some fancy important player inside the organization before she escaped or got burned, I'm not sure."

"How do you know that?" Roan asked.

"She's on the telly all the time, mate, and this isn't exactly the busiest pub on the block. I've got time." He gave a shrug.

"Good, we get in contact with this Tate woman and Fallout, and see if she can help Callie. We clean this mess up a bit tidier than the Escadrille business," Roan said.

"I would like it if it didn't require gun battles and borderline international incidents." I smiled.

"Me too, lad. Me too."

We finished up at the Black Watch and drove back to the captain's house. The view across the bay did something to me. Seeing the land fall away to the water, and the stands of trees almost erupting from the ground, it seemed almost primal. And to think it was his backyard. By the time the Aston was tucked away in the garage, we had switched from New Eden and raid tactics to something different, cryptocurrencies. There was something that the captain wasn't an expert on, and he was fascinated as I explained the intricacies of investing in one of the big offerings like CryptoCoin, and how it differed from the smaller more impulsive outfits like MemeCoin or one I had noticed during a fit of insomnia the night before, TwitCoin.

"So, what you are telling me is that a TwitCoin is blockchained from social media, and each coin is specifically a what now?" he asked, tapping the key fob, and locking the Aston.

"It's a non-fungible token, a digital copy of the tweet or status or whatever you posted, and the more it circulates and interacts with things on the internet, the more valuable it becomes," I said.

"So normally they're worthless?"

"Yes. My first TwitCoin this morning was worth one millionth of a cent."

"So how does this at any point become money?"

"I flipped one MemeCoin, and bought something like twelve million TwitCoins, which made the base price move, and other people started buying into it. I figure if the price gets as high as one thousandths of a cent, I cash out and have turned a sixty-cent Meme-Coin into something like... seven grand?"

"That's insane." He let out a huff.

"If I stay in at a cent, a laughable goal, my sixty cents turns into one-hundred-and-twenty grand, American, if I converted it to dollars."

"But you don't convert into dollars," he said.

"Almost never a physical currency. I tend to roll profits into CryptoCoin itself. It is the dog's bollocks. The only downside is that it's big enough that at this point, unless you are a high roller, you're buying fractions of a coin and not actual coins itself."

"And you have part of one?"

"God no, I have almost a hundred CryptoCoins. I got in when they were about seventy pounds each, and now," I made a gesture mimicking a rocket taking off, "they're stupid money now."

"What happens if a real bug-out happens?"

"Like what, nuke war or zombies?" I asked.

"Sure, what happens to all of that digital money?"

"Oh, it's fucking gone, mate," I said. "Then the only currencies worth a fuck are NATO .223 and cans of beans." We walked into the house, and the mood was greatly changed and much relaxed. I held the door as a pair of highly attractive professional-looking people in unisex scrubs left and found that the captain had another new guest.

Callie looked radiant, sitting at the table by the windows overlooking the bay. She had a rosy glow to her cheeks, and her fiery hair was clean and braided. I had the feeling that under the plump-looking robe she had on, she was nude. I felt something stick in my throat, and twitch in my pants. Miss Brooks looked equally content and almost bronzed in her matching robe.

"You just missed the masseuses, love," Sadie said with a languid smile. "But there is still plenty of mimosa in the pitcher."

"How's the leg, Mr. Roan?" the new guest, an older black woman, asked.

"It's doing well," he said. "Introductions though. Doc Max, this is a former Marine I served with, back in Afghanistan. Owen Worthington, but for some arsed reason we all call him Kurt. He remembers when I had two feet and would get into a fight with anything that had a pulse."

"Aye, that's Captain Roan, always ready for a bloody good scrap," I said. I had a moment to remember how he had been before the IED took out his vehicle and turned his leg into bolognaise. He had been a wild man. "Pleasure," I said.

"Doc Max is one of our specialized physicians, and has taken care of us more than once," Roan said. "When Sadie came into our lives, it was Max who patched her back together and got her through a serious case of double pneumonia. Saved her life, really."

"How are you feeling, Callie?" I asked. She held a cup of something in her hands, and knowing the captain and the company he kept, they could have given her a cup full of vodka as easily as herbal tea or plain American coffee.

"Better." She smiled. "Miss Brooks is a splendid and polite hostess."

"You don't need to call me Miss Brooks, we're friends here," Sadie said. Callie gave her a small nod. I saw a flash of color in her cheeks, and saw that *click* in her expression, that self-correcting behavior that Arik had beaten into her with his fists and his words.

"I'm sorry, Miss Sadie," she said. I saw Sadie give a small sigh and an accepting posture.

"I'll get directly to the point," the doctor said. "Calanthe has brain damage, but that can be managed. Sadie gave me the heads-up, so I came prepared. I've given her pretty much a thirty-day supply of several medications that will help her manage the condition. She will be fine. All she needs is some security, stability, and patience from the people who are around her. I think that the trauma from the emotional torture will be more lasting than the physical damage."

I saw Callie look down into her cup and I knew she was starting to blame herself, that she had deserved the abuse that Arik had poured out on her so liberally. I stepped forward and kneeled in front of her. "Callie." I took her hands in mine and looked into her eyes. "I won't let anyone hurt you ever again."

"Thank you, Kurt," she said. I could feel everyone in the room staring at me.

"Oh, he lays it on thick," Sadie said, and I thought she was talking to the captain.

"C'mon then, let's give them a little privacy," the captain said softly. The doctor agreed, gathered her bag, and gave Callie a pat on the shoulder before she left. The captain and Sadie went to each other, and something silent passed between them. I felt a little jealous of that connection. It was something that I wanted with Callie, and when I looked back to her, she was waiting for me. Her eyes were bright and intense.

"Your friends are really something else," she said.

"Yeah," I managed to get out.

"You don't have to stay on one knee, you know?" There was a bit of blush in her cheeks.

"I'm sorry if I embarrassed you," I apologized.

"You're so silly, Kurt." She leaned forward and kissed me on the tip of my nose. "And I am honored, and in no way embarrassed."

19

———

*C*allie…

    I hated how my cheeks flamed at the drop of a hat, especially considering once they started, they only flamed harder at how I felt about them flaming in the first place which could sometime lead, I kid you not, to me blushing all the way down to my knees... my knees which Kurt had carefully perched his hands on over the thick, luxurious terrycloth of my borrowed robe.

I was vaguely disappointed in myself that after such luxurious treatment, massages, and facials on Sadie's behest, that I was the closest to feeling *normal* since this whole ordeal began. Guilt crowded in and I resolutely tried to push it away.

After opening up a bit and confiding in Sadie about my fears about my mental faculties, she had immediately picked up her phone and called Doc Max. Doc Max had a much better bedside manner than the previous doctor and after reviewing the data from the previous doctors records and a few cognitive tests that she'd given me herself, she'd allayed the majority of my fears. Although I still mourned who I was and was still uncertain as to who I was going to be from here on out, it wasn't quite so terrifying of a thing that I was *completely* changed, you know?

I think that was what I was afraid of the most, that I was going to be deeply and irrevocably *changed* and would lose myself completely at the hands of what Arik had done, and I didn't want that. I so fiercely wanted to find and be the girl I had been *before*. I guess there wasn't any way to go back to that, at least not really.

Sadie had a way about her. A way of explaining things and providing a new perspective. She'd spent a lot of time, catching me up about her situation and I was so impressed by her. I mean, wow... I decided that I wanted that for myself. To have gone through something like I had and to, in her words, *choose to be a survivor rather than the victim that asshat tried to make you.*

I smiled at Kurt who was getting to his feet in front of me, holding down his hands to help me to my feet like some old-world and gallant gentleman. I wanted to make him proud as much as I wanted to prove to myself that I could be forged into something harder than steel after coming through such a trial by fire.

"Same room as last night?" I asked softly. We had arrived last night, and tonight would be our second night here. He nodded. "This place is so big, it might take me a minute to find my way back to it," I said with a bit of a nervous laugh.

Doc Max said I may have some mild memory impairment – forgetting words for things and things like directions and getting back to places I had just been. She'd also told me it was alright to be frustrated and that it may not even be all that bad given enough time for the bruising on my brain to heal. She'd given me a bit of unsolicited advice, to allow myself to feel things but to remember not to unpack and live in those feelings for too long. To be gentle with myself, which was honestly easier said than done.

"I've got it, Love. Come with me," he said with a smile, and he tucked my hand into the crook of his arm and led me away from the sitting room and through the expansive mansion, back to the room we shared.

It was nice. Kurt was at ease here which in turn put *me* at ease. Sadie had further put me at ease by telling me she was happy for the girl time and when I'd asked her if she was worried about New Eden making their lives miserable, she'd only grinned with a wicked light in her eyes and had said, *"That would be a very bad mistake on their part. Very bad."*

Something about the mix of confidence and the way she lit up with such a dark intention made me believe her with an almost shiver down my spine.

I liked Sadie, but some part of me also feared her a little.

I was glad when Kurt returned each time that he did to check in on me, and even more grateful still when we retired for the evening, and it was just me and him again. There was a comfort in his arms that I just couldn't say I found anywhere else.

He led me up the curving carpeted stairs to the second floor and along the long line of closed identical doors to the one that was ours. He opened it for me as he did just about every door he could get to before I did, and I slipped past him and inside.

The room was a suite of sorts, large with a bed and your typical bedroom furniture, but also with a nook area set aside for a desk – a little office space if you will – along with the room's own private bath.

It was nice, nicer than some of the mansions that even Arik owned, but that could just be because of the tasteful décor instead of Arik's penchant for a sort of gaudy baroque knockoff with its gold leaf saturating *everything* next to the garish deep burgundies he preferred. He thought it looked decadent and rich. I thought it'd looked like he was trying too hard, although I never in a million years would have said that to his face.

No, this room was done in light creams and muted pastels that made it seem airy and open. I wanted to attribute the design to Sadie, but to be completely honest, I thought her tastes might lean more to the wiry, sharp-witted and barb-tongued man she called her lover; Kyle.

No, this, I think was Kurt's captain's doing. This was all Roan.

They were an interesting trio to say the least. I don't think I could do it – have an actual *relationship* with two men at the same time. Especially two men as different as Kyle, sometimes called Lach, and Roan.

"You seem thoughtful," Kurt observed.

"You mean distracted?" I asked with a gentle smile, and an answering one graced his full lips.

"Accurate, I'll give you that," he said.

"I'm probably a lot of both," I confessed. "These three give a girl a lot to think about," I said.

"Oh?" That one word, that single syllable, sounded almost cautious. My smile grew. For a man so confident in just about *all things*, Owen "Kurt" Worthington did have his hidden insecurities and for some reason, I think I tripped a few of them and I didn't know why.

I went to him and wound my arms around his waist. He seemed almost too casually dressed for a place like this in his jeans and plaid-print, snap-button, western-cowboy type of shirt, but I secretly loved it. He was so at home and confident in his work boots, standing in the small sea of plush, high-pile carpet beneath our feet.

I tucked myself into his arms against his chest and felt the slight tension radiate through his muscles as I let my quiet confession slip about his friends.

"I could never do it," I said. "I'm glad your friends are happy and that their arrangement works for them, but I'm always glad when you come through the door and rescue me from feeling too awkward. I don't think their lifestyle is for me."

I felt some of the tension ease from him as he put his arms around me and tipped my chin up to face him with gentle fingertips.

"Aye," he murmured. "I'm glad they're happy, and that these things work so well for them, but I'm not one for sharing," he said. I couldn't help but grace him with a thousand-watt smile at that, relief flooding me to a degree. We both laughed a bit nervously and when the slightly awkward moment passed, I begged him, "Kiss me?"

"I'll do more than that, if you'll let me." His voice had dropped low into that sexy thrum that sizzled my nerve endings and sent a blot of electric shivers through me. I loved that he did that – asked permission before getting too physical with me, setting heart and mind at ease, *asking* instead of just *taking*.

"I'll always let you," I murmured just before our lips touched and my God, his kiss... it was better than any movie kiss ever produced. It made my toes curl into the thick, plush carpet and heat unfurled in the center of my body, *want* coursing through me for a deeper touch as his hands slid sexy and carefully over the thick lavish robe that probably cost more than I wanted to know about, from some crazy designer whose name is what garnered the price tag more than the actual make of the robe.

I loved how his big hands kneaded me so carefully through the rich cloth, easing minor aches and stiffness, and the way he reveled in the simple touches as though he were the one being treated rather than me.

He was so careful of me, but also firm; somehow leaving me feeling fragile but strong as well. I didn't really know how to describe it, I just knew I liked it and that I was grateful for it.

He kissed me carefully, an almost chaste thing until I parted my lips for him at which point, he groaned, and I can't tell you how much I loved that sound coming from him. It sounded to me, like I was a treasure, something long sought and desired and above all, it wasn't... it wasn't... *skeevy*. It didn't make my skin crawl. It made my heart soar and above all, it boosted my confidence, allowed me the space to do what *I* wanted, what *I* desired, which was to have as much of Kurt's warmth and strength pressed against me as possible.

"Callie." His voice was a desire-filled strangled whisper as my fingers went to the snaps on his shirt, swiftly unclasping one after the other, my fingers deft even if my mind couldn't be with how much he filled my senses.

I smoothed hands over his warm chest, and he stared down at me, between us, watching me do it.

"Cor, girl... you have no idea what you do to me," he said, and I smiled up at him, my hands gliding down his stomach, over his belt, to grip his thick cock through the denim of his jeans.

"I mean, I have some idea," I said with a slightly nervous laugh at my sudden boldness. He chuckled too and placed a hand against the side of my neck, caressing the line of my jaw with the pad of his thumb, his other hand gripping my upper arm on the opposite side through the thick robe. He held on to me as though he held on to a fixed point in a storm, swaying on his feet slightly as though drunk on the sensation of my small hand rubbing him through his jeans.

"You..." he gasped. "You, you, you!" He laughed and cleared his throat. I bit my bottom lip as I smiled, emboldened by the effect I seemed to have on him. The fact that just standing here like this, not even naked, not even really doing anything seemed to have him almost completely undone. It was both a powerful and really good feeling, I had to say.

He stepped into me, gathering me close, effectively trapping my arms between us, but rather than worry or send me into a tizzy, it had quite the opposite effect as his lips captured mine again. I sighed out in utter contentment as he pulled me tight against him by my butt and kneaded me through the robe.

One of the things I could appreciate most about Kurt is when we were like this, there was no hurry, no rush. He was always so gentle, but firm, so kind and so attentive to my wants and needs and I craved it, like a flower too long left in the shade, wilting from neglect, finally given a taste of the sun.

I felt like I bloomed fully under his tender touch, and I craved it so wholly – his gentleness, his kindness. A small part of me felt guilty for it.

"What's this?" he asked, caressing my cheek. I closed my eyes so I wouldn't have to look at the concern in his eyes, and turned my face into his touch, nuzzling the palm of his hand.

"Nothing," I lied and laid a kiss against the heel of his hand.

"That look wasn't nothing, Love. Talk to me," he murmured.

"I don't want to ruin the mood," I whispered, and he took a gentle half-step back from me.

"I'd like to think it's quite impossible to do that, Love... but we need to talk about this."

"About what?" I asked.

"What made you look so sad just then."

I sighed and closed the gap between us and nestled myself against him. He obliged me and put his arms around me, rubbing my back through the robe.

"I feel guilty sometimes," I confessed. "I feel like I've ruined your life, and... and even though I give you this, I'm so... so *broken* that it's not good for you. That..." I hesitated, forcing the words out was so hard.

"Oh, no, Love. I like this very much and with you I'm not wanting for anything."

I peeked up and his smile was both genuine and kind with no hint of amusement at my expense.

"Really?" I asked.

"Absolutely," he said and tipped my chin with a crooked finger, raising it so he could claim my lips again.

I didn't think. I just gave myself over to the sensations of him, the feel of him under my hands, in my arms, pressed tight against my body. How his lips moved over mine, gentle but possessive, urgently insistent, as though he would prove with his powerful body the sincerity of his words.

Boldly, he pulled the sash of my robe and I let it fall open. I was never shy about my body. It was impossible to be after how it'd been coveted, after how many others had seen it. Except now... now I wanted only Kurt to see it. Especially when he treated it and me so well.

He delved his hand beneath the thick cloth draping me, palming my waist. His hand curved around my body, fingers against my back and I loved that, that I could feel so delicate against him and yet so safe.

He guided me to the bed, and spun me around, so my back was to it.

"Is it alright if we take this off completely?" he asked. "Or might you be cold?"

I stuttered a bit of a laugh.

"Hard to be cold with you here to keep me warm," I murmured, and he gave me a slow smile.

"I'll keep you warm alright," he promised. I let the robe fall to the floor. He sat me on the edge of the bed and went to his knees in front of me. "Lie back," he ordered gently.

I did, but it took a while to take my eyes from him. He pulled me down, so that my butt rested just at the edge of the comforter, maybe even a little over, and hooking my knees over his powerful shoulders, he gazed up my body and flicked his tongue out to taste me.

I groaned and let my head fall back, closing my eyes, reveling in the feel of his lips and tongue over my most intimate parts. I don't know why I couldn't watch him go down on me. I was always so self-conscious, I guess. For some reason, watching made me blush and oh, how I *hated* to blush. Especially considering it was something that I had been prized for in New Eden.

I put a hand against my mouth and tried not to writhe against the fine bedding as he licked and sucked at my pussy lips gently, his tongue probing at my clit, sending fire racing through my nerve endings.

Sparkling light flitted through me like fireflies over the grass. I gasped, the gasp turning into a surprised "ungh!" as he slid one thick finger up inside me, but only one. He knew what I liked, paid attention. Even though I had never told him that was how I preferred it, he knew. He always just *knew*.

He teased the pad of his finger in a come-hither motion and whatever that place was inside me, that magic spot, he knew just how to find it, slipping in my wetness, gliding carefully and sweetly over it, raising that sweet blush of sensation from its sleeping state and encouraging it to lift me, levitate me, float me carefully out into the ether of that place that was neither here nor there before grounding me here with him with the use of his tongue against my clit.

The soft sweetness of what his finger did inside me was suddenly accompanied by a rich and decadent zing of purpose, and that purpose was to make me come, shaking, quaking, until I smacked my fingers against the forearm that he used to pin my bucking hips to the bed and even then, he didn't let up. He teased the orgasm into a lengthier thing until I tapped frantically on the edge of panic, afraid I would lose myself completely and all that good feeling would turn against me and twist into something akin to pain.

He gave a little self-satisfied chuckle and rose from between my legs to stand, and the way he rose, the way he smoothly gained his feet, it reminded me of a leviathan rising from the deep. A wise dragon, capable of great violence, but wise enough to know when it was needed. The way he stood looking down at me, pleased while I lay nerveless and panting from his ministrations left me aroused all the more.

He took his time disrobing, letting me catch my breath as he carefully unfastened the snaps at his wrists and the few I hadn't gotten to, seeing as they were below the waistband and belt of his jeans and had been out of my reach. Watching him shrug out of that shirt, pulling it from the denim capturing it at his waist... I didn't think there was anything hotter.

The something hotter came when he slid his jeans and underwear off, his cock springing free to stand smooth and perfect against his stomach, his length and girth both decent, just this side of too much to take for me and oh, how I wanted to take it. How I wanted him over me, inside me, and oh, how I needed him to feel as good as he made me feel... always.

"Up you go," he said, voice husky, guiding me into motion as I sat up and pushed myself back onto the bed to give him the room that he needed to join me.

He let me be bold and made me feel emboldened, so I reached between us, stroking his hard length that was scorching hot and velvety smooth against my palm. I used the slickness at the head of his cock to act as lube as I stroked him. He closed his eyes, jaw working as he lost himself in the sensation of my hand working him, even as he finished his climb and I parted my thighs, lying back so that he might settle between them.

He settled over me, and rather than it being overwhelming or intimidating, it was wonderful. I felt safe and protected, and certainly cherished as his gaze roved my face, looking for any signs of discomfort or unease.

Though my hair was braided, he still took a moment to smooth some of the stray, ever-present frizz in a halo around my face away, cradling my cheek as he looked over my face... dare I even think it? Dare I dream it? *...lovingly.*

"Oh, Callie girl, you are a sight," he murmured, and I smiled faintly.

I had been prized for my looks since forever. I was used to being complimented on them regularly but unlike all those people, I felt like Kurt really saw me. All of me. Not just the pretty face I'd won the genetic lottery of beauty standards with, but past that, further than that. When Kurt looked into my eyes, I could swear he saw my very soul.

"Make love to me," I whispered, beseechingly, and he smiled and very lightly, very gently, and oh so sweetly, he kissed the tip of my nose.

"I'll do nothing else," he vowed, and I bit my bottom lip, smiling.

We kissed, and with a few slow and lazy thrusts of his hips, he sank into me.

I loved the sounds he made, loved how he grunted and called out wordlessly and how pleasure filled that inarticulate noise sounded. I loved how he covered my body with his much larger one and pressed me into the mattress. I loved how he kissed me, how he smoothed my hair back from my face, how he thrust slowly and deliberately and how he hummed into my mouth with blissful satisfaction. Most of all, I loved how I pleased him in this way and how he made me feel like I was the only woman ever to make him feel this way.

I didn't know if that was true, I couldn't know for sure, but something in me appreciated it, nonetheless.

I wrapped my arms around him, raised my knees to give him better access and fell into the slow, deliberate, careful rhythm of his thrusting, that slight roll he gave to his hips, hitting just the right place inside me, building me up, keeping me on that exquisite edge for as long as he wanted to hold me there.

I sometimes wished he could hold me there forever.

I guess, in the end, the thing I loved the most about Kurt was that he made it so very easy to love him.

20

───────

Kurt...

Making love to Callie was a different experience than I was normally used to, and the more I was with her, the more I realized that it wasn't supposed to be the way I was familiar with. As I looked into her eyes and saw her bite her lip as we pressed into each other, this was the way it should be. Almost all the times before had seemed empty and shallow compared to this – just base coupling, using another person as a masturbation aid.

I wasn't there for me.

I was there for her, to make her happy and bring her the pleasure that life had too long denied her. I could only imagine how rough and cruel Arik had been, considering what he had done with his groupies, and how she had looked after their weekday visits. If everything she had said was true, Arik took her virginity, and there was no love or consideration there. He was an action star and stuntman in every other aspect of his life, why would this be any different?

I was sure he had never been gentle or loving with her.

Never went down on her.

Certainly, never looked into her bottomless eyes, into her soul, as they made love.

The captain's house was the safest I had ever felt. There was no sense of dread or urgency hanging over us, and there was nothing but time between Callie and me. I drew it out as long as I could. If I felt myself getting too close to finishing, I would pull out of her and just let myself *cool off* and occupied her with soft tender kisses. This felt strange at first, being so gentle.

I knew in some ways that I wasn't too different from Arik. I knew I was rough around the edges, and that was probably what drew that group of women I attracted to me. They wanted rough around the edges. They wanted someone who was masculine and strong, and knew things about discipline and authority. They wanted their asses to be hit, and to be taken roughly. I took them roughly, used them, and left them a wet mess, stepping out for a smoke before getting in my car and leaving.

Fuck, with one of those women, I never even took my sunglasses off. Had she been staring at her own reflection as I fucked her like I was tired of her shit and the moment I blew my load on her chin and neck, she was out the door?

I couldn't imagine those things with Callie.

There was no way I could treat her like that.

The thoughts of what I had done with those other women made my balls start to feel tight, and that meant easing out of her heavenly warmth before I lost my control.

In the large bed, I showed her positions that I was familiar with, and wrongly assumed that she would have been familiar with. Between transitions, I would kiss her again, cup her breasts and suck at her perfect nipples, and go down on her. She came, sometimes small, sometimes large, sometimes several times in quick succession.

I came once, my face buried between her thighs. I felt it coming, and despite how tightly I gripped myself, it still came out.

That was okay, it wasn't a lot, and I didn't lose my hard-on.

It almost gave me a second wind, once I felt confident that the moment I slid into her again, I wouldn't immediately shudder and blow everything I had inside her.

That was going to happen, just not yet.

I wanted this to last.

The moment was too perfect, and we were both so in the right mood.

Through missionary, then reverse missionary, to cowgirl, to reverse cowgirl, I learned that Callie knew two positions. On her knees with a man's hands on her head, or on her hands and knees with his two hands on her hips, with a jackhammer pace. It felt a little odd omitting doggy style from the moment. Almost every woman I had been with enjoyed that position, but they didn't have the same negative experiences with it she did.

The former was the only thing I had a shred of conflict over. As much as I loved getting head, and I doubted that there were any men who didn't like it, I couldn't imagine myself doing to her what he did. Maybe one day she might be interested, but that was a move she was going to have to make on her own. She might, if only because of how much I liked going down on her.

When I came, it seemed almost like an afterthought. Callie moaned softly, but her own rhythm stayed constant as I tensed and shuddered. She was almost insatiable. She managed another go of her own before lying tangled with me.

There was still no rush, and I stayed inside her until I had gone completely soft and slipped out. When I did, she made another soft sighing sound and kissed me again. I felt the mess we made start to run out of her and she giggled, of all things.

"Maybe a shower and you'll be ready to go again?" She nipped playfully at my lips.

"Again?" I asked.

"Yes, again. I can't get enough of you." Her voice was like honey. "I'm used to being treated roughly, and you're so gentle."

～

We retreated to the guest shower, a monster of river flagstones and a massive overhead rainfall showerhead. It quickly slicked her flaming red hair down against her body. There was something seductive about the way her hair ran over her shoulders, down her back, and even down her chest all but concealing her nipples. The hot water steamed the bathroom quickly, and the scent of fancy expensive soap was strong, but not entirely unpleasant.

She let me wash her hair. It was an odd feeling, massaging the shampoo through so much hair. I kept at the longest, a crew cut. Most of the time, I preferred a buzz cut. Several years in-country, where there were no casual barbers and something as simple as a hot shave was a pipe dream, I had long hair and a wild beard. I didn't enjoy looking like a desert nomad or a Jesus Christ Superstar cosplayer. I liked being clean, neat.

God, she was so clean and neat, even with that goddess's mane of fire-red hair.

I lost my breath when, as I was rinsing her hair, she took the soap and started giving me similar attention. What struck home was the way she cradled my cock in her hands, working up the soap until there was a thick lather. Her hands were small, but strong and confident. I thought after a half-orgasm on the floor and a full testicular evacuation inside her, that there was nothing left inside me.

In a few seconds, I was getting hard under her attention.

Fuck, that felt *good*.

"I keep washing it, but it stays dirty," Callie said, giving me the most devilish look I had seen on her delicate features.

"You're..." I swallowed hard, "...inspiring."

"I really liked when you let me get on top, earlier," she said. I could feel myself stiffening at the thought, and how forward she was about it.

"I liked that too," I said, shakily. She wasn't pretending to use the soap on me and was just stroking me, over and over. I was hard again. I let out a rattling gasp. I hadn't had feelings like this since I had been a dumbass teenager. Back then, I had been both an idiot and a beast. I could crank one out, see my girl at the time, give her a go, go back home, and crank out another.

"How did you work these knobs?" Callie asked, turning her back to me. She bent over to examine the gleaming chrome fixtures and pinned my increasingly urgent hard-on between my stomach and her milky-white ass.

I let out a groan as she shut the water off. She knew how to use the knobs; this was all show and tease. I knew it was, the way she rubbed her ass against me, my length caught between her cheeks. "Fuck," I groaned.

"Still dirty, even after that very nice cleaning shower?" Callie asked, turning to face me again. There was fire in her eyes. There in the shower, she kneeled carefully and wrapped one hand around the base of my shaft and started stroking me, slowly. As she neared the end of the stroke, she would give a squeeze. I groaned each time. My God, how could I not?

"There it is," she whispered, reaching up and giving my balls a shudder-inducing caress. "Yes, yes, there it is." I felt the lightest flick on the tip of my tool. I looked down to watch as she stroked and squeezed me again. A drop of clear fluid welled up from the head of my cock and she flicked it with her tongue.

It was so petite, so pink, so quick.

She kissed the end of it and laughed.

"Funny?" I asked, one hand braced against the side of the shower. I was thankful for the artfully rough texture of the river stone.

"Yes," she answered. Her lips were wrapped around just my head, and I could feel how hot she was, her tongue against me. "I think you like this, yes?"

"I do." I let out a breath. "Oh fuck."

She made a small giggling sound and put the head back in her mouth. I wasn't sure what all was going on in down there, other than the fact that it felt incredible. How could she be good at this? How did his cruelty allow for this sort of affection from her?

"You're too tense, relax," Callie said, and she caressed my balls again. "What's in your head?"

"That what you are doing feels really good," I said.

"Are you thinking about what he did?" she asked, hitting the nail on the head. She was fucking sharp as they came. I nodded, slightly. "That was a chore, this is not." She emphasized the point by running her tongue up and down my shaft. "This thing, this thing I like. It is nice to me and makes me have really special feelings."

She took me in her mouth, more easily than I expected.

I had to use both hands to brace against the rough rock walls of the shower. This place must have cost a fortune. The thought was fleeting, as she took my entire length down her throat, and I felt her nose buried into my stomach. Oh, sweet Lord. *Oh, sweet Jesus.*

My breathing was fast, ragged. She turned her head up and looked into my eyes. There was a spark of mischief there, and then I felt something – her tongue. Even taking all my length, she could still move her tongue.

Calanthe wasn't a mortal woman, fallible and flesh. She was a goddess.

Before I lost all semblance of self-control and balance, she released me. There was a flurry of lips and tongue along the bottom of my shaft, and even some attention shown to my balls. They were already tight again. Fuck, I must have been the one with the concussion, because there was no way this was actually happening.

That's what this all was, a delirium brought on by severe brain trauma.

The real Calanthe was still on the bloodstained carpet. She was leaning over a pink marble sink, spreading her cheeks so that I could see her almost scarlet red slit of a pussy and puckered little asshole, all but begging me to fuck her some more. I certainly wasn't putting a hand on her shoulder and one on her hip before burying myself inside said pussy. I was on the ground, also beaned in the head with a golden award.

But the truth of the matter was not that.

I wasn't on my back, I wasn't injured. Callie was far from injured, alternating between laughing and crying out with pleasure as I gave her my best.

This was real. All of this was real.

I didn't last nearly as long this time around. I tried to pull out and maybe change positions, give myself a moment to bring everything back down to a ground level. All I accomplished was to paste a few strips of my mess across her shower-reddened ass. I took her, pushing in to the hilt, before the last of my load was spent.

She let out a bright laugh and pushed back against me.

I wasn't able to stay up nearly as long as I had before, and we retreated to a second shower. This one was much more subdued, and while there was more kissing and she washed my cock again, it wasn't teasing, it was aftercare.

Shower done, and toweled dry, we went back to the bedroom and the invitation of the probably insane thread count sheets. Sleep came soon enough.

The first face-to-face meeting with Fallout was easily enough scheduled. The captain informed me that they weren't just a group of screaming heads on television; they were a full-fledged political-action committee. It seemed that after bailing from New Eden, Miss Marion Tate entered the political arena, and was working to not just bring down her old green cult, but the others as well. They were legit to the point that they had an office on K Street, the central avenue of lobbyists and PACs in Washington DC Miss Brooks seemed to have a handle on that. It seemed entirely too familiar to call her by her first name; it almost seemed rude.

It was sobering to learn that New Eden wasn't the only green cult, just the largest and most prominent of them, and close to being the first. Tate and the rest of her people were working as hard as they could to show what a group of assholes New Eden were, and that rather than trying to save the environment, they were only interested in looting peoples' bank accounts and pillaging their juvenile daughter's *nubile pussy*. It was insulting just how lacking in imagination they were. The captain stayed back at the base on this job, and it was left to his companion, Kyle Lachlan, Callie, Sadie, and me to complete this particular run.

The roles were obvious. Callie was the warhead. She had all the information that would destroy New Eden. She seemed to have reached some sort of bonding with Brooks, the way they sat next to each other. The thoughts of what we did not so many hours before tried to sneak into my mind. Sadie had spent a good deal of time on Callie's hair and makeup, making her look professional and slick for a meeting with the Fallout people, covering the vestiges of her bruising perfectly. I let out a sigh. This felt so strange, and I had seldom ever felt so vulnerable and exposed.

Kyle seemed so much cooler than I felt.

I was more comfortable with an earbud, a rifle in a three-point harness, and some body armor. Instead, I was sitting in the passenger seat of a massive SUV, with no weapons, no armor, no communications gear, not even a knife tucked in the top of my boot.

I wished that the SUV had been an armored infantry fighting vehicle, something packing cannons, grenade launchers, and all sorts of radios and scopes. I wanted an M2 in my hands, or the controls for a wire-guided missile – something that would let me reach out and touch someone. What I did have was a set of controls for the temperature of my seat, and how much and what temperature of air I wanted to blow on me.

The building was near the end of K Street. While they were the real deal, they were still small fry compared to some of the major government groups, whose buildings were registered as historic locations or were the cutting edge of modern design and innovation. The budget of Fallout was nothing – a raindrop versus the ocean – compared to the titans in the military, the medical industry, and petroleum. What were we thinking, coming here?

The Fallout headquarters was almost intimately familiar. I had seen this sort of building dozens of times. I could imagine the stairwells in it, where the mechanical areas were. More importantly, where to breach a wall to enter which section, or which pillar to blow to bring the whole thing down. Those thoughts were not very useful, considering that they were going to be on our side, and hopefully come up with a plan for Callie. She was the one with everything to lose on the line.

Me, I was just an ex-Royal Marine. The worst they could do to me was send me to jail for assault. No great loss there, since almost everything of value I owned was crypto or blockchain and beyond judicial authority.

The inside was nice, well-appointed, but there was obviously a budget at work. There was art on the walls, but it looked more doctor's office and department store than art gallery. Same went for the other small details – low-cost but durable Berber carpet in industrially generic colors. The satin finish paint on the walls was likewise probably picked for how long it would last and for easy clean up. The furniture all had a bit of a worn look to it as well. It wasn't at the point of being tossed up on a social media sales page, but that wasn't too far away.

Maybe I was being too critical?

Had all the time I spent working in Hollywood left me jaded to things like glass tables that cost thousands of dollars, and living room sets that were in the tens of thousands of dollars? Was this just a normal political-action office? It had the feel of a lawyer's office, but not one of the crazy powerful ones, just the sort that had an open door across the courthouse and a block up from the row of bondsmen.

I knew I was nervous. My eyes were moving too quick, and my hands were clenching. I felt like I was about to jump out of a helicopter or go charging out the front of a landing craft like it was fucking D-Day and I was on a mission to liberate France and kill some Nazis. But fuck all, it was just a meeting in an office building with a pretty woman with mousy-brown hair, freckles, and a penchant for screaming at Hollywood mouthpieces.

We didn't have to wait long.

While I was busy fidgeting with my pockets and my phone, Kyle had everything very smoothly in hand, gliding us through the process of secretaries and functionaries who existed to keep people like Marion Tate from being reached directly. It was a security cordon, a very polite one. The number of doors and the elevator required to reach her would have made her a difficult extraction, if the office occupants had been armed.

Knowing how things went down with the captain and his crew, they could have done it easily, but with a staggering body count.

I had heard about what happened in France and had been there when they went in after Kaijin and her inner circle.

Staying out of that had likely been the best decision of my life.

There was a lot of formality, hand shaking, polite introductions, all including full rank and title. It felt weird being addressed completely as Staff Sergeant Owen Worthington, former Royal Marines, 9th Commando Brigade. That felt like another person, some guy I had met once, and had a laugh that we had the same name. SSgt Worthington should probably still be in the Afghan highlands, or dealing with pirates out of Somalia, not standing here in this office.

Marion Tate was not an imposing woman in person – she was short and thin, and I could see the angular features that were not quite as important to the New Eden cult as say, being underage. She had probably been incredible before she gave herself a near-military haircut and traded her makeup and dress for a power suit and the posture of a BMW salesman.

"Calanthe Rex, I never imagined that I would have the honor. We have a lot to talk about," Tate said, extending her hand to Callie. They shook hands but it seemed awkward and almost strange.

"We do," Callie said, hesitantly.

"The first thing is Mrs. Rex's security and what Fallout can do to help us keep her safe," Kyle said.

"What sort of protection do you think we have to offer, Mister...?"

"Lachlan. What sort of threat does New Eden pose to Mrs. Rex and her associates?" he asked. He was as sharp as a knife, and just as fast.

"Physically, very little. New Eden is an unofficial church, an NGO, and some sections are registered charity organizations. If you're expecting some sort of armed-paramilitary response to Calanthe's defection, you might have watched too many action movies," she said with a soft condescension.

"It took a Royal Marine and a hell of a bug-out plan to rescue her from New Eden, and I'm sure in our correspondence, we made it known that Worthington was the New Eden head of security?" he asked, like an armor-piercing round.

"Yes, your emails did mention that," Tate said.

"We need to take this very seriously," I said, brushing my useless hands against the front of my borrowed jacket. "Arik's personal detail for filming and property security was nearly seventy men, and that's not taking into account the full resources of New Eden itself, which are not inconsiderable. They have helicopters, vehicles, and there are Class-three contractors who are familiar with the organization and involved in their overseas operations. In Beverly Hills, a five-foot stone wall and a few cameras will keep almost everyone out, but you set up a green center in South Africa, or Pakistan, it has a paramilitary force on par with a private military contractor."

"I wasn't aware," Tate said, suddenly looking more serious.

"I expect some sort of response," Kyle said. "This is a personal strike against New Eden and its leadership. With what Calanthe knows, this will be just shy of a literal assassination."

"While I would like to see the organization brought down, I am not going to condone violence or murder," Tate said firmly. Kyle pinched the bridge of his nose for a moment, a gesture of frustration that I could easily recognize, not knowing him more than in a cursory fashion.

"While few things would bring me more pleasure than violence and murder being heaped on people who are committing such glaring and obvious crimes, I will agree with you. Callie's evidence should be sufficient to severely harm Arik Rex's career, as well as implicate several key members of the organization being complicit with human sex trafficking and grooming minors for prostitution. There should be lots of jail time handed out, organizations raided and broken down by the Justice department, and maybe even some choice heavily armed raids from the FBI and other agencies better known by their initials than their actual names," Kyle said. His presence seemed to fill the room as he approached Tate and I could detect an almost physical change in her. Her posture changed, her facial expression, everything.

"I-I see," she said. "We have this building here, and there are Fallout halfway houses in several major cities, where we," she swallowed hard, "take care of women who've managed to get out of New Eden."

"Calanthe is not a rank-and-file member," I said, thinking to reinforce Lachlan.

"I was a First Among First Daughters," Callie said. Her voice was as soft as Kyle was intense. "Before I was sold to Arik, I was a teen goodwill ambassador to the United Nations, and had audiences with the governor of California, the state representatives and one of the senior state senators. My husband is one of the highest-grossing movie stars of the last decade, and when he married me, I was not of legal age by any stretch."

"Oh shit," Tate said.

"We felt it prudent to leave some of the details out of the written documents. I don't know how good your cyber security is," Kyle said.

"So, you want us to provide protection?" Tate asked.

"No, protection we can handle on our own," Kyle said. "We're here to deliver a deposition, a notarized confession and condemnation of New Eden, and name the people inside it, and their transgressions."

"So, I guess I need to call the lawyers, get a notary and scare up some recording equipment so that we have this properly documented and certified," Tate said. I nodded, and Sadie put an arm around Callie and whispered something in her ear. She nodded her head and seemed to stiffen. She reminded me of some of the women I had met in Afghanistan. You could see their eyes, calm and cool, and completely unmoved by emotion. They would cry and lament later, but in the moment, they would pull survivors of airstrikes or cruise missile hits from the rubble, dust off clothing and smooth down hair, and lead the children and the wounded away.

I learned that they had lost terrible things during the decades of war, their own friends and family, and digging a stranger from the rubble, and making sure they were okay was nothing compared to what they had lost, and the strength they had found in their own pain. I felt, at times, ashamed of this. That country was nothing to me, nothing to my country, but the war seemed to have a life of its own.

The most sobering thing was that for me, I knew men who had fought in the first part of the war, watching as their sons enlisted and ended up going to the exact same places, they had been years before. Nothing was changing.

I let out my breath.

"I need a smoke," I managed before standing. Tate nodded and gestured. One of her assistants showed me to the smoking lounge, aka a balcony off the fifth floor, overlooking K Street. I knew what was going to happen. They were going to drag a camera and a few other people into Tate's office, and then they were basically going to debrief Callie, and she was going to have to go into the details. The lurid details.

I couldn't sit and listen to that.

Just thinking about it had my blood boiling, and I was ready for a hell of a scrap. I wanted to bring their shiny building down on their heads and then leave the ground red with their blood. The people who would do this deserved it.

They were monsters, and that was half the reason for joining the Royal Marines – get out of North Yorkshire and to make the world a better, safer place. The first half was done. I was out of North Yorkshire. There was almost no chance I would ever get to return to England, never see my hometown or my family again. That was a *mission accomplished* right bloody there. The other half, well, that was in the bog. Afghanistan had been a horror show clusterfuck, but at I still had all my fingers, toes, and appropriate limbs.

Kyle came out somewhere between the third and fourth smoke.

"You alright?" he asked, leaning against the rail of the balcony.

"As much as can be expected," I answered.

"She's doing okay," he said after a long pause. "But, yeah, it's fucking ugly."

"I know some, at least a little. I'm guessing that if this is going to be, what, a bloody deposition, she has to go into detail?" I half-asked. He nodded, almost sensing that what I wanted was silence, peace from this entire ordeal, but to protect and care for Callie as well.

"When did you start smoking?" he asked.

"Year eleven," I said. "You know how when you're a teen, you have to do everything you can to fit in and be cool."

"Year Eleven?"

"Three years from graduation. Year thirteen you get your diploma and either join the military or go into the colliery."

"Roan hasn't mentioned what those terms are," Kyle said.

"I don't know what you call the third year from graduation, and the colliery is the coal mines, literal coal mines," I said. "Not a lot of prospects. Lots of kids in school smoked, dressed like we were badasses, and generally were a bunch of dirty-faced chavs."

"Sophomore," Kyle said, ticking fingers off, counting backwards I reckoned. "I get that. I remember what a bucket of hot shit that time was."

"The two worst places I ever served was in my last few years of school and in-country," I said. He nodded. He had been there too. Not someone I really knew or served with, he was a Yank after all, but he had been close to the captain before the IED took his leg. Lots of co-op back then. We were all in the same shit.

"Do you love her, or are you just infatuated?" he asked, gesturing for a smoke. I tapped him out one and then handed him the lighter.

"Sorry, I only light pretty girl's smokes for them," I said.

"When the situation comes up, I make a point of lighting it, and then handing her the lit cigarette," he said.

"I didn't know you smoked."

"I don't. But sometimes a cigarette is the perfect social icebreaker. Answer my question."

"I'm not sure," I admitted after a long pause. "But I think so."

"Is that why you're out here?"

"It is. I can't stand to sit there and hear what these people did to her. These were the people who hired me, and I thought they were bloody gits and silly wankers, playing at pretend church with their god of green land and blue skies."

"Don't beat yourself up over that. They fooled a lot of people. I didn't know they were like that, and I can promise you Roan didn't either. If we had known, there is no way we would have lined up an interview with them."

"I appreciate that," I said. "And here I thought that working security for a heroin cartel was going to be the low point of my career."

"Your career isn't over," he said, putting a hand on my shoulder. "Look, it took a seriously level head to extract Calanthe from that shitshow without turning it into a media disaster. If you had handled it wrong, an hour after the fact, it would have been on the celebrity news and a dozen state and federal agencies would have been on your ass like angry hornets."

"My career is a series of unfortunate events," I said.

"You got her out, and you *still* haven't really answered my question. Do you love her or is this some bodyguard infatuation?"

"I don't think it's an infatuation, it feels too real, too serious. I would and will do anything for her, to keep her safe. Even if that means me giving up my life."

"That's a romantic notion, and we're going to make sure that it doesn't come to that."

I grunted out, "Appreciate that."

"It is pretty rough, I had to leave too. It's nothing but women, and they are laying it out like blood eagles in there."

"What the bloody fuck is a blood eagle, mate?" I asked, almost feeling my neck pop from how quick I turned to look at him.

"Viking business," he said. "Something along the lines of cutting a man's chest or back in such a way that you pull his lungs out of his body but leave them still attached. Bastard is still alive but suffocates because he can't get air in or out of his lungs. That's what's going on in there. She's telling them everything, and I can only imagine what's not being held back now since I'm not there, keeping the space co-ed."

"I don't want to know. I just need names," I said.

"I'm sure there will be a chance for that," he said. "Are you familiar with any of the other women who've left New Eden and tried to blow the whistle?"

"I'm not."

"The cult comes after them with a smear campaign if they have a public face. If they're nobodies – not famous or important – some of them just go silent, vanish. Missing persons. There are dozens, if not hundreds of people formerly associated with New Eden who've gone missing and there is nothing that the police are interested in, or willing to do."

"So, what's the plan there?"

"You know they're going to send people to try to bring her back, to silence her if they can't?" he half-said, half-asked. I nodded in agreement. "So once this is out, they're going to come for her publicly, and that's where Fallout is going to be her shield. There will be shouts of divorce, annulment, infidelity, and all that, like almost any bad celebrity breakup."

"I totally expect that," I said, knowing that there was nothing I could do about it.

"Then they're going to come for her covertly. If I were them, and this were my job, I would find a way to paint this, making her the victim of her own actions, and the two fastest ways to do that are suicide or drug overdose. We'll keep an eye out for those sorts of words in their releases, and that will tell us what they're doing."

"That sounds like something the captain would lay out."

"Well, it should, because he did," Kyle said. "He has this all planned out and the only reason he didn't come himself is he said he has work to do, and he hates stairs."

"We didn't take any stairs, though."

Kyle shrugged.

"When he says 'no' these days, I don't push."

"Is there a real plan?"

"As a matter of fact, there is," he said. "This meeting is going to be set on a delayed release, so that Fallout's people should be able to get everything lined up. Then, if we luck out, they take a few hits and then the feds get involved. We see ourselves out and let the guys in the shitty off-the-rack suits clean up the pedos and false prophets."

"Do you think that is really going to work?"

"No fucking way," Kyle said, giving the cigarette a final puff before flicking it off the balcony. "That amazon warrior princess you told us about is going to try to take her back, while her friends in tactical black attempt to get rid of us."

"If you think this will fail, why are we doing it?"

"Roan said it's blood in the water. Something about *Moby Dick*, I'm not sure. He reads more than I do. But we do this, and deal with the scrubs that try to finish this like they're some fucking SEAL team. If they come hard enough, we go take care of them."

"You mean like... actually go to the New Eden Centre and bring it down?"

"That's ambitious, I love it. Do you know anyone who has a cruise missile for sale? That would be easier than breaching that big-ass building."

"I don't, no."

"That's fine. I know three assholes who know all about asymmetrical warfare. You don't mind that I call you an asshole like Roan and myself?"

"No, that's fine."

"Nice work on choking Arik out, by the way."

"Thanks."

WHEN I FINALLY DECIDED THAT enough time had passed, a fact that demonstrated itself by realizing that I only had two smokes left in the pack, I went back in. Kyle followed me, and there was something reassuring about it, how he did it. Despite the suit and the slick shoes, all the polish and posture, he still had the demeanor of an American special force's commando.

The scene inside Tate's office was not something I was prepared for.

All the women looked rattled, like a bomb had gone off. Callie's makeup, so artfully applied, was mostly streaked down her face. Tate looked like she had gone through a wringer, and her smart jacket was folded and on her desk. The AV people seemed to be wrapping things up and despite the level of emotional carnage, things seemed to be okay.

"This might sound rude, but thank you for stepping out when you did," Tate said, looking to Kyle and me. "By making this just us women, it made things..." She groped for the right word, but finally settled on, "Easier."

"You're welcome, and if this is easier, I don't think I want to imagine what more difficult would look like," I said. "But anything I can do to help, just let me know. Even if it's fucking off so you can have some privacy."

"It okay," Callie said, and wiped at her eyes with a tissue. "We're going to do good here, and everything that I had to go through, it's documented now. Maybe we can make sure no other girl has to go through what I did."

There were so many shining eyes looking at her.

I wasn't sure what had happened in that room, and what was on that tape or file, or whatever they recorded the deposition with. I didn't want to know either. I knew in my heart that it would just make me bloody angry. I steadied myself, taking a centering breath. I didn't need to let my emotions get me all hot and bothered, not considering what I had on hand. I sat next to Callie, and she gave me a smile. Her eyes were still puffy, and her face was red from crying. What horrors and abuse had she shared with them?

Fuck me, I didn't want to know.

"Are you alright?" I asked.

"Yes, yes I am," she whispered, and pressed her head against the side of my shoulder. I put an arm around her, and for all the world, I wanted to destroy the people who had hurt her. Thinking of it, I felt my cool trying to slip. Kyle put a hand on my other shoulder and gave it a squeeze before moving to engage Tate and her people.

I was thankful for him. He was a social assassin. He knew exactly what to do, and how to do it. Fuck me, I was sure that it he wanted to leave Tate's office with her panties in his pocket, he could.

I turned back to hold Callie. She seemed so small in my arms, but just being there soothed her spirits.

In that moment, with my arm around her, and my face pressed against the top of her head, I had an answer to Lachlan's question; I loved her.

Fuck.

This wasn't some riff on *The Bodyguard*, and I didn't care about her because I was some wanna-be White Knight looking for a princess to rescue. I didn't need to make myself feel like a big man with a little woman to save.

"So, what's next?" Tate asked.

"Dinner reservations at *Le Jefferson*," Kyle said.

"Oh, Lord, not like this," Callie said.

"There is plenty of time before our reservation for you to clean up and redo your makeup, and anything else you might need to handle."

"Duly noted," I said.

"We'll take a day or so," Tate said. "But our people are going to clean up that reel, and then we'll get everything ready to go. It won't take much to get this to our legal department and the public relations desk. Then, we go with everything at one time, hitting New Eden, Rex, and Triple E with this at the same time. We'll file the subpoenas, see what we can get for warrants, and the press release, all in sync."

"Is that important?" I asked.

"With a group as large and wealthy as New Eden, it's vital. We have to hit them with all we have as quickly as possible. Ideally, they will be cut off at the knees, tangled in legal and police procedure while trying to not look like the bastards that they are," Tate said, crossing her arms over her chest.

"Perfect," Kyle said.

ALMOST AN HOUR LATER, we were back in the car, returning to the house on the edge of the bay. Kyle handled the sedan like a fighter pilot, and I kept wondering if we were being chased. Every time I looked back, I saw nothing, but he continued his pace like a madman.

"Why are we going so quick?" Callie asked, gripping the armrest with tense fingers.

"Because one way or the other, we're out in the open now," Kyle said. "Roan said that the chance of someone working at Fallout being a mole for New Eden is so high that, yeah. They have a mole one way or another. If they don't, it'd be a shocker," he said.

"Unlikely," Sadie added.

"Then as soon as their plan hits, New Eden will know the general vicinity of where you are, and they will act," he said, sliding off the interstate and onto the highway that looped out toward the bay and the house. "But we completely expect them to act, so whatever they do, they're already chasing after us, and have no idea what they're getting into."

"Is this going to be a repeat of the Bootlegger Head incident?" I asked.

"No, no," Sadie said. "We have contacts in the local police, and a private security firm in the area. I'm sure by now that Roan has compromised Fallout's systems."

"Compromised?" Callie asked. "But they're on our side."

"They are, and we trust Tate, but Fallout is a group, and we don't trust that *entire* group. Roan will have his fingers inside their system, and we'll known everything they know by the time we get back. Then it will be showers. I know the dessert tonight at *Le Jefferson* is a *croquembouche*, and those are splendid."

"But what about Marion?" Callie asked.

"We aren't doing anything to Marion or Fallout, but we also aren't putting all of our trust and eggs into that basket," Kyle said. "Your safety is our number one concern."

"This seems like such a rollercoaster," Callie said.

"It is, but it will be over soon enough, with the things you told us, and the medical records from Carter and Doc Max. This is devastating," Sadie said.

"Roan says our reservation has been confirmed and we have our favorite table, love," Kyle said, and Sadie beamed. She gave Callie's hand a squeeze and a warm smile.

"You're going to love *Le Jefferson*."

21

———

*C*allie...

     I had my reservations about this *Le Jefferson* restaurant, no pun intended. Sadie was beaming at me as though she hadn't just shared some very dark and painful things about her own past with me to help ease me into talking more about mine. Or maybe it really was just to make me feel less alone. In any case, I wasn't alone. I knew I wasn't, and that was what I was doing all of this for.

The August and the rest of New Eden were going to kill me for it, too. I knew that. I was still wrestling with coming completely to terms with that knowledge, but I was honestly tired. So very tired, and so what would be would be.

I turned to look in Kurt's direction and he turned his head and looked down at me, his light-colored eyes unreadable behind the wall of mirrored aviator lenses that he had put up between himself and the world. Still, I could tell by the set of his mouth, the way it formed a grim line, and the hard edges that made up the rest of his expression, that he was on high alert and that he was worried for me.

I disentangled myself from Sadie's well-meaning grip and went to shelter in the shadow of Kurt's much larger frame, hugging his massive arm with both of mine and slipping my palm against his. His fingers curved around the back of my hand in a quick squeeze and then let go as the sleek silver sedan driven by Kyle Lachlan pulled up to the curb.

Sadie left out of the building that housed Fallout's headquarters and my nerves jangled at leaving its shelter. I mean, I highly doubted there was some New Eden sniper on one of the towering roofs around us, it wasn't August's style, but Arik... I fidgeted slightly and Kurt's hand returned to mine briefly.

"Easy there," he said, the timbre of his voice soothing. "Steady as she goes, now."

I sniffed and nodded and let his hand go, returning mine to the crook of his arm – just Calanthe Rex being escorted by her husband's bodyguard, nothing to be suspicious over. It'd happened before and would happen again. Everything was perfectly normal, or so I had been coached.

Give no one reason to suspect anything amiss and nothing was amiss. It was brilliant in its simplicity. We were hiding in plain sight to a degree, but I was sweating under my borrowed blazer and felt flushed to my knees below the hem of my borrowed pencil skirt. I was the picture of modern chic and businesslike in all the latest designer labels. While Ms. Brooks was by far more muscular than I, we were about the same size, though I was taller and she far more compact.

Sadie got into the front seat after I had slid into the back, Kurt slipping into the car right behind me with more grace than someone of his size should have been able to manage. He immediately laid his hand over the top of mine where it rested between us on the seats while Kyle smoothly pulled away from the curb and into traffic.

"You alright, Love?" Kurt asked gently, and I was snapped out of my private thoughts. I looked up at him and gave him a tight-lipped smile.

"I will be," I lied.

Truthfully, after the horrified looks and the equally haunted expressions of pity I had received from the other women in that room, I didn't know if I was ever going to be okay again.

I guess there was a point where the abuse and the life you were living all became so... *normal.* At least to you, the person living it. Like, you get trapped in this micro chasm of daily life and yes, it's awful, and yes, it's horrific to anyone that is on the outside who can look in – but that doesn't necessarily happen. And so, you have no frame of reference, at least not really. It all became, *so this is just my life now...* and now that it *wasn't* my life anymore, looking back and talking about it? I was finally getting the big picture on just how awful everything really was and I was having to look in the mirror that was the tears on their faces and... and *holy shit*, just what had I survived?

I mean, was some of it really so awful?

Yes. According to the rest of the women in that room, it really was, and I was left feeling so small, so ashamed, and goodness, wasn't that the thing?

I was feeling ashamed. Me. Over surviving what New Eden had done to me. I sat beside Kurt, my hand beneath his as we were being whisked away through DC and my skin just *crawled.* I wanted to *beg* for a shower before we did anything else after recounting the tales of how I'd been touched, how I'd been used, and how they had treated me.

As though I were the dirty one. As though I were the filthy one.

I mean, I knew that wasn't true. I knew that I was far from it, that I wasn't those things, that those things had been imposed upon me, my will subverted, and that I was a prisoner at the mercy of a group of fiends but I couldn't help the miasma of confusion that clouded my thoughts and feelings.

A few hours later, after I had received the requisite shower and freshening up – including a change of clothes into something quite a bit lovelier and fancier than I'd had occasion to wear in what felt like a very long time – I found myself sighing as Kyle piloted the new and much less non-descript vehicle we were in to the curb back in DC.

A hunter-green carpet on the sidewalk, edged in gold beneath an awning that was likewise, a perfect hunter green and likewise edged in gold, bespoke the level of opulence awaiting us at *Le Jefferson*. I fixed my eyes on the street number emblazoned on the arching front of that awning and for whatever reason, fixated on it.

A man with white gloves in a dapper hunter-green coat edged in more gold, twin rows of gold buttons on the front of his coat, stepped up to the door of the SUV, blocking my view of the awning. A white shirt collar, crisp and neat peeked over the fine coat's collar. He wore a military-esque captain-like hat, equally green with gold trim, the short black bill shading his eyes. Even his pants were a matching green for the carpet and the awning with a gold stripe down the side of his leg.

He opened Sadie's door first and then Kurt's. I leaned back where I had practically draped myself over Kurt's lap to see out the window. Kurt rose like a leviathan from the deep, drawing the front of his jacket closed as he stood, and the man's white glove appeared in the portal to the car to help me out. I rose with the aid of that steady hand, and I longed to be like the man behind it.

Simple, a blue-collar and essentially anonymous worker to the men and women in their power suits around us, notables being ushered in through the heavy wooden doors with its sparkling glass panes beyond into the sparkling marble and gilt lobby, only to be ushered past the Maître D's little stand and into the dimly lit restaurant and bar.

I knew this type of place. Maybe had even been to this one in particular before, although truthfully, they all seemed the same.

"Are you sure?" I asked Kurt softly while Kyle and Sadie went through the doors before us, the doorman holding the door for them and looking to us expectantly as I faltered in my smart, designer pumps.

How I longed to be anonymous. How I wished I were anyone but who I was right now.

"Aye, if the captain deems it to be so, it's safe," Kurt murmured, putting his hand to the small of my back and guiding me through the door into the glitz and glamour beyond.

I *had* been here before, a long time ago, in another life. A special dinner for the first sons and daughters of New Eden. There had been five of us, a delegation to the capital as teens in high school to lobby for the good congressmen and women to adopt greener policies and to enact more legislation designed to protect our planet, or so I had thought. It hadn't struck me then as it did now that the lot of us wore purity rings and had devoted ourselves to the planet, or that Scott, one of the two boys that had been with us, had a private meeting with a senator and how quiet he had been after.

I never did find out how that meeting had gone, just that Scott had changed. Gone from boisterous and smiling to subdued and haunted in the blink of an eye and then, I had just never seen him again. His family had been transferred to another state, a different division of New Eden in the state that the senator had been from.

My heart hurt for him, and I wondered now what had happened, but I think, deep down in my aching heart, I knew.

We were seated at a table near the bar and Kyle ordered himself a drink. Something fancy made with gin; I think. I didn't know. I was only recently old enough in the last few years to drink but my intake had been closely monitored. I didn't especially like the taste of alcohol and so I didn't know much about what was good versus what wasn't. The last time I had drunk was the wine with Kurt on the way here, states and states away. I liked it enough to have a second glass of it... but I didn't know what it was and to ask would only give me away... that I shouldn't be drinking at all.

"Have a drink, Kurt," Kyle ordered, and Kurt frowned.

"No, thanks," he said tersely, and his eyes drifted back to me. I smiled a bit and hid it with the wine list that Sadie had handed me.

"I don't know," I said, trying to sound indecisive. "What's good?" I asked when the woman looked at me expectantly. She smiled and narrowed the expansive list of wines down to two or three options while Kyle's tone shifted to slightly impatient.

"Seriously," Kyle said, eyeing Kurt sharply. "Have a drink. They don't have beer, but they have almost everything else you could imagine."

Something passed between the two men and Kurt nodded while Sadie and the Sommelier concluded helping me chose something to my taste. I was familiar with this back-and-forth, the *what will you be dining on,* and *the chef's suggestions for this and that.*

We settled and looked over the offerings for today. The limited menu printed on crisp expensive cardstock was something to behold and wasn't nearly as distracting enough as boisterous laughter from the corner that caused me to jump slightly. Kurt put his hand on my knee beneath the tablecloth and I flashed him a brief, grateful smile.

Our drinks came, and our orders were placed. I fought valiantly not to reach for Kurt's hand, to remain in the parts we played. Just the celebrity's wife accompanied by the celebrity's security – nothing more. Kyle and Sadie seemed to be intimately familiar with the menu and even seemed to know the staff. How often did they come here? At least Kurt seemed as nervous as I felt, his posture was stiff, his face was tight too. I recognized that body language – he was on guard. This wasn't a nice dinner out for him, and maybe if he felt wary, maybe my worries were legitimate, and that made me feel a little better.

Kyle was speaking though I had no head for truly listening as my eyes roved the opulent, yet still chic interior of *Le Jefferson.*

"Isn't it fabulous?" Sadie asked smiling.

I smiled in return and nodded. "They've updated things since I was last here," I said.

"Oh, you've been?" she asked.

I nodded. "A lifetime ago, as part of a New Eden teen leadership delegation while I was still in school. We were here in the capitol to lobby for tighter EPA restrictions and regulations on some of the titans of industry who are the worst offenders."

"Let me guess, a certain billionaire and his capitalism-driven online-ordering service?" Kyle asked lightly.

I nodded and said, "That would be one, yes."

"Did any of your bills pass or succeed?" Sadie asked curiously.

"As I rightly recall, they did not." I startled at the voice too close behind my chair. "As I live and breathe, Calanthe Hardy. Oh! Excuse me, it's Rex now, innit?"

I put on a tight-lipped smile and cast a look at Kurt that said *I told you so*, before I turned my face to the Texas senior senator, Hiram Emerson, the August's much older brother. As in there was an almost twenty-year difference between the two. Still... the brothers were close, and I was certain before Hiram even left the restaurant that the August would hear of this.

"It most certainly is, you know that, Senator," I said lightly.

He chuckled deeply and rested a hand on my shoulder, giving it a squeeze. Kurt bristled beside me, and Sadie and Kyle gave Hiram a flat and almost unfriendly look. Kyle's smile almost glacier in its coldness and certainly in its pace where it spread on his lips.

"Senator Emerson," Kyle drawled, and it was a sudden and almost too-perfect middle American, midwestern accent where there had been none before.

"I do apologize, sir, but I do not think I have had the honor of your acquaintance." Hiram smiled at Kyle, his friendly grip on my shoulder tightening to something almost painful.

"I don't have the honor of representing any of our fine states, but I do represent a number of *financial interests,*" Kyle said and that sounded downright chilly. He introduced himself with some fake credentials or other and I sat mute. Sadie's gaze fixed on mine, silently asking if I was okay. I telegraphed back silently, to the best of my ability, that I was alright and to not make a scene.

Hiram laughed and I jumped.

"Well, Miss Calanthe," he said. "You sure are keeping interesting company these days. I'm sure your husband knows all about it?"

"Of course, he does," I said smiling. "I don't do anything without Arik, you know that. It's just a shame he couldn't join us tonight. You know how Hollywood schedules are."

His thumb pressed the back of my neck over my collar, and he laughed. "Oh, I'm sure," he said. "I can't wait to tell Lil Eli I have seen you," he said. "Y'all have a nice dinner now, y'hear?"

"Of that, there is no doubt," Kyle shot back with a wink over the rim of his glass. Hiram almost paled under his spray tan at the mockery in Kyle's voice.

"Well, I'll let you be, Miss *Callie*. I'm sure I'll see you around New Eden real soon," Hiram said. "I'm still trying to get that brother of mine to put that next complex down in the Lone Star state. It would look right nice. Ought to get that Hollywood husband of yours and you down for the ribbon cutting." He let out another chuckle.

I gave him my brightest, emptiest smile and said back, "I'm sure it will," even as my stomach rebelled at the very thought.

He was several tables away when Kurt muttered for our table alone, "Over my dead body. Bloody git."

I pressed my lips together in a tight line.

"Cal, are you okay?" Sadie asked softly.

I shook my head and met Kurt's eyes. His expression softening some as he read what was in my heart.

I didn't want that. It had to be my worst fear at this point. *Over his dead body* was a distinct possibility and I was terrified of that eventuality.

Unfortunately, or fortunately, depending on how you looked at it, Kyle was keen on reading faces and mine was no exception.

"It's not going to happen, Callie. You can trust us on that," he said, downing the rest of what was in his glass and holding it up and catching our waitresses' eye. She nodded from where she was taking an order across the room and he lowered the base of the glass to the crisp, white tablecloth.

"What are you doing?" Kurt asked, taking my attention off Kyle and causing me to turn to Sadie.

"Texting Roan," she said lightly.

"The board is set, and the pieces are in play," Kyle said with a chuckle, and Sadie arched one delicate eyebrow in his direction.

Kurt's scowl got a scowl as his eyes bounced between the man and woman.

"Just what the devil are you playing at?" he demanded.

"That you'll have to ask Roan," Kyle declared as the waitress set down a fresh drink in front of him. "He's the mastermind of this job. And he wants to know if they will pack up an osso buco to go for him."

Kurt didn't look happy, which in turn made me nervous. Sadie smiled and patted my hand.

"It'll be fine, I promise," she said. "Roan will have it all in hand."

"Exactly," Kyle said. "So, all you gotta do is relax and enjoy the meal."

His words were punctuated by the arrival of our plates. I took a deep and cleansing breath and with an eye on Kurt, who seemed to trust Roan and by default these two implicitly, I decided to make a leap of faith. I spread my neatly pressed cloth napkin in my lap and tried to enjoy my food.

Still, I couldn't help it. I couldn't shake the dread that this was serving as some sort of *last* meal after the appearance of Hiram Emerson. I already knew he had tattled to his brother, if he hadn't yet then it was beyond likely he was doing so right now and that was scary. Hiram may be the older of the two, but Elijah? August Elijah Emerson was by far the smarter.

22

urt...

There was only one word for this – insanity.

We were supposed to be hiding from attention, so that New Eden wouldn't find us, and instead, we were sitting in the middle of a large restaurant, surrounded by dozens of people that I recognized. I recognized them because they were on the news regularly – senators, heads of committees, celebrities. This was probably one of the worst places we could have come, and maybe the captain and his compatriots didn't understand what was going on.

Their lives weren't on the line.

There was also a chance that there was a plan in the works and the captain hadn't seen fit to tell me, but I wasn't so sure.

Seeing Senator Emerson was sobering. He was part of the reason that New Eden was strong and only getting more powerful. I knew enough about American politics that the fact that he was in Texas and supporting this, and not getting run out of the state, spoke to his popularity and influence.

"I mentioned this was a bad idea," I half-growled, half-whispered to Kyle.

"Relax, Kurt, relax," Kyle said. "This is all in hand."

"I fail to see how you've got this *all in hand*."

"Have some imagination, and faith," he said, offering me a toast from his absurd gin and whatever cocktail he was having.

"That is the older brother of the leader of the New Eden Centre, and he knew her on sight, you might have noticed."

"I am fully aware of that, and as we're somewhat regular guests here, we have an idea of the people who come here. This place is among the most elite regular restaurants. Elite enough that you and Calanthe alone wouldn't be able to get in here," he said, his voice low. "And I'm sure that you didn't even know about this place."

"Make your point quicker," I said.

"Calanthe's general location was going to become general knowledge as soon as the Fallout stuff goes live, but now, the people who might be willing to try something will know that she has powerful friends," Kyle said. "The sort of powerful friends who have the ability to have a table at a restaurant that hosts the president of the United States, foreign heads of state, and the guys who run banks and military industrial companies. This restaurant hosts those ten-thousand-dollar-a-plate dinners that the Washington elite enjoy so well."

"So, this was deliberate?"

"It was a calculated gambit, according to Roan," Kyle said.

"A calculated gambit?" I asked, and my voice started to rise. I felt my fists clenching and the urge to action starting to boil up inside my chest.

"Staff Sergeant Worthington," Kyle said, and it was with the tone of a superior officer. "I'm going to need you to stand down."

"But—"

"But Calanthe is safe. New Eden isn't going to send commandos, or ninjas, or assassins after you. When they respond, it's going to be through press releases and conferences, and legal missives. This battle is going to be played out in courtrooms and news briefings. There isn't going to be a running multi-state gun battle with car chases and a helicopter with a guy shooting a rocket launcher out the side door," he said.

"Pardon?" a woman, sitting at the next table over, looked over at our conversation.

"He's a big Bruce Willis fan," Sadie said. "He was telling us about one of those movies he did, the action one." The woman gave a polite smile, and nodded, and Kyle looked back at me. His charisma was palpable, and I couldn't unclench my fists.

"It's okay," Callie said, her voice wavering softly. She said the words, but the look in her eyes shared my fears and concerns. Seeing that, I felt my jaw clench. I would *not* let anything happen to her, and this entire thing felt like a bad idea. A series of bad ideas, and if there was anyone who knew anything about bad ideas, it was me.

I was the king of bad ideas. Why wouldn't I know one when I saw it?

I stared Callie in the eyes and guilt gnawed at me.

I had told her that it was safe...

THE DRIVE back to the house was tense.

Maybe it was because she sensed it, or maybe it was part of their plan, but Sadie showed us a part of the house we hadn't seen before. The mansion had a panic room. Not a tiny, armored box with a panic button, but a regular-sized room with armored walls, an arsenal of weapons in wall cases, and a full suite of electronics and communication equipment.

"What if they cut the power?" I asked.

"Solar panels on the roof and about half of the windows in this place generate electricity through piezoelectric principals," the captain said. "Plus, there is a small outbuilding behind the house that houses a diesel generator, and there are battery packs lining the walls of the basement. Despite how big this house is, its carbon footprint is almost zero."

"Almost?" Callie asked.

"We're still attached to the grid, state law, and in certain situations, we do draw a small amount of power. Most of the time, this house is putting a modest amount of electricity into the grid. It's when we hit a long period of overcast weather that also happens to be hot, and the solar isn't running full capacity and the AC is. Rather than drain all the batteries down, we meter in electricity. When the sun is out, the panels are charging capacitors and batteries, and the house can run on what's been gathered throughout the day."

"That's surprisingly green of you," Callie said, her eyes wandering across the room, bulging a little at the large variety of guns and other weapons lining the walls.

"When we recommended our mutual friend Worthington to New Eden, it was because we had been fooled by them and assumed that they were what they appeared to be – a group interested in saving the earth," Sadie said.

"Let's not get preachy," Kyle said. "We thought they were green. Roan did a lot of green stuff in this house, and it's saved money, and gave everyone warm fuzzy feelings, and now we know what they're really about."

"Is that why you're doing this?" Callie asked.

"It kinda is," Sadie said.

"I'm going to get a drink. Does anyone else want anything?" Kyle asked and excused himself.

"He drinks a lot, doesn't he?" I asked.

"Not as much as it appears. The drinks are smaller than you think," Sadie said.

"So why did we make an appearance at *Le Jefferson*," I asked. "It seems like a foolish and pointless risk, and if it was for some dish, they obviously make to-go orders."

"You are familiar with the concept of a strategic feint?" the captain asked.

"This isn't the Royal Marine Corps, sir," I said as calmly as I could. "And we aren't tanks and helos."

"It isn't and we aren't," he agreed. "But that's what we are doing. We want New Eden to make a play, to show their hand. Fallout and Tate have a timetable on their press releases and subpoenas that they're going to be firing into New Eden like torpedoes."

"And what does that have to do with us exposing ourselves?"

"Because it's part of the plan," he said. "In the morning, Sadie and Lach are going to pack up and go stay at that cabin of yours in the park. There's some accidental intel in the Fallout missives that is going to refer to it. We both know that there will be moles inside Fallout who are still faithful to New Eden, and they will know that Kurt and Callie are going to be at a remote and secure location."

"You're putting Kyle and your girlfriend in my cabin as decoys?" I asked.

"Yes, they are highly capable and competent, plus we have a few other friends we reached out to, for an assist. If New Eden sends some sort of package to find you and the lovely Mrs. Rex, they're going to find an elite paramilitary force waiting for them in an entrenched position, well-armed, well-equipped, and highly informed."

"You're going to kill them?" Callie asked, her voice a little strained.

"While there is certainly that chance, the plan is non-lethal apprehension. We want to, ideally, take them prisoner. We shall then turn them over to DHS, since human trafficking and sex crimes are involved. They'll likely treat them as terrorists operating in the United States."

"That's... that's not a terrible plan, actually," I said.

"I'm glad the staff sergeant agrees with his captain," he said. "Because the subpoenas and media firestorm are going to be a kick in the knackers for New Eden. Capturing and interrogating a New Eden paramilitary force operating in proximity to the U.S. capital, that will be a knife in their heart. This has to be public and visible, because the real heavy hitter that is going to take New Eden down isn't us, or the Justice department or even Homeland Security."

"Public opinion?" Callie said. "New Eden has a huge PR wing, and public opinion is a major concern for them."

"Exactly," he said. "So, Sadie and Lach are going to go camping, and you two are fully welcome to all the amenities of the house for the duration of your stay. Full kitchen – I like to cook for company – a pool, a hot tub, a boat down on the dock, a full library with a billiards table, and a pretty solid gym."

"Home delivery takes care of the rest?" Callie asked.

"It does indeed, my fiery angel," he said. "With the bum leg, I'm not super keen on going to the market, but there are plenty of apps that bring everything I could want right to me. And the house is registered under an LLC, so if you're still concerned about security, you shouldn't be."

"You do seem to have a lot of guns," Callie said.

"These, bah, these are trophies and prizes we've collected from the missions we've done. There are weapons and armor lockers scattered throughout the house and grounds; certain walls have been reinforced with steel plating so that anything less than a vehicle-mounted machine gun won't penetrate them, plus the outer wall was seriously reinforced when we renovated."

"Learned some lessons from the Escadrille?" I asked casually, muscles unknotting themselves the more my captain spoke.

"Indeed. I'm not going to lay out all of the house defenses, my good man, but be assured, they are impressive," he said. "Better than the setup I had down on Bootlegger Head, and that almost stopped a triple alliance of cartels and organized crime syndicates before going up."

"Bootlegger Head was a beautiful house." Sadie sighed.

"Historically registered residence," he said. "This place is nice, and upgrading it was easier, but there's nothing special about it. It was built by some local shipping mogul, utilizing a local fancy architect imitating Hollywood and Beverly Hills – big windows, open space, and some surprisingly cheap building materials."

I nodded, and Callie seemed to be hanging on to his every word.

"I'm digressing," he said. "You really don't want to hear about how this place had white pine flooring, and how I got rid of that mess. You're still dressed to the nines and would probably like to get cleaned up and relax. Have a drink or two, enjoy each other's company, and don't worry about anything for a little while. I've got the best security this side of Fort Knox, and my drones are armed for parties of ten or more."

I saw the beginnings of a smile creep across Callie's face. She was hesitant, and I knew that she was worried, because admitting things might be okay was a good way to invite the universe to come give you a tap between the thighs, a reminder that everything was supposed to be terrible.

"I think that is a good idea," Callie said. "You said there was a hot tub?"

"Indeed, I did." He smiled. "Enjoy."

23

---

*C*allie…

"Come with me," I breathed and tugged on Kurt's hand.

"What?" he asked distractedly.

"Come with me," I repeated. He looked up from his phone and tossed it on the bed.

"Come with you where, Love?"

"The hot tub."

"What?" he asked, frowning. "You serious?"

I nodded and he loosened his tie. We were back in our borrowed room and were supposed to be relaxing but all I could think about now was the clean smell of chlorine and the hot water soothing the tension out from around my spine. But I didn't want to go alone. I wanted Kurt. I wanted to sit on his lap to keep my chin above the water and I wanted to feel his strong arms around me.

"I sometimes don't understand the way you think," he said but it was with a smile curving his lips.

I pulled mine down, trying to hide my smile and smarted off, "Well, I do have drain bamage," I said. He laughed at that then stopped himself to check that I had meant to say it that way and at my giggle started laughing again.

"You are a treasure," he said, shaking his head as though he marveled at me and it made me glow from the inside, like any time he praised me.

I tugged on his hand lightly and towed myself closer to him, tipping my face up for a kiss. He kissed me, and I closed my eyes and swooned into his chest. I couldn't help myself. In all the time I'd been married to a big movie star, not once did he ever make me feel like it was *in* the movies.

No, that was Kurt – his hands on my hips, his lips against mine, making me lean in, one foot popping up off the ground like some ridiculous heroine in some ridiculous romantic movie. Except our story, as crazy as it was, wasn't any sort of movie, it was our life. Maybe, someday, it would be a film. I mean, stranger things *had* already happened.

He drew up out of my reach and I blinked up at him in surprise. His light blue eyes were heavy lidded with desire, and he murmured, "Keep at me like that, we'll never make it to the hot tub."

I smiled and giggled a little, and he traced a tendril of my hair that'd escaped my smart French braid off my forehead and behind my ear. His eyes bounced back and forth over my face as though he were memorizing every line and curve to paint it later. Which it struck me then, just how little I knew about Kurt Worthington... I mean, did he draw or paint? What did he do besides read?

"What?" he asked me as the realization chased across my mind behind my eyes.

"I just realized how very little I know about you," I whispered.

"Oh?" he asked, raising an eyebrow.

"The way you looked at me just then..." I trailed off and he cocked his head.

"Like what?" he asked.

I smiled gently and said, "Like you were memorizing me, almost like to draw or paint me later."

He laughed then and I grinned, but I quickly lost that grin when I said, "And I realized, I don't even know, do you draw? Do you paint? What is it you love to do besides read?"

He looked down at me thoughtfully and finally said, "Go find a swimsuit, and let's continue this discussion in the hot tub, yeah?"

I smiled and nodded, and he let me go.

I found a black one-piece in the wardrobe in here that Sadie had filled with some of her things that suited me. Meanwhile, Kurt found a pair of black-and-blue swim trunks amidst his things.

We both covered up with the thick white terrycloth spa robes that seemed to be on hand in every guest room or bathroom in the mansion, and it made me secretly wonder if they were there because our two hosts and one hostess spent a lot of time naked or what?

Truthfully, Sadie was the type that I could probably just ask, and she would tell me. I pictured of the three of them only Roan getting flustered.

Kurt and I wound our way through the expansive mansion, and I asked as we padded barefoot over marble floors and through plush, high-pile carpets, "What had you frowning so over your phone?"

"Oh, that was a good frown," he said.

I laughed and asked, "How is any frown a good one?"

He chuckled and held the door for me to the back patio. The sun was starting to set, and even though we were on the opposite shore, and it wasn't setting over the water but rather land, the sky was still a beautiful shell pink and yellow over the water as the sun dipped behind the mansion.

I slipped out onto the plateau of the back patio, raised and made of rock, the pool a lapis lazuli in the deepening shadow, the hot tub already frothing and lit. Kurt turned to the nearest camera and gave it a salute and I laughed.

"I was merely concentrating on some investments the captain took a liberty to make on my behalf with some of my cryptocurrency," he said.

"Ah, wait... you don't sound mad."

"I'm not. He cashed out a substantial sum like I'd asked, and the few and small investments he made are already seeing gains. Some quite impressive gains. It's hard to be mad about that."

"Oh, I see." I thought about it for a minute and said, "If we get out of this alive and I somehow manage to see any money from a divorce or whatever, maybe he could help me. I'm afraid I don't exactly have any marketable skills. I'm afraid I don't know how I'm going to survive in a world that I've never really been a part of, you know?"

He gripped my shoulders and looked at me, a small and almost, I don't know... proud, smile on his lips?

"You asked me what I liked to do," he said, and I nodded, untying the sash of my robe. He pushed back the thick, warm material and a breeze off the bay was brisk.

"Ooo!" I gave a slight shiver, and he held my hand and helped steady me as I stepped down into the steaming water. There was nothing for it. With a braid past my waist and hair to my knees when it was unbound, it was going to get wet, so I didn't worry about it.

I sank into the water and sure enough, when I sat on the bench, it came up over my mouth and tried to invade my nose. Kurt slid in with a hiss and a sigh and sat down with some of the jets at his broad back and I drifted over to him. I slipped my arms around his neck and settled on his lap, the extra few inches keeping my neck to my shoulders out of the water.

"So, is this why you dragged me down here, Love?" he chuckled, and I giggled and shook my head.

"No, I mean, I sort of knew I needed you as a... shit. What do you call it? Um, tower seat?"

"High chair?" he asked, and I shook my head.

"No, a high chair doesn't – booster seat! That's the word for it!"

He nodded and shook his head at me, his expression charmed.

"Don't change the subject," I murmured. "You were just telling me..."

"Oh! Right, sorry, Love." He massaged the back of my neck and craned his to kiss my temple.

"Survival is what I like to do, is what I'm passionate about, I guess."

"I'm sorry?" I blinked and felt like my eyes maybe went crossed, I thought about it so hard for a moment.

"You know," he said. "Hunting, fishing, foraging, and living off the land and the like. You want I should teach you?"

"Me?" I asked a bit incredulous.

"Well, yeah!" He nodded, palming my hip beneath the waterline, and massaging it gently. "Why not?"

I laughed a bit. "You and me in a cabin in the woods somewhere, what foraging for mushrooms and shooting?" I sputtered, looking for the right word for it failing and falling back on my childhood with "Bambi's mom?"

He laughed outright the. I mean threw back his head and *laughed.* Deep from his chest – no, lower from his belly. He laughed and laughed, the sound rich and joyous like a fountain of chocolate cascading around me, warmer than even the water we sat in.

I smiled and waited for him to calm down and answer me.

"Well, yeah," he said, wiping a tear from the corner of his eye and it almost mollified me. I don't think I had ever seen him so relaxed and just, *happy,* and it struck me...

You. You are what makes him this happy.

I bit my lips together, overcome with emotion at that.

The two of us honestly couldn't be more different and yet, and yet somehow our love was finding its way.

I shifted, laying my hand against his cheek, resting my forehead against his and closed my eyes asking softly, barely audible above the bubbling jets, "You really think I could? That I could master it?"

"Oh, Love," he said, bringing his hands out from the water and cupping my face in his hands. He pulled my forehead from his and replaced it with his lips, kissing me soundly and I melted.

"You can do anything," he said, bringing his forehead back to rest against mine and holding me close. I shifted and put a knee to either side of him on the stone bench beneath the frothing white, blue waters, and my arms around his neck. I was taller now like this.

I kissed him then and he hummed out. I could feel he was growing hard between us, and I loved that whenever he and I were alone like this, he almost instantly grew hard for me. It was almost as though I could think his erection into being and it was an honestly powerful feeling.

I loved that I was beautiful to him, and that he believed in me, and I knew it when he looked at me, that it wasn't my face that he found lovely. That Kurt loved my mind, and my spirit such that it was, before he loved me for my looks.

"Hey, you two! Can you hit the pause button on this fuckery for just a minute?" I jumped and turned. Kyle and Sadie strode toward us in... in forest camouflage tactical gear.

"Oi, what's that?" Kurt asked and I loved that the longer he spent with his old captain, the more pronounced his British accent became.

"Need the keys to your cabin if it's all the same to you. We'd like to post up," Sadie said with a grin bordering on feral.

"Red Queen over here hasn't had any action in a minute. She might be a little too excited," Kyle muttered into his wrist.

Sadie rolled her eyes.

"What White King said, Black King. Now shut up."

I turned back to Kurt whose eyebrows were raised and he was trying not to laugh.

"Key is on the ring with my truck keys up in our room, bedside table. It's the one with the green rubber gasket, brass key. If you don't mind, take just the cabin key, and leave me the rest, yeah?"

"You got it," Kyle said with a smirk.

"Enjoy yourselves," Sadie sang out and they turned and went back toward the house.

"Why do I think I should be scared of them?" I asked.

"Because you should. Everyone should."

"But Sadie is so nice to me—"

"Aye, and we'd like to keep it that way, Love." He sighed and his hands went to my hips and gave them a squeeze. I resituated myself so I was sitting across his lap again. "You've not got anything to fear from the likes of them, but I think New Eden does."

"God, I hope so," I said.

A bird flew overhead and swooped down to the water and Kurt stiffened under me his eyes sharp as he looked at it. His hands tightened with excitement.

"That's a Double-crested Cormorant, that one," he said, nodding in its direction as it settled out of sight, likely in the shallows of the Chesapeake.

"It was big," I said, eyes wide.

He nodded, grinning.

"You like birds?" I asked.

"Oh, aye."

I smiled faintly. "Is that how I got the moniker Cardinal?" He lifted a hand out of the water and traced a finger along my braid.

"It is," he said. "Ever seen one?"

"Once, I think. I glimpsed a flash of red in a tree on a winter DC trip. It was dusk, so I don't really know if it was one or not."

"Likely it was." He nodded.

"I think I'd like to watch the birds with you," I murmured.

He smiled. "No time like the present, Love," he said. I settled back against him as he held me and we looked to the surrounding trees and property for birds and listened for any stray song.

It was nice.

Peaceful.

I think I could like this.

24

—————

*M*adeleine Oberisk...

Canvassing was slow work, but it had to be done right, otherwise there was no point doing it. We had been in Indigo City for a day and a half, cruising through neighborhoods that seemed to fit Kurt's profile for privacy and independence, as well as checking campgrounds and the cabins we could find. There was no luck on picking up the trail of his truck, and just finding the sole truck was problematic. There were tons of the vehicles here, and even being a decades-old model didn't help. It seemed like for every twenty normal trucks, there would be a retro or vintage model cruising around.

It made my eyes hurt; my head hurt. There was so much riding on this, and I had to find Calanthe. I had to be the one to rescue her.

I almost dropped my coffee when my phone rang. It was Alexander Soren, the August Emerson's high priest of misogyny, and the man that was going to have my ass exiled from New Eden if I didn't bring Calanthe back safely.

"What?" I answered, sharply.

"I have two bits of wonderful news for you, Oberisk." His voice was tight, but cordial. "We've gotten a lead on our missing pet and your hunch was almost correct." The way he was speaking, there were probably people in the room who weren't cleared at this level of security.

"Go on." I had to prompt him.

"It seems they have a place in Maryland, on the opposite side of the Chesapeake. It's a cabin in the middle of one of the parks over there. There are so many of them." I bit my tongue to not curse. I was right but was on the wrong side of the bay.

"I told you I was going in the right direction," I said.

"And so you were, which is why I have some good news for you. If you are able to give Sigma Team support when they move in for extraction, I'll let you remain at the New Eden Centre."

"You'll let me stay in security?" I asked.

"Oh, absolutely not. Either way, this is your last job. Screw it up, and you're gone. If you do it well, you'll get to come home to a lateral transfer to a job more suited to a woman."

My fist clenched and I heard the faint complaint of the metal and plastic in the phone case.

"Is that so," I said.

"It is indeed, and two pieces of good news, we've located, what did you call her, *Cardinal*, and you get to remain in New Eden's good graces."

"I consider myself blessed," I said through gritted teeth.

"And don't bother trying to contact your friend Mackenzie. She is no longer working in tech and communication, but you'll be able to see her if this works out for you. She's already accepted her lateral move."

"What did you do with her?" I asked, louder than I intended.

"Temper, temper, Oberisk. Housekeeping. Don't worry, you'll have overlap with housekeeping, but you won't actually be violating anyone's private quarters with your presence. Groundskeeping, if you were curious."

"Goddamn you, Soren," I said, but instead of defiant I felt defeated. That fucking asshole.

"You need to be in position in about an hour. I'll send the coordinates in a secure text. Don't be late."

"An hour?"

"An hour. Sigma Team is already on the ground. They took Rex's G700 and might have set a record for LAX to BWI. Now, move your dump truck of an ass and get into position, or start considering what you're going to do with a pink slip and a blacklisting."

Clicking end on a call was never going to be as satisfying as slamming a phone down on the receiver; there was no cathartic violence to the disconnect. That was just fucking frustrating as hell. Soren had pulled an end run on me, and Sigma was already on the ground and well ahead of us. "C'mon, we've got an addy on the other side of the bay, and we need to be there in less than an hour."

"There's no way," Lisa said from the driver's seat of REX3. She gestured to the GPS screen. The distance was certainly far enough, but the traffic we had to get through, and then crossing the Chesapeake Bay Bridge... We couldn't make that. As heavy and slow as REX3 was, it would be a struggle to meet that deadline with zero traffic and closed roads, and a fucking police escort.

"Doesn't matter. Sigma Team is on the ground and will be moving on target in an hour, and we're their backup." I let out a breath, and my stomach felt tensed and wadded into knots. This was going to cost me everything. I was going to be unemployed, homeless, and blacklisted in less than twenty-four hours. It was a shit trade, but what was the alternative? Leave Sigma to handle Kurt and whatever he had planned? What if Calanthe was harmed?

What if Sigma failed?

Kurt was a decorated former Royal Marine, and had spent years in the Afghan highlands. This could very easily turn into a bad fanfic of *Rambo*, but it would be a bunch of guys and few women who believed in a green and pure earth, trying to rescue as close to a princess as there was in America from a British commando.

This was going to be bad for them; no one on Sigma had military experience. They were paramilitary cosplayers with connections inside New Eden.

Fuck.

If we got there in time, we might be able to pull some of them aboard the RV and evac. Maybe my team and I might be what it took to turn the tide and ensure that Calanthe was rescued.

Lisa put the hammer down and all the green lights on the dash of the RV went out, and the crimson lights started blinking. We weren't running in economy mode, or fuel-efficient mode. The RV's electric motors were driving one axle, and the big diesel engine wasn't idling to power the batteries, it was pumping raw power to the rear axles. The big beast rolled down the interstate quickly, and Lisa white-knuckle drove it like a demolition derby-ace.

We crossed the Bay Bridge with nine minutes left.

By the time we reached the edge of the park, we were fifteen minutes late.

When we found Sigma Team's trio of rented black SUVs, we were almost an hour late. I wasn't prepared for what I found. I expected a jubilant Sigma Team, and Soren's mocking phone call that I was shitcanned, not even good enough to take out New Eden's trash and mow its grass with a reel mower.

I found just the three vehicles, no sign of the ten people in Sigma.

I flipped through my contact info, none of their phones connected, everything went straight to voicemail. That was a bad fucking sign. I called Soren, and there was no answer there either. The fuck was going on?

"So, here's the plan," I said, addressing the rest of my team. "We have a single Royal Marine, one hostage, and ten missing members of Sigma."

"There are only four of us," Cullen said. "If he was able to take out Sigma, I don't think the three of us, and Lisa will be able to do anything but end up as notches on his belt."

"He's got a point," Lisa said, the look on her face showing that she had no interest in being a notch on anyone's belt.

"We're going, and that's it," I said. "We don't quit until Calanthe is safe."

"I don't think I'm willing to risk my life for a movie star's wife," Jacobsen said.

"There's no reward here," Cullen said.

"Call Soren again, tap out," Lisa said. "We aren't prepared to deal with this."

"I just need you to fucking back me up because I am going to talk to Kurt, not threaten him with guns and violence. If I am alone, I've got nothing as leverage. I need all of you with me," I said, my voice rising.

"I'm just here because I want to save trees, Oberisk," Lisa said. "I'm not a fucking mercenary. I feel like I need to shower and change my pants after that drive just getting here, and this looks like a goddamn death trap."

"We need to call up for reinforcements," Cullen said. "That's as far as I am willing to go – hold this position so that he doesn't take off on the road again."

"What do I have to do to get you on my side?" I asked, my voice sharp, and entirely too much frustration and desperation boiling over into it.

"Call Soren, tell him we are standing down," Jacobsen said.

"You can tell him I fucking quit. The chief is scary as fuck and I'm not going to try facing him," Cullen said.

"This is just a job and not worth my life, Oberisk," Lisa said. "I mean, I know it's more than that to you, but Jesus, we don't bleed green."

"My blood is as red as yours," I said, but I felt the betrayal already. They didn't bleed green; they wouldn't suffer or sacrifice for New Eden. This just showed how shallow their devotion was. It was just a job, just money. I knew a defeat when I saw one, and this was just another in the campaign of my fucking miserable life.

"Fine."

"That's it?" Lisa asked.

"Yeah, take REX3 back to the paved road, the big service station just outside of the park. I'll be in touch soon enough. If you don't hear from me in two hours, you can assume Kurt won. If I call, you burn the rubber off those tires getting your asses to the addy because I will want evac for Calanthe as fast as fucking possible."

"Okay," they agreed. I don't know that I will ever feel that abandoned again in my life.

I hope I never feel that again.

There were no keys in the SUVs so there was nothing to do but walk to the address given. It was an estimation, and the gravel road only went a few hundred feet before it turned into a two-lane rutted path through the trees and undergrowth. Everything was thick and green, closed in. There was plenty of cover, but that went both ways, and this was his home ground, not mine. If he had traps laid, I would more than likely find them the wrong way.

Had he had the time to dig tiger pits and line them with Punji sticks? The thought of a six-to-eight-foot fall onto a bed of sharpened wooden posts made me shudder, my imagination filling the silence with phantom feelings of a sudden lurching fall and the sharp stab of raw wood into my thighs, my stomach.

He might have had claymores. The upside of those would be if I found one, I probably wouldn't realize it – just a bright light and no more Maddy.

There was no sign of damage to the plants, no screaming, no blood. It seemed like nothing had happened here. That made it all the more unnerving.

Something crunched under my foot.

A pair of polarized sunglasses. They were high end, and my foot had completely destroyed them. A few feet away there was a discarded fancy water, the bottle empty, and a black New Eden snap-back. Sigma had been here, and there was no sign of them now.

What the fuck was this? Was Kurt the Predator? Had he hung them from the trees?

I shuddered again and felt a liquid gurgle in my stomach.

When was the last time I had eaten?

The last time I had taken a shower, or more than a piss?

My head throbbed, and that was when I realized I had been clenching my jaw the entire time I had been walking up from where the SUVs had been parked.

"Kurt!" I shouted.

Silence.

"Kurt! Are you out there?"

More silence.

Then there was a crack, a twig breaking, a few leaves crunching. I froze and held my breath. I couldn't see whoever it was, but they couldn't see me either. The fact that I was unarmed suddenly loomed very large in my mind. Why in the fuck would I leave my pistol in the RV? Ehy hadn't any of my team thought to mention that my gun was very conveniently not on my hip?

For fuck's sake. I let out a breath.

"Kurt?" I asked again.

The other person moved. They were quick and quiet on their feet. I doubt I could move as quietly as they were. I took a few steps and then threw the hat I had found. The other person struck as I threw, much closer than I expected them, and they didn't go for the hat. It wasn't Kurt. He knew better than to try and take me down at the waist – my balance was better than his, and there was a chance that I was stronger than he was.

We grappled. I tried to find his shoulder, to put him in an arm bar, but he was too fast.

It was a man I didn't know who came face-to-face with me, but I recognized the eyes of a soldier, and reacted. The way he moved suggested he was expecting a knee to the crotch, so the hip throw worked well, and the stranger went ass over tea kettle into the brush.

"Who are you, where's Kurt?" I shouted.

"He's nowhere near here," the man said. "But you must be Oberisk, I've heard a little about you."

Before I could answer or ask another question, he was under me, fast as a cat, and less friendly. I didn't lose my feet, but it cost me bruises, and a hard elbow to the stomach, but I caught him. The grip was poor, nothing I could translate into a grapple, but I could redirect. Instead of smoothly moving into my space and peppering me with knuckles and elbows and then out, he came in, delivered violence, and then I almost threw him into a tree.

I wanted to hear the crunch of bone, a broken nose, but all I got was a grunt.

"I'm all out of darts, so we have to do this the old-fashioned way," a woman who was very much not Calanthe said. I looked up to face where she had appeared from the brush, brandishing a pistol at me. It wasn't some small thing, but a large frame revolver, likely a .357 by the look and size. Her grip was professional, and despite her small size, I had no doubt that she knew how to use the gun.

"I had this under control," the man said.

"We can argue later," she said. "You, on your knees."

"That's a first," I said, but there was no hint of amusement on her face. "Where's Calanthe, where's Kurt?"

"Not here," the man said.

"Give me one reason," the woman said. "One reason I shouldn't leave you here for the crows and the crabs."

"I'm only interested in rescuing Calanthe Rex. I want to find her and take her home, to where she will be safe," I said.

"She's safer here than she ever was with New Eden," the woman spat.

"You don't understand," I said, and the woman moved closer, the barrel of the gun suddenly closer to my face than I was comfortable with. For a split second, I had thought to disarm her just as soon as she was in range. She crossed that space too quickly; there was no hesitation. I knew if I moved, there was a really high chance that I would end up with a bullet in the face.

"No." she said and pressed the barrel against my forehead.

"Easy," the man said, more to her than to me.

"Either you are completely ignorant, or you're completely complicit," she pushed the gun for emphasis, "of what your organization does."

"We are an ecologically minded organization that works to reclaim the Earth from pollution and environmental destruction," I said, softly.

"New Eden traffics minors, and that's all it's about – underage pussy and money."

"No."

I had heard some of these lies before. The exiles who made Fallout said these things, and there were a few dissenters who spouted these lies. It was such a common lie.

"Callie is two years younger than you think she is. You falsified documents so that Arik Rex could marry and fuck a minor for several years, and that's not even talking about what other people inside your fucking cult did to her." I could see this woman believed every word she was saying, and there was fury in her eyes.

"What happened to the others?" I asked. "Are they dead?"

"No, they aren't," the man said. "They've been taken into custody by agents from the DHS and the Coast Guard. They left not too long ago. They're going to be treated as domestic terrorists."

"It was not smart of you to come alone," the woman said. "And DHS isn't coming back, they got everything they needed."

"I'm going to bind your hands behind you if you surrender. No one has to be shot in the head. We've made it all day with zero fatalities. Let's keep it that way," he said. I mouthed an *okay*, too petrified to nod my head. I let the stranger put my wrists behind my back and heard the soft whisper of cable ties binding me.

I felt shame at the sob I let out when the woman took the gun away from my head. He patted me down and took my phone. He seemed surprised that was all I had. The expression on his face, I felt sick with humiliation. He made me feel like a child pretending to be an adult, the way I had felt when I failed to measure up to become a First Daughter.

He tied me to a tree, and left me alone, for a while.

There was hushed conversation between the two of them, and I could only imagine it was over the fact that the woman really wanted to kill me, and that she hadn't, and he wasn't going to let her.

I didn't recognize her. She wasn't New Eden or Fallout.

My hands went numb, and my wrists ached from the cable ties. I would have killed to wipe at my face. I knew I looked awful, my eyes red and swollen from the silent tears I had shed.

Fuck.

"Hey," I said, my voice startling me with how raw it sounded.

"What?" the woman said.

"Can I have a drink, and I need to pee..." I croaked.

There was a long pause – silence that lasted for minutes, an eternity of minutes. Some sort of insect crawled across my leg and wiggled its legs at me before moving along.

"Hey?" I repeated.

"I don't care," the woman said. "If I bring you water, you'll just have to pee more. Hold it, you'll balance out."

There was another long silence, and then a hushed discussion.

The man walked to where I could see him, and he looked down at me, gauging me, seeing what condition I was in. Fucked, fucked was the condition I was in. I hadn't eaten properly in two days, just junk food and energy drinks, and not a full night's sleep in a week. I was ragged, and exhausted, and I could feel where we had fought before and now. I knew I had to be on the verge of dehydration.

He let me drink from a water bottle, and as absurd and insulting as it was, the water was cold, and I felt tears in my eyes again.

"We're leaving in the morning," he said.

"Please don't leave me tied to this tree," I said.

"We're not going to," he said. "You'll be blindfolded and driven to an undisclosed location, and then we're going to turn you loose. You'll be on your own to get back to your people. My companion is a little upset because we aren't going to do anything to you. I consider it... mercy."

"I don't want to die," I whispered.

"We're all going to die, every one of us, eventually," he said.

"Please don't *hurt* me," I managed. I couldn't even say the word. He certainly had the ability to do anything he wanted to me.

"Why would I harm you? You're disarmed, and detained," he said. "Does New Eden have a habit of harming people it apprehends?"

"No, we don't apprehend people, we're just private security," I said. He let out a chuckle, and I felt his eyes bore into me. "And I don't want my first time to be like this—"

"Wait... what?" He looked genuinely surprised. "Do you think I'm going to take advantage of you?"

"I don't know," I whispered.

"Well, I'm fucking not. Put that out of your mind. The only thing I'm here to do is walk you to the latrine so you can have a piss, and then back to the tree," he said. "Then I think we need to have a talk, just the two of us."

I nodded.

"Are you going to untie me?" I asked.

"No, I'm not. Your reputation is well deserved. I've not been thrown like that in a long time. I don't feel like having my head knocked in, thank you."

"So how I am going to do this?" I asked.

"I'll walk you to the latrine and will have to assist you with your pants. Other than that, I hope you can manage." His words had a hint of humor to them, but I could only feel my face flame with heat and a clench of fear between my legs.

"What about your companion?" I asked.

"Her words were, I believe, *she can piss herself for all I care.*" He gave me what I supposed was a disarming smile, like this was all quite amusing. "She's had experiences similar to what Calanthe has endured. She was a victim, once. She sees you as a willing accessory to what has been going on at New Eden. You being a woman makes her consider you a gender traitor."

He untied the rope from the tree and helped haul me up by a shoulder.

It was not often that a man dared to touch me – most were intimidated, or offended by me, just being there, taller than them, or stronger. He seemed respectful, but not otherwise bothered by my sheer existence.

"This is humiliating," I said as he walked me to their latrine. This was a fucking primitive campsite, and they weren't even using the cabin itself.

The tree laying smashed through the building explained that fairly simply.

Their car was a white-on-white Range Rover, and they had a mossy oak tent big enough for maybe four to sleep inside it.

There was no sign of Calanthe or Kurt.

This had been a fucking ruse, a trap, the entire time.

I looked up into the trees and the now almost completely dark sky as he unbuckled my belt, then my pants, and they fell around my ankles. The humiliation was almost complete. The air was cool against my legs, and there was nothing between my inner secret and his eyes other than the off-the-shelf cheap panties I was forced to buy if I'd at least wanted clean panties on this mission.

He slid them down.

I trembled when he touched my legs, but his fingers were quick and easy, and there was nothing awkward from him. He was a piece of ice for how cool he was.

I wished that I could be as indifferent as he was, as calm and unaffected. This nameless man scared me more than so many others I had met. He wasn't excited by violence and having me completely vulnerable and at his mercy seemed to give him no thrill. The only explanation that came through my mind was that he was a sociopath, to the bone.

If he decided to kill me, I'd never know, and he wouldn't lose a wink of sleep.

The woman I could understand – she was furious. She had an emotional investment. She had emotions and motives, and the sociopath seemed to be the one calling the shots. I shuddered, my imagination filling in the lurid details of the .357 firing, the way it would rock her skinny wrist back, and how the massive slug would penetrate my skull in slow motion.

"Do you have bathroom anxiety?" the man asked.

"What?" I stammered, shocked out of my reverie.

"Bathroom anxiety, you can't go if someone is too close or is watching you?"

"No, I was just distracted," I said.

"Can we get on with things? I have a number of kinks, and this involves none of them," he said, and there was a hint of humor in his voice. I closed my eyes and concentrated on relaxing. That was an absolute paradox right there, but it worked, and almost like cracking open a rusty spigot, I was finally able to go. I felt heat rush to my cheeks again and almost clenched off mid-stream. I in front of a handsome sociopath, pissing like a horse.

I finished, with my face almost pressed to my knees.

Maybe being shot wouldn't be as awful as this.

"Wipe? Or are you a drip dry?" he asked.

"Wipe, if you don't mind," I said.

He was quick, and it was done. I tried not to shudder, because there were feelings there that vibrated through my entire body. Shamed, bound, and now a strange man, whose name I had no idea of, was now the person who had come the absolute closest to me. Only this piece of tissue prevented his strong fingers from caressing me down there.

He helped me back to my feet, and then pulled my panties back up, then my pants.

His breath was warm against my neck as he did the zipper and button of the pants, and then the belt. I didn't resist as he walked me back to my tree and tied me to it again.

"I appreciate the fact that you've decided to not scream," he says.

"Hadn't considered it. Who would even hear me out here?"

"Fair point, I still appreciate it. Would you like some more water?" I nodded, and he held the bottle while I drank the better part of it. I would pay for that later, but it seemed to be a modest inconvenience, considering everything else that was going on.

He left me alone after that, and there was some soft conversation between the man and the woman. They very carefully omitted any names, just pet names for each other, generic, babe, for the most part.

Then there were different noises.

She moaned.

I bit my lip.

She hissed and made other noises. God, they were fucking.

She wasn't very quiet, not a screamer, but there was no attempt at stealth.

He was more of the silent sort, but I could hear what he was doing, the sounds she made, and I could hear the wet slap of their skin. How turned on did she have to be for me to hear it? I stared up at the stars and tried to remember their names, the constellations. I couldn't see leaves well enough to try playing at forest guide.

She came.

I felt myself clench, a hint of warmth tingling between my legs.

This was so not the fucking time for that.

He was a machine, and each time she let out those noises, each time she came, I felt myself getting more and more turned on. This was beyond humiliating, and stupid as fuck. Tied to a tree, job gone, home gone, mission completely failed, just nothing but a fucking washout, and my face was burning with shame. I was aroused enough that it was completely uncomfortable.

"Don't make too much of a mess," I heard her voice say. "We don't have a shower out here."

"The mess is up to you," he said, and I heard amusement in his voice.

She didn't say anything, in fact, she was completely silent. I could only hear him, and for once he was the one making noise and being loud, dropping f-bombs like confetti. Then she made a muffled, loud moan, then wet sucking sounds.

I knew what he had done.

He came in her mouth.

I shuddered, but I wasn't sure if it was because the thought repelled me, or because I was jealous.

The only silver lining of the day was that my brain was still inside my skull. If I was alive, there was always a chance to make things right. I wish I had caught on to meditation better, that would have likely been a nice way to distract myself from my aching back, numb hands, and my crotch being all hot and fucking bothered.

If I got out of this alive, I was going to buy one of those vibrator things.

"I still don't know why we haven't dealt with her," the woman said, and I lifted my head. My neck creaked, and my entire body felt awful. Why shouldn't it – spending the night tied to a tree, hands behind my back, after almost winning a fist fight?

"Because we are a lot of things, but we aren't murderers," he said.

"We still kill people," she said.

"She's awake, mind what you say," he said. I looked up, the two of them standing over me. "And I don't think we should do anything to harm her. She came with no ill intent."

"She's one of them," she said.

"I don't think so," he said. "You came alone, unarmed, and you know Kurt personally, yes?"

"I had a team with me, but they refused to engage. I was left alone to try and complete the mission," I said, my voice cracking and raw.

He offered me more water, and it was a godsend. "I didn't bring my sidearm because I wanted to talk to Kurt. I considered him my friend, and I wanted to understand what happened, and why he abducted Calanthe. I wanted to talk sense into him so that he would surrender her, and I could take her home." I closed my eyes and turned my face away, braced to be struck. She had that look in her eyes.

"What did your team do?" the woman asked.

"They fell back. I told them that if they didn't hear from me before dark to go back, tell the Dragon that I was gone, and that Kurt was much more dangerous than we'd given him credit."

"Big ugly RV, California tags?" the woman asked.

"Yes." I sighed.

"Maryland Highway Patrol detained that vehicle this morning and arrested three people," the woman said, holding up a phone. "Looks like you avoided being arrested."

"Lucky me," I groaned.

"So where are we going to turn her loose?" the woman asked.

"We aren't," he said. "She wants to talk to Kurt and came with what looks like good will. I say we take her to where he is, let them talk. Then we decide what to do."

"Take her back to the house? That's just walking an enemy through the front door," she said.

"A potential enemy, but maybe not," he said.

"She could cause problems."

"Naturally, but she also knows that we are more than capable of handling ten of her own men, and that we're professional assassins. Too much trouble is easily managed with a small caliber round, and a large plastic bag." I shuddered because there was no threat, this was just a man talking about a regular day at his day job. He was a sociopath. *Jesus, please help me get through this alive.*

"I won't cause any trouble," I said. "I like being alive."

"Alive is good," he agreed. "We're going to put a hood over your head. No reason for you to know where we're going. You'll be properly looked after when we get back to the house, and we'll all have a nice talk, answer some questions, and have some cake."

"Cake?" I asked, that seemed to come out of nowhere.

"He's making the chocolate gateau," the man said, and the woman seemed to beam with delight.

There was no point fighting them, as they pulled a sack over my head and put me in the back section of the Range Rover. My hands were still secured, and now I was cable tied to the cargo hooks. At least it was laying down, and my hands and wrists weren't in such agony. We drove for a long time, leaving the park, then crossing the Chesapeake Bay Bridge again. The sound it made under the tires was familiar.

There was traffic.

Then a long stint on the interstate.

More stop-and-go as we exited. The vehicle pitched up, and I kept rolling back and thumping against the hatch as we climbed several hills.

Then a darker darkness as we entered a garage and the mechanical door slid shut behind us. I felt a moment of panic as both the man and woman left, shutting the doors, and leaving me in the back. How long would I last back here, tied with cheap pieces of plastic that I couldn't break, and not having the strength of action movie conviction to do something like dislocate a shoulder or break the ties with a heroic bulge of strength?

The hatch opened, and I could smell the hint of sea air. We were near the coast, much closer than we were in the park. Strong hands moved me, cutting the cable ties, all of them. My arms were free, and fire lanced through my back and shoulders. I didn't cry out. I wouldn't give that level of satisfaction.

"So, this is the fearsome Madeleine Oberisk," a man with an accent like Kurt's said.

"Don't underestimate her," the familiar man said. "She can fight, and even odds, she could probably beat me."

"That's high praise," the likely Englishman said. "Let's get this ugly bonnet off of her."

The sack came off my head and I blinked back the bright light of the garage.

"Hardly a proper greeting, but welcome to Indigo City, my dear," the Englishman said. "Let's get you inside, cleaned up, and we'll have a little chat."

"I want to talk to Kurt," I said. "Where is Calanthe, is she safe?"

"Oh, in good time, yes," he said. "And the wee lass prefers to be called Callie. She is here, safe, and quite comfortable. We have a lot to discuss."

"Like what?" I asked.

"You were Kurt's second-in-command, and how this level of abuse went on inside New Eden, and no one was the wiser to it," he said.

THE LIVING ROOM of the house was enormous, and the full-length windows faced the bay. Their property must run right up to the edge of the water, and that would mean a pier and a boat. There was no way they had a house this big and no boat.

The brunette woman had supervised me taking a shower, using the restroom properly, and then dressing in men's clothing. This wasn't new. I was more familiar with button-up shirts and denim than anything feminine. The fact that she had that massive revolver on her, that was disconcerting.

Being clean, I felt better.

I know I smelled better, thank fuck for that.

"So, Kurt said that the house in Hollywood had multiple layers of security, including cameras that had onsite storage and were backed up to the New Eden main facility," the Englishman said. I nodded, this wasn't a breach of any of my NDAs, yet.

"There is ample evidence to demonstrate that Arik Rex routinely abused his wife, physically. We have X-rays, and MRIs that show a history of broken bones and multiple concussions. How did you not know about this?" he asked, his voice calm and even.

"Calanthe is a very slight woman, and she is both easily harmed and accident prone," I said. That was what we were told.

"Callie is a slight woman, but that doesn't mean she has the skeleton of an eighty-year-old woman, or a medical history that looks like a professional boxer," he said.

"I've heard this propaganda before," I said. "It's the same story – New Eden has made some people mad, and the two go-to items for smearing an organization are sexual abuse and exploiting children. Neither go on at New Eden. Keep your lies and propaganda to yourself. I don't know who you are, and I want to talk to Kurt, and to know Calanthe is okay."

"It's not propaganda," the Englishman said.

"I don't care what anecdotes you have, and anything you can print or show me is going to be something anyone with a computer and a decent hand at Photoshop could make. Fuck you. You could use deep fake AI to make a video of whatever you wanted, so I don't care about your bullshit evidence."

"Let me go get Kurt," he said, the sighed and stood up.

Slight limp.

That was the weak point when the time came.

"Obe?" It was Kurt.

"What the fuck, man," I almost snarled.

"There's a lot to explain," he said, holding up his hands in a defensive gesture. "But there are things you have to know—"

I interrupted him. Hearing his voice, seeing him looking clean and healthy, fire boiled inside me. We both hit the wall, and there was a crunch of drywall caving in. Everything came up at once, and I turned and slung him onto the tasteful coffee table. There were cracking noises, and part of the table gave way.

The air went out of Kurt in a gust, and I saw his face turn red.

Those were broken ribs.

Fire lanced through my back and there was the familiar crackle of a taser. The brunette was there, jabbing the device into my side.

Far from the first time I had taken a taser.

I knocked the thing from her hand and sent her tumbling over the sofa. There were shouts, and I paused long enough to kick the taser away before grabbing Kurt up off the table.

"You son of a bitch, do you know what you've cost me?" I shouted at him.

"Put him down," the sociopath said. He was unarmed, but the look on his face was murder. He helped the brunette back to her feet and gave her a handkerchief to wipe the blood from her face.

"Maddy, wait," Kurt rasped. "Please."

I didn't listen, I couldn't listen.

I refused.

He grunted loudly as I put him in a head lock. "Move again and I'll dislocate your shoulder, again."

He tapped at my arm, the signal to release when we were sparring. But we weren't sparring now, this was real. I turned so that he was between me and the sociopath. Would he shoot Kurt to get me? I didn't really want to find out, but this confrontation, taser aside, had been really gun free.

"Madeleine?" I looked to see Calanthe standing at the doorway, her hand covering her mouth. I saw distress.

"Calanthe, I'm here to rescue you. I won't let them hurt you! Let's go. Get to the Range Rover in the garage, and they can keep the rest of this... mess." The sociopath gestured for the brunette to stay where she was.

"I'm safe, Madeleine, they're my friends." Her voice was soft.

"C'mon, I don't know how long I can hold this stalemate, let's go." I grunted. It was true, with little sleep, and hurting all over, the only thing keeping me moving was fury and adrenaline.

"Madeleine," she said, leaving a pause. "Please, stop. Let Kurt go. I don't want you to hurt anyone else. Stop being the bad guy."

I blinked.

"What?"

"Stop being the bad guy. These are the good guys," she said.

"No, New Eden are the good guys. *We're* the good guys. These people are murderers, they said as much. Please, Calanthe, *please...*"

"Let Kurt go. He's turning purple," the sociopath said. "No one is threatening you, and you're destroying our house."

I ignored him as Calanthe walked up to where I was still holding Kurt. Her eyes were big, like I remembered them. Everything else about her was small and perfect. This was why she was the First Among First Daughters. Why else would she have been a goodwill ambassador to the UN, and to Congress. Calanthe was everything we were supposed to be.

She was everything that I had wanted to be but had failed.

"Madeleine?"

"Yes, Calanthe."

"Please let Kurt go. You've hurt him. You're breaking things and hurting people, and that's not what New Eden is supposed to do." I felt a knot in my throat, and my eyes burned. Fuck. Hesitantly, I let Kurt go. He all but fell to his knees, and Calanthe, of all people, propped him up.

"I'm sorry, Kurt, let's get you down on the couch." Her voice was like silk.

I felt a new round of shame.

"I'm not mad at you, Madeleine," she said. "We were lied to, all of us. We were lied to, and we were abused. Some of us in different ways. They didn't touch you, like they touched and used me. But they didn't insult me and treat me the way they treated you."

"I'm not a victim," I said.

"You've been wronged, and I'm sure you know the names of the people who've done the most harm to you, emotionally and physically," she said.

I trembled.

I did know, Alexander Soren, the man with the audacity to call himself the Dragon.

Majordomo Maxson, the man who looked at me when I was twelve and decided that I was too tall to be a First Daughter, and that I wasn't feminine enough.

Jacobsen and Cullen for abandoning me.

No.

This was just getting inside my head.

"Madeleine, you're almost there," Calanthe said. "Arik is a bad person, no matter how much money he gives to New Eden."

I wanted to refute that, but I knew there was truth there.

How many women had Kurt and I gathered up and removed from his trailer?

Some of them had bruises, bright and fresh.

The makeup Calanthe sometimes wore, thick almost pancake-like, and the oversized glasses.

There was a spark.

"My phone has the encrypted files from the house security system," I said.

"Does it now," the Englishman said.

"That will show the truth," I said. "It recorded what happened in Calanthe's puzzle room, and you wouldn't have been able to alter it."

"So, you'd accept that evidence?" the Englishman asked.

I nodded.

The sociopath had my phone and handed it to the Englishman. I told him the passcode, and he took it into another room. I wanted to follow him, but I couldn't turn my back on this room of fiends.

"I'm glad you didn't shoot her," the sociopath told the brunette.

"It's only because she was standing in front of the Van Gogh. There is no way we could get blood off of the *Poppy Flowers*." Her tone was matter of fact, and she was indeed, still carrying the revolver. The color on her face where I hit her was also hard to not notice.

Regardless of what happened, I was going to pay for that one.

"I've got the files downloading," the Englishman called from the next room. I moved closer to the door, giving Kurt room, and

Calanthe sat next to him and put her arms around him. He would probably need a doctor from that last hit.

The Englishman sat at a computer rig with multiple screens and the hum of electronics. I could see the files popped up on the screen while several progress bars seemed to be running.

"What are you doing?" I asked, keeping an eye on the rest of the room.

"Running several decryption programs. I'll have this cracked quick enough. Looks like commercial stuff, and I have tools for those."

"I'm going to call Max," the brunette said. "I think Kurt has broken ribs, and hopefully this shaved sasquatch didn't damage his spine."

"Watch it, Barbie," I shot at her.

"I have the revolver, missing link," she quipped.

"And you don't want blood on your cheap paintings," I fired back.

"That's an honest to God, Van Gogh," she said, and pointed to a painting of some yellow flowers in a vase.

"I really don't care," I said, swapping back and forth between the banked monitors and the room full of hostiles.

"Here we go," the Englishman said. He hit a few buttons and the feed popped up, the four rooms that were the inner zone of the house – the bedroom, Calanthe's puzzle room, the solar, and the media/entertainment room. I saw Arik and Calanthe, but they were moving jerky and fast.

"Replaying at twice the normal speed," he said. "No need to watch real time."

They seemed to avoid each other, at high speed. Calanthe had her small space she stayed in, and Arik was almost manic moving through the rooms. He left, came back with coffee, watched television, then more coffee. Other things happened but the feed was too fast to pick up the fine details.

When he pulled Calanthe out of bed and pulled her clothes off, I didn't need fine details to see what was going on. God, it was rough, but thankfully it didn't last long.

There was nothing tender about what he did.

She left the bed, went to the bathroom, showered, took something from the medicine cabinet, and then Arik was in the room.

Jerky movements, but the confrontation was obvious.

Then it turned into violence.

He was throwing her around like a doll, striking her, making her flee from him.

When he hit her, the couch spattered with blood. It was almost black on the replay. He kept hitting her, and I could sense the malice and hostility through the low-resolution imaging. Kurt came in and grabbed Arik, and they grappled.

The headlock was clean, and then Kurt took a dive through the glass table, sparing Rex any injury.

It was tender the way he put Rex on the ground, and then checked Calanthe, and took her out of the room.

The award laying on the ground, partially bent, and dark with blood was a telltale heart, a smoking barrel. I felt sick.

I let my guard down, shoulders slumping and my hands unclenching.

He all but raped her. Maybe he did rape her, there was no audio. He assaulted her, and looking at the blood on the couch, the damage done to the room before Kurt appeared, Arik might have killed her in a fit of rage. This didn't make sense. Sure he was a womanizer, but wasn't that supposed to be one of the perks of being a celebrity?

"No," I whispered.

"I'm sorry, Madeleine," Calanthe said. "I wish it weren't true, but it is."

"Please, no," I sighed.

"New Eden is a lie. It's a cult for a bunch of assholes to get rich and have all the underage sex they want," Calanthe said.

"They're done," the brunette said, her posture relaxing as well. "Fallout is going to kill New Eden in the courts, and what they don't get, the DHS and a few other government agencies are going to chop up over money laundering, sex trafficking, and domestic terrorism."

"They're the bad guys, Madeleine," Calanthe said, putting a hand on my arm. Reflexively, I stepped back and bumped into the wall.

"I don't have anything left..." I choked back the sob. "I gave them everything, and there's nothing left..."

"It's okay, you can start over, but you have to stop. They're the bad guys, and you aren't a bad person. I know that," she said, her eyes peering into mine.

"I think Kurt would beg to differ," Sadie said.

"I'll live," Kurt groaned.

"I can't believe this." I felt numb.

"Give her a minute, all of you," Calanthe said. "This is a lot, and I think we've destroyed her worldview. She's going to need a bit to put it all back together."

"I don't know what to do," I grasped. "I've always known what to do. There were always guidelines and all that."

"New Eden has always been there, and now it's not something you can go back to," Calanthe said.

"I couldn't even if I wanted. By now I've been blacklisted for failing to bring you back safely," I said.

"I can't extend the hospitality of my hosts, that would be rude, but if there is anything I can do for you," she said, a hand on my arm.

"You were perfect." I felt tears start to burn down my face. "You were everything that I couldn't be. You were everything that New Eden stood for."

"I was, at first," she said. "Back when I was part of the National Honor Society and did things like speak in front of world leaders. You saw what I did after that. I did puzzles because that was what I was allowed – no crosswords, no television, no internet. The only books I was allowed were the ones August Emerson approved for the New Eden education. I used to be smart, and I could do some gymnastics, and now I stumble over words. I can get so confused trying to remember things that I burst out in tears of frustration."

"What started the fight?" I asked, grasping for anything.

"Birth control," she said. "That's all I ever was to Arik – a tight wet place to put his seed. His broodmare. I was supposed to give him handsome sons and beautiful daughters. Once I was spent, I would be shuffled off, and another teenager would be trotted up to take his *affections*."

I felt my shoulders slump.

I gestured and the Englishman rewound the file and I rewatched it at regular speed. In the entertainment room, I watched Arik pop a handful of pills into his mouth. I didn't know what they were, but he chased them with a small glass, the sort that whiskey goes in. It was morning, and he was drinking and popping pills.

He was so violent.

Tearing her clothes, slapping her, fucking her face like she was a piece of celebrity-chasing trash.

This was all wrong.

"I want to leave," I whispered, as I watched Arik pound her furiously from behind. "Turn this off, and I want to leave."

"Where are you going to go?" she asked.

"I don't know," I whispered.

"Let me give you my phone number," she said, and added it to my phone, before handing it back to me. It was almost dead, and I had no charger.

So what?

"Thanks," I said.

"Let her go," Calanthe said.

"She could tip them off to our location," the brunette said.

"Call the New Eden contact number," Calanthe countered. I handed the phone off to the brunette and she thumbed through my contacts until she found Soren's, after I mumbled "recents" at her.

"It's been blocked, or disconnected," she said, looking up from the phone.

A message blinked across the screen, *service terminated*, and the phone powered down on its own. The brunette pressed buttons on the screen, and on the side, and it refused to respond. She handed it back to me, and I shrugged. I turned and flipped it into the waste bin near the Englishman.

"I've been burned, now," I said.

"You aren't a prisoner here, Maddy. You can leave if you want," Calanthe said. "I think you could also stay if you wanted."

I looked at them, at this weird unit they had going on, and shook my head.

"No, I want to leave, or at this point just shoot me. I've got nothing left." The sociopath gestured at the brunette, and she took her hand away from her hip where the revolver was and looked annoyed.

Calanthe walked me to the front door and opened it.

"You're a good person, Madeleine, and I'm sorry."

I nodded, and when I stepped through the door, she shut it behind me.

Fuck.

25

———

*K*urt…

The captain ran a strange ship and made really questionable decisions. He hadn't seemed like that back in-country, but then again, in-country was a few years ago. The fancy restaurant seemed like the craziest thing they could consider doing, but then they brought Madeleine Oberisk through the garage door, not knowing what she was.

They meant well, and being both veterans, there was that certain overconfidence that veterans had when dealing with civilians. Maddy was a civilian, and a woman, but she was a zealot. She was the best hand-to-hand fighter I had ever met, and she learned fast. Each lesson was only required once, and after a month of CQC training, she was the one teaching lessons.

When she opened up, the only surprise was when the coffee table didn't shatter under me.

It felt like my ribs obliged instead.

The good news was that the floor was there to catch me, the wood cool against my face. Maddy and an expensive piece of furniture was like being hit by a bloody tank.

Breathing hurt, especially on the right side.

I drew in a shallow breath.

Stay calm.

They talked her down, and of all people, it was Callie who brought her to earth.

Then, stunningly, Maddy just... left.

I could feel my feet, and I wiggled my toes. I could see them, they were still there, and I flexed my foot. My spine was intact; I wasn't a paraplegic. That was good news.

"Oh God, I hope you're okay," Callie said, kneeling next to me.

"I've had better days." I let out a cough and tried to force a smile. I didn't want her to worry. "But not the first time I've lost this particular dance."

"They've called the doctor who looked after me – the nice black lady," Callie said. "She's going to make sure you're okay."

"That sounds splendid." I smiled grimly.

Doc Max was a handsome woman, and exceedingly polite. Polite enough that I felt a mild tingle of surprise that she wasn't from London or Liverpool and was just a Chicago girl who found a special place, where she could do the medicine she wanted, and not have to deal with the paperwork and the lawyers.

The introspection came easy.

It was the morphine.

Enough morphine and a woman could be massaging my broken ribs, and I could let my mind wander to things like what song had been playing on the radio the first time I saw Calanthe. It had been an internet playlist, classic American rock. Gary Wright had been crooning "Dreamweaver" in my ear when Rex pulled up for our first face-to-face, and Calanthe had been with him in the car.

The car had been a convertible Ferrari, and possibly the only thing in the world a brighter shade of red than his wife's hair.

That's when she became Cardinal.

He would become Tomcat after the first time I had to drag a half-naked chippie out of his trailer.

I hadn't fallen in love with her then.

The opioid haze made me want to be saccharine and nostalgic, like she was some dame who came sashaying up out of an exotic car and I knew at that moment I would burn down the world to have her.

But that wasn't true.

That first impression, with the PA bringing her a low-cal dairy-free decaf latte, with her little nose and huge glasses, I thought she had to be the most shallow, self-obsessed Hollywood tart I could imagine. I had met a few of that type, with their designer tits and sculpted noses and threaded eyebrows. Vacuous, bland, boring, and Rex had mentioned a few things about them. He had called them anorexic sticks, that the only things going for them was that most of them had no gag reflex left, and that their egos were so fragile that a little negging and they would go from being starfishes in bed, just holes in the middle of a spread-eagle figure, too willing to humiliate and debase themselves in a vain chance of being further insulted.

Diseased people.

I felt a groan escape my lips as I was suddenly very hot.

The captain was on one side of me, and Kyle was on the other and I was being eased down into the hot tub.

"Are you sure this is safe?" I asked, as I felt the hot water swirl around me.

"Heat is not ideal at this point," the captain said, then there were a large number of other words, and Kyle said a few too. That was okay. For some reason, my concern seemed to involve sharks.

That didn't make sense, hot tubs were fresh water, not salt water.

Calanthe put her arm around me, and I felt myself relax.

Her embrace was really nice.

"You're going to be okay," she said in my ear, and that was good. I felt like I was starting to dissolve in the water, and for a moment, I was concerned about clogging the filter.

<h1 style="text-align:center">26</h1>

*C*allie…

I was worried, no – *scared* for Kurt when I watched him crash into that table from the doorway. They had told me to stay out of sight for the time being, that my presence could or would only galvanize Maddie further into violence and they didn't want that. I stayed out of sight in another room, but all too soon, I found myself drifting in the direction of their voices. Stealing away in the opulent halls of the mansion, pressed against walls, and listening outside doorways as I had done countless times while ensconced in New Eden, under their eye, under their thumb, wondering what was next.

I had been so naïve even then, even after what the August had done at my presentation. So damn naïve I hadn't realized that meeting Arik Rex wasn't an accident but had been just as thoroughly engineered as anything else.

I swallowed hard and listened and had turned the corner just as Maddie, who had always been strong, lifted Kurt's massive frame clean off the floor and *slammed* him down into the table.

The sound had been horrendous, and I couldn't get it out of my mind. The table cracking, but not giving way, and there was honestly no telling if that awful, terrible sound had been the table or if it had been Kurt.

Doctor Maxine had come and given him a hefty dose of morphine. She recommended cold and then hot therapy to promote healing but said that Kurt's body needed to do the work. Beyond pain management, there wasn't anything she could do except wrap the ribs.

Kyle and Sadie went to work, and it was left to Roan and me to get a stupefied Kurt out of his clothes and into a pair of swim trunks.

"Get yourself ready," Roan told me. "We may need you in the hot tub. Ideally cold to start but we need him a bit more lucid than this for that or he may fight us."

I nodded and changed swiftly into a swimsuit, leaving Roan to swallow his own tongue when I didn't step into the bathroom to do it. His cheeks flaming redder than his hair, we helped Kurt to stagger downstairs, holding him up between us.

It was difficult moving a man of his size without holding him around his ribs. I was scared, his back already starting to purple and bruise around the side where he had taken the brunt of the hit.

"I got him." Kyle rushed forward and dipped low to take Kurt up on my side.

I turned and Sadie was dumping ice into an aluminum... what looked like a horse trough they had produced from somewhere, a garden hose running into it, water splashing, ice sloshing and rattling.

"You're going to put him in *that?*" I asked incredulously.

"Aye, after a bit in the hot tub. Loosen him up some. As I said, ideally ice first but I'm afraid he'd cave our bloody heads in right now." Roan looked amused and I had my misgivings. How did any of this present as funny?

Poor Maddie had been devastated and they'd just let her go out the front door. I would be lying if I said I wasn't just as worried about her. It wasn't her fault. All of this was clearly to be laid at the August's feet and I was so hurt but more importantly, I was *angry*.

I got into the hot tub at Kyle's gesturing and raised my arms to receive Kurt as they lowered him into the swirling steaming waters.

"Are you sure this is safe?" he asked, as I sank in up to my chin.

"Heat is not ideal at this point," Roan said, and Kurt muttered something about sharks.

I must have looked stricken when I looked up at Roan who just winked at me with a smile and said, "He's always had a rather *unique* reaction to morphine."

I took Kurt into my arms, and he sort of lay suspended in the water, his head lying back against my chest between my breasts.

"You're going to be okay," I whispered into his ear and that seemed to satisfy him. He leaned back against me, and I barely kept my feet and his head above water, but I managed.

"How long?" I asked, looking up. Kyle set out a patio chair for Roan and he sank into it. Sadie went over to him, and he pulled her down onto his knee.

"A fair bit," Roan remarked and nodded to Kyle who nodded back once and disappeared into the mansion.

I held on to Kurt and murmured to him when he stirred or started to struggle a bit in his drugged stupor.

"You have a knack with him," Roan said after a bit. "None of us could keep him half so calm in-country the one time we had to administer him morphine."

"What happened?" I asked.

"Oh, I'm sure you've seen the scars," Roan said with a smile as Sadie cuddled into him. "Took some shrapnel about two months before I lost my leg. Superficial, merely flesh wounds, but had to administer the old boy some morphine in the field. Turned super soldier on us after that. Tried to fight us when there wasn't any enemy left. That's how we found out he had a slight allergy to morphine. Messed with him up here a fair bit." He tapped his temple with a middle finger. "Came out of it within an hour or two, still — nothing better than the old milk of the poppy to handle pain."

I nodded and Kurt groaned slightly, and... and I think he was asleep! Asleep and dreaming.

Oh, shit. I took my responsibility doubly as seriously so that he wouldn't drown on me.

"That's it." Roan nodded. "He'll sleep for a while and when he comes out of that, he should be lucid enough."

"Don't worry," Sadie said with a smile. "We won't leave you out here with him alone. He won't drown and neither will you."

At that, Kyle returned in some obnoxious bright blue speedos. I blushed and looked away as he jogged back our way, things... uh... bouncing, and he slid into the water opposite me and Kurt and took a seat on the bench.

"You can relax now," he said with a grin and a wink. "I'm here to spot you."

I gave him a tight-lipped smile and nodded.

Oh, goodie?

We didn't have much to talk about after that. At least I didn't. Roan, Kyle, and Sadie talked about some old times and Roan told a few stories about Kurt. Eventually, after about an hour, Kurt stirred and though his words were slightly slurred, he sounded much more with it when he said, "You need some new stories, Captain."

"Ah, there he is! Bloody brilliant. You ready for your ice bath, then?"

"Bloody hell, *no*, but let's get it done."

Kurt found his own feet and stood. I smiled up at him, and he reached out and touched my face, his eyes unreadable as he stroked a thumb down my cheek and he asked, "You alright then, Cardinal?"

"I'm alright." I took his hand between mine and kissed his scarred knuckles.

"Think you can lever yourself out of here or you need help?" Kyle asked, standing by.

"What d'you think, you fucking namby?" Kurt asked with a grin and Roan laughed.

"No offense meant," Roan assured Kyle. "He's just taking the piss."

"Aye," Kurt rumbled, and Kyle got out of the hot tub. Kurt almost went cross-eyed at what he was wearing.

"Or maybe I ain't," he said, his accent as thick as I'd ever heard it.

"Come on, man. Up you go."

"Callie," Kurt called, and I lightly touched an unbruised part of his back.

"I'm here," I said.

"Come out of there, girl," Roan declared, and Sadie was suddenly just tub side holding out a giant bath sheet of a fluffy white towel.

"Okay." I got out and she wrapped me up in it and rubbed my arms briskly with a smile. Roan and Kyle both helped Kurt out of the hot tub, and I grimaced as he stood shaking like a leaf with the effects of the drugs and hot water, staring down at the trough of ice water.

"Bloody hell," he muttered and then he let the two men help him into it. I grimaced and cringed, and *Lord Almighty,* did I feel for him.

That had to be absolutely miserable.

"God save the Queen, that's cold!" Kurt said through chattering teeth and Roan said, "Just hold it as long as you can. You know the drill."

"Aye, aye, fuck you, mate." Kurt laughed and it was everything in me not to cry. Cry for Maddie, cry because it was because of me that Kurt was even injured, but also cry with relief that he was going to be okay because seeing him out of sorts? That was honestly the scariest thing of all.

27

Kurt...

The worst part about being modestly allergic to morphine and opioids in general wasn't that I had to deal with the flu-like withdrawal symptoms, or how sharp the pain of an injury might come back when the meds faded. No, the worst part was that I had two bad habits when doped – I would become combative, and there were some hallucinations. These weren't immediately noticed the few times I was injured and given dragon juice. Being amped up from an ongoing firefight proved ample explanation for my lack of acceptance or passivity after being hit with the needle. The hallucinations, audio and visual, were easily ignored in the context of a good fight or taking cover from some dangerously close artillery or air strike.

In the civilian world, it was different.

The people around me weren't trained to deal with high stress and combat situations, and instead of being a guy just keeping it together, I was what they called a *problem patient*. The answer to this was simple, don't get hurt, and if I did get hurt, no painkillers were better than giving a nurse a cuff to the neck or a close-quarters knife hand.

Thankfully, after my brief stint as a piece of living room table literature, my antics were not violent, and no one earned a black eye from me, no sprains, strains, or bruises.

All in all, that was well enough.

No one had mentioned anything funny about my time under the influence so maybe most of those things I was remembering hadn't actually happened, and were only dreams, or morphine fantasies.

We waited for something to happen.

There was no follow-up strike team from New Eden. There was no follow-up from DHS or the Coast Guard, but then the captain mentioned that all the things he had done to get them involved and on the scene, had been anonymous. Even Sadie and Kyle's presence had been covered and accounted for. There was nothing against a little survivalist roleplay out in the woods.

The thought was weird, but for some reason, I could see them out by my cabin, pretending the world had ended and they were the only people left. There was something actually kind of appealing about that.

I didn't want the world to end, but I did want to live a good deal apart from it.

The counterattack came three days after Madeleine Oberisk cracked three ribs and left me with a bruise the size of a dinner plate. Anyone else would have gotten an email over it, but since Arik hadn't allowed Callie to have one, New Eden had to post their legal missives in the LA Times. It was buried in the business and announcements section and detailed in fine print that Calanthe ne Hardy Rex was officially estranged from her husband and that Arik Rex was filing for separation. In retaliation for domestic assault and sexual infidelity, she was divested of any and all legal rights to alimony or any other compensation.

The captain's web trawler programs sniffed the article out.

The next article didn't need a web search bot to find, it was on the bottom of the front page.

"It's a smear campaign," Callie said, looking at the screen. "They've decided that I'm *fair game*, and no longer offered any of the protections of New Eden."

"You'll be safe," I said, "I promise."

"It's not something that a fist or a gun can stop," she said. The captain nodded, sagely.

"So, what do we do?" I asked. "We don't just let this happen?"

"We let Fallout's lawyers and people do their job. They're desperate if they're swinging like this. Once those subpoenas have struck home, then Miss Callie follows suit, filing criminal and civil charges against the lot of them," the captain said.

"And that's it?" I asked.

"Pretty much," the captain said.

"Her fate is in the hands of... lawyers?" I asked. I could almost taste bile. "They'll ruin everything, leave everyone broke, and congratulate themselves on a court case well wasted."

"What would you do?" he asked.

"Punish the people who hurt her," I said, my hands balling into fists.

"Lad, are you going to go try and kill Mister Hollywood action star, and the leaders of a multinational environmental crusade?" he asked. He knew I fucking wanted to.

"I already had that chance, and didn't," I said.

"You were thinking," the captain said. "Keep thinking and be patient."

I felt completely useless.

Ribs broken, a good chunk of my retirement plan finances were just gone – my cabin apparently had a tree laying through it. Despite everything surrounding me in the captain's house, all the wealth and conveniences, I felt something growing on me. A restlessness that was pervasive, like a fungus.

Just because I had nothing to do didn't mean everyone else was just sitting around. The captain seemed to stay relentlessly busy. He would spend hours at his multi-screen workstation, doing all the different things he did. I watched a little, as he did his business investing, moving things, buying, and selling. It seemed whatever money he had; it didn't stay in one place long.

I did a little of the same, getting my own finances sorted back out. I thought I had been clever digging into the cryptocurrencies, but in a day, the captain caught up to where I was, and in another day, passed me. I took what he found and put it to good use. Flipping a few of my precious CryptoCoins to cash let me start throwing money at interesting investments, some jackassy, some legitimate. I never really knew which was going to take off. I had lost money on things that seemed like sure bets, and then made bank off the dumbest fucking shit I could imagine.

Kyle, Sadie, and my Calanthe were remarkably busy.

They were constantly going to this place and that place, speaking with people, lawyers, giving affidavits and briefings to legal teams. There were seemingly endless meetings with Tate and the Fallout people. There was a divorce lawyer team who Kyle had convinced to work on some sort of delayed payment.

None of if involved me.

I went to a few, to be there for Callie, and she was thankful I was there a few times. Once she found her feet and her courage, I just really wasn't needed. It was obvious I wasn't needed. I had no legal experience. There was no pretending I was legal counsel, or an advisor. I wasn't even a passable bodyguard with the injury I had.

The captain and his own seemed to be masters of relaxing at the end of the day. The hot tub, the in-house bar, basically a mini theatre in their living room, and the pier out to their boats and the bay.

It was nice.

It wasn't really for me though.

"I know Callie is safe when you all go do the lawyer things," I said, looking at the captain over a cup of breakfast tea. "Is there a risk if I go out and do something?"

"That depends, I guess," he said. "What do you have in mind? I know you've been getting that stir-crazy look."

"Aye," I said. "I was thinking about going and looking at how bad things are at my cabin. Callie said there's a tree crashed through it."

"You're not in much shape to do much about that," he said.

"I've got some cracked ribs, I'm not on my death bed."

"Still, you should be resting, more than anything."

"Aye, you're spot on, but I can't just bum around and do nothing for six to eight weeks, I'll go mad."

"That's likely true," he said. "It wouldn't be wise to be off by yourself, in case something went wrong, and you were injured, or the New Eden people tried to be arses again."

"I'm not worried about that," I said. "How did you put it, all the torpedoes aren't just in the water, they've all hit home?"

"Aye, they have, but that doesn't mean New Eden is done. A ship can still have a lot of fight left in it, even if it *is* on fire and sinking."

"Then come with me, unless this is the only thing you do," I said, and gestured to the bank of monitors.

"It's not the only thing," he said.

"I recognize some of those icons – those are games, the funny ones."

"I don't know what you mean," he said, and I could see his face tighten, a guarded expression.

"You know, funny like with wizards and shite," I said.

"Oh, well yeah," he admitted. "I do play those, when I sometimes have time."

"Come on, get out of the chair, or let me off by my lonesome."

"You drive a reasonable point," the captain said, rubbing his face. "All this business with the legalese has me sitting on the bench now. We've got some of the best on our team, and now the only thing to do is make sure all the payments that need to be made are made."

"Perfect," I said. "Wherever Sadie and Kyle are, will they be fine with this?"

"They're away on business, and they'll have to be. Is there cell reception up by your cabin?"

"Of course, it's just on the other side of the bay, not the arsehole of nowhere," I admitted.

"I'll let them know the plan, and then we'll see about this green boot camp of yours."

"Leg up to it?" I asked.

"Even down one leg, I can still keep up with you, lad." He gave me a grin.

"So, you're going to spend days out at your cabin, working to fix what Kyle and Sadie said was wrong with it, and Roan will be going with you?" Callie asked. She looked stunning in some smart wool-blend blazer and pencil skirt, a pair of power heels making her calves pop and adding a few inches to her height. Given the way her breasts seemed higher and more pronounced had to be Sadie's handiwork, some fancy brassiere or something. Callie radiated confidence and sophistication.

"Aye, that's the plan," I said.

"But you'll be back here, at the end of the day?" she asked.

"We both will," the captain said, his eyes meeting Sadie's. It seemed like it was ultimately her consent that mattered here. It was a strange dynamic they had between them. I could see Kyle's complete indifference. It wasn't a cold indifference, like apathy, it was the vibe that those American Army Rangers shed like condensation from a freezer.

"I'm not sure that I'm a fan of the idea, but I can tell he's getting restless," she said and gave me a head nod, and then back to the captain, "And I can see that mister fix-it gleam in your eye. No point trying to stop you?"

"None," he said, a polite smile on his face.

The drive to the cabin seemed to take forever, but it was a different perspective when I was in the passenger seat, rather than driving. The captain insisted on taking his big white Range Rover, and we made a brief stop at a mom-and-pop hardware store, the place looking like it was about two years from going out of business. When we left, the back of the Rover was loaded down with all the tools and hardware we might need for the task, and the people that ran the place seemed like they were going to break down in tears.

The captain said that was something he did. He didn't spend money at the big box places, especially now that he could afford not to.

The cabin was worse than I expected.

The tree that fell on the cabin was a century white alder, and the angle of the fall crushed the porch, the front wall of the living room, and smashed the entire roof. Everything inside had been exposed to months of weather, a Maryland winter, and possibly a big bloody storm or two. I let out a sigh, and the captain clapped me on the shoulder.

"Do ye remember the Wolfhound the Mad Lads put together?" he asked.

"Aye, that beast truck they put a pair of 20 mil cannons over the cab?"

"Oh, that's the one." He smiled. "You remember what happened to it?"

"Sure, some Talibani flipped it with an IED and hit it with small arms and a few RPGs."

"How bad was it?"

"Well, no one died, and we took care of the cunts with the guns. The lads had the 'hound running in like a week," I said.

"This here is a lot less complicated than a shot to shit Wolfhound, innit?" He gave me another encouraging grin.

"You know a lot about repairing and rebuilding houses, Cap?"

"Oh, fuckin' aye," he said. "I've given two the business now, putting armor plating inside drywall and plaster without damaging it, that's a fair trick. The last place had a drone launcher, an automated gun system, a bloody minefield, and more electronics than you can imagine."

"The current house?"

"Oh, shite no," he said. "Better armor, a bigger and better panic room, and it has active security from a private company, and the local police."

"The local police?"

"Oh, yeah. Dropping a hundred grand into the local police fund and shaking a few hands was quicker and cheaper than what I spent on drones and Soviet surplus. We have a discrete hotline to ICPD, about as close to the Bat Signal as a bloke could want."

"But what about the business?"

"To the ICPD, our business is being rich, and that's all that matters to them."

"Fair, fair," I said.

We set to work. We both went after the alder with chainsaws. Debris was cleared, and I ended up getting a good fire going. It was easier to let the trash burn than try to haul it all out. The good news was that a few of the guns were perfectly safe, and the liquor supply survived.

Having a few sniffs of proper Irish spirits wasn't the brightest thing when handling fire and chainsaws, but there were a few times over in-country when we were manning million-pound vehicles, lit up on stimulants and local hashish. A little of the old country spirits just gave us that camaraderie.

The second day, we had something the locals called a bobcat brought out, so that as we cut the big tree up, this comically small mock-construction vehicle could pick up the pieces and move it away.

It proved useful again when the truck of treated lumber arrived and we used its attachments to unload the wood, and then to set beams for the new roof.

This felt right – the routine, morning tea and proper breakfasts, then working on the cabin, with nips of whiskey here and there, and then coming back to the house for showers. It was almost a contest, who would get back to the house first, the construction crew, or the legal team.

One thing I was certain of, the cabin would be fully rebuilt before the first case went before a judge.

But there was something that didn't feel right.

Callie was tense, most nights. Sadie was as well, though I wasn't putting my hands or lips on her. Things in the legal realm weren't going smashingly, and the women weren't in the sharing mood.

I let out a sigh.

This wasn't going to end anytime soon.

28

---

*C*allie...

"I just need to use the restroom," I murmured, deflated. It had been weeks and weeks of this with no forward motion in sight.

It was an endless vicious cycle of testimony and depositions, and I was getting discouraged, disheartened, like you wouldn't believe. The laws in place to deal with these sorts of situations were an absolute joke when it came to victims, and the more I gave? The less it seemed like anyone at New Eden would suffer any consequences, not only for what was done to me, but to so many others as well.

"You want me to go with you?" Sadie asked me quietly and I shook my head.

Honestly, I just wanted to clean up my makeup and get the two minutes of blissful solitude that was the time it took me to pee.

I missed Kurt with a fierce, aching longing. He hadn't been able to come today. Something needed to be done at his cabin where his presence was absolutely required and I didn't know... it was harder and harder to focus on anything other than the next videotaped interview or legal proceeding. I just wanted to get to that grand jury.

They told me that if I testified in front of a grand jury, that was it. Even if New Eden somehow got to me or made me disappear, my grand jury testimony could be used at trial. The prosecution could easily argue my disappearance or murder was to keep me from testifying and that would automatically make my grand jury testimony admissible at any given trial.

I didn't want it to come to that, obviously, and everyone swore I was as safe as safe could be... but I knew better. Just because Madeline was disillusioned with things, didn't mean that New Eden would stop, didn't mean that Arik or the August would ever stop.

Not unless they were locked up, which I was beginning to think would never happen.

I sighed and pushed my way through the restroom door and stopped in front of the mirror, huffing a disgusted laugh at my reflection, at the muddy tracks of makeup running down my cheeks.

That had been one of the things I had been prized for... the fact that, for whatever bizarre reason, the August and Arik both held it in their opinion that I somehow managed to remain pretty when I cried which made absolutely no damn sense to me.

I went in and used the bathroom, stepped out and stopped at the sink again and sighed.

I couldn't go back out there like this.

I turned on the tap and splashed cold water on my face, scrubbing at it to clear it of the offending mud spackling my looks that'd turned into this crazy Rorschach painting with my tears. I groped for the nearby paper towel dispenser and said "Thank you," when someone pulled some for me and put them into my hand.

I blotted the water and makeup off my face and glanced in the mirror at my unlikely savior and froze, eyes fixating on the reflection of the very shiny gun barrel of the pistol pointed at my back.

"Good afternoon, Mrs. Rex." Alexander Soren's mouth was pulled into a line of grim satisfaction, and it made him look like a toad wearing calico horn-rimmed glasses. He always looked so pretentious, too. Always wore a suit, always had his hair parted to the side and slicked down, and *always* had on a freaking science teacher bowtie. He wasn't very old, either; maybe forties, but the whole almost-nineteen-fifties getup with its modern flare made him even creepier somehow than he already was. And that was saying something because Alexander Soren was and always had been so very creepy. His very presence made the hair on the back of your neck stand on end.

I stared at his reflection in the women's room mirror and my own mouth was the one that could catch flies with how it hung open in horror.

"I'll take this," he said, reaching out and relieving me of my purse with the hand that wasn't draped in his suit jacket and wasn't holding that gun with its gaping maw at my back. I swallowed hard, my mouth so dry from the combination of crying and the new situation at hand, my throat very nearly audibly clicked with the motion.

I stood motionless and just tried to breathe through the soul-crushing panic.

"You are living proof that if a man wants something done right, he must do it himself," he said and the horror of the implication of his words sank in slowly. *God, no, not again...*

"Come now. We are going to walk out that door and turn to the left. At the end of the hall, we are going to take the emergency stairs to the first floor. Do you understand?"

I just stared at him frozen in the mirror and his face crumbled into bad mood and impatience.

"Nod, Calanthe, nod that you understand," he ordered and I nodded a bit too quickly, my head swimming.

"Very good." He stepped up beside me and jacket concealing his hand, shoved the barrel of the gun into my ribs. I jumped.

"Open the door, and to the left," he ordered.

I automatically tried to go to my *other* left because – hello brain damage, there's a gun in my ribs and my heart is *hammering* into my ribs and my throat feels like it's closing up and *oh, God! He's going to shoot me, and I'm never going to see Kurt again, and what do I do? What do I do? What do I do?*

He shoved the gun into my ribs a little harder, indicating which way I should have been turning and I whimpered and moved in that direction instead, casting a longing look at the knot of people in the hallway just the opposite corner of us as they talked softly, likely about me and next steps. I didn't want Soren to shoot me, but I *really* didn't want him to shoot anyone else, and so clutching and wringing my long braid over my shoulder in both hands, I complied with everything he said.

We were only on the second floor, so there weren't a lot of stairs and this monster marched me bold as brass right through the front doors of the building's lobby to a waiting eco-friendly SUV idling at the curb. He opened the back door, and I dropped the paper towel wadded in my hand against my braid at the curb.

It had my makeup on it, and hopefully... hopefully, I don't know, Sadie would find it? She had done my makeup for me that morning. She knew what lipstick and eyeshadow I'd worn. Maybe it would help. Maybe it would tell her I'd been kidnapped. I don't know. All I knew was that I didn't want to die, and I needed to do everything to stay alive, so Kurt could come get me.

For a brief moment, I had a flash of *l'appel du vide*, which was a crazy thing to remember the name for right now. It basically meant that I had that split-second flash of wanting to do something I knew to be detrimental or stupid, like a person swerving their car into oncoming traffic, or sticking their hand into a running garbage disposal – except in my case, I saw myself crying out, running, screaming, or even grabbing the gun and forcing him to finish me... but I did none of those things.

Instead, as calmly as possible, I got into the back seat of the SUV and slid over. I owed it to too many women, to Kurt, and to *myself* to survive. I had endured so much, and I would continue to endure, in hopes that someday, someway, we would all have justice.

Still, I jumped when the car door shut behind Soren and my

stomach dropped out when he told the man behind the wheel, "Drive."

I also have to admit, my hope dwindled the further behind the SUV the lawyer's offices got.

Damn.

What were they going to do to me, now?

29

***K*urt...**

"I need you to say that again, slowly," I said through gritted teeth.

"Callie was taken from the lawyer's building," Sadie said, her arms across her chest. "A man in glasses and a bow tie. It looks like he might have had a gun in his pocket."

"Doesn't the Fallout HQ lawyer's offices have, I don't know, metal detectors and basic fucking security?"

"There are a dozen ways to get around metal detectors," the captain said, rubbing the sides of his face with his hand.

"And the most obvious one is that he never had a firearm, only something he could jab into her ribs and make her think he had one. It's called a bluff and they're actually pretty effective," Kyle said. "But assuming the building was completely secure is on me."

"The man in glasses and bow tie, the sort that looks like he swallowed a baby lemon, that's Alexander Soren. He's the right hand of August Emerson. He dresses like a jerkoff science teacher and insists that his callsign is the Dragon."

"The Dragon?" Sadie asked.

"Yes, Soren was the *Dragon*. Emerson was *Arhat*. It's a title from some Eastern religion. Rex was *Tomcat*, Callie was *Cardinal*," I said, feeling my hands clench in frustration.

"I have to ask," the captain said.

"You've been quite the fucking spider the last few weeks, so maybe you should have a plan for how to deal with this instead of asking me about my handle," I snapped.

"Yes, there is a plan." He sighed. "As soon as we know where Soren and Callie are going, then we mount a rescue mission."

"There was a contingency plan for this. The official name for that was Heimdall, the all-seeing guardian of Asgard. The plan covers the rapid removal and protection of high-level assets of New Eden, people like Arik Rex. Callie and Fallout would be a direct and total threat to both Rex and the entire organization, and they can't really compartmentalize this."

"I'd say not," Kyle said.

"Arik and other potentially threatened people would rendezvous in a *secret* location before a collected evacuation plan went into effect. They will meet in a place of tangled jurisdiction and overlapping areas in influence, so that any attempt to detain them will fail because of agencies fighting each other instead of working together."

"BWI?" Sadie suggested.

"Correct," I said. "Which means Callie was likely taken to a safehouse to be held until the other people showed up for evac, and then they'll all leave on a private chartered flight. The August, I mean Emerson, personally owns a Chinese Xi'an Y-20 cargo plane. It's pretty much a parallel design to the American C-17 Globemaster – large, powerful engines, advanced electronics, and it can carry something like seventy tons of cargo almost anywhere in the world."

"Jesus," Sadie said.

"The VIPs would literally drive their personal RVs and other vehicles into the aircraft and at final count, it's wheels up and gone for a New Eden compound, likely somewhere in Africa, or any of two dozen islands. If we can't catch the jet on the ground, there is no way to stop them. They could go anywhere in the Caribbean, any of the Atlantic islands, fuck, they could vanish into the cold islands in the south Atlantic or Antarctic Sea."

"So, we need to move quickly," the captain said.

"Hanger seventeen at the cargo terminal, not the private terminal," I said.

"Cargo?" Sadie asked.

"The Y-20 is a massive cargo jet, not a Lear jet," I added. "The private terminal isn't set up for anything that heavy."

"But they have those too?" she asked.

"Absolutely, and part of Heimdall is that these jets all launch at the same time from their respective home fields and start filing increasingly random flight plans, some even violently deviating from them to draw attention to themselves. There is a Lear 3 based out of Houston, Hiram Emerson's backyard, and it has a preplanned path of launching from the airport there, heading for LAX. Then, as soon as it is out of Texas airspace, the plan has it suddenly deviating toward Mexico. They call it the Reverse Coyote. Everyone goes chasing a Lear 3 making a bandit run into Mexicali or Mexico City, and the entire time, almost everything is in the guts of a Chinese cargo jet going God knows where." I let out a breath.

"If it's that simple, we call ATC and have them hold the flight," Kyle said.

"Easier said than done. You make that call and all those federal agencies want to know who made the call and everything about them. It's one thing to call the ICPD, when we've pretty much put them on our payroll and another to mess with BWI customs, the FAA, and ATC. Things get really ugly there," the captain said.

"Of course, it does," Sadie said.

"It will take a bit of time for them to get everything in place, before they can go wheels up," I said.

"But they know you know, right?" Kyle asked.

"Probably, but a plan that big, it would be nigh impossible for them to change it," I said. "It took years to get it in place. They can't just up and pop out a contingency for their contingency plan," I said.

"So, we're storming a jet?" Sadie asked.

"Well, I think so," I said. The captain made a sour face but nodded. "I mean, unless any of you have an interceptor jet or something at BWI that we could use to follow them to another country and then take them down commando style."

"No, we don't own any aircraft," Kyle said. "Too expensive, I was told."

"They *are* too expensive, and we can handle this," the captain countered.

"I just have one question. Why are the three of you willing to do this? You don't have a stake in it, there's no payout, and they've not done anything personally to any of you. I need to know motive."

"I know what they did to *her*, Kurt, and if I can do this and protect even one girl from going what she went through, or even what *I* went through, it's worth it," Sadie said. "You can all talk the rest of this out, but if we're going to storm a plane, that sounds like we need toys."

"She does love her toys, now that she has them and knows how to use them," Kyle said, with a hint of admiration in his voice. "As for me, abuse is abuse and I won't abide it. Not like this. I might be a hitman by profession, but that doesn't mean I don't have standards. Men like this deserve a place in Hell, not in a sanctuary state."

"They pretty much covered the hard points, and I feel responsible for getting you the posting at New Eden, back when I thought they were tree-huggers with a better PR department. I don't have a personal stake other than they deceived me. Is that enough for you?" the captain asked. I nodded.

"Let's get geared up. Roan, can you throw something in the jet's way, slow them down a bit?" Kyle asked. The captain nodded.

"While I'm covering that, grab my party bag and put it in the Rover. I'm thinking we might have to do a little off-roading," he added.

We split, and I followed Kyle to the house armory. He was quick and handed me a dragonscale vest and then gestured to the racks of guns. I had a moment of admiration. These weren't trophies and prizes, these were the tools for an entire company of Royal Marines, everything from bullpup shotguns and Belgian P90s to AR-15s and Uzis. Kyle looked over at Sadie, already kitted out in a tactical harness and body armor as she hefted an antique grenade launcher.

"Not the place for that, airports aren't grenade friendly," he said. She gave the weapon a wistful look, patted the stock and put it back in its rack. The two of them packed themselves out with more guns and knives than I expected a half-dozen people would carry. Kyle grabbed a nylon duffel and slung it over his shoulder. "Come on, you said time was short."

I was about to grab one of the AR pattern rifles when I saw her.

FN FAL, the right arm of the Free World, chambered for .280 British. My heart skipped a beat as I grabbed the rifle and the belt of magazines to go with her. *God save the Queen*, I sighed, and felt for a moment, all could be right in the world.

It certainly could be.

We left the house in two vehicles. Kyle and I took point in his Lamborghini, while the captain and their... *girlfriend?...* brought up the rear in the Rover.

This felt normal, in a startling fashion – riding shotgun in a high-speed vehicle, an automatic rifle in my arms. Kyle was stone silent as he drove, weaving through traffic like it was non-existent. Even more impressive, instead of getting bogged down in the main traffic arteries, he knew all of the ground streets. We exited the main road and tore through subdivisions, housing projects, and through avenues of strip malls and low-end businesses.

More than once I thought we had lost the Rover, but a moment later, it would appear hopping a curb or crossing a grassy median to rejoin us. We were faster but had lower ground clearance. The Rover was no slouch but by no means nearly as fast, but it had ground clearance, and it seemed like the captain was attacking parking lots and greenspace like it was his own personal path.

The dash touchscreen lit up, and Kyle tapped a button on his steering wheel. "Go ahead."

"I've tapped into BWI ground control, and it let me listen in on their ground chatter. The Y-20 got the notification to go wheels up in fifteen minutes. We won't have any time on the ground, but we might get there before they're in the air."

"Copy that. Still holding firm that those former Talibani Stinger missiles were a bad investment?" Kyle asked.

"They were throwing money away. There was no way the fuel cells were still good after this long. That's buying our gear, not ex-Soviet stuff."

"You guys buy a lot of Sov gear?" I asked.

"We do. There are tons of it, and it's surprisingly durable. Not the point though."

"So, what's the plan now?"

"We figure that out in the next fifteen minutes. We need to find a way to keep that fat bastard on the ground," the captain said.

Kyle waited until the captain ended the call before he spoke. "There is a way to do this, but it's going to be doubly dangerous."

"I'll do anything to get Callie back."

"I figured, but getting on the plane is going to be Hollywood dangerous, and then there is a good chance you'll be on your own after your in."

"Alright, tell me how," I said.

"The Y-20 is starting its taxi to the runway. We've got minutes," the captain said, his voice sounding strained through the Lambo's audio system. "We're out of time."

"We've got a plan," Kyle said. He pushed the exotic car through the access road, cutting through a parking area, and into the cargo terminal. We passed several blocked entrances before he found one that was open. Security here was nowhere near as tight as at the main terminal but getting on a cargo or military aircraft meant much better checks at the plane itself. Plus, as Kyle mentioned, crashing a cargo plane was not an effective terrorist technique.

The Y-20 was next in line. I could feel my heart racing, and the weight of the insanity I was carrying in the ultralight bag in my lap. Kyle gunned the motor and the car accelerated like a missile. The cargo jet, with its New Eden logo gleaming bright green and blue on the tail, started rolling too.

"Remember, once you're in, you won't have long before it gets up to altitude and it will be lethal cold and super low O2, you don't have long to do this."

"I got this," I said. "For Calanthe..."

"You pull this off, mate, I'll give you and her a weekend in Monaco, my treat."

"We'll enjoy that."

The next three minutes were the most terrifying seconds of my life. He accelerated until he matched speeds with the jet. It was ponderous and slow, but by the time we caught up with it, it was already clocking a solid hundred miles an hour. The good news was that the Lambo could probably reach near 200, but the Y-20 only had to get to 175, maybe 150, and it would lift.

Seconds.

With the bag secured, I crawled out the window into a wall of roaring air. Everything seemed to vanish in the roar of the engines and the scream of the car. He held it steady and moved closer. I slipped my leg free and braced against the slick carbon-fiber shell, and I could see what I wanted, the thick landing strut. If I could get to it, I would have more than I needed to hold on to. It was right next to a freight-truck worth of howling rubber, the jet's wheels.

Look before you leap, leap before you stare.

The shadow changed, the engine pitch changed, and I saw the front of the wheel assembly start coming off the ground.

I leaped.

Something hit me like a truck, but my hands caught the strut. There was some vibration, and I felt it run through me. The ground rapidly fell away, and Kyle's Lamborghini executed a perfect hand-brake turn and shot away, making for a hot exit from the terminal. I could see emergency vehicles attempting to chase, but that was just a gesture.

There was a grinding noise, and I felt the strut start to move. They were pulling in the landing gear. I looked around. I had to make sure I was in the open space, not where I was going to be caught between the scorching hot wheels and the inside of the compartment. Everything held the stink of hot rubber. After a few seconds, the landing gear locked into place, and with a loud whine, the doors closed, pitching me into complete darkness.

I wasn't dead, but the jump hadn't been free. Before I could assess how badly I had hurt myself with that stunt, I had to get out of the wheel well. Kyle had mentioned that at altitude, I would be experiencing subzero temperatures, and if I didn't get into the plane quickly, they'd find me frozen, if I didn't fall out the moment that they dropped the landing gear on approach.

I had a one in four chance of surviving that ordeal.

I fumbled with the zipper of the ultralight bag, careful to not drop anything. If that happened, whatever was dropped would be pretty much gone forever. I found the first tool, a torch. I flicked it on and panned around my sub-economy seating area. I had barely enough room to do what I had to, and it only took a minute or so to work my way around to a tiny square in the wheel well. It was a viewing port. The crew could open it and look into the well to see if the gear was actually up or down, if there was a problem in the cockpit. The metal would be the thinnest there. That was important, because the toy in the bag only had a limited power supply, and if it ran out before I was through, well, then I was well and completely fucked.

The cutter felt like a large flashlight, but much heavier. The instructions were simple, and according to the brief guidelines, it had more than enough power to cut a person free from a damaged vehicle, or in extreme circumstances disable a door, or, if switched into the secondary power output position, weld such a door shut.

Where did they find shite like this?

I placed the tip of the device near the side of the access panel and pressed the button. There was no sound at first, but there was a wash of heat, and thankfully not that much light. The laser made quick work of the aluminum well housing. The metal turned to a quicksilver consistency and flowed away from the laser. I moved the beam as quickly as I could. I couldn't run out of power and be trapped in the wheel well. That would be some Poe-esque tragedy on par with the *Cask of Amontillado*.

The cutter managed to cut almost the entire span before the beam faded to a pencil light and then went out. I dropped the spent device and pushed against the section I had been working on. The metal didn't move, and I felt a surge of panic. If I died in the wheel well, whatever, I didn't matter. If I died, no one would be able to save Callie.

She would be alone in their power.

I pushed again, not feeling the rough edge or the heat still in the metal. There was a shudder, and the last few inches of aluminum gave, like a hinge. I pulled myself through the hole, and out. I could smell gasoline fumes, and the curious gray line and chlorine smell I associated with caravans and campers. I was in the crawl space under the loading deck of the jet. There wasn't enough room to stand, but if I bumped along far enough, I would find the access door where the ground crews inspected the insides of the jet.

Fuck, this place was cramped.

It did bring Kyle's point that the FN FAL would be the wrong tool for the job, and the Beretta 93Rs he loaned me were a much better choice.

I felt like an absolute madman, cutting my way into a jet, after jumping on the wheels, with just a couple of pistols. What sort of action movie hero did I have the bollocks to think I was? Even Arik Rex didn't do stuff this batty in his flicks.

Finding the access door took longer than I expected. It didn't help that I was starting to feel the bruises and burns I had gained jumping onto the landing gear. One of my pants' legs was torn away, a boot was gone, and my foot was several shades of purple. It bore my weight, so it didn't feel like anything was broken, but I wasn't going to be winning any footraces anytime soon.

The hatch lifted easily, and I looked into the cargo hold. I was looking into the wheel well of a large deluxe RV caravan. As I looked around, it was more of the same. The light was dim, and several of the vehicles – there might have been eight – had lights on. Considering the size and cost of these vehicles, they were probably scales more luxurious inside, compared to anything that a Chinese-built cargo jet could offer.

The amount of money inside the jet, and the jet itself, was offensive. These guys were supposed to be green, eco-friendly, all that. Green communists, or some shite like that.

"I can believe they called Code for this," I heard a man say. There was the familiar flick and scritch of a lighter.

"You're not supposed to smoke in here, Cam," a woman scolded. "But if you are, give me one too."

"This is stupid. The merch wasn't ready to be moved. They were still in basic."

"I agree, half of them still cry constantly. They aren't ready. We should have sent them to a different facility, or on a goddamn boat."

"Yeah. Can I ask you a personal question?" he asked.

"No, I won't go out with you. I'm in a long-term relationship with several vibrators and a Hitachi," the woman said.

"No, nothing like that."

"Shoot," she said, and I could hear her take a long drag on the cig before puffing it out.

"How do you compartmentalize it?"

"What?"

"How do you rationalize what we're doing to those kids?"

"They aren't kids, Cam," she said. "And you're still hanging on to that progressive petroleum mindset. Everything we've been taught since we were kids is a social construct created by the industrial sector to be productive laborers scalded into powerlessness and weakness."

"I took the same accelerated classes you did," he said.

"They aren't children, they've physically matured. What's that expression, if there is grass on the field, play ball?"

"That's the expression, yeah."

"Besides, you don't have to deal with them on a day-to-day basis. They're lazy, entitled, remarkably stupid, and their self-esteem is so non-existent it's frankly insulting. The only thing I have in common with those mewling, sobbing animals is the same chromosome pattern." Her voice was acid on glass.

"That's harsh," he said.

"It hasn't prevented you from being a training stud when needed, has it?"

"Well, no," he hesitated.

"I think you're just having a relic crisis, and when we get to the islands, you should talk with one of the Ministers. They can probably help with that. Don't make that face, I'm not turning you in because you're having second thoughts about how we're treating the cattle. That's just proof that you're almost ready to completely embrace August Emerson's teachings. You're right there at the door, man. I am actually very happy for you."

"Really?"

"Enough," I said, pointing a pair of pistols at the both of them. "One more word and you're both worm food." They both looked surprised and raised their hands. Both were armed, but neither had a hand near their guns.

She had a bundle of cable ties in a back pocket, and I assumed it was for dealing with troublesome *cattle* and felt my blood boil. My injuries seemed less severe, and I had a burning urge to shoot both of them. "Take some of those cable ties and bind her hands and feet." I gestured the pistol at the man, Cam. He nodded, and when he didn't move fast enough, I gave him a motivational cuff with the butt of the pistol. He let out a small sound and fumbled faster with the cable ties. After the woman was trussed up, I did the same to the scared man. There was something satisfying about the way his hands shook as he tied his own feet and surrendered the ties so I could bind his hands.

"You disgust me," I said softly. "But I'm going to let you live, if you answer my questions." He looked terrified, but her eyes were bright with defiance and anger.

"I won't tell you anything," she hissed.

I pressed the barrel of the Beretta against her forehead, right above the bridge of her nose. "Are you telling me the truth, because if you really won't tell my anything, I have no reason to leave that pile of shite you call a brain inside your skull. Ever see what a nine mil does to a human head?"

She made a whimpering sound, the guy let out a gagging noise.

"Oh, you might be familiar with that?" I asked. "So, do you want to answer my questions, or will you?" I turned my attention to the guy. "After I pop her skull like acne, will you talk?"

He had a sheen of nervous sweat on his face and looked close to vomiting.

"Your pal here looks like the canary I need." I raised the angle of my hand, flexed my fingers, and she let out a sobbing noise.

"I'll talk." Her voice wavered, but there was no mistaking the sudden darkness between her legs and the look of liquid fear in her eyes. She believed every word, down to her core. That was good because I had meant every one of them.

"Where is Calanthe Rex?"

"The forward section has a VIP cabin, mess, and bathroom. She is being kept there with a few other dignitaries," she said quickly.

"She's not on one of the caravans, here?" I asked. She shook her head vigorously. "She telling me the truth, sport?"

"Arik and his wife are in the VIP lounge, the VIP section behind the cockpit," he agreed.

"I'm glad to see you didn't piss yourself," I said and gave him a tap between the eyes with the end of the barrel. He groaned and chose that moment to do just that. I sighed.

Gagging them proved a bit more difficult, but I managed to make do. He had the pack of smokes stuffed in his mouth, and then bound with one of my shirt sleeves. She got a wad of shirt and the other sleeve. Easy enough, considering how rough they looked after my daredevil antics getting on the plane.

"What are you going to do?" the scared guy asked before I put the gag in his mouth.

"I'm going to rescue the girls you have here, and Calanthe, and I'm going to make sure this doesn't happen again." I gave the cable tie an extra tug, and he looked away. I could feel the shame radiate from him. Perhaps a different Kurt might have had a change of heart, a moment of mercy. I felt the opposite, something inside me hardening. A point of hatred so intense that it stopped being black like coal and started to gleam like a diamond.

They were going to pay for this.

I was a ghost, slipping from RV to camper, SUV to luxury car. I quietly removed each of the ratchet straps and tie-down chains. One by one, I made the vehicles free, only their brakes and transmissions holding them in place. They were going to pay, pay in blood and terror.

After a half hour of this, I circled back to where the two were tied up.

He looked sick as I had ever seen a person, and the stench told me a quick story. He had tried to puke, but the gag prevented it from coming out. Too fucking bad. I went to the woman and pulled the gag out of her mouth. She coughed a few times, but slammed her mouth shut and swallowed all the coughing when I jammed the barrel of the Baretta into the side of her mouth.

"How many, and where are they?" I asked. "If you say who, I

swear to Christ and Satan, I'll cheese your skull and ask the pants shitter where they are."

Her mouth was dry, and she chewed that cottonmouth for a moment. "They're in the big RV, the Halcyon Cruiser."

"How many?" I reminded her.

"Thirty-nine," she said.

"Are you fucking kidding?" I asked.

"No, please don't hurt me."

"Whatever happens to you, you deserve worse," I said. I slipped the gag back in place.

The Halcyon was an older RV, a forty-footer, and when I opened the door, the man sitting in the driver seat seemed surprised to see me. He was even more surprised when I cracked him in the head with the gun. Two more strikes split his forehead and broke his nose. Before he could slump over the steering wheel and lay on the horn, I gave him a rib-cracking kick to the ribs. He slumped into the driver-side window, and I debated shooting him in the head. I turned to see several dozen glassy eyes staring at me, and I was glad that I hadn't.

"Ladies, I'm going to need you to all do what I ask, as quietly and calmly as you can."

Silence.

"If you'd like to go home, nod, and follow me," I said. They moved forward, hesitantly. "I'm here to help you. I'm here to rescue you from all of this. I'm a Marine, and a friend. C'mon, freedom is close." My foot ached. Pretty sure there were some broken toes from kicking the driver in the guts. When this was all over, I was going to need a nice long vacation, maybe in the three-to-six-month range.

They followed me, a trail of wet eyes and sniffles, a few quiet sobs.

"Are you really a Marine?" the lead girl asked.

"Aye, Royal Marine Corps, formerly of the 2nd Commando. I am alone, but it took an Army Ranger and a Marine Captain to get me on this plane. I promise you, all of you, that when this plane is on the ground again, you'll all be safe, and will get to go home."

I gestured for them to wait at the base of the ladder going up to the forward cabin. The door wasn't locked, and when I opened it, there was no one hanging out. That was a complete tactical mistake. A single man here with a SMG could hold the entire front of the plane secure from what I was going to be doing.

Rookie mistakes.

The doors to the sides of the corridor were marked with masking tape and note stock signs – stateroom, VIP bunk 1, VIP bunk 2, head.

I opened the door to the head, and it was empty. No stall lurkers were going to blindside me. I had seen enough action and horror movies. There was always a lone zombie, or a goon with a gun who came out of the bog to get the drop on the hero and company. I listened at the doors, and I heard voices – three in the first bunk, none in the second, and most of the people were in the stateroom. I opened the door to the bunk and found something I hadn't prepared myself for.

I recognized August Emerson from his smiling pictures, and Arik Rex was an international celebrity.

The naked woman tied down to the bunk had a mane of beautiful red hair.

Calanthe.

My blood was fire, and I almost pulled the trigger.

I didn't care about puncturing the hull of the plane, I was more concerned with a ricochet or the round changing course going through Emerson's body and hitting Callie. I cracked Emerson in the back of the head, and he dropped faster than his track pants. Arik turned to face the sudden intrusion.

"Worthy!" He looked surprised

He was even more surprised when I broke his nose with the slide of the pistol. Callie let out a scream as I gave him several more, harder strikes to the head and face, as he backed away. His last step faltered, and he hit the side of the bunk and slid to the floor, boneless and bloody.

"I'm here, Callie, it's me," I said.

"Kurt? Is that you, oh my God..." Her eyes suddenly brimmed with tears. I was going to turn and cut her loose, but the door opened, and Alexander Soren stepped into the room with a look of annoyed superiority. His eyes bulged when I put two rounds through his chest. Callie screamed. There was a commotion in the corridor and then people crowded around the door.

VIPs and dignitaries of New Eden, the majority men, a few women. I knew the look they had in their eyes. These were the members who knew full well about the sex trafficking, training underage girls for sex work, and handling all the money that went with it. I fired a few more times, delivering stomach and chest wounds to anyone who presented themselves as a target.

Toes definitely broke when I kicked Soren in the middle of the chest and knocked him back into the corridor. There was so much adrenaline in my body I didn't feel it. I didn't have words, only fury.

I sprang into the hallway, all elbows and waving pistol barrel. They fell back, their bravado and numbers giving them zero advantage against my complete lack of self-preservation, and the willingness I had to shoot them.

A brunette with a sculpted nose and bright pink fingernails pulled a compact pistol from a shoulder holster, a hot pink job matching those nails. I put a round through her right cheek, which exited through the back of her head. A thin man with a pedophile's pet mustache flipped out a knife and I put a 9 mil through his chin and sternum.

There was so much blood.

Two more rounds fired and those who were still standing quickly adopted submissive body postures, surrendering.

"What's going on back there?" The intercom from the cockpit buzzed.

"Everything's fine back here, just having a restructuring discussion." I clicked the intercom.

"We heard gunfire," a different voice said. Copilot?

"The discussion has been intense," I said.

"Is that you, Kurt?"

"Arizona?" I asked.

"Yessir. I heard…"

"I'll talk in a few."

I clicked the intercom off.

"Listen to me, you pieces of human waste," I said, resting my foot on Soren's chest. His eyes were getting a glazed look, and there was a lot of blood. He was bleeding out and would be dead soon enough. "You're going to exit the forward cabin and go to whatever RV you want. You're going to lock the doors behind you, and if I see one head poke out for the duration of the flight, I'll shoot that person. I have more than enough ammo for everyone on this bloody plane, you understand me?"

They nodded.

"Take these pieces of shite with you." I waved a pistol at the bodies.

They did, and there was a lot of confusion at the ladder. The important people made their way down, and I never took the gun off of them. Then, the girls started coming up while I covered them from the top of the ladder.

I counted them until all thirty-nine were in the front cabin.

"Who is the bravest among you? Who is your leader?"

"If there was a leader, it's Cass," one of the girls said, and pointed to a quiet girl with hair so blond it was almost silver, a set of black eyes, and her arm in a sling.

"I put up the most fight," the silvery blond said. "I'm Cass."

"Can you handle a firearm, Cass?" I asked.

"I know how, yes. My dad used to be a police officer," she said.

"We'll get you back to him," I said, and handed her one of the two Berettas. "The safety's off, and you've got eight… nine rounds in the clip, and one in the chamber."

"I hope I'm not reunited with my dad, at least not yet. He's dead," she said.

"We'll delay that reunion then. There's still work that needs to be done here." She smiled, and the others seemed to brighten. This was becoming real for them.

"No one will come through this door... sir," she said. I gave her a salute and hurried back to the first bunk. Callie was still tied to the bed, her eyes red from tears. I untied her quickly and pulled her into my arms.

"I'm here, I'm here," I said. "I've got you."

"Kurt, I can't, I don't, I can't believe it. Am I hallucinating? Have I finally gone completely mad and living out an insane fantasy?"

"This is real, and we're going to be going home real soon." I gathered her clothes back up and helped her get dressed.

"Where are all of the rest of them?" she asked.

"The girls are here in the forward cabin. All of the New Eden people are in the cargo hold, and one of the girls is holding the door with one of my pistols. Do these people have guns with them?" I asked.

"Probably not. They're all top-echelon people, and they were forced to leave their security people behind. The only people with weapons were Soren and Brynn."

"Pink nails, blonde hair?" I asked. She nodded. "They're both taken care of, and disarmed."

"Are we really going home?" she asked.

"We are," I said. "I've got to go talk to the guys in the cockpit, but it's cool, I know them and they're alright."

"What about them?" she asked, gesturing to Rex and Emerson, both unconscious. "You know you'll go to jail for this, regardless of what they did. They'll have the media and money on their side."

"They won't, I promise."

"What are you going to do?" she asked.

"There's an American song, *don't ask me no questions, and I won't tell you no lies,*" I said. She saw the dark intent, but not speaking the words made it different, not real. She nodded.

"Be careful, Kurt," she whispered. "I love you."

"I love you too, Callie."

I pulled the unconscious men from her room, only pausing long enough to pull Emerson's track pants up. It wasn't a matter of modesty or dignity, the last thing the traumatized girls in the cabin needed was to see the August's bruised cock hanging out of his pants like a gross joke.

There was a general uproar when I opened the door and rolled his fat ass down the ladder. He crashed into several angry people. These were all wealthy, self-important and powerful people. They were not accustomed to being made to wait, and it was only the arrogance of the August who made them board this plane at all.

Total cult bullshit, and I saw nothing but the eyes of angry zealots.

"Where are my girls?" a man in the front shouted.

"What did I say about anyone sticking their heads out?" I brandished the pistol. They fell back quickly, bumping and trying to climb over the people behind them. "Any of these girls your daughters?"

"I paid for my ticket, like everyone else," he said.

I put a round through his neck, spraying the side of his RV with blood.

"I said get back in your shit wagons, yeah? Or does someone else need a new mouth to breathe out of?" They scurried like angry rich cockroaches, fury and fear in their eyes.

"If any of them touch the ladder, shoot them," I said to Cass. "That's an order." She nodded grimly.

When I came back, it was Arik's limp but still breathing body I let tumble down the ladder. He landed like a bag of potatoes, but he was still breathing after he finished tumbling arse over teakettle.

"Cass, is this everyone? Is there anyone else down that deserves to be saved? Do we have all the monsters in the cargo hold?" She looked around at the other girls, and I could see the structure starting to sort out. She was as close to a leader as they had, and I could see that there were six, maybe seven others who were functionally lieutenants.

"This is it," she said.

"Any sympathizers down there?"

"Anyone who pretended to be a sympathizer was just working the inside and was the person who would turn you over to the handlers. Sympathizers are the worst sort. They'll pretend to be your friend and that all of this is just sad but inevitable. I hate them the most."

I nodded.

"Shut the door and lock it. Everyone," I raised my voice, "find a safe place, somewhere you can sit, maybe have something to hold on to. We're going to change course and the flight might get a little bumpy." They nodded and started moving.

"C'mon, Callie," I said, and offered her an arm. Her eyes were wide as she was finally able to take in what shape I was in. I was going to hurt in the morning, when the adrenaline was completely gone and I crashed. Not yet, not yet, there was still a lot to do. I thumbed the intercom at the cockpit door. "Arizona?"

"Yeah, chief?"

"Mind if I come in?"

"Strapped?"

"I can leave it with someone if that would make you feel better."

"Bring it, I could use the support."

There was a buzz and a click, and the cockpit door popped open. We stepped in, and Arizona, that splendid sunburned aspiring cowboy actor, was sitting in the copilot seat with a revolver poked into the ribs of the cargo master. The pilot was dripping sweat, nerves rattled.

"Need a hand?"

"Always, sir," he said.

"Are these guys on their side, or just unconvinced?"

"I'm not part of New Eden," the pilot said, swallowing hard. "I got nothing in this, but a wife and kids—"

I cut him off. "You're fine, just follow instructions. We're going to turn this bird around and head back to BWI, same runway we took off from. You'll get to be a hero."

"The fuck you will turn this around," the cargo master snarled.

"Oh, Chester, I didn't know they let you out of the kennels. Are you allowed to be within five hundred feet of normal humans now?" I asked.

"Fuck you, Worthy, you piece of shit," he growled.

I hit him the face with the butt of the pistol, and he screamed, spitting out a few teeth and a mouthful of blood. I reached over and thumbed the intercom. "Cass, you there? Send me someone you trust. Whatever girl picked up the pink pistol, I have a prisoner who needs to go in the cargo bay."

"Yes, sir," she replied. A moment later, a pretty, pale girl with black hair popped through the door, clutching the pink pistol in a death grip.

"What's your name?" I asked.

"Levi," she answered.

"Mind your finger on the trigger, the safety is off. You don't want an accidental misfire, especially when you're escorting Mister Dog Fucker to the cargo door. If he offers you any problems, feel free to shoot him, especially down low, through the kidneys. That's bloody and it hurts a lot. He deserves it, don't you, Chester?"

"That's all bullshit and you know it," he said with a hand over his bleeding mouth.

"Chester here got in trouble for running a dog-fighting ring, back before reforming his wicked ways and joining New Eden. What did you do for these guys, again?"

"Trained dogs," he said.

"Lose any?"

"That's something that happens," he said. "Just part of the job."

"Were you still running an eco-friendly dog-fighting ring?"

He shook his head in denial, but I could see his eyes. His eyes were afraid, guilty as fuck. I gestured and he unbuckled his belt, and let Levi lead him down the corridor. I heard the door open, some shouting, and then the door shut again. Levi came back and gave me a nod.

"So, what's the plan, Chief?" Arizona asked.

"I'm going to take the trash out," I said. "Which button opens the loading ramp?"

"We can't open the ramp in mid-air," the hired pilot said. "It's against regs."

"I've got a gun and don't give two shits about regulations. I've already shot seven people today. Do you want to be number eight?" He shook his head. "If the ramp is dropped, will it make us crash?"

"It won't make us crash, but we'll be exposing everything in the cargo bay to low oxygen and low temp."

"Well, that's the plan," I said. "Which button? I'll do it, so your conscience stays clear, how about that, mate?" He pointed at a button on the console. I reached over and flicked the cover up and pressed it. I could feel a moment of hesitation and the plane shuddered. Both men had to hang onto the controls, but it evened out.

"I don't think we're high enough," I said. "We need to climb, urgently."

"Sir, what are you trying—" the hired man asked.

"Those animals in the hold are going to be held accountable for that they've done. This is the only way you get people like them," I said. "I want you to climb, steep as this bitch can go."

He swallowed and nodded. He seemed to pop out a fresh layer of sweat. I felt the deck start to pitch as both pilots pulled back on the yokes. I clicked the button on the intercom. "Ladies, everyone grab a secure seat, or grab a spot on the rear-facing wall, we're going up for a bit."

The plane groaned as the engines pushed it higher. Both men reached and pushed all the throttles forward, more power. "Is there a monitor for the cargo bay?"

"At the cargo master's seat. Should be on now," Arizona said. I slid into the seat, which was now preferable with the steep climb angle. I could see a black-and-white view into the cargo area. The door was open, and things were moving. I could see the people trying to find something to hang onto.

"Why are you doing this?" the hired man asked.

"Did you know that in recent history, people like that were only held accountable twice? The French Revolution, that thing they called the Reign of Terror, and the Bolshevik Revolution. They're rich, and influential, and that means they can pull all of the strings." I watched as the pitch became too much and the largest of the RVs started rolling backward. The Halcyon pitched upward, and the front windshield grazed the top of the cargo compartment. It all seemed to be happening in slow motion. As it moved, it crashed into the smaller vehicles behind it, all in black-and-white silence.

"That's why common assholes like you and me get hit with forty-dollar fees when we run out of money in the bank, but they can run millions into the negative and in a year, the government will bail them out, or they'll play some cash game and suddenly they have more than before they lost it. They fly away in jet helicopters to private islands while people starve or choke on industrial waste."

The Halcyon finally came free, slid down the ramp, and fell away from the jet. Several SUVs and luxury cars tumbled out with it, and in a moment, all the vehicles were gone, shrinking as they plummeted to the ocean below.

The people were like action figures as they followed.

Arms and legs outstretched, some grasping at the ramp, others in various states of being broken and mashed by the stampede of cars and buses.

I felt cold.

"You'll go to jail for this," the hired man said.

"I'm not worried about that. I've done the best work of my life today." My voice felt hollow. "You can level us off and turn back for BWI. Drop down to maybe ten thousand before we get to the coast."

"You're going to hell. That was fucking murder, those were people," the hired pilot said. His hands were white as he leveled us off and turned the jet back the way we came.

"Mate, I'm going to hell for things I did years ago. I killed innocent people in another country for the crime of being in the wrong place at the wrong time – women, children, people who were no threat, no harm to anyone. This was taking out the trash, and keep that in mind, so you remain a mercenary pilot and not trash like them." He looked at me and I saw him swallow hard.

"Feel free to call the tower, tell them what happened, that an armed man held a gun to your head and made you do all of that. I don't especially care. Call me a terrorist, that would be even better. Then you can start explaining to the powers that be what you're doing involved with these people."

"I think we've got everything covered up here, Chief," Arizona said. "Looks like thirty minutes to the coastline."

"You got parachutes on this bird?"

"Yeah, Chief." He gestured to a locker. I dug inside and pulled one out.

"Perfect."

"You're hurt," Callie said, stroking the side of my face.

"Ah, nothing an ice bath and some painkillers won't take care of." I gave her a smile. "Are you okay? That's the only thing that matters to me."

"Yeah, I'm okay, now." She put her head against my chest. I felt eyes on us.

"Excuse us." It was Cass. I nodded for her to go on. "What are we doing?"

"The crew is going back to BWI, the same terminal we left from. I'm sure it will be swarming with cops and guys in black jackets with big letters on them. They will take care of you and get you back to where you need to be. The people who hurt you, they're dead now. The cargo area should be empty now. We climbed long enough that none of those wastes of flesh should have been able to stay conscious and hold on."

"You dumped them in the ocean?" Cass asked. I nodded. "The cops are going to make an example out of you."

"They'll never know who I was," I said. "Unless you know my name and tell them what I look like and all that. I'd prefer it if you didn't."

"We won't," Cass said. "They taught us about keeping quiet. We can keep this secret."

"You know I'm cool as a cucumber, Chief," Arizona said. "I'm pretty sure our pilot-for-hire doesn't want any scrutiny of his record. It's a little unusual finding a young guy like this who knows how to fly big Chinese jets, eh?"

"I'm just doing a job. I can't recall what you look like, and I legit do not know who you are," the rent-a-pilot said. There was sweat on his forehead.

"We appreciate it. Neither of us was ever here," I said with a smile. I could feel Callie squeeze her arms around me, and I returned her embrace with my good arm. I was feeling myself stiffen from the beating I had taken.

"Are you leaving?"

"We are. In a few minutes, my girlfriend and I are going to play D. B. Cooper and bail out of the plane. We have friends waiting for us."

"We do?" Callie asked, her eyes suddenly bright and full of renewed hope.

"We do. They'll be along to pick us up in the cigarette boat. We'll just bob for a little while."

"I can't believe this." She looked up at me. "It's too insane."

"Why?"

"Because even the movies aren't like this," she said.

"Ah, the movies are imaginary, and this is real. If this were a movie, I wouldn't have more than a bloody lip and we'd already be making out." I laughed.

"We will be doing that, just as soon as you're able." Her eyes were like diamonds.

"We've got one more stunt to pull first," I said. "Do you know how to skydive?"

"No, I don't," she said. "I didn't realize that's how we're getting off the plane."

"Don't worry, I've done a batch of tandem jumps, and you'll be completely safe. What do I always say?" I asked.

"I've got you?"

"Always."

Arizona paged the intercom, that we were down to twelve thousand and that he was lowering the ramp. It should be good for us to go. I looped the chute over my shoulders and pulled the harness tight.

"I don't know that I can hold on like that," Callie said, her voice worried.

"You don't have to," I said. "You'll strap to me and have this across your chest." I showed her the other half of the chute. "This one is for one or two people."

"Be careful," Cass said, as she opened the door to the cargo hold. It was loud, the wind roaring around the ramp. I nodded, and at the bottom of the ladder I made sure that the hold was empty, that none of the bastards had managed to hold on for their lives. Good riddance.

Before we got to the ramp, I pulled Callie to me and hugged her tight. I felt her shake a little, then she pressed her back to me as I hooked the straps of the harness and backup chute against her chest. She felt nice, her ass tight against my crotch.

We duck-walked to the ramp and I turned at the last moment. Cass and several of the other girls were crowded in the door and their eyes were almost lost and far away. I gave them a salute and leaned backwards.

Callie screamed as we plummeted from the plane. It turned into a rapidly moving gray cross in an endlessly blue sky.

Once we were well and clear of the jet, I pulled the cord and the chute came out perfectly, snapping against the air and dragging us to a much slower drop. This wasn't a combat drop or a thrill-seeker escape. It was getting both of us to safety.

We drifted down, and it wasn't long before I had to make a decision – island or water.

Given how my leg felt, I didn't think I could stick and walk off a dry landing, so I brought us down into blue water a few hundred feet from the sandbar island.

"That, that was... wild," Callie said.

"Let's cut the chute free and get to land." I felt weird.

"Kurt?" she asked.

I reached and tugged the harness release, popping her free from me.

"Kurt!" Her voice was higher now.

The last thought I had was pulling the release and coming free from the spiderweb of nylon lines that connected me to the chute. Gotta get free of those when you hit the water or the current will drag you away.

30

$\mathcal{C}$**allie…**

The water was warmer than I expected, but it wasn't what would be considered *warm*. Maybe it was because the air rushing past us as we hurtled back to earth had been so bitingly cold through our meager clothing. Almost as soon as we hit the salty brine, the tangle of strings and the parachute disengaged from us, and Kurt? Kurt went alarmingly limp behind me and the weight of him dragged the both of us under. I struggled and kicked, fumbling at the buckles and straps of the strange and unfamiliar rigging locking us together.

"Kurt!" I screamed, barely getting my head above water and having just enough time to suck in a breath before being dragged under once more.

I fought for the surface and screamed again, "Kurt!"

He sputtered behind me, and I was loosened from the tangled web binding us together. I swished in the water, giving a swift kick, spinning and reaching, trying to keep his head above the surf. We were close to a spit of land, very close, but Kurt was having a hard time. I got behind him, shook him lightly, and cried out, "Float! Float damn you!"

He finally caught my meaning and stopped struggling and just lay back against me.

"Yes! That's it! That's it!" I kicked, powerful strokes that I hadn't committed to since my days on the swim team. Kurt cried out and flinched when one of my kicks encountered one of his feet as I towed us bodily toward the shore.

"I'm sorry! I'm sorry!" I cried. "Just stay with me, try to stay awake, let's get on the ground, that's it! That's it!"

I got us to ground, but it was hard. Kurt was so *heavy*, and it was taking all of my strength which was quickly being sapped with the chill starting to seep in. Plus, I was small and he was so large it was a near impossible task to drag him bodily onto the shore of what was little more than a sandbar that was – well, I didn't know where.

"Kurt?" I asked, and kneeled beside him, putting my ear over his soggy dress shirt, which was missing buttons. "Kurt?" I asked again, relieved at the steady thunder of his heart. I kneeled up and touched his face, putting it between my hands, lightly smacking him in hopes of somehow waking him.

"Kurt!" I cried and finally gritted my teeth and slapped him.

He jolted, jerking with a sound like "Ungh!" and demanded of me, "Did you just slap me?"

"Kurt, I don't know where we are. I don't know what to do!"

"Pocket," he mumbled. "Left pocket, the beacon."

I rifled through his pockets, found his phone, and pulled it out – it was wet. It wouldn't work. I sniffed, and said, "It's wet. It won't work."

"Twist it, they'll be... they'll be here soon." His head lolled on his shoulders, and I looked up and out over the darkened waters, shivering with cold, the slight wind in wet clothes combining to create misery. The night was black as pitch, and I didn't know what to do. How would twisting a phone do anything? I dragged Kurt into my lap and held him. I held him and despaired... how would anyone find us out here?

I finally gave into my weeping, and just hugged him close. *If I were to die, at least it was like this, with him, free and not in New Eden's clutches,* I thought.

He stirred, and said, "The beacon, left pocket."

"All I found was your phone." I sniffed.

"Other left, Love," he said, fumbling at his other pocket.

"Oh!" Curse my wretched brain and slow thinking for not having thought of *that* sooner.

I found it, twisted it, and it flashed brightly, pulsing into the night, chasing back the dark.

"Okay, okay!" I hugged him tight, and he almost cuddled back into me.

"Just going to have a rest," he murmured, and I nodded.

"Okay... okay..."

Relief flooded me, but it was a fleeting one as the time dragged on and on. The night gave way to the false light of first dawn on the horizon, which shifted to full dawn, the sun crawling up from the horizon, clawing its way across the sky.

Kurt wouldn't wake, both of us shivering violently with no protection from the elements. His lips were bluish in the morning, but the sun warmed us up marginally.

My failing hopes were propped toward dusk the next night, the high-pitched grinding whine of an engine broke through the surf, cutting above the sound of the constant wearing wind. Eventually, that whine became louder and louder and eventually the irregular *"whump! whump! whump!"* of a boat bottom smacking into the surface drew closer, the motors whining down as it pulled up alongside the sandbar.

"Kurt! Callie!" a woman's voice, *Sadie's* voice, cut over the sounds of the water.

"Here! We're over here! Help me!" I cried and I *did* cry, my tears of despair turning on a dime to tears of joy as the shadow of a boat cut across the glare of the setting sun.

"There!" I heard Roan's voice and the motor kicked up as I shielded my eyes from the light behind them.

We were saved.

Kurt lay in a hospital bed in the basement of the mansion. It was a state-of-the-art ICU, one that Roan had said they'd "Blessedly never had to use."

Doc Max had met us at the house's garage with a full nursing staff and gurney, swiftly wheeling Kurt away, down a ramp that switch backed under the house, to a full surgical theatre and this room right here.

I didn't know what to make of that.

Kurt hadn't needed surgery, thankfully, but he would be staying a while. I held his hand by the bedrail, his wrists wrapped in soft but thick buckled restraints. They'd needed to give him morphine and he'd reacted even worse on it this time than the last and his "altered mental status" as Doc Max had called it, led to one of the nurses being tossed aside like a broken toy.

"That's going to cost extra," Kyle had said flatly, and Sadie had punched him in the arm and looked my way as we'd watched everything on the monitor. I knew my face was pinched with worry but Kyle's soft "Sorry, Callie," had made me crumble and cry.

I was so worried for Kurt, and they wouldn't let me in there. Instead, I was wrapped in one of those crappy and sparse wool blankets like you saw on television watching my lover *on* a television struggle with the medical personnel charged with saving him.

It had been a nightmare. I just wanted to be with him but "not until he's stable" was the rule and I *hated, hated,* living by other peoples' rules anymore.

Look what it'd gotten me.

"Come on, sweetie," Sadie urged in a soothing low voice, rubbing up and down my shoulders. "Let's get you cleaned up and warm. They'll take good care of him, I promise. Look, Roan is there now."

And he was and I was grateful, and I think that was the only thing that had allowed me to get up from my seat and let Sadie lead me away.

I had bathed, and she had helped me get the seaweed out of my hair and had helped me wash the stink of petroleum products that'd been floating in the water we'd landed in out of it. Now, here I sat in an expensive satin nightgown and matching robe, looking far more glamourous than I had a right to, willing Kurt to just wake up and look at me with my mind.

Of course, he didn't. On top of the opioids, they'd had to sedate him. *Heavily.*

"How's he doing, Love?" Roan asked from the doorway. I looked up and over and wiped my eyes with the heel of my hand, refusing to let his go.

"Sleeping, um... I don't know, really. I mean, I don't know what's wrong with him."

"Remarkably, nothing too terrible," Roan said dryly. "The worst of it is some broken toes, the rest?" He gave a little blasé shrug. "Soft tissue damage, he'll hobble for a bit, but he won't look like me." He used the cane he had a hold of to tap on his false leg twice for emphasis.

I turned back to Kurt's bruised and sleeping face. "I wouldn't care either way as long as he's here, as long as he stays with me."

I reached up and caressed the stubble on his cheek and muttered, "What were you thinking? *God,* you crazy idiot." But of course, there weren't any answers except the soft sound of the blood pressure cuff around his bicep doing its automatic inflation. He was under monitoring and observation. Just to be safe.

Safe... I didn't feel like it. Not with Kurt unconscious. I didn't know that I would ever feel it again if he didn't get healthy. Safe was the only thing I felt when in his arms and nowhere else.

"Come now," Roan said, limping into the room.

"I don't want to go," I said. "I won't."

He chuckled and said, "A bit vague of me, yeah? No, I meant to help you into bed. You look exhausted."

"What, with Kurt?" I asked, surprised. "Won't the doctor—"

Roan chuckled and shook his head. "This isn't a hospital in the traditional sense of the word, Callie. No one is going to scold you here."

He came over and hung his cane on the bed rail and held out a hand to steady me. I took it and stood, and he raised it up gently, indicating I should step on the chair and use it as a ladder. I did and I got into the surprisingly wide hospital bed, lying down beside Kurt carefully, and gingerly laying my head on his shoulder.

He slept on and didn't even stir.

"I'll fetch you a blanket from the warmer," Roan said kindly and taking up his cane, limped out of the room. I closed my eyes for just a moment, exhausted, and feeling safer already, startling when the warm, but rough hospital blanket was laid over me.

"That's it, just try to get some rest yourself," Roan said, tucking me in. I nodded against Kurt's shoulder and sighed out, lulled to sleep by the ticking of his heart, his deep and even breathing, and the quiet rhythmic hush of the machines around us.

I don't think I was even aware that Roan had taken the seat I'd vacated, standing watch over us both.

I JOLTED awake with a soft start I don't know how much later, unsure at first as to what had woken me in the first place. It was only when the soft press of Kurt's lips left my forehead that I realized what it'd been. He was awake. What's more, he had been released from his restraints and had his arms around me.

"Hey," he said in that soft, half-accent of his, the British a little richer now that he wasn't thinking about it.

"Hey," I whispered back softly.

"You alright, then?" he asked me, and I smiled and sniffed, my eyes welling with happy tears.

"How can you ask me that when—"

"Oh, hey, shhh, none of that now, Love. I'm alright."

I sobbed anyway, caught in a maelstrom of emotions, and he gathered me close. I clung to him, my rock in a storm-swept sea, and I let it out because he let me.

Because he gave me a safe place to do so. One of no judgment and gentle support.

"Look at me," he ordered gently. "Look at me now," he insisted when I didn't right away, embarrassed.

I looked up and with a gentle hand at the edge of my jaw, he took me in, searching my face, the depths of my eyes with his carefully considering gaze, finally bowing his head and pressing his mouth to mine. It surprised me and didn't, caught me off guard, but also sent such a *relief* coursing through my veins.

I kissed him back, desperate to be as close to him, *with* him, as possible. He urged me to straddle him with his hands which were free of restraints, and I paused, asking against his mouth, "Should we?"

"Oh, *aye*," he murmured against my mouth. "Afraid you'll have to do most of the work, but aye, I need this," he said. I nodded. I needed it too. I pulled up his hospital gown beneath the sheets and sat up, slipping a leg over his hips, shoving the blankets and covers down behind me. He was covered to the cameras by my nightgown, as I straddled him, and I was careful about not settling my weight just yet.

Kurt reached between us, pressing on his cock to stand it for me, and I bit my bottom lip and eased down on him, bending forward as I became fully seated, not quite ready or used to having him inside me, but desperate to have him there, to erase...

I banished the thoughts from my mind and focused on kissing him, on his lips underneath mine, of the feel of him inside me, his broad hands on my hips, smoothing over the satin of my gown, gripping my body through the thin material as he grunted slightly and whispered against my mouth, "If I've died, this is my heaven."

I wanted to laugh, I wanted to cry, his words they were so sweet to me.

"Move for me, Love. Take your pleasure. I'll get mine."

I nodded and kissed him and he put his hands palm up beneath mine to help me find the leverage I needed without hurting him. I sat up, gasping slightly as it forced him deeper, moved him against my walls, and I held his hands and he held mine and braced so that I could roll my hips and, *oh yes...*

He sucked in a breath and groaned out. I stilled, and he shook his head and said, "No, no, no, don't stop, Love. Please, I beg you, don't stop."

I smiled and moved slowly, deliberately, and sucked in a deep breath of my own, tilting my head back, closing my eyes, and giving myself over to the *feeling*... oh my, oh *yes*, it was both insane making love to him in a hospital bed but also, insanely *exquisite*.

I moved for myself as much as for him, that tingling glow of pleasure building at the apex of my thighs, deep inside me, that feeling like my womb was expanding and that warm heavy golden feeling... yes. *Yes, yes, yes, yes, yes!*

Before I knew it, I was close, so very close, fingers twined with Kurt's, our bodies so warm it was hard to imagine the bone-chilling depths of our exposed cold out on that tiny spit of land we'd managed to find ourselves on. The rushing wind of our descent, the fear, the abject terror faded into a distant memory already.

I thought we were going to die. I thought I *was* dead, that they would kill me, that all was lost but then there was Kurt – impossibly, on that wretched plane, and I couldn't believe my eyes. I wondered if it was some sort of dream, if it could even be reality, or if I had gone completely insane, but the insanity...

"Stop, come back here with me, stay here with me, Love. Look at me." I bowed my head and looked at him and he disentangled one hand from mine and caressed the side of my face.

"This can wait," he said dully, and I shook my head, gripped him with my pussy, and began to move all over again.

His eyes all but rolled into the back of his head in his pleasure and I smiled, loving that I could have such an effect on him.

I was so wet, and I didn't remember that happening, at least I wasn't right away... just enough to fit him inside me, but now? Now I could feel it between us, slicking our skins and making things so much better the more I ground on his cock. I panted, the pleasure rising again, expanding like the heat death of the universe from the center of my being outward and I let out a strangled almost sob with how desperately I wanted to come. With how much I wanted to feel something *good* and Kurt? Kurt wanted that for me almost as much as I did.

"That's it, Callie girl," he murmured, encouraging, voice pitched low and husky, sexy and seductive. "That's my girl, come for me," he murmured, and it put me close and closer still.

"Yes," he moaned as I tightened up just that little bit more and reached between us, gathering my gown out of the way, putting my fingers against my clit.

"That's it, *yes*," he encouraged and I touched myself, pressing in tight, making rapid circles, massaging my clit to drag the pleasure out of the dark and releasing that light inside myself. Kurt worked his hips as best he could beneath me and touching off that spark that set the fire that burned me from the inside out, unmaking me, consuming me, turning me to a pile of panting ash against his chest as his strong arms went around me and held me tight.

I lay there, gasping, slowly coming back to my senses, as Kurt whispered gentle praises against my hair and kissed the top of my head... and through his love, I rose once more, a phoenix rising; a new life ahead of me if only I was brave enough to seize it, and I would *not* disappoint.

There was still so much to do to unmake New Eden and with Kurt's continued strength, continued grace, I knew what I needed to do, and I would get it done.

I had such a fire inside and I was going to use it to burn New Eden to the fucking ground.

I sat up and looked down into my lover's eyes as he smoothed back some of my red curls and he smiled.

"I love you," I murmured, and his smile grew.

"I love you, too."

I lay back down in gratitude and cuddled against his chest. He held me tight and tighter still.

I could do anything... anything... but it would all be nothing without Kurt.

Thank God, he was safe.

31

*K*urt…

"You know, if I had done that in the service, I would be getting a Victoria Cross," I said.

"Aye, or you'd be getting court martialed for mass murder and looking at a few dozen lifetime sentences at Wakefield or Millbank Prison," the captain said. The look on his face was complicated.

"You want to give me the bit about not being the, what's the Yank phrase? Judge, jury, and executioner?" I asked.

"Oh, the thought is foremost in my mind," he said.

"Aye, I'm sure it is," I said.

"How are your feelings on this, mate?"

"Clear as a bell and steadfast as the Queen. The world is a lighter place for however many creatures went into the pond. If there's anything that might trouble my conscience, it's that one of those big ugly caravans might have hit a turtle or a whale on its way to the bottom."

"Can you be sure they were no other innocent people in the cargo bay when you had them dumped from twenty-five thousand feet?"

"No, I cannot say with complete and utter certainty that there were no other innocent people, but it seemed at the time, if there were any civilians in the strike zone, that was an unfortunate accident on their part," I said. I could see his eyes harden.

"You know it galls me to have my own words handed back to me," the captain said.

"We knew for a certain that there were multiple civilians at that bridgehead. The call was made, and the Yanks turned that place into a burning crater, because of that call." I carefully left out that it had been his thumb on the mic. It was Captain Conan Roan who called the Yank's B-52s to change course and carpet bomb a nameless village. We both knew the place was crawling with Talibani, and that it wasn't just Jihadis with AKs and IEDs, they were serious combatants with machine guns, RPGs, and several field guns.

"When the bill comes due," I began. "I'll settle up with the bloke at the Pearly Gates, and either he'll decide I did enough good to let me in, or he'll give me a shake of the head and down I'll go, right back to North Yorkshire."

"Pretty sure Saint Peter sends you down to hell," he said.

"If Old Scratch had North Yorkshire and Hell, he'd rent out the York and live in Hell." I gave him a grim smile. "Besides, it's hard to have the high ground when you've retired from Her Majesty's service and are a freelance killer in the colonies."

"It is a gray area," he said.

"My conscience is clear. If there were people inside those caravans that didn't deserve what happened, well, the bastards can get in line and give me the finger when it's my time. But I don't think there were any. I got all the chippies in the clear, and the rest that went in the pond, they were the sort that justice never gets."

"Fuck all, mate," the captain said and leaned back in his chair.

"What did the news say, seventy-seven people missing, associated with New Eden, lots of wealthy people, power brokers, Hollywood types?" He nodded. "That sort, even when they're caught, if there is any legal action, it's a slap on the wrist. Give 'em a few years and they're back at the awards' shows, pressing lips against the pretty girls and not long after that, you know they're back to the old dirty business."

"You think it was a community service?"

"Aye, I think it was as near to Godly work as I'll ever do. I feel like when they make the posthumous biopic for Arik Rex, I should get a cut of the box office and a shiny gold naked bloke for it."

"I assume you're talking about an Oscar?"

"The one with wings," I said. "I had to get stitches because Rex hit me with one."

"That's an Emmy, and it's not a bloke," he said. "The Emmy is a woman holding an atom, with lightning bolts for wings."

"Bitch will cut." I laughed.

"You have to give up the high ground," Kyle said. He offered me a glass, and I accepted. "Besides, it doesn't matter how much you enjoyed Rex's remake of *The Valley of the Spiders*, they were all scum."

"But..." the captain protested.

"Mate, the only reason we could honestly have to be pissed is that he got to rack up those kills instead of us," Kyle said, saluting me with his glass. "Besides, he did it for the greatest thing in the world."

"Love." The captain gave a chuckle.

"I was going to say pussy, but that works too."

"Lach, that's crude, even for you."

"Don't act like it isn't true. Sure, you might have started with noble purposes, but the moment you fuck, everything changes," Kyle said.

"Don't let Sadie hear you say that," the captain warned.

"I'll tell her to her face." He gave another toast.

"I guess that means we aren't the good guys," I said, giving the gin a swirl before draining the glass.

"No, we aren't. But we are the sort of people the world needs. We kill the people who need to be killed, and along the way, we enjoy the good things in life. It's the payoff for the fact that the world would punish us for what we do, and there is always the chance we don't come home, because the bad guys will sometimes win."

"That's damn near a monologue from you, mate," I said.

"It is, now tell him the interesting part," Kyle said. "And stop trying to lecture him."

"What's the interesting part?" I asked.

"There were a few interesting things that have been going down in the cryptocurrency world, some stuff in the news about a few crazy billionaires shooting themselves into space, and a few major crypto investors vanishing into the Atlantic," the captain said. "And thanks to a few discussions we had, we all made a nice bit of money."

"What's a nice bit?" I asked.

"You made back everything you spent getting Calanthe here, and then some."

"He's being modest," Kyle said. "Fuck all, I just threw a little cash at that TwitCoin mess and it made me enough that if I really wanted, I could get that Bugatti now."

"Oh, that's smashing," I said.

"What you do with your shares are your own business but I have a new potential business venture," the captain said.

"Better than New Eden?" I asked.

"Absolutely. It's a mining startup down in South America, precious gemstones mostly."

"I'm no geologist, mate," I said.

"Look, this company is basically taking advantage of the fact that Venezuela is a few years away from being the next Somalia. We get in on the ground floor, and when the mines start paying out, we're virtually partners. I've got a meeting with the guy behind the venture. He seems legit, but reminds me of that Afghani general, the one who always had a riding crop."

"Oh, that guy. I think he was working both sides," I said.

"I'm sure he was," Conan said. "He made a ton of money too."

"Right up until he caught all that shrapnel," Kyle said.

"You're tense," Callie said, her hands on my shoulders.

"I know," I said, looking out at the ocean. I could see night hurtling toward us, the sun turning into a memory in the west. "I'm at a bit of a loss."

"I don't see why, tell me," she said.

"There isn't any more plan."

"Sure there is."

"Nah, it's all done," I confessed. "There isn't a next job, there isn't another looming disaster."

"Hush, you don't have to go hunting for a job," she said. "Tate and the Fallout lawyers are still working for us, and worst-case scenario, I only get ten percent of Rex's estate. That's still in the multi-million-dollar range. Best case, I get everything. He had no legitimate children, no one to contest the will, and if there are any agreements between his estate and New Eden, they're burned bread now."

"Toast?" I asked.

"Yes, toast." She kissed my cheek, and for a moment I thought I could smell lavender. "And I've been told you've made a lot of money with internet coins?"

"Aye, I've made enough to be comfortable for a while," I admitted.

"In your cabin," she added.

"I'd like to take you to see it once it's finished being repaired. I'm still a bit miffed that the captain has had some contractors head out with a crane and saws to finish that, since I'm a little worse for wear."

"Aren't we quite the pair?" Callie asked. I could see a look in her eyes. She wanted to be close to me, to sit in my lap, but knew that my leg was still tender. There was nothing broken that could be cast or splinted, but the bruises would take a while to clear up. Doc Max had me loaded with painkillers and some meds that would make sure that none of the bruises turned into a blood clot.

"I like us," I said.

"I do too. You're different from Arik, and he's the only other man I've been with."

"You know I've done horrible things, and have issues with PTSD, and I don't celebrate Independence Day or Thanksgiving," I said.

"Arik celebrated himself. Every movie was its own holiday, and the awards' show season was his Christmas."

"I'm not him," I said.

"He did horrible things and had issues with narcissism and was about one pubic hair away from being a child abuser, so there is no comparison between the two of you. You made the world a better place. He made terrible movies and was even worse in bed."

I let out a small laugh.

"Don't laugh, you're good at all of that bedroom stuff."

"That's not what has me tickled, Love," I said. "God, his movies were bloody awful."

"At least we won't have to see any more remakes and sequels to movies made sixty years ago, and you've made me enjoy the only two things he liked, so you are by far the better man."

"Don't," I said.

"I'll do as I please, Mister Worthington," she said, planting another kiss on my lips this time.

"Aye, that you will."

She smiled at me, and suddenly the future which had seemed bleak on my end the moment before, was brighter than her eyes.

ALSO BY A.J. DOWNEY

The Sacred Hearts MC

1. Shattered & Scarred
2. Broken & Burned
3. Cracked & Crushed

3.5 Masked & Miserable (a novella)

4. Tattered & Torn
5. Fractured & Formidable
6. Damaged & Dangerous

The Virtues

1. Cutter's Hope
2. Marlin's Faith
3. Charity for Nothing
4. Stoker's Serenity

The Sacred Brotherhood

1. Brother to Brother
2. Her Brother's Keeper
3. Brother In Arms
4. Between Brothers
5. A Brother's Secret
6. A Brother At My Back
7. A Brother's Salvation

ABOUT A.J. DOWNEY

A.J. Downey is a Pacific Northwest girl living in an East Tennessee world who finds inspiration from her surroundings, through the people she meets, and likely as a byproduct of way too much caffeine. She specializes in real and relatable romance stories featuring that real-life kind of love that everyone craves.

Stalker Information:

Website
www.ajdowney.com

Sign up for her newsletter at
http://eepurl.com/dkQiIH

Facebook Group - AJ's Sacred Circle
https://www.facebook.com/groups/authorajdowney/

facebook.com/authorajdowney

twitter.com/authorajdowney

instagram.com/ajdowney

bookbub.com/authors/a-j-downey

ALSO BY JARED KINGPACAL LAIN

Indigo City Darker (with A.J. Downey)

1. Triple Threat

2. Double Shot

Paranormal Romance (with Timber Philips)

The Water's Edge

ABOUT JARED KINGPACAL LAIN

Jared KingPacal Lain hails from the Great Smoky Mountains, a place of both beauty and dark things, where he explores strange fiction, hidden secrets, and venturing away from the main path to find hidden pleasures, wonders, and horrors.